The House of Christina

of

Christina

A NOVEL BY

BEN HAAS

SIMON AND SCHUSTER · NEW YORK

PUBLISHED BY SIMON AND SCHUSTER
A DIVISION OF GULF & WESTERN CORPORATION
SIMON & SCHUSTER BUILDING
ROCKEFELLER CENTER
1230 AVENUE OF THE AMERICAS
NEW YORK, NEW YORK 10020

DESIGNED BY EVE METZ
MANUFACTURED IN THE UNITED STATES OF AMERICA

1 2 3 4 5 6 7 8 9 10

LIBRARY OF CONGRESS CATALOGING IN PUBLICATION DATA

HAAS, BEN.
    THE HOUSE OF CHRISTINA
      1. WORLD WAR, 1939–1945—FICTION. I. TITLE.
PZ4.H112HO [PS3558.A17] 813'.5'4 76–30373
ISBN 0-671-22526-X

This book is for Jim and Anna Henderson.

And for the Taube family, René, Renate, and Vivian, and our mutual home in Kritzendorf.

And to Bill Reiss, with gratitude for favors rendered when his client was half a world away.

AUTHOR'S NOTE

The Ferntal, Ferndorf, and Altkreuzburg, as well as the Christina Hof and the Schellhammer Hof, together with all their inhabitants, are fictitious, and no resemblance is intended between these locales and actual ones and none between characters in this book (except obvious historical personages) and actual persons living or dead.

At the same time, I am more deeply grateful than I can say to the Austrians, friends and otherwise, who generously and frankly shared with me their recollections of the way *it seemed to them* during the era covered by this book, and for their assistance with my research. Naturally various individuals had wholly different perceptions of the era. The choice of angles of perception for my characters has been wholly mine, but it is based in fact. In any event, I am immensely grateful to all who took such a deep interest in the project, and who were so helpful. Special thanks are due Joel Haas, Lawrence Bliss, and Russell Herman for their extraordinary help in putting the manuscript in final form. Without the faith and encouragement of my editor, Peter Schwed, it would never have been written at all.

PROLOGUE

1923

THE PRINCE'S AGENT, Dr. Rainer, could hardly bear the tension. His body stiff with it for days, at night, sleepless, he had swung between optimism and despair. Now, with the moment of decision almost at hand, he was frightened by the way his heart began to hammer. Pounds sterling! If the General bought this property, payment would be in solid, honest money worth a sum unimaginable in inflated Austrian currency. Only one word, a single *ja,* and for a few months more the Prince's current mistress could go on wallowing in her scented luxury. But, far more important, in a single stroke the fortunes of Herr Hofrat Doktor Ludwig Rainer would be restored, because his commission would also be paid in pounds. His family's survival insured, again he could walk the Kärntnerstrasse with head high; no more slinking down back streets dodging creditors. Only *ja,* he thought. Dear Jesus, he must say yes!

He studied the General's face, with its high forehead, arched nose, wide mouth, and felt a caustic surge of envy. He, once so prosperous and proud, now went about in shirts with frayed cuffs, suits with telltale darns, shoes with .worn-through soles; while Kurt Helmer, part of the crowd that had ruined him so, ruined the Empire, and brought the world tumbling down, remained not only unscathed but had everything a man could want—a wife of striking beauty, a fortune he'd not had to lift a hand to acquire, and, at this moment, perhaps literally the power of life and death over Dr. Ludwig Rainer. Because, Rainer thought, if he doesn't buy, I think I will kill myself. He was reaching the point that so many former friends had already passed, so constantly exhausted and desperate that death seemed preferable to the continuing struggle for survival in a world where all verities had been swept away overnight. But his voice was smooth, persuasive, steady, as he said, "Of course, it's one of the Prince's minor properties, but it's always been one of the most profitable. And so conveniently near the city while"—he emphasized the last words—"still offering abundant game and excellent shooting."

"Yes, I am sure," General Helmer said with that unfailing affability.

"If there's anything else at all . . . You've inspected the house and buildings, the vineyards, fields, cellars. You've met the servants, workers, tenants, and audited the accounts. But if you have one single question more, please don't hesitate to ask it."

"Thank you, but I have no more questions." Helmer smiled. In his forties, he was not quite six feet tall, only a trace of gray showing in hair the color of a crow's wing. His figure made the most of his beautifully cut English suit: wide shoulders, flat stomach, the erect posture of a soldier. He seemed wholly self-possessed and competent, but, for a military man, deplorably easygoing and democratic. This subtly bothered Rainer; like most Viennese, he defined men by rank and class, and a former brigadier general, especially a member of the Maria Theresa Order, was a personage of status and owed it to society to act the part.

"Your presentation," Helmer went on, "has been most thorough. However"—he glanced at his wife—"if you would be so kind as to allow us a few moments of privacy . . ."

Dr. Rainer's heart kicked violently. The decision was at hand. "Certainly, Herr General." His knees watery, his throat tight, he excused himself, leaving the Helmer family on the terrace.

"Well," Kurt Helmer asked Christina, "what do you think?"

She hesitated, and he watched her closely. God, he thought, how beautiful she still is! They had been married ten years; she had borne one child, was pregnant with another, and still just the sight of her could make something clutch and grab within him, leaving him breathless with the same painful, delicious emotion he had felt at first sight of her in the ballroom of the royal palace in Bucharest. At forty-five, he felt every year of war and exile and knew that each had laid its mark on him; she had suffered, too, but, sixteen years his junior, showed no sign of it.

With pale gold hair glinting in the morning sun, the bone structure of her face exquisite, with just the right dash of coarseness to keep it from seeming too delicate and fragile, she might have been their daughter's older sister. A kind of miracle, he thought; but, then, she had always seemed miraculous to him, quicksilver to his dull, rusty iron.

The breeze riffled the rich fur of the silver fox draped lavishly around her, setting off the fairness of her skin. "Well?" Helmer repeated. "After all, it's your money."

"No, ours. And ... Kurt, it's fine, it's lovely. Only—" She broke off, blue eyes cloudy.

Helmer swallowed disappointment; he had hoped for enthusiasm to match his own. "Only? All right, Christina. You're still afraid, aren't you?"

Slowly she nodded. "Yes, I am. I'm sorry, but I can't help it. Once we buy this place, we're committed once and for all to Austria. And ... that frightens me. Not for myself, but for you, for Christa, for—" She touched her swollen abdomen. "I know I shouldn't feel that way, I know how unhappy you were in Rumania—"

"I wasn't unhappy there. I won't be if we go back. Or we can try England, maybe even Canada or the United States."

She shook her head. "You'd still be an exile. Austria is your homeland. I can't imagine you really content anywhere else. And ... I don't want to be the one to deny you what means so much to you. But—"

"But you're still afraid. Well, I can't blame you. Maybe we'd be fools to come back now. It's true; if things go wrong, we could lose everything. On the other hand, though, this is our chance, *our one chance*, to acquire property, lots of it, and build an estate for our children. With the inflation here, our pounds will purchase a hundred, a thousand, times more than they ever could before or ever will again, for they're bound to reform the money soon. If we strike while inflation's at its peak, and if things do work out, it means a whole new life for us. And for Christa and our son." He was confident the second child *would* be a son, sure it could not be otherwise. "They're the ones I'm thinking of, not just ourselves."

"I know. I'm thinking of them, too." Christina bit her red underlip; her teeth were large, very white. "*And* of you, and what they did to you before and what they might do to you again and . . ." She paused, looking intently into his eyes. Then, slowly, she smiled. "You love this place, don't you? Owning it would make you happy."

"Yes," he answered simply after a moment.

"Then I think the decision is up to you. Because I know that whatever you decide will be the right thing, the best thing, for all of us. And I think you ought to make it now, with no more waiting; Dr. Rainer is entitled to an answer." She took her daughter's hand. "Christa and I will leave while you make up your mind. And whatever you decide, I will be for with all my heart. Come, darling. Let's pick some of the Prince's lovely flowers."

Helmer watched his womenfolk go down the terrace steps and cross the wide lawn of the *Schloss* park, beneath huge old linden trees. The child was an astonishing duplicate of her mother, containing the older woman's beauty within her chubby form as the bud contains the flower. Helmer felt a thrust of fear mingled with an intensity of love. Years of combat had instilled in him a kind of superstitious pessimism; knowing the random brutal ways of fate, he sometimes feared that his feeling for his family was so great it might actually tempt the gods, draw down evil on them. At such times he felt small, helpless, and inadequate, a frail shield between them and the world.

Christina had been right; he had fallen in love with this place. It had everything he had always dreamed of—three hundred hectares of rich land in the Vienna Woods, wholly rural, yet only an hour from the city itself. Once more he took inventory of its assets, beginning with the house, towering three stories above the crest this hill.

A century before, Rainer had said, the Prince's great-grand-father had razed the last crumbling walls of a ruined castle on this high plateau and built on the ancient foundations a hunting lodge which was also headquarters for one of the family's minor holdings. Since its original purposes had been simple, homely ones, the *Schloss* was, by the standards of those times, rather plain, not so much a palace as the word implied, but rather a substantial country house, painted the imperial yellow of nobility, its steeply pitched roofs of tile, its walls fortress thick to withstand brutal winter winds. There were sturdy matching outbuildings connected with it to enclose a courtyard, deep wine cellars, all the appurtenances of a working farm. Yet within there was space and luxury enough to satisfy a woman of Christina's tastes, mingled with areas of the kind of simplicity he liked. It was, in short, a nice balance of the elegant and functional; and it had struck a chord within him immediately.

Not as strongly, though, as the land itself. For he himself had been born and raised in the Wienerwald. This was the country of his childhood, and his return was like a homecoming.

Below, the mountainside fell away in a long, gentle sweep to the valley of the Fernbach, a small clear stream foaming down out of the far hills to join the Danube a few miles away. Beyond the park's walls, the orchards—plum, pear, cherry, and apple—made a frothing sea of white and pink at this season of the year. Interspersed were lush green meadows blazing with the bright yellow of thousands, maybe millions, of enormous dandelions and the plumage of countless other kinds of flowers. And beyond the meadows, row on row of staked vines, in new leaf now, marched in formation toward the valley floor—the vineyards, the heart of the whole estate.

The lifeblood of eastern Austria was wine; those sorts maturing now in the Prince's cellars were superb and valuable, and the success or failure of the family Helmer would hang on these vineyards. With hard work and close attention, he intended to make them the foundation of a fortune.

His eyes moved on, crossing the little stream on the valley floor—it marked the line of his property—and sweeping up the opposite wall, a couple of miles away. Nearly the mirror image of this side, it was superbly tended, owned, Rainer said, by a rich farmer named Max Schellhammer, a man of common origins. Schellhammer, Helmer thought, knew his business, lowborn or not. Then he turned, looking up the valley, and within him his heart lifted. Beyond, the rugged, seamed hills of the Vienna Woods rolled away as far as the eye could reach: the last dying convulsion of the Alps before the Danube plain began. For Helmer, these were more than ordinary hills and more than ordinary forests; they were something in his blood.

Curving in a vast crescent for miles around Vienna's western flank, there was something secret, dark, and mythic about them, a world within a world—endless reaches of forest; lost green valleys silvered with swift streams, dappled with isolated farms and villages; and here and there, on a hillcrest or in a sheltered lowland, a castle ruin, a *Schloss,* or one of the rich ancient monasteries of the various orders of the Church; and, of course, in the meadows and the dark coverts of the woods, the game: deer, wild boar, pheasant, hares, and foxes. All was as it had been in his childhood and for centuries before, immutable, unchanged. The Wienerwald, at least, Helmer thought, had survived the end of the rest of the world.

Which had begun in 1914, although none of them had known that yet. Only nine years; it was incredible, a half-remembered dream.

Nine years ago, Austria, as it had for centuries, sprawled across central Europe—the Dual Monarchy, the Habsburg Empire, a great power with fifty million subjects. And then something beyond comprehension had happened. What should have been a simple, quickly won war against a tiny country had been taken over by the Germans and Russians and the French and English, exploding into world catastrophe. And Austria had lost, and the House of Habsburg had collapsed. Generalmajor Kurt Helmer, once a feted hero, had returned to a Vienna caught up in seething, brutal chaos. And, like other professionals, was a target for the vengeance of the masses, urged on by the Socialists and Communists. Attacked on the streets, his wife and child threatened, and catching wind of trumped-up charges being drawn against him, he had fled.

Christina was Rumanian, and they found asylum in her homeland. There, through family connections, Helmer had won a post on the staff of King Ferdinand's corps of Royal Huntsmen, with the rank of a Rumanian colonel. Thus they had survived, while Austria was torn to bits like a hare by a pack of hounds. And when the vengeance of the Western Allies was done, there was almost nothing left—only a tiny rump of six million German-speaking people, burdened by the great city of Vienna, an imperial capital without an empire.

Helmer watched that from afar with sinking heart. In Rumania they lived well, had prestige and perquisites; in poor, shattered Austria they would have starved. And yet no day had passed that he had not yearned for home, drawn by something as mystical and powerful as a tide. When, slowly and painfully, an uneasy order emerged, a constitution was drawn up, a shaky republic established, he still dared not go home. At any moment things might collapse, the house of governmental cards fall in; and besides, the Helmers had no money.

Suddenly that last had changed. Christina's maternal grandmother was English; she died, and the Helmers received a substantial share of her estate. Only a modest fortune in British pounds, it was enormous in the devalued currency of central Europe, and new choices opened. Inevitably, that tidal pull had drawn Kurt Helmer back.

Now, though, he had to decide whether to stay. Everything in him cried out to purchase this place at the ridiculous distress-sale price offered, at last put down roots, and then use all his strength and energy not only for his family but for Austria. He could do that, stay here and gamble. But if he lost the gamble, his family lost, his children lost.

To emigrate was cowardice, he thought rebelliously, and not only cowardice but a kind of betrayal. Christa had been born in Vienna; she was Austrian. Ernst—he had already named his unborn son, for his father—deserved a homeland, too. He deserved—

Christina and his daughter reappeared through the gate, clutching bunches of the yellow flowers called keys of heaven. The girl laughed, looking up at her mother, and Christina laughed, too. In a far meadow a cock pheasant ratcheted its harsh call. A cloud passed across the sun, muting the colors of the distant hills. Then the bell of the parish church in the village of Ferndorf farther up the valley began to ring, clear and brazen. Almost at once it was drowned by a deeper, more virile, more melodious chiming from farther away: the bells of the huge ancient monastery of Altkreuzburg, near the Danube. It was exactly noon.

Helmer watched them there, against the dappled pattern of the lawn beneath the lindens, and he looked off across the valley, and his decision then was made. He belonged here; *they* belonged here, and they would not leave. To stay was risky, not to was a greater risk. He knew that now.

Christina and the child came up the steps, a question in his wife's eyes. He did not answer it directly. He touched his daughter's cheek.

"Christa," he said, "please run inside and tell Herr Hofrat Doktor Rainer I'd like to talk to him."

She ran off, and Christina leaned against him for a moment, and he put his arm around her. Then she drew away as Dr. Rainer trotted out on the terrace, face pale and contorted with the agony of *his* question.

Rainer closed his eyes, opened them again, feeling light, weightless, almost young again. For the first time in months he could see the sunshine, hear music in the distant sound of bells; indeed, they seemed a celebration of his resurrection. "All," he said as they walked toward the parked Mercedes in the drive, "will be as you direct, Herr General."

"Good," the General answered. By the trim black car they halted, and Helmer turned to look at the high, yellow flank of the house. He cleared his throat. "There is, I think, one more condition."

Rainer felt suddenly cold. He should have known it; too easy, too good to be true. And now the whiplash, the one impossible condition, probably, to which the proud, stupid Prince would certainly not agree. His gaze followed Helmer's pointing hand.

It was on the house's flank, a great colorful tile mosaic inset in the yellow plaster: the Prince's family name and coat of arms, like a banner.

"You will have skilled workmen remove that," Helmer said, "and install a new design at my expense."

Rainer leaned against the car, knees suddenly weak. "That will be no problem, Herr Generalmajor." Somehow he masked the tremor in his voice. "What design will be your pleasure?"

Helmer looked at his wife, smiling. "Nothing difficult or ornate. I think a blue background and a single word in white: *Christina*." He took her hand. "Every estate must have a name. From now on, this will be the Christina Hof. You will see to it, Herr Hofrat Doktor?"

"I shall see to it," said Rainer.

Helmer opened the door of the auto. "I shall," he said, "want the letters to be very large."

16

BOOK ONE
The
Black Peacocks
1936-1938

1 IT WAS AN ABSURD THING to have done, but he had got himself lost here in the Vienna Woods. Stupidly, he had left a marked trail to wander along another, and that had branched and branched again, and, coming back, he'd taken a wrong turn; and now he had no idea which way out, what direction to travel toward the car. But, Lan Condon thought, he had in a sense been lost in darker woods than these. And so he said aloud, using one of Ross O'Donnell's favorite phrases, "Not to worry." There was brandy left in the rucksack and a bit of daylight, and he was in no hurry to go anywhere anyhow. He had, in fact, nowhere to go, except back to the hotel room in Vienna, or the hotel bar. So the hell with it. Maybe he would just stay here until the robins covered him up with leaves.

Sinking on a tuffet of bright green moss, he leaned back against the bole of a beech that must have been young when Napoleon was still barefoot on Corsica. He was a man of thirty-three, tall and lanky in hiking clothes. His face, beneath a damp shock of dark brown hair, was lean, exhausted, with dark circles beneath dark eyes. He lit a Lucky Strike, inhaled, stared down the slope at the green infinity stretching before him.

It was, he thought, more pagan temple than forest. As if acolytes had cleared its floor of fallen limbs and underbrush, there was only a smooth carpet of leaves and a spatter of bright blue wildflowers between the thick, gnarled bluish trunks rising like columns to support a vast arched, filigreed canopy of foliage.

Yet, for all its beauty, there was a quality of wildness, too. A far cry, he thought, a long way, from the sere brown hills around Los Angeles.

Los Angeles . . . Phyll . . . and Ross. No matter how far he ran, it seemed, he could not outrun that, the memory of catastrophe. Guilt was a hound that could trail even across an ocean. Violently he shook his head, but the image was already there: Ross standing in the doorway of the bedroom, round face as pale as tallow, eyes wide with shock and horror, mouth gaping. And his wife, naked, bent over Lanier Condon's body, also naked, her swirl of hair still not long enough to mask what her mouth was doing. And then that strange, incoherent cry breaking from Ross's throat, raw agony and— He could have come on in, Lan Condon thought; he should have! He could have beat hell out of both of us; I would never have raised a finger! Instead—

He drank some brandy from the pack. It helped a little, not enough. He remembered shoving Phyllis sprawling off the bed, springing up. "Ross!" he'd yelled, but there were already footsteps on the stairs, going down, the slam of the outer door, the roar of a car's engine starting. And Phyllis, standing there, robe pulled about her, in the bedroom when he returned, pale and shaken. "He's gone?"

"He's gone."

Phyll poured two drinks, hands trembling, gave one to him, tossed hers off, lit a cigarette. "Damn him," she said with husky fury. "Damn him to hell! How dare he do that to me! He was supposed to be in New York until Monday! He didn't even wire or call." She turned on him. "Deliberately! He did it deliberately! It was a trap!"

Lan Condon's first impulse had been to hit her. Instead, he drained his glass. "No," he said dully, "it wasn't any trap. It was a joke, a dirty joke, the oldest dirty joke in the world. Husband comes home to find his best friend and his wife— God damn it!" he roared and threw the empty glass against the wall and with hasty, fumbling hands began to pull on his clothes.

Her voice had been metallic. "Where're you going?"

"To find him," Lan had rasped.

"Find him?" She laughed harshly. "What then?"

"How the hell do I know? All I know is I've got to find him. He'll probably head straight for Frenchy's place." He turned toward the bedroom door.

"Lan!" Phyll caught his arm. "Don't. Don't leave me. Suppose he comes back while you're gone?"

Condon looked down at her, the pale lovely face framed by the touseled fall of dark rich hair, the enormous eyes, the red love-swollen mouth. A half hour ago it had been the most desirable face he had ever seen, worth any risk, any betrayal. Now it might as well have been a skull. "You know," he said wearily, "that Ross wouldn't hurt you. You know him better than that."

"But he'll have been drinking. And— Lan, for God's sake!" But he was already gone.

But he had not found Ross, he thought now, letting more of the strong dark brandy trickle down his throat. Not at Frenchy's, not at any of the usual places, not at the studio. And finally, exhausted, trembling, he had gone home to his own bungalow at the Garden of Allah. When he had entered, he'd half expected to find Ross there waiting for him; it was the way they would have paced the script, written the scene. But he was not there either and had not been there. And Lan had not known what to do, what to say when he and Ross finally confronted each other. What could he say? "Well, O'Donnell, it was this way. Phyll and I couldn't help it. It was bigger than both of us."

He had quit making scenarios for the meeting in his head, and driven back to the O'Donnell house on Camden Drive. By then Phyll had somewhat recovered. "Well, there's nothing to do but wait. He'll be back eventually. And then we might as well have it out. Maybe it's all for the best." She took his hand. "I can't understand it, but I'm getting hungry. Come on in the kitchen, I'll make some sandwiches and coffee."

In there he'd watched her—trim, graceful, and as cool and businesslike now, he thought, as Lady Macbeth—and he could not imagine how desire and revulsion could so intermingle. Well, he could not lay the blame on her, it had been his fault as much as hers. Restlessly he'd moved around the kitchen. "I'll take this garbage out," he said, not even knowing he was saying it. He went outside after turning on the floodlight, dumped the smaller pail in the big can, closed the lid. Today had been a hot one, now a cool breeze blew. He straightened up, drawing in deep breaths of freshness. Then he heard it, the steady pulsing sound, muffled, of a car's engine running, idling. Had Ross come back unheard, was he—?

Then he understood. The sound came from the closed garage. "Oh, my God," Lanier Condon whispered. Then he was running across the drive, heart pounding, bile stinging in his throat, already knowing what he would find.

Worst of all was the recollection of that twenty minutes after he had rolled open the door of the garage, pulled Ross's huge inert figure from the front seat of the car, dragged it to the pavement. "Call an ambulance!" he'd screamed to Phyll, and then, there in the floodlit night on the asphalt of the drive, had begun to give Ross artificial respiration. He was still at it, begging, pleading, crying out to the unresponsive body to move, to stir, to awaken enough to hear contrition, when the ambulance screamed up. They dragged him off, clamped on the respirator, but it did not help. Still hope lingered until, in the echoing, feverishly lit hall of the hospital's emergency corridor, the doctor came to tell Phyllis she was a widow. The police were there, too, by then. They questioned her first, and he heard her coolly tell the story that he had not even known she had devised. It was all neat and logical: she had been alone when Ross had returned unexpectedly from a visit to his family in New York, where his mother had been ill. He had been depressed and weary from the trip, had acted even more strangely than he had been acting lately. They had quarreled. He had, she thought, driven away. For a long time she had been afraid of suicide. Upset, she had called his collaborator and best friend, Sidney Lanier Condon, and Condon had searched for him, ineffectually. Had returned to the house on Camden Drive to comfort Phyllis. Had put out the garbage, heard the motor running in the garage. Ross hadn't driven away at all. He had driven into the garage, left the engine idling, closed the door, and ... They knew the rest. Mr. Condon had worked tirelessly to save him, but hours had passed and it was too late. She did it marvelously, every nuance exactly right; but, then, she had been a damned fine actress until she'd married Ross and he'd taken her out of circulation.

The detective turned to Condon. "Is that right, Mr. Condon?"

"Yes," he heard himself say, as if he were standing at the other end of the long hall and watching all of this. "Yes, that's exactly how it happened."

Phyllis did not even sigh. Or if she did, the handkerchief she held to her face masked the sound. "All right," said the cop. "There may be questions later. You'll take her home?"

"I'll take her home," said Lan.

In the house, she poured each of them a stiff drink. "Thanks, Lan. There'll be no problems, of course. The studio will see to that." Phyll looked at him a moment, then turned away. "Christ," she said, "don't you think I loved him, too? I slept with him and gave up my career when he insisted and I tried to be a good wife—"

"I know you did," Lan said gently.

She drained her glass. "Look," she said, "I'll be all right. Understand? I'll be perfectly all right." She hugged herself as if very cold; and now, three years older than he, she looked every year of her age. "I just don't think," she said almost briskly, "that we should come near each other again. Except at the funeral. You've got to comfort me in public. You understand? But I don't think we should come near each other again ever, not for a long time anyhow. Besides, after they bury him, I'm going home to Maryland for a while. I'm not superhuman either; I need my family around me."

Condon slid the brandy back into the rucksack and wearily stood up. Well, somehow or another, he had better get out of these woods. Slinging the pack, he strode on through the silent beech forest, following a narrow winding trail. Where it would take him, he had no idea. All he knew was that he was somewhere in Austria, for no particular reason except that Willi Orlik had been right.

"A hiding place," the lean, handsome little man had said, looking around the bungalow's living room—a hog wallow of books, scripts, empty bottles, and soiled clothes—out of which Condon had barely stirred since Ross's funeral. "A place to think things out, recover from the shock. So . . . any place in mind?"

"No," Lan said. He had not invited Willi here and wished he would go away.

"Well . . ." Willi helped himself to a drink. "Where could be a problem, all right. London, Paris, the way they are now, they're no cure for depression. My God, in London every day is

23

gloomy Sunday, and Paris is even worse. Why not Vienna?" He smiled. "Short of joining the Foreign Legion, it's the best place to forget that I can think of."

Condon only grunted.

"Of course it's Fascist, too, now—Austria. But it's a typically Austrian kind of Fascism, more of a defense against Hitler by cuddling up to Mussolini than an ideology. The Austrians have, really, only one ideology—to survive with as much grace and enjoyment as possible, however bad things may get. Oh, it's no bed of roses, either. No place is these days. But there's still gaiety there. And, I'll guarantee this: it's totally unlike any place you have ever been before, and the people are totally unlike any you have ever met, present company excepted. How much money do you have?"

"About twenty thousand."

"So. Not much by our standards in this madhouse, but there you could live like a king for five years anyhow. Wine, Lan, song, and women. All the ingredients for forgetting."

"If it's such a paradise, why did you leave it?"

"Two reasons. Who in Austria's going to pay me sixty thousand dollars to direct a picture? And I'm a Jew. In Vienna a Jew, no matter how successful, must take a lot of shit. Here in the studio it's the other way around. *We* hand it out to *goyim* like you. But that has nothing to do with Vienna from your standpoint. So?"

"I don't know," Condon muttered.

"Lan," Willi said sharply. When Condon looked at him, he raised an empty bottle. "I was Ross's friend, and despite it all I am still your friend. You didn't kill Ross, not completely. This ... this had already killed most of what he had and you know it." Then Orlik's manner changed completely. "Well, I've had my say. Now I've got to rush; a young lady is waiting for me. She thinks she's going to play Sandra in the picture. Of course she is impossible, but for the moment, for my own purposes, I have convinced myself that I will cast her. I do this with all the best will and good intentions and lightest heart in the world. Are you listening carefully? You have just heard the Viennese mind at work. My capacity for deception is exceeded only by my capacity for self-deception, and so my conscience is always clear."

He went to the door. "Go to Vienna, Lan. Stay a while. Write

24

when you can. Not scripts, but another novel, a good one. Then you will see a lot of things in a different light." He nodded. "If I can help you, Lan, just call on me. *Wiederseh'n*." And he went out.

After he had gone, Lan Condon had poured himself another drink and looked around the stinking little room. Why not? he found himself thinking. Why the hell not?

The path began to slope downhill. The silence, the lifelessness, of the forest was almost eerie; the woods strangely unreal. This was the forest of myth and fable, of witch and elf and gnome, woodcutter and werewolf, and he was alien here. He smiled at the combination of the brandy and his imagination; but the fact that it was getting late and he was a long way from his car was no joke.

Below him the path dropped steeply down a hillside into a deep ravine through which ran a trickle of muddy water. It looked forbidding, that dark gulch, but it was the only path he had, so, with the brandy still working in him, he skittered down the slope. Just as he reached the bottom, something large and nimble dashed off through the woods farther down the ravine, breaking twigs and rustling leaves. Lan whirled, tensing. He'd heard there were wild boars living in the Wienerwald. Then he laughed, relaxing, as a frightened blat drifted back to him, unmistakably a goat.

Well, he thought, if you had a goat, you had a farm, and if you had a farm, you had people, and people could tell you how to find your car. The woods were less hostile now as he slogged along the muddy bottom of the ravine. Presently the path led across the stream and up the far bank.

He still could not see the goat, but it blatted again, somewhere far to his right. The path led toward the hillcrest; probably the farm was not far behind it. Bent forward, he trudged on upward.

One moment he was alone, the next a man blocked the path. Lan Condon gasped, jumped back, stared, short hair prickling on his neck's nape. "Hello—" he began, then broke off as he stared into fierce blue eyes belonging to what could only be a hallucination.

Out of a nightmare or a childhood book of fable, the figure

was short, squat, iron-gray hair a frowzy dirty bush, gray beard hanging matted to its chest. A square leathery face was contorted in a snarl, the eyes, like chips of bottle glass, had fire behind them. Thick gray hair crawled up across the being's chest from beneath a low-cut leather shirt; and stubby solid legs were wrapped in shapeless leather breeches, bound around the calves with thongs, vanishing into high leather boots, obviously homemade. The creature glowered at him, and in its right hand was an unsheathed sword, bronze blade glinting in the soft slanting light; in its left it brandished forward a bronze-pointed spear. Lan backed away two paces more. Either he had gone mad or he was confronted with a primitive Teutonic warrior.

Making a sound in its throat, the thing stepped forward, brandishing the sword. From it roiled a string of guttural words, of which Condon recognized a single one: *Verboten*. Then the wild man gestured with the spear, unmistakably ordering Lan back the way he'd come.

"All right." Lan backed down the hill. "All right." The man in leather stood there scowling, sword and spear both upraised. Then he fired another word Lan understood. *"Wiederseh'n!"* With that dismissal, Condon turned around, hurried back along the path. Finally he saw the goat, standing on the slope nearby, watching him with bright curiosity.

Down in the ravine he turned and looked up the hill. The creature in leather clothes had vanished. Lan shook his head unbelievingly, feeling silly after such headlong flight. But what else to do when some misplaced Cimbrian or Helvetian brandished a broadsword and threatened to divide you in three parts? He heard a rattling laugh from his own throat.

"Absurdity, not sin," Ross had said once, "is the normal condition of mankind."

Then he sobered. Be that as it may, he had better put some distance between himself and the evil genius of these woods. He scrambled up the opposite hill, retracing his steps. Presently, breathing hard, he reached the level again. There he stood indecisively, not sure yet of what he had seen. Wearily he went back the way he had come, often turning to look behind him, but seeing nothing to alarm him. Presently he reached the edge of a kind of glade, where the forest opened out a little, and there he halted. A few yards away, where a shaft of blue-gold light splayed down through a foliage rift, a man dressed in somber black sat on a log, his back to Condon, a curl of cigarette smoke wreathing itself around his head.

And what will he be? Lan wondered. A leprechaun? Cautiously he moved forward, careful to scuffle leaves to give ample warning of his coming.

The man in black heard and stood up, turning. Not tall, very slender, he had a long thin face nearly as white as the clerical collar at his throat. Seeing that, Condon relaxed. Priests he could cope with.

As Lan came up, the man nodded, smiled. He was not old, younger than Lan, perhaps in his late twenties. He wore thick-lensed glasses, eyes dark, soft, and friendly behind them. *"Grüss Gott,"* he said, voice unexpectedly deep and mellow. *"Guten Tag."*

"Grüss Gott." Lan groped for German. *"Ich bin Amerikaner ..."*

"Oh, an American! Well, how do you do?" the priest said in perfect English, coming forward with hand outstretched.

"Oh, good." Lan felt sanity returning; the hand was small and fragile, yet firm. "You speak English."

"Of course. As a matter of fact, I teach it. I am Chorherr Doktor Martinus from the Stift—the monastery—of Altkreuzburg. At your service, sir."

"Well, Father, I can use some service. My name's Condon, Sidney Lanier Condon, and I'm lost. I left my car at a little place called Oberfelsdorf, I think, to take a walk, and I got turned around somehow—"

"Oberfelsdorf? Oh, dear, you *are* turned around. It's nearly ten kilometers that way." He pointed at right angles to the path.

"Oh, Lord. I knew I was lost, but not that lost." Lan sank down on the log.

"You're on the wrong side of the valley." Dr. Martinus looked at him a moment, then smiled reassuringly. "Ah, well, don't worry, Mr. Condon. I'll be glad to show you a well-marked path that will take you there." His English was fluent, British-accented, musical.

"Thanks. I hate to put you to so much trouble."

"No trouble at all. I'm just strolling in the woods, and one direction's as good as another. An American—I say. We don't get many of you this far from the city. And your great country has always interested me. May I ask where in it you are from?"

"Louisiana originally."

"I am not sure ... Ah, yes. Longfellow's poem 'Evangeline.' Of course. But speaking of poets, your name was—?"

"Condon. Sidney Lanier Condon."

"What I thought I heard. Sidney Lanier? The Georgia poet, no? 'The Marshes of Glynn'? And, yes: 'Into the woods my master went, Clean forespent, forespent ...'" He jerked his head ecstatically. "So beautiful and apt."

Lan stared at him. Dr. Martinus looked shy. "Well, as I said, I teach English in the Gymnasium at Altkreuzburg. And I write some poetry and essays myself, usually in English also. I've had a couple of slender volumes published in Great Britain. Sidney Lanier ... How did you get that name?"

"He was a cousin of my grandmother's."

"Then ... is it possible you've inherited—? Perhaps you write yourself."

"Yes," Lan said. "Yes, I write—a little."

The young priest stared at him with penetrating and sophisticated intelligence. "Somehow I thought so. Perhaps more than a little?" He tapped his temple with a slender forefinger. "Somehow, I think ... Ah. Ah, yes!" He straightened up. *"Sup with the Devil!"*

Lan Condon's mouth dropped open.

"Ah!" the priest crowed triumphantly. "You *did* write it!"

"Yes, but—" Lan gestured. "Six years ago, and—"

"Of course! And I have a friend in London who sends me new books of consequence as they are published! And I pride myself, Mr. Condon, on never forgetting any book I have read, or the author." He put out his hand again. "This is indeed an honor! And may I say that my memory of your book is not just a fluke. It was indeed a memorable piece of work. There are scenes in it which I recall as clearly as if I had experienced them myself, and some appalled me and some moved me deeply. Ah. Ah, yes." He shook Condon's hand vigorously.

Lan smiled wryly. "Well, I guess that's fame. When you meet a stranger in the woods eight thousand miles from home and he's read your book." He knew now what kind of day this was turning out to be. *Slantwise,* Ross had called such days. "The day turns this way"—he'd jerked one hand higher than the other—"and when you tell somebody, nobody believes it and neither do you."

Then his brief pleasure faded. "Dr. Martinus, it's getting late."

"Yes, I'm sorry. We'd best be getting on. Perhaps I'll walk all the way to Oberfelsdorf with you." He gestured toward the ravine. "This way is shortest." He took a step, but Condon touched his shoulder.

"Wait a minute," Lan said, and when the priest looked at him inquiringly, Lan told Martinus about the apparition with sword and spear. "Anyhow, that's what I *think* I saw."

"Professor Busch." Martinus smiled.

"Professor?"

"*Ja.*" Martinus sighed, a little sadly. "He was brilliant once, one of the world's leading authorities on the bronze- and iron-age cultures of old Germanic tribes."

"He looked it."

"Yes, it's a pity, but these things happen. There are many pressures on certain people here in Austria and . . . much has happened in a short time. Some minds, not fortified by Christianity, find it hard to cope. Professor Busch's was one of those. A few years ago he suddenly resigned his chair. Civilization as we knew it, he proclaimed, was doomed; the only salvation was to revert to the old pure Germanic way of life to appease the ancient gods. Then he turned up here in the Wienerwald. Up there on that hill"—Martinus pointed—"he built a wattled hut, authentic pre-Christian Germanic construction, right down to the last twig, and settled down to living as nearly like an ancient Teuton as is possible these days. He even has a woman with him, a misguided former student." Martinus shrugged. "I daresay it was dismaying to bump into him like that, but really, he's quite harmless."

"You wouldn't have thought so if you could have seen him wave that sword. '*Verboten!*' he said. I caught that much."

"Odd." The priest's eyes clouded. "Usually he has no objection to visitors, provided they'll listen to his ranting. He ordered you away, threatened you?"

"With decapitation, the way I understood it."

29

"Hmmmm." Martinus rubbed his chin. "Maybe it's better if we don't go that way after all." Suddenly he smiled, pale face lighting. "Never mind, Mr. Condon. I have a better solution. Don't know why I didn't think of it at first, but I've a friend living not far away who has a motorcar—a couple of them. I'm sure he'll be happy to send you to Oberfelsdorf in one of his to pick up your own." He pointed up the trail, away from the ravine and Professor Busch. "It's only a couple of miles, and the walk's a scenic one. We can be there in less than an hour."

2   As USUAL on a Sunday afternoon, they came in droves —the invited and the uninvited. Now, at *Jause*—tea-time—the trickle of visitors had swollen to a flood, and Christa was nearly exhausted from playing her role as hostess, while Aunt Alma kept the servants busy replenishing the food and drink on the tables on the terrace. *Oh, my dear Herr Hofrat, how nice to see you! Frau Doktor, it's been so long! Yes, of course, Herr Colonel! You are always welcome here!* Like a trained monkey at the Prater, she thought: gesturing, smiling, chittering, performing. The whole house was packed with flowers, mostly wild ones from the Wienerwald. No caller but must bring flowers, candy, or some other gift; and it was astonishing how many elderly couples just happened to be taking a Sunday stroll in the woods and had, on impulse, decided to favor the General and his family with a wildflower bouquet . . . just at mealtime.

Well, she did not mind, really, the poor old things. Some of them were aristocracy and some were military and some were simply middle class. But they all had one thing in common: the world they had lived in no longer existed. And the world that succeeded it had no place for them.

For so many of them, what they would eat here this Sunday afternoon would be the only square meal of the week, unless, as he so often did, Papa saw that they departed burdened with tactful gifts. *Herr Doktor Kommerzialrat, I must ask a favor. We are experimenting with a new formula for seasoning our bacon.*

Would you be so kind as to accept a kilo of it, taste it, and give me your valued opinion? Perhaps there is too much paprika ... And a liter of our Grüner Veltliner? I am sorry, last year was really not very good. Oh, these cucumbers! We simply have more than we can use, the season is at its height ... And off they would go, Herr Doktor Kommerzialrat and his tottering Frau Doktor, trying to mask the relief, joy, and gratitude they felt, trying to save face and dignity by taking it all in stride.

"Herr General," Uncle Max would say, "you'll bankrupt yourself."

"Nonsense!" Papa would reply. "A liter of wine, a kilo of bacon, a few cucumbers? Read your Bible, Max. Bread cast upon the waters. Or do you remember the fable of the lion and the mouse? Yes, these people are old and now they are poor. And while I'm out here in the country, they are in Vienna, sitting in their coffeehouses or gossiping with their relatives. And what they learn in the week, I learn on Sunday, sometimes sooner if they know it will affect me. Friends, Max. If you look after your friends, they'll look after you. Myself, I think the price is cheap enough to know what will happen before it happens."

"It must be nice to be rich," Uncle Max would say. "Giving good food away to find out who sleeps with whom."

"And when, in Austria, has that knowledge ever been unimportant?" Papa would laugh. "Max, Max. Maybe you could buy and sell me twice. But you have your way of doing things and I have mine."

And Uncle Max would growl and pour himself another glass of schnapps.

Now, for a moment, there was a lull. I simply must freshen up, Christa thought, and she dodged into the downstairs bath. There she touched up her lipstick, made a quick pass at her hair, added another touch of 4711—Jicky was too heavy for her taste—behind each ear, at the cleft of bosom. Usually they talked politics, she thought, out there on the terrace. Today, though, they would be talking about Christa Helmer.

Leaving the bath, she dodged into her father's study, a large room full of his hunting trophies and military decorations, wholly masculine. There on his desk this week's issue of *Die Bühne,* with its usual lurid, sophisticated cover, looked out of place. She thumbed it open to a spread of photographs. The magazine was an amalgam of society and theatrical gossip, and there, the largest picture in the spread, was she, in the two-piece bathing suit she had bought without his knowledge. "Fräulein Christa Helmer, daughter of Generalmajor Kurt Helmer ... one of the beach nymphs at Baden ... models the latest bathing dress."

All right! she thought. I *didn't* know he was taking me that way on the diving board ladder, bent forward. Yes, a little more and one could see my nipples. Still, she had no regrets. There was, somehow, a deep satisfaction in knowing she had scandalized all of Austria and maybe half of Germany. At least it gave her some identity of her own. And the sight of her own nakedness in the picture obscurely thrilled her. No denying it, she was lovely, prettier than any of the actresses or the show-girls in the other pictures. Even Auntie Alma, purple-faced as she had been, grudgingly admitted that.

And, of course, she had been the first to show the picture to her father, realizing that things would be much simpler that way. For a moment he had stared at it, and slowly his face had turned brick red. "Christa," he finally managed, while she waited tensely. "How could you?" He drew in breath. "What would your mother say?"

"Papa, Papa." She smoothed the hair along his temples. "You always said yourself, Mama was the most fashionable woman in Vienna. Don't you think she would have worn it at my age?" She kissed him. "Papa, don't be fierce to me."

"I'm not being fierce. Only ..." Then she felt his body relax. "Only, I'm still not sure it's proper and ..." He raised his head and looked at her. "Come around here."

She had yielded to his grasp. Now, he could look into her eyes. She looked back, directly, proud, lovingly. And, as she had known he would, suddenly he laughed. "All right," he said. "You've done it again, haven't you?"

"Done what?" she asked with all the innocence she could muster.

"You know what." He looked at the picture again, eyes clouding in a way that touched her. "Yes," he said. "Yes, she would have worn it if it were the fashion. And she *could* have worn it, too, even at her age. She was like the Empress Elisabeth; she had the kind of beauty that never fades, only deepens with the years." He had closed the magazine. "And you are so much like her. So . . . it will be a minor scandal, a tempest in a teapot, and next week there'll be something else in this rag and it'll be forgotten."

"Of course it will." She kissed him solidly. "Thank you, Papa, for not being mad."

She had started to leave then, knowing exactly when to let well enough alone; but his voice halted her. "Christa."

"Yes, Papa?" Apprehensively she turned.

But he was smiling. "You *are* the prettiest girl in the magazine. I looked at all of them and decided that."

Christa laughed. "Thank you, Papa. So did I." She threw him another kiss and went out.

Now she closed the magazine, touched her hair again, and left his office. She'd heard enough conversation this afternoon to know that the older people indeed were shocked, the younger ones admiring. The degree of scandal was absolutely perfect. After all, a Viennese who had reached the age of twenty-one without creating *some* sort of sensation, well, what a poor dull creature she would be!

Somewhere in the house a bell rang as she stepped out into the corridor, and she smiled. Another rickety *Gemeinderat* and his Frau, salivating; more wildflowers as a hostess gift, the price of the meal. Slowly she wandered to the foyer, prepared to receive the newcomers; there would be a time lag, for the bell was wired to the gate.

Traudi, one of the servant girls, was waiting there to open the door. Out on the terrace the throaty voice of Zarah Leander husked a love song as the younger people played a gramophone. Christa smoothed the silk summer dress from Bertha Farnhammer, with its floral pattern. Then the doorbell rang, and Traudi opened the door and Christa gasped, feeling her heart kick beneath her breasts with terror and excitement. The man in the doorway was Josef Steiner.

Entering, he handed his hat to Traudi, strode forward, a tall, angular, almost spidery man in a black suit, his face pale, exhausted, and very handsome, his eyes lambent pits of blackness. As she stood motionless, he came to her, and automatically she raised her hand and he bent gracefully, touched his lips to it. "Your servant, *gnädige Fräulein.*" Straightening, he handed her a bouquet—a dozen roses, velvety black.

Christa swallowed hard. "Herr Doktor Steiner." She wondered if Traudi caught the tremor in her voice. Then, blessedly, Aunt Alma called from somewhere in the back of the house, "Traudi! You, Traudi! Come here, please!"

Josef Steiner stood motionless, as did Christa, until the girl disappeared. His eyes darted around the foyer, into the adjoining rooms and passages. Then he said, *"Du,"* and embraced her. Pulling her hard against his lean body, he crushed his mouth down on hers, penetrating it with his tongue.

For one second Christa was absolutely rigid. Then something dissolved within her, and suddenly she returned the kiss, fervidly, left hand digging through his coat, nails biting in. Then she broke away, appalled at the risk she'd taken.

"Josef!" she whispered. "Have you gone mad?"

He smiled, in that weary, wholly confident way that made her feel as if she stood naked before him and more than naked, as if he could read everything inside her, like some pagan priest divining the entrails of a sacrifice. "Of course. Ask my brothers. They'll all testify that I am mad."

"But to come here—"

"Your father banks with my family. If we are good enough to handle his money, are we not good enough to drink his wine?" Then, earnestly, "Listen, don't worry. I won't embarrass you. I'll not come near you. But I couldn't stay away. I thought to myself, I must see her. So, now, I will greet your father, your aunt, stay only a little while. You may be as cold and distant as you choose. But at least I can look at you for a few moments and . . ." His voice dropped to a whisper. "I shall be in Vienna all this week. Please. Monday afternoon, at our place?"

"Josef, I don't *know.*" She was also whispering now, looking over her shoulder. "I—" Then she saw Aunt Alma coming down the corridor.

"I shall wait," he said. "Monday, Tuesday, the whole week if necessary." Then he turned, took a step forward. "Ah, good afternoon, *gnädige Frau!*"

Kurt Helmer's sister smiled, then stopped dead, recognizing him. "Oh," she said. But Josef, still smiling, moved toward her; and as he did, she stared at him like a bird fascinated by a snake. Somehow he seemed to will her to raise her hand, and she did, and he kissed it with perfect grace. Aunt Alma was seventy, withered, harsh, direct, and tough; yet Christa saw how, for an instant, she batted her eyes almost coquettishly and moved her tongue along her lips.

"Good afternoon, Herr Doktor Steiner." Her voice was shaky, cracked, uncertain. Her eyes lanced to the bouquet Christa held. "Oh, what beautiful black roses!" she blurted.

"A pathetic offering from Schloss Schwarzgipfel," Josef said, and she saw the glint in his eyes, knew he was handling Aunt Alma firmly and expertly. "I should have brought twice as many."

Christa's paralysis broke. "Auntie." She thrust the roses at the older woman. "Would you see to these? Herr Doktor Steiner wants to speak to Papa."

"Of course," Aunt Alma croaked. But now she had recovered, lips set thinly, eyes turned cold. "Yes, I'll see to them." She turned, marched back down the corridor.

Steiner waited until she had disappeared. "A charming lady," he murmured ironically. "But her niece is much more charming." And for just an instance his hand touched her waist as if, again, he would embrace her.

Frightened, yet profoundly excited, Christa pushed the hand away. She had not bargained for this, she had not bargained for this at all. It was one thing to meet Josef Steiner in some secluded coffeehouse, to ride with him in his black roadster along back roads where they would not be seen together; and there had even been that afternoon early last week when, finally, reluctantly, yet unable to resist, she had gone to the address he had given her, the small apartment in a workers' district where she would certainly not be recognized, and which, within, had been furnished luxuriously, bizarrely, with black damask, black velvet, and only here and there a touch of blood red, and where she had let him go much too far in kissing her and caressing her. All that was one thing. Quite another was to have this Jew show up bold as brass at the Christina Hof on Sunday afternoon; it was embarrassing and downright dangerous, a sign either of great love or fierce desire, and she did not know what to make of it.

"Come," she said firmly and led him through the house to the

35

crowded terrace, where the guests had curdled into groups and cliques by age and rank. The young people she'd invited from Vienna were foxtrotting to music from the gramophone; the older women sat gossiping on the wicker outdoor furniture, again dividing themselves according to their husbands' titles, and their husbands stood talking politics or hunting. Thank God, Christa thought, neither Robert Schellhammer nor his father, whom she knew as Uncle Max, were among those present this afternoon.

Her own father was in a group of leathery men at the far corner of the terrace, avidly discussing guns, bullet loads, stalking methods, or the like. They did not look up as Steiner entered, but others did; and then, like an infection, a diminution of the chatter spread. Then her father raised his head and saw Josef Steiner.

The instant surprise in his eyes was immediately masked by hospitality. Excusing himself, he strode across the flagstones. "Good day, Herr Doktor Steiner," he said in a loud, clear voice. "This is an unexpected pleasure."

"Herr Generalmajor. I hope you will forgive the intrusion. I was on my way to Vienna from the Wachau and I thought I would call and pay my respects. I hope I am . . . welcome."

"You are, of course, quite welcome." Kurt Helmer's voice was, if not warm, courteous. But what else could he say? Christa thought. Next to the Rothschilds, the Steiners were perhaps the most important and soundest family banking firm in Vienna, and the Helmer accounts had been with them for years. These days, as even Christa knew, a financial connection with the Steiners was too important to be damaged by discourtesy to any member of the family, even a black sheep like Josef. "Come," said the General smoothly, "and try my latest bottlings. I know they're inferior to your Wachauer wines . . ."

Christa drew in breath, her cheeks hot, her palms moist. Papa was not stupid, and he must be wondering why Josef had stopped by. If Steiner paid her any undue attention, the game was up, and then there would be an explosion that would make the scandal of the picture in *Die Bühne* a bagatelle, the kind of thing Kurt Helmer could not gloss over. Quickly she turned, merged into the protective covering of the group from the University around the gramophone. "Rudi"—she took the hand of a handsome boy in white flannels—"will you dance with me?"

He stirred nothing at all within her, but his embrace was like a refuge. As they moved together to the lovely American song "Blue Moon," she had time to think. In a sense, she told herself, it was Papa's own fault that she had got mixed up with Josef Steiner. The increasing pressure he had put on her, subtle yet unrelenting, about marrying Robert Schellhammer, had upset and dismayed her, so that she was already rebellious and vulnerable that night Josef had approached her at the Opera.

It had been a performance of *Don Giovanni,* which she loved for its beauty, sensuality, and eroticism. She and Luisa Kraus, whose father was something important in the government, had gone together unescorted to the great gray opera house on the Ringstrasse. She had not told Luisa anything about Robert; she was puzzled and embarrassed by her father's obvious approval of the son of a farmer, even a *Grossbauer*—a rich farmer —as a potential husband for her. Not that Robert was a clodhopper; he had his *Matura* and was a graduate of the Wine School at Klosterneuburg. But she had known him all her life and knew him well enough to be sure that she would not marry him, no matter what. When she married, finally, she knew how she wanted it to be, and she had no intention of some flat, dull, earthbound union with poor earnest Robert Schellhammer.

For a while, once inside the Opera, she put it all from her mind, savoring as always the grandeur and excitement of the crowd, the music, and the magnificent building itself. She knew that, in the blue dress, low-cut, with the bow between her breasts, the high heels which she managed gracefully, without a thought, and the special care given to her hair, she drew her share of masculine attention, female envy. At the interval, she and Luisa went to the smoking hall, with its parquet floors and crystal chandeliers to have a cigarette and a glass of *Sekt,* after which, of course, they would promenade, seeing and being seen. The buffet was crowded, though, and after one attempt they stood aside to wait until the crowd diminished. That was when the tall, pale young man in faultless evening dress had strode toward them, a glass of champagne in each hand. "Allow me," he said, smiling. There was something strange about his eyes, large, absolutely black, unreadable. He seemed not quite well, totally fatigued, as if possessed of knowledge so vast, profound, and bitter that it had drained and enervated him. When he introduced himself, Christa barely suppressed a gasp of shock and excitement, for Josef Steiner was legendary. The Viennese were dedicated gossips, and his affairs with women high and low had provided grist for their mill. There was talk of strange rites and rituals, even orgies, at his *Schloss* in the Wachau, far up the Danube; but then Jews, especially those enormously rich, went in for dark, strange pleasures, as everyone knew. Somehow, not knowing how it happened, never remembering afterwards any conscious decision, she had agreed to meet him the next day for lunch at a restaurant she had never heard of in the Sixth District. Then the bell rang, and they returned to their seats.

Luisa had been simultaneously atwitter and appalled. "Christa, you aren't really going?"

She felt strangely cool, superior. "And why shouldn't I?"

"But *Josef Steiner!* He'll . . . he'll seduce you, rape you!"

Christa had raised a brow. Someone else seemed to be speaking from within her. "Do you really think so? That should be interesting."

"Oh, Christa, don't be impossible. Besides, he's a Jew!"

"They say he doesn't work at it. That's one reason he and his brothers aren't speaking." She smiled as applause broke out, the conductor returning to the podium. "I shouldn't think a luncheon would ruin me."

"But that restaurant he mentioned. Why should he invite you to a place like that? Away from everything—"

"To protect my reputation, goose! No one I know will see us there!" She turned on Luisa. "And if you spill a single word—"

"Of course I won't. But you must tell me all about it." Then the music had started and they sat back to see the opera.

3   SLIGHT AS HE WAS, Martinus seemed totally inde-
     fatigable; and Condon, with much longer legs, was
hard put to match his pace through the woods.

A *Chorherr*, the priest said, was a member of the Augustinian order resident at the Stift, the monastery, at Altkreuzburg. "You must have seen it on your way to Oberfelsdorf. High up on your left, above the Danube, just where the river makes a bend." Lan nodded, with a fleeting memory of a gray stone massiveness, like a huge old fort, sprawling across a beetling ridge above the river. "It was founded in the thirteenth century," Martinus continued. "I'd be happy to take you through it someday, if you should have the time. We have some remarkable treasures there, many of which the general public is not aware of."

"So you're a monk," said Condon.

"Well, not precisely. Strictly speaking, we are a community of clergymen whose duty is to go out into the parishes of our canon and serve the people as ministers or teachers. As I say, I teach English at the Gymnasium in the town. *Chorherr* is a rather antiquated term—gentleman of the choir. It stems from our belief in the choral celebration of our divine office. The restrictions on us are considerably less onerous than those of other orders, and we are, perhaps, a bit more worldly."

Condon nodded. As if abhorring silence, Martinus went on. "I've been very fortunate. My parents were poor country people living in the mountains south of here. As a child I loved to sing, had a rather remarkable voice. Word of it reached the Stift, and they recruited me for their boys' choir. They guaranteed my support and education even after my voice changed. Really, it was the only chance for me, and I shall always raise my prayers of gratitude for my dear parents, who were willing to make the sacrifice, give me up. Otherwise I should be stacking hay in some mountain field, or tending bar in some country *Gasthaus*. Instead, the Stift saw that I got my doctorate; and six years ago, in humble thanks, I took my final vows." He smiled. "Now you see why I know these woods so well. The Stift owns much of them, and I've been roaming them all my life."

A little farther on they saw a crone, bent almost double under an enormous bundle of twigs and sticks, a scarf around her head, a basket on her arm. She shuffled with tiny crippled steps through a glade, never seeing them, eyes riveted on the ground. "Firewood and mushrooms," Martinus said quietly. "Gathering both today. Poor creature. Times are very hard here for many people, Mr. Condon."

"Not only here."

"In America as well?"

"In America as well." He thought of the endless maddening sway of a boxcar, the rank musty smell of the unwashed humanity piled and clustered in it, of hobo jungles and of deputies and railroad bulls: things he had known so well and managed to bury after having struck it rich. "Better now than four, five years ago, but bad enough."

"A judgment," Martinus said. "Perhaps a judgment on us all. Maybe poor Busch is right. In his prediction, not his answer." They emerged from the woods, then into an open sunlit meadow. Vast deep valleys fell away on either side, gilded by the special light of late afternoon. As Condon goggled, Martinus raised his arm and pointed. Ahead, the big yellow house towered on the crest of an even higher hill.

"There," Martinus said. "That's where we'll get a car. The residence of General Helmer: the Christina Hof. But first we must pick some flowers. Never, here, does one come calling without flowers for the hostess."

"I'll tell you, Mr. Condon," Martinus said as, fifteen minutes later, they walked toward that big house on the hill, the priest nearly hidden behind a bouquet, "General Kurt Helmer would be a good subject for any novelist. We all think our lives are strange, dramatic, but his truly is. General Helmer's father was an obscure forester and gamekeeper of a royal hunting lodge. Of course, it's a position with a certain status. Hunting's not only a sport here; it's an art, a kind of mystique, and a good hunter and gamekeeper is respected. They serve a long apprenticeship and usually their sons follow in their footsteps. By all rights, Helmer would be a *Jäger* now, not a general—a rich, honored, influential man—but God touched him with His outstretched finger."

A little wryly, Lan said, "And how did God touch this man with His outstretched finger?"

"Almost the same way He touched me," Martinus answered soberly. "Helmer came to the attention of a colonel in the Imperial Army who was shooting with the Archduke Rudolf. And, like the Church, the Army was always alert for promising material. Helmer, at the age of twelve, must have been very promising. The Colonel sponsored him at a gymnasium in Vienna, then at cadet school, and finally at the military academy in Wiener Neustadt. And he must have had a natural talent for soldiering, for he rose very quickly to become the youngest colonel in the Imperial and Royal Army." Martinus laughed. "You must remember that our army has always been more show than substance. We Austrians love parades and uniforms, but actual warfare goes against our grain. Anyhow, in an army of parades, a fighting man was a real rarity—and Helmer was a fighting man."

He paused to accept a cigarette from Condon, inhaled sensually, then went on.

"Later, Helmer was sent to Rumania as a military attaché. There he married Frau Helmer, who was Rumanian by birth but of German stock. He brought her to Vienna, and almost immediately thereafter the war began, and he was sent off to command a regiment in Galicia, now part of Poland, against the Russians."

Their way led uphill, toward the big yellow house.

"In 1915," Martinus chattered on, "the Czarist Army mounted a tremendous attack against the Austrian line. The old generals lost their heads and ran around in panic, but Helmer kept cool. He flagrantly disobeyed orders to retreat, and his regiment attacked instead. The story is that his momentum drew in other units and soon, more or less by default, he was the real commander of the Austrian forces in the field. At any rate, he smashed the Russians, turned defeat into victory."

"And he probably got court-martialed for disobeying orders."

Martinus laughed. "Oh, no, that's not the way things work in Austria. We have a special medal for soldiers who disobey their orders and win—the Maria Theresa Order. Helmer was awarded that and promoted. But after the war he *was* forced to flee and take refuge in Rumania. Anyhow, he and his wife came back several years later, bought this place—the Christina Hof, named for Frau Helmer. She died several years ago. The General took it hard, of course, but he's himself again now, and you'll find him a most hospitable and likable man. He and his family all speak fluent English, incidentally." The path circled, brought them to a steep, broad drive, and they went up it in silence until Martinus said, "Well, here we are. And I'm sure

41

the General will be happy to send you to Oberfelsdorf in one of his cars."

Before Martinus could ring the bell, an attendant opened one leaf of the high wrought-iron gate. From the way he and Martinus greeted each other by name, Lan could tell that the priest had been a frequent visitor to this place, and a welcome one. Then they passed on through, following the drive across a wide grassy park shaded by giant trees, studded with statuary, dimpled with pools. In its center was the house itself. People were on the terrace at its rear, and Condon caught the sound of dance music. Following the drive, they passed through a lofty arch in a wall that seemed a continuation of the house's flank, and then they were in the courtyard. Condon halted, impressed.

He was no stranger to manor houses: he had seen the great old plantations of Louisiana: Rosedown, Greenwood, Afton Villa, and their like, in Steamboat Gothic and Greek Revival; had been a guest, too, in the big pseudo-Spanish houses of Beverly Hills. But the Christina Hof was of a style new to him, and captivating.

Seldom had he seen a place so welcoming, inviting. Dr. Martinus led him up the steps to the front door and rang a bell.

Dressed in old-fashioned black, a plump servant girl opened the door, smiled, curtseyed, and to Lan's amusement, kissed the priest's hand. Then, after a few words in German, she scurried off.

The entry in which they waited had a parquet floor and plastered walls hung with paintings. The ceiling was high, wreathed and medallioned with plaster ornamentation; from a plinth in one corner, a gleaming suit of armor, halberd in its hand, glowered at them with slotted visor. Then the terrace doors opened, and a girl came through them smiling. Lan Condon tensed, suddenly aware of his rumpled hiking clothes. For, like Phyllis, she was one of those.

By *those* he meant a kind of woman one met rarely, who, just at first sight, took a man's breath away, stirring something in him beyond defining that had only partly to do with physical desire. It was not a quality that had to do with beauty even, for the loveliest women often lacked it. As eerie and unexplainable as electricity, it was nevertheless as tangible and potent: star quality they called it at the studio.

42

"Dr. Martinus." Her voice was a little husky, yet bell-clear and resonant as she spoke in German. Her smile, her whole face, was open, undevious. Her hair was blond silkiness, gently waved, her blue eyes large, direct, and clear, lashes very long. Her skin was flawless, with an outdoor cast of tawniness. Her face's bone structure was delicate, yet durable, striking rather than exquisite, the kind that would last on into age. Her body, in its silken summer dress, was slender, long-legged, athletic, yet well rounded; she bore herself with grace, energy, and pride. She was, Condon guessed, hardly out of her teens, and yet somehow neither too young nor too old for any man past puberty. One sensed immediately a vast realm of possibilities within her, waiting to be discovered, explored—a maddening wealth. Then he became aware that she had turned to him, was speaking to him in English.

"Mr. Condon." She put out her hand. "How do you do? I am Christa Helmer. Welcome to the Christina Hof. Dr. Martinus says you are an American and a writer, so we are doubly honored." She had taken the flowers from Martinus, and they enhanced her looks. Her hand in Condon's was slim, firm, and strong, her handshake straightforward, neither lax nor reticent. "He also says you have difficulties. Of course we shall be glad to help you. But first you must come out on the terrace and meet my father and have a bite to eat and something to drink." She handed the flowers to the servant girl, who had reappeared. "This way, if you please." And she led them through the drawing room.

The terrace was broad and the view that it commanded was magnificent. Martinus was recognized and warmly greeted by several people, but, loyally, he stayed close to Lan, as did Christa Helmer. "There's Papa over there." She gestured.

Helmer was a man better than medium height, body somewhat thickened but still ramrod straight. His gray suit trimmed with velvet and with silver buttons seemed half uniform, half folk dress. His English was more heavily accented than his daughter's, which was nearly flawless. "Of course, of course, Mr. Condon. We'll be happy to put a car and driver at your disposal. I'm terribly sorry you've had difficulties, but you're lucky to have met Dr. Martinus." He clapped the priest on the shoulder with affection. "But first both of you must have refreshment. And, please—" He turned to the tall, dark young man in black

43

with whom he had been conversing. "Mr. Condon, Dr. Martinus, may I present Dr. Josef Steiner?"

"Mr. Condon." Steiner bowed slightly. As they shook hands, his pale and saturnine good looks made a phrase pop into Condon's mind: *jeweled serpent.* There was something coldly elegant, complex, reptilian about this Steiner; behind those large dark eyes one felt a complicated personality coiling inward on itself in mysterious, intricate convolutions. His English, too, was easy, fluent. "An American. A coincidence. General Helmer and I were just discussing France, England, and America."

"Oh?"

Then a servant girl appeared with a tray of glasses. "Some wine, Mr. Condon," the General said. They all took glasses and Helmer raised his. *"Pros't."* The wine was dry, tangy with earth, sun, and grape. Over his glass's rim Condon saw a glance pass between the girl and Steiner, something complicitous, secret. "Do you like it?" Helmer asked.

"I'm no expert, but I think it's fine."

"Every man should be his own expert." The General smiled. "Should drink what suits him. Tastes are as various in wine as in women, and it's unreasonable to expect everyone to agree on either. But—" He turned as a short man with a face and beard like that of a mournful goat touched his elbow. They spoke in German. Then Helmer said, "Please excuse me, gentlemen, but Herr Gemeinderat Körner has a private matter to discuss." He drifted away as the old man kept a tight grasp of supplication on his elbow.

For a moment, silence. Then Josef Steiner said, "As I mentioned, America was just under discussion. I would be most interested to know, Mr. Condon, what do your people think of Herr Hitler and events in Germany?"

America . . . your people. Lan hesitated. Suddenly, from this perspective, he saw the country, broad, sprawling, various, impossible to speak for. Besides, he had not lived in America for more than two years; he had lived in Los Angeles, in never-never land. The Americans for whom he'd written movies were not supposed to think. They were supposed to have the minds of children, wanting everything made simple, innocent, and clear and always with a happy ending. He shook his head. "I really don't know. It's hard to say. Foreign affairs. Most Americans are too busy to think about things over here. We've still got problems of our own. It takes a lot of work just to stay alive."

"I see. But surely there is *some* opinion."

Again Lan paused. "Yes. Yes, but it's divided. Some people think Hitler's fine, that he's got all the answers to what's wrong. Naturally, others hate him, are scared to death of him. But the main thing over there is the Depression. Everybody says it's over, but it's not; it's still going on, and ... I guess by and large most people think Hitler's just not our problem."

"Oh," said Steiner, and he drank. Then, lowering his voice, he said almost angrily, "Mr. Condon, I assure you, Hitler is very much your problem."

"Not as long as we've got the Atlantic and Pacific oceans."

Steiner sighed, as if exasperated at such stupidity. "Not even they will save you. Believe me, Mr. Condon, you Americans had better be concerned with Europe and particularly with Austria. Because what happens here within the next few years may well determine whether you and your friends and relatives in America are still alive ten years from now."

Lan Condon stared at him, surprised by his intensity. "I hardly think so," he said finally, a bit riled by Steiner's condescension.

"No, of course not." Steiner's dark eyes flared against his paleness. "Nobody thought so, either, on July twenty-eighth, 1914, when Austria declared war on Serbia. How could a little Balkan war affect America? How many of your American cowboys, coal miners, or college students laughed and drank *their* wine and kissed *their* girls, not knowing that four years thence they would be blown to bits on foreign soil? Because of a decision taken in the Imperial Palace in Vienna."

"Don't get me wrong. I don't sympathize with Hitler. I hate everything he represents. All the same, you were a world power then—"

"And now we are not," Steiner snapped. "Only a tiny country, defenseless, in the heart of Europe. Believe me, sir, Austria is even more important. Unless we get help—help from England, France, and, or, America—there will be another war, and you may count on its making the last look like a children's party in a nursery."

"I don't follow you." But Lan was interested.

"All right. After the Great War, your country and its allies broke up our empire. Now what's left is a clutch of separate little countries, all quarreling, none really capable of standing alone, all suffering from economic chaos. The destruction of the Austro-Hungarian Empire created a vacuum, a power vacuum."

Christa Helmer, Lan saw, looked at Steiner raptly as he went on.

"Sooner or later any vacuum must be filled, and the answer's obvious: either the Germans or the Russians will fill it. So far the main danger's not from the East; it's from Adolf Hitler. Remember, he's Austrian by birth. And he's proclaimed a thousand times he'll not rest until Austria's part of Germany. When that day comes, war will be inevitable."

"Josef, why?" Christa asked.

"Because," Steiner said. "Because Austria's the key to central Europe, the Balkans, and the southern flank of Russia." He gestured with his glass. "If Hitler's blocked off from Austria, he can't expand, and sooner or later he will fall. So the time to stop him's now, before he seizes Austria, the key he'll use to unlock Pandora's box."

"I hadn't thought of it that way," mused Lan.

"No, but we here must always think of it that way. We are the target of the pointed gun."

"I had the vague impression that Austria was under Italy's protection."

Steiner's mouth twisted. "A flimsy shield. Yes, to some extent we are, we hope. In fact, to gain it was one reason Chancellor Dollfuss abolished Parliament in 1933 and set up a Fascist state. That was the price for Mussolini's aid. But things have changed since then. First, Hitler approved the Italian adventure in Ethiopia when the League of Nations condemned it. Secondly, this past March, Hitler marched into the Rhineland, reclaimed it for Germany, and neither France nor England raised a hand to stop him. That made Mussolini stop and think. The writing on the wall is clear; Hitler's maneuvering Italy into a position where she must choose between Germany and Austria. And I hardly think she will choose Austria."

He shrugged. "So, when Hitler thinks the time is ripe, why, then, unless the Western Allies help us, we are doomed. And, sooner or later, so are you. There will be a war. And, Mr. Condon, like me, you are the perfect age for cannon fodder."

Lan shrugged. "Well, I'm sorry, but personally I have no intention of dying for Austria or any other part of Europe."

"Yes. Well, I hope you never have to. And I am sorry if I've bored you. Sometimes I tend to get carried away when I discuss international affairs. Now I am afraid I must run; I have an appointment in Vienna. Awfully nice to have met you, Mr. Condon. Dr. Martinus."

"Dr. Steiner." There was a strange hostility in the priest's voice.

"So. *Wiederseh'n.* Fräulein Helmer—"

"I'll see you to the door, Doctor. If you gentlemen will excuse me . . ."

Condon watched the two of them move off across the terrace. Again he had that sense of something secret linking them, but it was none of his affair. Then he was aware of Martinus speaking to him. "What?"

"I said I shouldn't pay too much attention to Steiner's diatribe. He has an ax to grind, you know. After all, he's Jewish."

"Oh, is he?"

"Yes," Martinus said with some asperity, turning toward a long table laden with food. "His family is one of the old, powerful Jewish banking families of Austria. Josef himself, however, takes no part in the family business." Martinus raised his head, watched Steiner and Christa vanish through the door. "In fact, he has a deplorable reputation."

"For what?"

"For debauchery," Martinus said bluntly. "One scandal after another, but, of course, his family has money enough to cover it all up. Certainly I was surprised to see him here today. He's not the sort one expects to find at General Helmer's."

"I see." Condon understood now those secret glances. So Steiner was after Christa Helmer. He felt an unexpected twinge of sadness, but again it was not his affair. He joined Martinus at the table.

"Anyhow, Steiner exaggerates. His appraisal of the situation's naturally colored by his Jewishness."

Lan stared at the priest, who was helping himself to *Käsewurst* and a huge slice of dark bread. Martinus, feeling his gaze, turned.

47

"My preference, Mr. Condon, is for the present regime, which is staunchly Catholic. Austria has always been a bastion of the Church. But suppose the worst does happen? Given a choice between the Nazis, who at least arrange an accommodation with the Church, and the Reds, who would stamp it out altogether, what is a clergyman to do? If we must fall, let us fall to the West, to Germans, our own folk. Anyhow, much of Dr. Steiner's lecture was merely Jewish propaganda."

"I can't judge that one way or the other."

"No, of course not. The fact remains, Austria is poor; out of six million people, nearly a half million are jobless. People are literally starving. I have seen things that would break your heart." He stacked pickles and pickled mushrooms on his plate. "Meanwhile, Germany prospers. If we become part of Germany, maybe we could share that prosperity. In any event, one comforting fact is clear. The Church can live with Hitler and he with the Church."

"Which is all-important," Lan said tonelessly.

"Certainly." Martinus looked at him keenly. "You are not a Catholic?"

"I'm not an anything. Except hungry." Cutting off the conversation, Lan turned to the table. "What's this stuff right here?"

"*Blutwurst*," Martinus answered. "Sausage made of blood. An Austrian favorite, truly delicious, and nobody makes it better than General Helmer."

4   AFTER ALL THE OTHERS HAD DRIFTED off into the woods, bound for home, Robert remained behind inside the smoky dimness of the wattled hut, sharing his pocket flask of schnapps with the man from Munich. Busch's place, as always, reeked of woodsmoke, drying herbs, and the goats that wandered in and out with perfect freedom. It was a smell to which he had long since become inured, a small enough inconvenience, he thought, considering the safety Busch's madness—if one

48

could call it that; it could also be considered an exquisite form of sanity—provided.

"Forty," the man from Munich said, jotting something in a little notebook. His name was Holz. "Forty Party members in a place so small. Herr Ortsleiter Schellhammer, I congratulate you."

"Thank you. Remember, these are only the *active* members. We have as many sympathizers again who don't dare to join the Party yet. That includes all three policemen in Ferndorf and two of the six in Altkreuzburg."

"A most remarkable performance. I'll see that it's included, with special mention of you by name, in a report that will come to the attention of der Führer himself. I must say, this has been one of the most impressive meetings I've attended on this assignment."

Robert nodded modestly, accepting the praise as his due. Still, he could not suppress an inner glow, a quick vision of der Führer in the Chancellery in Berlin or the Eagle's Nest at Berchtesgaden poring over the report, then raising his head. *Schellhammer,* he would say. *I remember him.* Then, to an aide: *Schellhammer: make a note of it. Men like him will be needed to administer Austria when the time comes. He once came to see me in Munich, years ago, only a child then. But I knew immediately there was something special in him.*

"This place stinks."

"What?" Robert stared, then laughed. "Oh, sure. That's part of the reason we meet here. It's a lot more secure than meeting out in the open, even in the Wienerwald. You never can tell when some dim-witted hiker will blunder in. Or maybe the Sozis"—he meant the outlawed Socialists—"will get wind and put the police on your tail. Just as we did to them once a couple of years ago, when they were meeting in the woods west of here. Anyhow, all the locals avoid Professor Busch. You can see why now. On the other hand, he and his woman are like Red Indians in the woods; nobody's going to sneak up on us while they're on guard." He gestured to a wooden box in one corner. "I even keep the records here, what few I have."

"God grant the goats don't eat them," said Holz, stowing his notebook in his rucksack. "Well, Herr Ortsleiter, I must be on my way."

"Thank you for coming, Herr Sondervertreter. You explained a lot of things, answered a lot of questions for the boys."

"That's my business. I'm sorry some of them were disappointed. But, as I explained, for the time being you people must pull in your horns and lie low. Der Führer has certain important negotiations under way which must not be hampered by any incident. A burned haystack, a broken shopwindow, bagatelles like that. Let them know you're still around. But at the same time, be damned sure you leave no hard evidence around to connect anything to the Party. Do you understand?"

"Perfectly." Robert pocketed the flask and rose, a man of medium height, in his early twenties, with a big head, broad sloping shoulders, a barrel chest, legs somewhat disproportionately short, but sturdy. His hair was blond, his eyes the color of a razor's blade, his face square and handsome, mouth thin, strong, and confident, chin massive. Yet he was light and graceful on his feet as he came off the split-log bench by the rude homemade table, for his muscles had been tempered by hard work, and his body bore no ounce of fat. "We'll be careful in every respect."

"Good. So . . ." Holz's right arm shot up. "Heil Hitler!"

"Heil Hitler!"

"*Wiederseh'n,*" Holz said; they shook hands and he went out.

Robert sat down again, lighting a cigarette. *Absolutely the best local organization I've seen so far in Austria.* High praise from a man like Special Party Representative Gustav Holz. But, then, he'd earned it with hard work and risk and dedication. And, if the truth be known, not for his own glory—though that was important—but for his country. *Ein Reich, ein Volk, ein Führer!* A goal worth any risk. Then he looked up as Busch came in.

The accumulated sweat of weeks or months and other dirt suspired from in him stomach-turning rankness. He rammed his broadsword into its homemade sheath, greased with goat fat. "The meet is over?"

"Yes, Professor," said Robert gently.

Busch, well past sixty, hung the sheathed sword on the wall, placed his spear between pegs designed to receive it. Going to a clay pot on the table, he dipped up a cow's horn of mead, sweet, potent fermented honey. He drained it, dragged a grimy hand across his mouth. "A stranger came. I sent him packing."

"What kind of stranger?"

"I don't know. His clothes were peculiar. He didn't seem to understand me. An *Auslander*, I would guess." He smiled. "Not a policeman, I can assure you. Some tourist, I would think, who'd lost his way." He dipped another horn, offered it to Robert, who shook his head. "What did the Special Representative have to say?"

"He was much impressed by what you've done. He called it a unique distillation of the Teutonic spirit."

"Ah?" Busch's gray-blue insane eyes flared. "And further? What about the money?"

"He took a copy of your proposal with him. He promised it would receive der Führer's personal consideration."

"Ahhh." Busch expelled a gusty breath and sat down on a bench. "Then it is done. Because, believe me, der Führer understands the German soul as only I and Richard Wagner have heretofore perceived it. Imagine, Robert"—he spread his hands—"in every *Gau* in Germany an old Teutonic village where people can go on their vacations or as part of Party indoctrination to re-establish contact with the German earth, the Ur-Deutsch way of life from which all of us sprang! Think what a rebirth of the German soul that would bring about!"

"It will be considered, Holz assures me."

"Good." For a moment his eyes focused on something distant that only he could see. "Well, I must call the woman in. Time for her to cook."

He shambled out to get the thin, wild-eyed, pinch-faced girl who lived with him, shouting "Heil Hitler!" over his shoulder like a war cry. Robert shuddered slightly, answered in kind, and then he left, too.

He followed no trail through the woods, and needed none, for he had grown up here and knew every fold and hollow. He liked the dark, secret places, the magnificence of hidden glades with their ancient oaks and beeches, and he did not hurry. When he emerged from the forest, the sun was going down, its slanting light throwing into exquisite relief every tree and vine on the opposite wall of the Ferntal, limning like a sculpture the yellow bulk of the Christina Hof on its peak. Sunset on the Ferntal was something he had viewed nearly every day of his life, and yet it never failed to stir him. Now he sat down on a grassy hump of ground and lit a cigarette, and it seemed to him that the earth was part of him and he part of it, one being.

This was one of the days, one of his moods, when he was acutely, almost painfully, aware of his own power, all the force contained within him. One could not go around boasting to others that he knew that someday he would change the world; he kept that precious certainty locked tight within him. Most men were manipulated by events; Robert Schellhammer had long ago decided to shape events to suit his dreams, and so far he had succeeded.

Take the matter of the Gymnasium. His father had been opposed to that, wanting him to go to the village *Hochschule* instead—where his education would have ended at the age of fourteen—fearing that too much learning would spoil his son for life on the land. But Robert had set his mind on a *Matura* and more than that; he wanted the prestige and rank education yielded. So, though academic subjects came hard to him, he had studied, worked, and striven to raise his grades so high that his teachers had put pressure on his parents to let him matriculate at the Gymnasium. He had won that battle and received his *Matura* after making respectable, if not the highest, grades. And meanwhile he had found the cause to which he would dedicate his life, the lever he would use to change the world.

That it needed changing, he had long realized. When Max Schellhammer had come home from the war, he had been loud and articulate on the betrayal of Austria and of Germany: by the stupid generals, the corrupt politicians, and, of course, the moneymen, the Jews, who gloated over the downfall of the last bastion of staunch Catholicism. As a child Robert had listened and absorbed, feeling outrage and indignation. It grew as he became conscious of the chaos around him. The traitors were in the saddle—the godless Socialists, the Communists, the kikes and Christ killers. And they had robbed him and every Austrian of his rightful heritage. Something must be done, revenge taken, things somehow set to rights. And somehow, he knew, he would do it—or play his part in doing it.

Then, when he was sixteen, he found his instrument. It happened on a *Schulausflug* in the Styrian Alps in March, a class excursion to a mountain lodge where they received the ski instruction that was a mandatory part of their education. Robert had been on skis since he was five, already could ski rings around most of his instructors. And being in the company of his classmates bored and nauseated him.

Most were wellborn or they would not have been in the Gymnasium, and he had always been something of an outsider among them anyhow. But that had suited him, because they were so mediocre, such light-minded, unserious, ill-informed dolts. They had no *Weltanschauung* at all. And after two days he had to get away from them, have solitude, absorb the majesty of the mountains. So, giving his teachers the slip, he worked up a high bleak drifted slope to a stout Alpine shelter hut on a saddle, where at least he could be alone and think. But, to his dismay, there were two other youths already there. Eighteen, blue-eyed, blond, and handsome, they were not Austrians, but the next of kin—Bavarians. And they were as different from his classmates as stallions from geldings. For the first time, he realized he was not alone. These young men were serious, clean-cut, and he could tell by their gear that they did things right. A favorite saying of his father was *You can tell the man by his tools.* Their equipment spoke volumes to Robert Schellhammer.

He skied and talked with them all day, and by late afternoon they were like the brothers he had never had. And he was immensely flattered when the tallest, Werner, said, "Do you know, Herr Schellhammer, you're the first serious-minded Austrian we've met so far?"

Drinking tea with rum before the fire, they talked, he listened, with excitement rising, a sense of discovery. And then Moritz, the shorter one, had taken a book from his rucksack. "Here. Read this. It'll explain it all."

Robert turned it over in his hands. "*Mein Kampf.* Yes, I've heard of it, but I've never read it. Only . . . I couldn't take your only copy."

Moritz laughed. "It's not our only copy." Then he was serious. "I think this book will change your life; I really do. It has changed ours. We're organizers, don't you see? That's why we're here in Austria, organizing the National Socialist Youth Movement. If we young people don't take the lead, who will? Read

53

the book, Robert. And if you have questions, write us in Munich or come to see us. Now, let's have one more downhill run before the snow crusts."

It had taken him five days to read it, slowly, thoroughly, as was his wont. Then, more swiftly, he read it again. By then he knew Moritz had been right: the answers he'd been seeking were all there; and his life was changed. That summer, after considerable maneuvering, he managed to arrange a trip to Munich. By then he had been in correspondence with Werner and Moritz for months.

They met him at the Munich train station and then—beyond belief—they took him to a palace in the Brienner Strasse, the Munich Brown House, headquarters of the National Socialist German Workers Party, and of Adolf Hitler. And there he met der Führer.

The man was both less and more than Robert had expected. Despite all the pictures, one thought of him as tall and towering. He was not. Of medium height, possessed of vigor but seemingly no real physical power, he would not have lasted a day on an Austrian ski slope or a working farm. But that did not matter. He granted Robert fifteen precious minutes, and nothing mattered then except the personality, the magical personality, compounded of the piercing blue eyes, the voice that could ring all the changes, and something else, something beyond belief, that gave Hitler the power to look directly into the soul of Robert Schellhammer, divine his deepest, most secret dreams, yearnings, and ambitions.

"Work," he said. "Work, Herr Schellhammer. That's the ticket. *Arbeit macht Freiheit*. Work brings freedom."

Robert laughed nervously. "My mother always says, 'Work's the only way to beat the Jews.' "

"Your mother is a clever woman. There's a wisdom in mothers found nowhere else. I remember my own dear mother—" He broke off. "I am sorry, Herr Schellhammer. I would love to talk with a countryman all morning, but the demands on my time . . . May I just say this: Remember, National Socialism is a German philosophy. Austria is a German country. And there should be no rest for any of us until all Germanic peoples are united in National Socialism." Those marvelous eyes flared.

Robert suddenly loved this man as he had never loved another human being, not even his own father.

"That is our aim, yours and mine. And you and I will work and fight and sacrifice to reach that goal, together, and let nothing stop us, ever!" His voice rose, full of steel, determined. "And we warriors who took the field early and led the rest will be joined in a bond nothing can dissolve. You are young, but the time will come when you can say, 'I am an old soldier of the Party; I was with Hitler in the early days.' " He paused, letting the words ring in the room. Then, with warmth and friendliness, he smiled. "My greetings to your parents, and to our comrades in Austria. Thank you for coming to see me, and I shall expect to hear more—much more—of you in the future."

Robert had left the Brown House in a daze, feeling as if he had just had sex; he was drained, exalted. Returning home, he threw himself into what he knew now would be his real life's work.

At first he recruited farm and village youths his own age. Bored, restless, penniless, they were ripe for anything. Galvanizing them to action, he was so successful that soon older men were drawn in; for a brief period they wrenched leadership from Robert. That did not matter, for he had to leave anyhow to go to the Wine School at Klosterneuburg, where there was a stronger Nazi element, and where he could make contact with Party members in Vienna, too. By graduation, he had learned more than expertise at raising grapes and making wine. Wholly mature, thoroughly indoctrinated, an expert organizer, he came home and won back leadership of the Ferntal group.

As Hitler rose in Germany, so did the Nazi Party in Austria. When der Führer became Chancellor, then dictator, Robert scented victory. Money, material, support of every kind flowed into Austria. Germany put on pressure, imposing surcharges that nearly destroyed Austria's tourism. It restricted imports; and as the people suffered, the power of the Nazis grew.

Robert, looking across the valley, smiled. The Austrian Chancellor Engelbert Dollfuss had tried to dissolve all rival political parties, both Socialists and Nazis; but when the wearing of the Nazi uniform had been prohibited, Robert's group, like most others, retaliated by uniforming themselves in the most ridiculous possible way—top hats, frock coats, knee pants, and white stockings—and parading in mockery of the police. But they'd done more than that; they had shown their teeth. His own group had traveled up the Danube to another district, twice blown railroad lines there with the ample dynamite supplied by Germany, had firebombed a Jewish store, and burned the barn of a vocal anti-Nazi farmer. Simultaneously, another group from far away had hit targets in the Ferntal. It was happening all across the country—a campaign of sabotage and terror.

Robert was now known in the inner councils as a young man to watch. When the new Austria was built, part of Germany, yet ruled by Austrians, Robert Schellhammer would become a man of power.

And then, he thought, staring at the Christina Hof, he would need a wife. Not just any woman, but the one he had to have—Christa Helmer. For him there could be no other.

He had loved her from first sight, when she was eight and he eleven, stunned by the most beautiful, dazzling creature he had ever seen, as different from the village children as a butterfly from caterpillars. But there was an enormous gulf between them, unbridgeable. Her mother was a baroness, her father a famous general; Bertha Schellhammer was the daughter of the village butcher, and Max a farmer and a farmer's son.

Still, these were no ordinary times, and hard economic necessities leveled barriers. His father and Christa's had been drawn together by common interests. So, despite the disapproval of her mother, he and Christa were allowed to play together, roaming the fields and woods like brother and sister, he watching over her, doing his best to keep her out of trouble.

Childhood could not last, and over the years they'd grown apart; but he never ceased to love her. Aging into various schools and patterns of living, they had seen little of each other until recently, when Christa, having first dropped out of the University, gave up her private art lessons, too. Tired of her aimlessness, the General had brought her back to the Christina Hof for good; and then Robert had begun to court her seriously.

It was hard, though. He was nothing like the dashing, colorful, simple-minded Viennese twits she was accustomed to. Nor was love for him a game to be played for fun. Politics and government were his obsessions; she had no interest in any of that. He thought in eternities; she lived for the moment. Yet she was neither stupid nor shallow, only a little spoiled, and once they were married he would soon fix that.

Night before last, he'd almost proposed to her. After a couple of refusals, she'd consented to go with him to a *Heuriger* in Altkreuzburg.

These were taverns where vintners and their families could serve their own new wine and simple food without elaborate licensing arrangements. When the wine was ready, a green pine bough was hung over the door of the establishment and it was *ausg'steckt*—stuck out, open for business. The wine at Meissner's had been good, though not so good as the Ferntal wine, and there had been musicians playing the good old songs in the lamplit garden where guests sat on wooden benches at trestle tables. Christa drank two *Viertels,* a half liter, and was warm and gay, for a change, and heartbreakingly lovely. It took all his restraint to keep from kissing her there in public. As her laugh rose, light and musical, at something someone nearby had said, he put his hand on hers. "Christa, I have something serious I want to say."

The laugh trailed off. She looked at him a moment strangely, then briefly kissed him on the lips. "Oh, Robert, please, this is no night for being serious."

"You don't understand. I—" He drew in a deep breath. Then his courage failed him. No. The time was not ripe. She would not take him seriously; to speak now would be only to draw a premature refusal. Besides, he could wait. The day could not be far off now when she would have to take him very seriously indeed, look at him with new eyes and see him in a new light, not as good old Robert Schellhammer, the farmer's son she'd known so long—too long—but as a man of power, one of the aristocrats of the New Order. The General, Robert knew, saw him that way already. Without saying it, he had made it plain, that day weeks ago in the Helmer cellars....

Kurt Helmer was his own *Kellermeister,* and a good one, but not too proud to call on Robert for advice. In one tunnel of the vast stone-lined labyrinth of cellars beneath the Christina Hof he and Robert had sampled several working wines, and Robert had made a few simple recommendations. Then, pausing in the cool darkness for an *Achtel* of one of the best, Helmer had broached the subject.

Blunt when he chose to be, more often he preferred to be oblique. "Robert, you've got your father worried."

"Sir?"

"We were talking just the other day. Here you are, twenty-four years old, still no wife, and he's itching for a grandson. What do you propose to do about it?"

Robert had stared at him, trying to guess what was in his mind. He laughed shortly, embarrassed. "Not much I can do—until I find the right woman."

"God in heaven, boy, you've got the whole district to choose from. The way I hear it, you could have your pick of any *Dirndl*—"

"And maybe," said Robert gravely, "I don't want just any *Dirndl*."

"Well, I don't blame you for that. Marriage is an important step. And..." Helmer's eyes met Robert's. "And you deserve the best. Perhaps you're wise to wait for it."

Schellhammer's hand tightened on his glass. "And what if the best I want won't have me?" A wild excitement rose in him. Because he could see now what Helmer drove at. The General paused an instant before replying, and now Robert was *sure*.

"I'd imagine, Robert, that in the long run you could get anything you want." His words were slow, measured, significant. "Certainly, if I can ever help you get it, you can depend on me."

Robert tried to speak, but Helmer went on. "Of course, you must remember that young girls are strange creatures indeed. Most of the time they don't know their own minds. Slowly but surely they must be led to see where their best interests lie. Sometimes they can be like the dog and the piece of meat in the fable; they'll drop what they already have to seize at a mere reflection in the water. But eventually they learn their lessons." He went to a spigot and rinsed their glasses. "But I've known you since you were a brat so high. In many ways you remind me of myself when I was young. You're certainly different from most of the young men I see around the Christina Hof and in Vienna these days, and I'm just as proud of you as Max is."

"Those are kind words, Herr General."

"I don't say things unless I mean them."

Robert gathered courage, was about to speak Christa's name, but the General turned off the spigot, straightening up. "So if I were you, and I'd picked out a girl, I'd keep after her, not feel any sense of . . . inferiority. I'd hope that her father recognized my worth, would speak in my behalf, recognizing, of course, that it must be done cautiously. I'd be patient, knowing such things take time. And I'd hold to my belief that it will all come out right in the end. That's what I'd do if *I'd* picked the best and would settle for no less. Now"—he slapped Robert affectionately on the shoulder—"let's go up. You've got work of your own to do. Thanks for helping me."

"It's quite all right, sir. You know that I'm always glad to do what I can for you." And nothing more on the subject had passed between them.

Robert had thought it all out. Helmer was no fool. His son Ernst, only thirteen now, had no interest in or aptitude for managing the estate; his only interest lay in music. Helmer, looking ahead, had like Robert already imagined what a magnificent thing it would be if someday the Schellhammer Hof and the Christina *Gut*—the Christina holding—were merged under the expert management of a man like himself.

More than that. Helmer kept his ear to the ground, knew what was happening day by day behind the scenes in Austria almost before it happened. So far, he had seemed to back the Kurt von Schuschnigg regime, expressing neither approval of nor opposition to the Nazis, neutral, fence-straddling. But he knew Robert was a Nazi, and their conversation could mean only one thing. Helmer had appraised the situation and had himself come to the conclusion that the New Order was inevitable. And when it came, he would not be caught short; he would have taken out insurance—on himself, his land, his family. There could be none better than his daughter's marriage to an old fighter and a man of power in the Party.

So, Robert thought, moving on, that was a sign of how far they—he—had already come. So he would not be impatient, premature; he would bide his time, and it would all be his. He halted, looked up and down the vast, sprawling Ferntal.

All of it.

He laughed aloud with sheer exuberance. The meadow was

59

fragrant with the mists of evening. Swiftly he strode home through the dew-wet grass, whistling the "Horst Wessel Lied," the Party marching song.

5 NOTHING, Christa Helmer thought, was ever certain in Vienna, least of all the weather. Within an hour the temperature had dropped a good four degrees centigrade, and the thin rain falling as she parked her little Steyr in the Dorotheergasse was as cold as the apprehension in her stomach. Turning up the collar of her raincoat, opening her umbrella, she slid out of the car and locked it. A gibbering creature dodged out at her, arm extended. Clad in sodden Army greatcoat, it had only one arm, half its face was a gruesome mass of scar tissue: one of the omnipresent beggars of Vienna, a man wrecked years ago by war. It was bad luck to refuse a beggar and today she needed all the luck she had. She fumbled in her pocketbook and dropped a couple of schillings in his cup. He mumbled something, turned away. Swallowing hard, Christa hurried toward a taxi stand.

Maybe the donation had worked; there was a single cab. She gave the driver the address off the Hernalsergürtel, settled back into the anonymity of the tonneau with relief, and lit a cigarette, shivering, not entirely from the chill. Why was she doing it? Why was she in this cab riding toward a rendezvous with Josef Steiner?

Women, of course, were not supposed to be responsive to risk and danger; safety and security were all they were supposed to crave, especially Austrian women: the warm well-ordered house, the full-stocked pantry, the well-raised children, the well-cooked meal, the good provider, the comfort of a life lived in a neat enclosure of space and soul. But the very thought of such a life wearied and oppressed her, just as did the thought of poor old Robert, who represented that whole scheme of things. He was a fine man, true, and she felt affection for him. But what a massive weight he was upon her spirit, as, she was sure, he would be upon her body in a marriage bed! Couldn't Papa see that? Why did he keep trying to push her into such a union?

So Josef was escape; and seeing him, if nothing else, was a way of rebelling, declaring her independence. Robert was one extreme, Josef the other, and she knew no one in between, no one exciting, challenging, yet with the qualities Papa would approve. Maybe no such man existed, one who could challenge all of her, bring out her best and worst qualities together, and understand them both, as no one ever had. Maybe there was something wrong with her, maybe she was too complicated, aimed too high, wanted too much. Sometimes she did not even know who this creature Christa Helmer was at all; it was almost as if she searched for someone to show her, tell her. She was Briar Rose, waiting for the magic kiss to wake her; more truth than poetry in those old fables if you analyzed them.

Her hands were cold; she rubbed them together, put them beneath her arms. That American—the one Dr. Martinus had brought on Sunday—now *he* had interested her. It was too bad he had left so quickly; she would have liked to know him better. But after Josef's leaving, she'd only had a few minutes to spend with him before his own departure.

"Tuesday," Josef said firmly. "I shall await you Tuesday afternoon, the same place."

"I—" Then she heard herself say, "Yes. Yes, I'll be there Tuesday."

"Time will crawl," he whispered. He smiled and then was gone.

Feeling dazed, frightened, yet exhilarated, she returned slowly to the terrace. Martinus had been captured by three dowdy old women, and the American, Condon, was leaning against the balustrade sipping wine, looking out at the valley. Almost with relief, he joined her.

"I'm so sorry you were left alone, Mr. Condon. Please excuse me."

"It's all right." He smiled faintly. "Just admiring the view." He looked tired, haggard, she thought; and there was something in his manner that put a distance between them, as if he did not want anyone to come too close, to touch him.

Suddenly she was intensely curious. After all, he was a writer, which meant he was no ordinary person. It was a profession highly honored here, setting its practitioners apart, making minor gods of the better ones; and the few she'd met were fully aware of that, haughty, self-important, or affected. Even the young ones who had never been published somehow felt themselves superior to everyone else; he seemed quite the opposite.

"What do you think of Austria?"

"Well, I've only seen a little of Vienna and this area out here. The scenery's magnificent, so far. And, I must say, so's the hospitality."

She smiled. "We always welcome strangers and hope they'll love our country as much as we do. I wonder . . . Please, would you mind if I asked you a few questions? Dr. Martinus says you're a writer, and we're great readers here; Papa and I both read in English. My great-grandmother was English, and we often go there on holidays and business trips."

He hesitated, with a shyness wholly un-European. Then he told her that he'd written two novels, whose titles he jotted on a scrap of paper off a small notepad taken from his shirt pocket, where he carried also a pen. *Sup with the Devil* and *Road to Nowhere* by S. Lanier Condon, she read. "The first one came out about six years ago. I'll write my publisher to send you a copy of each."

"Oh, that's too much trouble, surely."

"Not as much as your father sending a car to Oberfelsdorf. A couple of letters is all. Where should I have 'em sent?" He handed her the pad and pen. "You write it out for me."

She did. "Now," she said, "may I ask what they're about?"

"Well, *Sup with the Devil*—it's about Louisiana. That's a state in the South—"

"I know. New Orleans. It must be fascinating."

His brows lifted, surprised at her knowledge; she was flattered. "Right. Well, my father owned a little country newspaper in Louisiana, a place called Temple Mound. And he . . . we . . . got involved in politics. A man named Huey Long took over the state, almost the way Hitler took over Germany; he got elected governor, then senator . . . He practically made himself king. In fact, he called himself the Kingfish."

"Kingfish?" She giggled. She could not imagine Hitler calling himself such a thing.

"Somebody shot him last year; otherwise he'd be running for President right now. Well, not to drag it out, *Devil's* mostly based on the Long regime."

"I see. And the other?"

His face shadowed. *"Road to Nowhere?* That's about the Depression. About people with no jobs, no money, riding freight trains—goods trains, I guess you call them—empty cars, back and forth across the country, desperate, getting thrown in jail, beaten up by railroad men, living any way they could. Hoboes they are called in America, tramps. It's not a pretty book; you probably wouldn't like it. But it's the way things were, still are, only not as bad."

"You mean the proletariat—"

"They weren't the proletariat. Just Americans, all kinds. The first boxcar I was ever in, there was a bank president who'd lost his bank, a defrocked priest, two partners in a house-building company..."

"The first one you rode in? You mean you—?" The idea startled her, a writer reduced to such expedients.

"I sure did. For about a year." His voice was grimly wry. "You see, my first book was a mistake. I thought it would make me rich, but it didn't. What it did do was turn the Long regime against our newspaper. They broke us, just wiped us out. Took everything we had. And writers have to eat like anybody else. So—" He shrugged. "Then finally *Sup with the Devil* was reprinted in England. I got some money from that, which bought me time to write *Road to Nowhere.* After that things went better. For the last two years I've been writing screenplays— scripts for movies—in Hollywood."

"Oh!" Now she was excited. "How marvelous! I never miss the cinema if I can help it! I'm mad about Garbo! And Charlie Chaplin. Have you ever met them?"

"I'm afraid I've only seen them at a distance. Writers don't move in those circles very often. But—" His eyes shadowed as if suddenly he had tired of her inquisition. "You know, it's getting pretty late."

"Oh, do please stay for dinner."

He shook his head. "Thanks, but I've got a rented car somewhere over *there.*" He swept out his arm. "I'd better pick it up and get back to Vienna before it gets completely dark. Otherwise I'll get lost again, sure as fate."

"Then maybe you'd come back again. Will you be in Vienna long?"

"I don't know. My plans are ... uncertain. But"—his smile

was strangely mechanical—"thanks anyhow for wining and dining me. It's been most enjoyable. Now, do you suppose your father . . ."

"Of course. I'll speak to him and he'll have the car sent around right away." She was both disappointed and a little angry at the easy way he'd detached himself. A Hollywood film writer! Well, glamorous as his occupation was, there was certainly nothing sparkling about him. He looked exhausted, maybe on the verge of getting sick. Compared to Josef . . .

Her taxi turned off into side streets where, without trees or gardens, people lived like wasps in nest-cells. The rain was falling harder as the vehicle entered the cul-de-sac that was her destination. Christa's throat was dry, her heart pounding; now was the moment of decision, last chance to change her mind, tell the driver to back out and take her with him.

She paid, opened her umbrella, got out in the rain. On the sidewalk she halted before two big wooden doors, iron-strapped, set in the blank front of a grimy building. The right one was unlocked and she pushed through, into a grubby entry, as stony, dim, and chill as a cave, with stairs running up to right and left. Here again she halted. Suppose . . . Suppose today . . .

Luisa had been reassuring. *Really, it's nothing. Wasn't for me, at least. The pain was no worse than sitting on a tack in school and the bleeding stopped very quickly. And then afterwards . . . Well, you can't imagine how good it feels.*

But that was not the point, she thought: the pain or pleasure either. The point was that like all girls of her class she'd played at love for years, allowing liberties, though remaining always in control. She had desires, yes, strong ones, but always in the end she could master them.

But this, though, was different. Josef Steiner was no fumbling boy, no idealistic stolid Robert. And this was no game, or if it were, she might find herself hopelessly overmatched. And— She was like a beggar woman with a single coin: to spend it wisely or to squander it on a single whim? Once gone, it could never be retrieved. Something rebelled in her, and her knees were weak with fear.

Nevertheless she climbed the stairs.

The door was one flight up, in a narrow paint-peeling corridor.

The handwritten name above the bell was Schmidt: J. Schmidt. Christa stood before it folding her umbrella. How many women, she wondered, had delivered themselves, almost against their will, to him in secret in this place, just as she was doing now? She hated to be like all those others. But with a gloved finger she pushed the bell.

Instantly the door swung open and he was there, in black cardigan, the rest of his clothing just as black, only the shirt crisp and white. His eyes lit in the paleness of his face. "Ah," he said, "you did come," and he stepped quickly aside to let her in. Closing the door, he took her hand, pressed his lips lightly to it. No more than that, which surprised her. Then he said, "Let me take your coat."

He helped her out of it, bending forward to touch his lips to the place behind her ear as he did so. A shiver rippled down her spine. She stripped off gloves as he hung the coat on a hook in the small tiled entry. Then, as she reached for the buckles of her galoshes, he said, "Let me, please." Kneeling before her, he stripped the overshoes from her feet and set them beneath the coat. Then he rose. "Come in."

The sitting room of the apartment was as she remembered from the previous visit: large, the walls done in a filigreed damask pattern of black predominating over scarlet; the furniture was upholstered to match the walls; it and rows of bookshelves were all lacquered glistening black. The carpets on the floor matched; the paintings on the walls were sinuous black-on-white designs, fluidly erotic. One lamp in a corner provided soft indirect light; a blue flame hissed beneath a samovar on the table before the divan.

"Incredible weather," Josef said. "What about hot tea with rum to warm you?"

"Thank you." The steadiness of her voice surprised her; she sounded as if she were quite accustomed to coming secretly to men's apartments. "While you're making it, I'll do something about my hair."

From her previous visit, she knew where to find the bath, with its sunken tub, golden fixtures. She touched her hair, renewed makeup. Her hands were cold. There were no servants here; they were totally alone. Last time, when he had brought her here, he had explained: "There are times when a man in my position needs total privacy. So, while I keep my dwelling on the Singerstrasse and the *Schloss* in the Wachau in my own name, I purchased this building through an agent and have three rooms incognito. Not even my brothers know about them." He'd smiled coldly. "Least of all my brothers."

The Josef Steiner touch, she thought with mingled admiration and revulsion; needing a love nest, he'd bought an entire building. On the way back to the sitting room she passed the bedroom, its door open, the bed enormous, canopied, all in black of course. Straightening her shoulders, turning her head forward, she marched on by.

Pouring tea, he looked up as she entered, and appreciation gleamed in his dark eyes. "Lovely," he said quietly. "You're absolutely lovely, did you know that?" He motioned to the divan. "Sit here. Your drink is ready."

He had been liberal with the rum; after the first revivifying swallow, she felt its warmth spreading through breasts and loins, melting apprehension. To her surprise, though, he did not sit down beside her, but stood facing her, cup and saucer in his hand. For a moment he did not speak. On the walls a clock ticked loudly; rain hissed against the windowpanes.

"I hope," he said at last, "my visit Sunday did not embarrass you."

"It was . . . a surprise."

He smiled. Sometimes his smile could be surprisingly free and pleasant, almost boyish. "To me as well as you." Then his face was serious. "What I mean is this: I had not intended to go there, only to get in touch with you through Luisa, as I usually do. But"—he frowned slightly—"going through Altkreuzburg, passing the road to the Ferntal, knowing you were only minutes away, something happened. I couldn't help myself. I simply had to see you. Not to make this . . . arrangement. Just to see you. Do you understand?"

Something in his tone took her aback. "I'm very glad you came," she said automatically.

"Were you? I didn't know how you would feel—or your father. I tried to be discreet, and I must say he was very gracious."

"He always is. But he wondered. He didn't say anything, but I caught him looking at me strangely several times that night."

Josef nodded. Then, suddenly: "And if he knew about us, what would happen?"

Christa stared at him, surprised, searching for words. "He would be most unhappy," she said finally.

"Yes, I suppose so. Josef Steiner, the roué, seeing his daughter. Even worse than that, Josef Steiner, the Jew." His voice was bitter.

Christa looked down at her cup. She could not understand what was working in him. Somehow it had never occurred to her that he, too, could be hurt. That smooth, burnished exterior had seemed impervious. All at once she was no longer afraid and she liked him better. "Josef," she began. She wanted him to take her in his arms, and she would hold him, too, and—Then from the bedroom came the buzzing of the telephone.

Steiner frowned. "Excuse me." He rose and went down the hall. She heard the bedroom door close, but not tightly, for Josef's voice came to her: "Schmidt here."

Christa set down her cup, lit a cigarette. She rose and wandered around the room that was so deliberately decadent, somehow epicene. Josef's voice went on: "Yes. Yes, that's possible. I'd rather spend twenty thousand schillings less, but ... If that's the only charter available just now. No. No, not through my brothers, absolutely not." Then his voice became a murmur.

Inevitably Christa was drawn by the shelved books. She'd not had a chance to inspect them before, and yet one could read another's personality from his books, almost like a glimpse into his soul.

To her surprise, most were heavy, abstruse volumes on science—biology, genetics, it seemed—thick, forbidding. One by one she glanced at half a dozen, put them back. Then her hand slipped down to another row, bound uniformly in black calf, no titles, only volume numbers. She pulled one out, opened it—and gasped.

It was an album containing photographs, two to a page, each large, brilliantly clear, and totally obscene.

Hands trembling, eyes wide, Christa turned the pages slowly. Pornography she had seen before—art students' drawings and books of satire with fat mustachioed *bürgerlich* males doing awkward things to monstrously wide-hipped females in black

67

stockings. But this was like observing the acts themselves, and all the acts were there, all she had ever heard of and some she had not imagined. Revolted and aroused simultaneously, she stared in fascination, knowing some of them would be etched in her mind forever.

"Oh," Josef said behind her. "So you've found those, have you?"

Christa jumped, slammed the book shut, turned with flaming face. Josef smiled, took it gently from her hand. "You see? I *am* a monster. Most of those I had commissioned especially for my own collection. The expense was not inconsiderable. I'm sorry if they have shocked you. Or did you find them interesting?"

When Christa did not answer, he shrugged, slid the book back on the shelf. "Some do, some don't. Men always do; with women it's a matter of taste and experience. I suspect most women enjoy them as much as men but are ashamed to admit it. But that's not the point. I need them neither to increase my potency nor to aid in the seduction of the innocent or not-so-innocent. They have quite another purpose, which I am not at liberty to explain. You'll have to take my word for it that they're a kind of . . . business investment."

When she did not answer, he took her arm and led her to the sofa. "Sit down, Christa," he said. "Forget the pictures. They are, perhaps, part of my personality, but not an important part." He took her cup, poured in more tea, and added a tot of rum as, trembling slightly now with reaction from the pictures and being caught, she sat. Passing the cup to her, he stood over her, looking down. "So," he said. "General Helmer wondered why I came to Christina Hof. What would he say if you and I got married?"

Christa's hand jerked, the cup turned over, and its contents spilled across the table, trickling off onto the carpet.

"Let it go," said Josef. In the oyster-colored light from the window, his face was tense. "Christa, this is a proposal. I want to marry you."

She stared at him, dumbfounded.

"I know." He smiled faintly. "This is not precisely why you thought the spider had enticed you to its web. And I must confess that I am as surprised as you—and have been since the last time you came here."

68

"Josef, there'll be a spot on the carpet," Christa heard herself say inanely.

"Damn the carpet. Please. Please just listen to me for a moment and don't interrupt."

He lit a cigarette, hand shaking slightly. "Very well, my original intention was ... what you thought it was, what your father would have thought it was had he known about us. But along the way something changed. I knew that when you left here last time; there was a moment then when I could have ... pressed my advantage. You weren't perhaps aware of it; I was, and I could have had you then. But I didn't, and I did not know why; and after you left, I was still wondering. Presently, though, I understood. Shocking as I found it—it's a new experience for me—I wanted more of you than I could get that way. Excuse me." When he saw her fumbling out a cigarette, he was there instantly with burning lighter.

Christa drew the smoke in deeply, staring at him.

"I do," Josef said quietly, looking at her. "I do want more of you, Christa, than I can have here in this place. That's something I understand, now, something I have come to terms with. And so, I'm gambling. All or"—he made a strange, vague gesture—"nothing."

"Josef, I don't know what to say." The cigarette had steadied her a bit, but this was more than she could grasp; a trick, a tactic, or did he really mean it? And if he did, what did she feel, what should she answer? Her mind refused to work.

"I told you, say nothing until you've heard me out. There is much about me you don't know, much I must explain, but this you must believe—I love you. And I do not say it lightly. Or to put it another way, the trapper's caught in his own trap.

"Now," he said crisply, beginning to pace, his manner almost that of a classroom lecturer. "I am aware that there are objections that must be dealt with. We'll begin with my somewhat towering reputation."

He paused, mouth twisting. "Well, it's earned, and I'll not deny it. I have my virility, and I have time and money plus an insatiable curiosity about women and, believe it or not, a liking for them. Given all that, I have done what any other man would do; and any who denies that is a hypocrite, which is one vice I've never claimed. Except to protect others, I've never tried to cover up anything I've done along that line. I will say this in my own defense: I have tried one way or another to *teach* something important or to *give* something important to each of my, ah, victims, so that they do not leave me poorer than when they came. You, for instance. You are a virgin. It was—still is—my intention to make a woman of you in every sense, to uncover, to reveal to you the depths of your capacities for feeling and pleasure. But in a different way, under different circumstances, than I first had planned." Then Josef shook his head. "That sounds pompous, foolish. As a matter of fact, you've wound up teaching me. Anyhow, let me finish with that: I've sowed my wild oats. I think I can promise to be faithful, even more so than some steady, upright type whose fantasies are still unfulfilled. Marry me, Christa, and I'll willingly embrace monogamy."

Thank you, she felt the nearly irresistible impulse to say ironically, but she held her tongue. Josef's face was almost grim now.

"The next obstacle's much more serious." He ground out his cigarette. "I am a Jew. That's quite true and there's nothing to be done about it. Even though I don't pursue the ritual of it—I abhor all that, the hocus pocus—my Jewishness is a fundamental part of me, a heritage I can't deny."

His expression turned sardonic. "However, it's mitigated by two factors. First, my family's old and, Jewish or not, thoroughly Germanic, Austrian, Viennese. The Steiners have been here nearly as long as the Habsburgs and have played almost as important a role. We were received at court when your father's ancestors were still hewing wood and drawing water in the wilderness. My older brother has a string of titles longer than your arm, my next oldest was ennobled by the Kaiser himself. I came along too late for any of that, but it doesn't bother me; I know who I am.

"The second factor's even more important: I'm a *rich* Jew. Extremely rich. And almost—not quite—that erases class distinctions. Rich Jews seem to be made of more pleasant substances than ordinary ones. They sweat, we emanate perfume. There is no sweetness greater than the perfume of a billion schillings."

He took out another cigarette. "Besides, you would not be required to convert to Judaism, as I would not convert to your religion. We would be married in a civil ceremony, legal, even if not valid in our respective churches. And you would find few doors closed to you that are now open and many open that may now be closed."

He went on, eyes meeting hers. "As I say, I'm rich. So much so that even I sometimes am startled. So, of course, there would be no question of a dowry. On the other hand, there would be a marriage contract, a settlement on you of, say, a hundred thousand pounds sterling, in a Swiss bank in an account over which you'd have complete control. More if you should like or General Helmer should require it; the amount is immaterial."

Christa's jaw dropped. "You live well," Josef said. "Of course you do. But your style of life now compared to what it would be as my wife is, with all due respect, as a Strauss waltz compared to a Beethoven symphony. I can think of nothing material that you could want which I could not afford or would not be prepared to give you. No doubt about it, Christa, there is a kind of magic in great wealth; it can make the impossible possible, miracles happen, dreams come true. What I have would be at the disposal of your happiness."

"Josef—"

"I know. You can't be bought. But it's a fact of the life you—we—would have, just as if I had to confess to you that we were poor and would have to live in a garret. It's part of what you should know about me. And there is more."

He sat down in a chair across the room, leaned forward, elbows on knees, pale hands twining and untwining. "I also have the reputation of being an idler, abhorring productive work of any kind. That's absolutely false, a rumor that began when I did indeed drop out of any active part in the family business. I had neither the taste for banking nor the aptitude and no intention of wasting my life in the dreariness of the counting house. But believe me, I am far from idle. I work much harder than the people who accuse me of laziness. You have never been to Schloss Schwarzgipfel."

"No."

"Neither have most of the others who spread all sorts of stories about my activities there—an orgy every night with the village girls, or boys, according to the taste of the gossiper ... that I sleep in a coffin in the cellar, that sort of thing. Well,

71

I've never troubled to deny their rumors; they even amuse me. But, of course, there's a kernel of truth to the story. My, ah, supposed sex life aside, what's the strangest thing you've heard about the *Schloss?*"

"I don't know," said Christa numbly. Her eyes swept the room. "Black. That everything there is black, the furnishings, the decor, even the animals and flowers." She remembered the black roses he had brought on Sunday.

Josef nodded. "True—or almost so. I have an affinity for black, always have since childhood." He smiled wryly. "You see, I am partly color-blind. My preference for black in dress and surroundings has the effect of simplifying many aspects of my life. With black, white, and scarlet I always know where I stand. Naturally, I don't go around admitting this to everyone, so I suppose there is justification for sinister interpretations. That, too, amuses me." He rose, went to the bookshelves.

"As for the black animals, yes, that part's true as well. You see these books? No, not the lurid ones, the others. Genetics, an interest of mine which I pursue in a serious scientific manner, and my holding in the Wachau is my laboratory. There I breed white and varicolored plants and animals back to black strains—and admittedly I chose black arbitrarily, partly again for simplicity, partly because it's consistent with the *Schloss*'s traditional name. Of course, black's the color of evil in the peasant mind, so—" He shrugged. "But I'll point out that I run my estate just as your father runs his, and it makes a profit; so I'm at least as industrious as General Helmer, and as busy." He paused. Then he said, "No, no, I— There are, beyond that, other activities and interests, demanding and extremely important, crucially important to a lot of people. But those I can't discuss until we're married."

Married. That word sounding again dispelled some of the numbness; she looked at Josef with new eyes, and now he no longer frightened her. She felt a strange sense of power and amazement at her possession of it, that suddenly the tables were turned, that she, quite involuntarily, unwittingly, possessed the power to conquer Josef Steiner. It was a heady feeling, and yet somehow disappointing as well; she had expected more strength from him, more shrewdness, more forcefulness. But for all his articulateness, his poise, he was the weaker, the supplicant, no stronger than any other man in love. When she had come here, her life had been in his hands; now his was in hers. She liked him better; but, she realized suddenly, his magnetic attraction had quite dissolved.

Staring tensely at her, he must have read something of that in her face. He turned away, went to a cabinet, brought out two glasses and a brandy bottle. He poured splashes in each and handed one to her.

"Well?" he said. "Surely you're not engaged to anyone else, or you wouldn't be here." He smiled. "Is the idea really that mind-boggling? Yes, I suppose it is. I'm still quite amazed myself, and, God knows, my brothers will be just as shocked and outraged as your father, not that I care a damn. Still, I can't get around it, Christa. I am just quite helplessly in love with you."

He sipped his brandy. "It's not that you're a gentile and I'd be getting something unattainable; I could marry any of a half dozen tomorrow, all titled and some wealthy. It's not your beauty, although, whether you know it or not, you're gaining a reputation as one of the great beauties of Vienna. It's not even" —he smiled—"your virgin fairness to flaunt against my sinister swarthiness in triumph. All that, of course, is part of the attraction, but not the vital part."

He paused. "The closest I can come to it is this. There is so much less to most people than meets the eye. They're like beautifully wrapped gift packages that when opened are empty. But you . . . one senses in you so much, so many possibilities waiting to be discovered, put to use. Maybe you yourself don't even know they're there. But they are, challenges and riches enough to occupy a man a lifetime in exploring them. All the women I would ever need from now on are there inside you. And I can't bear letting someone else have them. So, I'm taking the supreme gamble." He smiled. "Another tea with rum, some brandy, a few kisses . . . I could have had part of you and let the rest go. But I'm sacrificing the part in hope of gaining the whole. Now. I am finished with my amorous monologue. And I am in a species of agony wondering what will be your answer."

Christa stared at him, and he looked back, smile set, a vulnerability she had never suspected in his eyes. "Josef, I don't know what to say," she answered finally. "I am . . . flattered, complimented. No one else has ever spoken to me like that. I would like to think I'm what you say, but maybe I know myself

73

better than you do. Maybe you've seen things in me that aren't there."

"No. I know what I see." He took a deep breath. "Christa, I know you must feel something for me or you wouldn't be here. Whatever you feel now, time will increase and deepen it, I promise you. Christa—?"

She stood up, knees weak. She was in over her head, and she had to fight clear, get out where she could breathe and think. As he moved toward her, she raised a hand; he stopped. "Josef, of course I feel something or I wouldn't... wouldn't have let things go this far. But there's so much to think about before I could even begin to give you an answer. Papa, for instance—"

"Yes?"

"I don't know what he would say. Whether he'd agree—"

"If he doesn't, we present him with a *fait accompli.*"

"I couldn't do that."

"Why not?"

"Because I love him."

"Perhaps you will find you love me more. Or is it your intention to let him arrange a match in the old way and meekly marry whoever he says, with or without love?"

She thought of Robert. "No. No, I'll never marry any man I don't choose."

"And if you chose me?"

"Then I'd marry you, regardless."

He drew in breath. "Ah. Then it must be my business to make you choose me. But I am rather at a disadvantage. I can't play the infatuated lover in the usual way, I take it. Can't call on you at your home, send flowers, gifts, telephone every day, take you out in public. My style is rather cramped. Christa, is that fair?"

When she found no answer, he nodded slowly. "Fair or not, it must be that way? Well. Then you must come to me. Again. Here. You owe me that much anyhow. To give me a chance. Will you come tomorrow?"

"No, not tomorrow."

"Then the day after."

She stared at him a moment. "Yes. Yes, I'll come then. After I've had time to think. Josef"—she turned toward the door—"I'd better go, now."

74

"But, I do have hope. Tell me I have some hope."

"Josef, I can't tell you anything. My mind's all mixed up, my brain's just a whirl."

"I'm sorry, but I'm also glad. At least you're not unaffected. Very well. My car is in the courtyard. You wouldn't want me driving you back to the First District, so I'll have the building superintendent do it. Put on your things while I ring him. He'll meet you at the entry."

Numbly she put on her things, Josef kissed her hand, then she hurried down the steps; the *Hausversorger*, a dark man with long black mustachios, waited in the entry. She gave him the address on the Dorotheergasse, and he did not speak a word as he drove her there through the rain.

6   LIKE A DEFEATED ARMY, the clouds fled eastward, driven before a fresh wind charging down the Danube. By seven the sky above Vienna had not only cleared but was tinged with a lavish glow of pink and pearl which, washing over the city, transformed its stony grayness into muted lambent radiance. Condon, sipping a Scotch and soda at the Hotel Sacher's sidewalk cafe, watched the streams of well-dressed people flowing toward the Opera across the way from all directions, and felt a touch of awe at the sudden beauty surrounding him. He could see now why Willi and others had said there was something magical about this place. It seemed to exist not only in other space but in other time, especially at this twilight moment, a place out of misty saga, legend, designed to awe, stimulate, and nourish all the senses. Nothing in it had ever been planned for efficiency, only esthetic pleasure; to his American eyes that made it wholly exotic.

He leaned back in his chair and reread the cable from his agent. After all, his contract with the studio still had a year to run; now they wanted him back or there would be trouble, a lawsuit, maybe, or tying up of his funds. Matthews wanted to know what he intended to do so he could negotiate.

Condon lit a cigarette, signaled for the white-jacketed waiter, and folded the cable. No hiding place, he thought. Today with radio, there was no place they could not eventually bring you to earth. Still, maybe this was a jar he needed; decisions must be made. He had a life to get through somehow, and it could not be spent hiding in a hotel room or a bottle.

But the thought of going back to the studio filled him with nausea. Of film writing he had had enough. He could do the scripts, easily, proficiently. But they were not why he called himself a writer. The novels were the real challenge, the real reason for his existence, and he had been away from them too long— the books around which his life was built.

"God-blessed books," Big Alice had used to grumble, trying to bring some order into the house on Cypress Street in Temple Mound for fifty cents a day and reasonable pilferage. "Ain't no excuse for nobody havin' so many God-blessed books."

But Ewell Condon, Lan's father and owner-publisher of the Temple Parish *Register,* was a hopeless case, totally addicted to, unable to resist, anything printed and bound, from the complete works of Bertha M. Clay to the tragedies of Euripides, with way stops for the *Decameron,* Zane Grey, Gibbon, and the yearbooks of the Department of Agriculture between. Ewell drew books the way a magnet draws iron filings. Consequently, the Cypress Street house was one vast mulch of books, in which Lanier Condon had grown to manhood, browsing unrestricted through whatever took his fancy, be it Shakespeare, *Nana,* or a Johnson & Smith catalogue.

Thus, he absorbed words almost through his pores, and by the time he reached puberty he knew what he wanted to be and what his father wanted him to be: a writer, a novelist, a Twain or an Owen Wister or an Alexandre Dumas or a Stephen Crane. There was a compulsion in both of them to make Lan a writer.

In 1928, when Lan was twenty-five, Huey Long was elected Governor of Louisiana. By then Lan knew precisely how things worked; he could have quoted, as if from a catalogue, the going price of every politician in Baton Rouge and New Orleans. And where once he had wholeheartedly supported Long's reforms, now he felt only a queasy, horrified fascination. Because there were no limits to the man's craving for power; deftly, brutally, he had transformed the state into a dictatorship: Maybe it had been necessary, maybe it was the only way things could change, roads and schools get built, children educated, the power of the oil companies curbed, but it made Lan's gorge rise. Still, the alternatives were worse, and so the *Register* kept backing Long. But the philosophical questions about power raised by what was happening would not let Condon rest.

He worked them out by translating them into fiction. Without even telling Ewell, he wrote a novel, working nights and weekends in his room. He called the state Evangelina, the politician Buddy King; and it was not an *exposé*—though he poured into it much of his inside knowledge—but a serious questioning examination of a unique man in a corrupt society. And whatever Lan proved about Huey Long, one thing he did prove about himself—he was indeed a writer. It was his calling.

He finished in a daze compounded of ecstasy and exhaustion and sent it to a publisher. Not sure he could share the shame of rejection, he told no one about the novel, not even Ewell.

Five weeks later he received a letter of acceptance. Huey Long was already a figure of national interest. Lan had unwittingly produced the first *roman à clef* of many to hit the market. The book created enemies for him and Ewell with the Huey Long crowd, and the *Register* suffered from that. But *Sup with the Devil* turned out to be a modest success for a first novel during the Depression, earning Lan something over a thousand dollars in royalties. It was nothing compared to what they lost when, in revenge, Long set out to destroy the *Register*.

It was so easy to kill a little country paper then, in the spring of 1930; the ripples of the Wall Street crash were not ebbing as they spread throughout the country, but growing into waves. It hardly required more effort than stepping on some small soft creature with a booted foot. No thugs came to threaten, no one tossed dynamite. Advertising simply dried up, job work became nonexistent, a third of the subscribers canceled, and neither suppliers nor banks would any longer offer credit. The Condons had no reserves, the royalties Lan poured into the paper were swallowed at a gulp, and within three months the *Register*'s doom was clear.

So he ensconced himself in his room in the house on Cypress Street and went to work, plotting now a novel of the old South, a swashbuckling romance which he hoped would be colorful and commercial enough to redeem their fortunes. But before he had even finished plotting, Ewell, returning home from a conference with the editor of a paper in Mississippi, was caught en route by a freezing rain. The worn tires of the Model A failed to hold on an iced-over bridge, and the vehicle skidded into the still black water of a bayou. Ewell drowned.

He was twenty-nine now, alone, with no money to finance the writing of another book even if he'd had the heart for it. Ewell left nothing but debts, which the sale of the mortgaged house and all its contents barely satisfied. The books, sold every one at auction, brought a pittance. Lan, having to eat, sought a job, any job.

But his enemies had long memories and were as implacable as the Depression that now in 1932 gripped the country with cold iron fingers. He was blacklisted in Louisiana, poison, but he had no money to get out of it. That was when he hopped his first freight train.

For a bitter year then he had drifted back and forth across the vastness of a country once strong and vital, now nearly paralyzed and snapping at its own parts like a diseased mongrel. He lived as best he could, doing whatever was necessary to stay alive, sometimes despairing of the human species, sometimes marveling at its magnificence and its resiliency in adversity. And the whole while, pressures were building in him, the need to pour out what he had seen and learned in another book.

In 1933 he got the chance. Huey Long was larger in the public eye than ever now, spouting panaceas for the Depression. *Sup with the Devil* was picked up by another publisher—the original one had gone bankrupt—for a new reprint edition. That supported Lan for three months while, holed up in a room in San Francisco with a rented typewriter, he almost literally slammed out *Road to Nowhere*. Full of rage, bitter, he wrote a shocker—taut, honest, brutal. It was bought immediately; and when it came out, it touched a nerve, selling well, if not phenomenally. That was when Tom Matthews, the Hollywood agent, traced Lan to the room in San Francisco. "I'm asking seven hundred to start," he told Lan. "When we've got them hooked, we'll jack up the price."

"Seven hundred a month?" Condon goggled at him.

Matthews laughed. "Seven hundred a week, my friend." As Lan sat stunned, he went on: "Look, it's a seller's market down there now. Sound has been in over three years now, and they still don't have enough good people who can write dialogue. You can; your books prove it. And you've got the cinematic imagination; even your scenes in *Road* are arranged like shots."

Lan rubbed his face, thinking of all those nights in the Alhambra in Temple Mound with Ewell.

"The question is, yes or no? I'll shoot for a one-year contract with option and escalator. I get ten per cent. Give the okay and I'll have papers for signature within ten days."

Lan thought of Ewell, of the *Register*. "God damn it, why couldn't you have offered me this three years ago at half the price?"

"Three years ago nobody knew you were alive, and the studios didn't know whether to shit or go blind when it came to sound. Well?"

Lan turned away. *Seven hundred dollars a week!* In a year he could save enough to support him for the next five, while he wrote three, four, half a dozen books. This was his chance. Once more he faced Matthews. "Yes," he said. "Hell, yes."

Four weeks later he was shown to his office in the writers' wing of the studio main building. A week of idleness followed. Then one afternoon he opened the door to his cubicle in response to a solid, peremptory knock.

The man who stood there was tall, nearly six-four, and must have weighed two hundred and eighty pounds. His hair was a mass of black shaggy curls around a huge head, like a lion's or a bison's, his eyes bright black sparkles in a doughy face. His brown suit was expensive, stained, and rumpled. His smile was strangely sweet; his voice had a faint lilt of Irish. "Well, you'll be Condon. My name's Ross O'Donnell." His breath filled the room with a taint of gin as he entered, putting out a soft enormous hand. "And, bucko, I have news for you, good or bad as it may be. We're to collaborate on a script, you and I. And, God help you, wait until you see the story outline. A flaming insult to the intelligence of any male old enough to pick his own nose. Of course, what we'll do is to render it null and void in the writing and produce a script we can both read without losing breakfast. Now, I'm an old hand at this sort of mercenary work

79

and you're the recruit, so it's up to me to take the lead and show you the ropes. I warn you now, I'll pick your brains and exploit your youth and innocence quite mercilessly. And now it's time for O'Donnell's collaborator test; and if you fail, may God have mercy on you. It will be administered in the wee bar across the road from the prison gate, and if you're still on your feet at closing time, you pass and are my lifelong friend. Now, bucko, shall we go?"

"Sir? Sir?"

The voice, the flame before his eyes, brought Condon back into the present. He realized that he had taken a cigarette from a pack, and now the waiter at the Sacher's sidewalk cafe was trying to light it for him. He leaned forward to meet the flame, drew in smoke.

"Will you have another, sir?" The waiter made to pick up the empty glass.

"No. No, nothing else. My check, please."

"Of course." The man hastened off. While Lan waited, he shifted restlessly, drummed his fingers on the table, tried to damp the vivid memories—Ewell, Ross...He could sit no longer; he needed action. No more drinking, get out and walk, as he had done on Sunday, only this time around the city. Wear himself down, clear his head—and make a decision. The head-waiter came; he paid and left the Sacher.

7   THE GIRL WAS SLENDER, but the breasts beneath the clinging silken blouse were large and round. Her skirt was cut much shorter than the fashion, and a handbag with a long strap dangled from one shoulder. Her face, in the glaring light of the Kärntnerstrasse shopwindows, was pale beneath its garish layer of cosmetics, and very young. A pink tongue moved across painted lips as she lightly touched Condon's arm. What she whispered was in a language he did not understand; but he comprehended.

Nearly tempted for a moment, he shook his head, pulled his

arm away, let himself be carried along by the crowd promenading and window-shopping on the street of expensive stores. The girl faded back into the alcove which was her station, but, ahead, her sisters were popping out of theirs to accost passing men; the whores were as numerous along here as mosquitoes in a swamp. And most, like the one who'd just propositioned him, were young and genuinely pretty. He shook his head. Check clearings, car loadings, employment figures: good enough maybe, but the best indicator of the economic temperature was the prevalence of prostitutes. The greater the poverty, the larger their numbers and the lower their average age: a fact of the Depression. Using that yardstick, things here in Vienna were miserable. But what else could girls do who could find no jobs? Starve? He did not condemn them; he had whored himself for the past two years.

But there was money here, too. Well-dressed, well-fed couples strolled the Kärntnerstrasse as if putting their prosperity on display. The women's clothes in the shopwindows were almost lasciviously luxurious; jewelry, petit point, furs, and leather; rich Oriental rugs; antique furniture and some also insolently modern; like the whores, all part of the strange and seething mix of this exotic place.

He crossed the street. He could stay here in Vienna. Let the studio do its worst, this place was so far from everything, so insulated not only by distance but by its very atmosphere, that he could not believe Los Angeles, Hollywood, could touch him. Anyhow, he could transfer his money to a numbered account here or in Switzerland and let them sue and be damned. Learn enough of the language to get along, find a decent place to stay, give his thoughts and emotions a chance to sort themselves out—and maybe even write another novel. If he could. If he had the courage.

Turning down a sidewalk, he wound away from the Ring. It was nearly dark now, and there was a different atmosphere here, a modest, respectable neighborhood settling down for the night: no ladies of the evening, in fact almost no one abroad. The little shops were shuttered by iron grilles. Lan walked slowly, weighing decisions.

The thought of returning to California filled him with a kind of sickness. The studio, Phyllis, that strange seasonless

81

perfervid paradise—it was all like some dimly remembered nightmare that inspired a dull gorge-clogging weary horror. This dog, he thought, was not yet ready to return to his vomit.

And yet, not to return would cost him the balance of his contract—sixty thousand dollars and a lawsuit, probably, on top of that. No sane man could in these times shrug off such considerations. But . . . he did not know. To go back now, he would have to deliberately kill something within himself, like a doctor destroying a nerve that carried pain. With the nerve gone, the circuit broken, you could do anything and it would not matter.

He ambled on, the cobbled streets curving, turning, narrowing, and growing even shabbier. A fat woman on a bicycle pedaled by laboriously; lights gleamed through curtained windows above the shops. A door opened, a pretty girl in a summer dress stepped out onto the sidewalk, her body thick, voluptuous. Without looking at Lan Condon, she crossed the street beneath a lamp, disappeared around a corner. He noticed that, like many women he had seen here, she had not shaved her legs; her calves were covered with thick whorls of hair. For some reason he thought suddenly of the girl on the terrace last Sunday, Christa Helmer. He wondered if she shaved hers; he had not noticed. Surely she did, or if not they would bear only a thin, fine golden down, nearly invisible anyhow. He conjured up her image, standing there by the terrace rail, limned against that breathtaking swooping view. Again the stirrings of desire; he found himself mentally undressing her, examining that fine and slender body.

If he stayed, he just might take advantage of her invitation to visit that country house again. Somehow that interval on Helmer's terrace had struck a chord. Give the guests Southern accents, a different style of dress, and it could have been a Sunday afternoon at a plantation home in Louisiana. There was that same openhanded hospitality and courtliness, the doctrine that the guest was king, the lavishness with food and drink. It had been the first time, really, that he had felt even temporarily at home since leaving Temple Mound.

Back to the decision. Well, he would not push it. Only feed the data to his subconscious mind, let it marinate a day or two; then the solution would emerge into his consciousness, perfect and elegant, a trick he'd used regularly with knotty problems.

Now he'd forget it, walk a while, have another drink somewhere, and . . . The desire was still in him, and he thought about the girls on the Kärntnerstrasse. And that, maybe, was part of what he needed, too, a good piece without complications, bought and paid for.

An hour later he had roamed deep into a section of Vienna neither particularly picturesque nor lively and had turned back toward the Ring and the Inner City, but reaching them was easier said than done. He was not lost, he knew the general direction to take; but these people had never heard of any grid system for laying out a city; the narrow streets coiled like twisted gut, sending him doubling back, so that for every block he gained he lost half of one.

Well, he had plenty of time, and the exercise would do him good. He went on briskly, still watching his surroundings and the few passersby with the instinctively keen observation of the writer, something in his mind recording everything, so that later it could be retrieved whole, intact. That was part of the writer's gift—that memory like unwinding photographic film—and a personality that was, in a measure, permanently split. One segment was himself, Lan Condon, who laughed and cried and loved and hated, was wise and foolish like any other human. The other was the Observer, a creature grim, emotionless, dispassionate, watching everything Lan Condon did, analyzing and dissecting his responses, and recording all. Even when he had made love to Phyllis, had given artificial respiration to Ross there on the driveway, completely distraught, mindless with his own emotion, the Observer had been there watching, probing, pondering: was this ecstasy real, the keening an outpouring of genuine grief? What lay beneath the surface, what falsities and hypocrisies were masked? Only alcohol could kill him, the Observer, for a while and give the real Lan Condon rest and freedom; and even that did not always work. But that was a reason, undoubtedly, that every writer he had ever known had to have the bottle sometimes, to gain a measure of peace and freedom from that endless monitoring and to feel emotion unanalyzed and genuine.

Even now— He halted before the one lighted shopwindow in the whole district: a mere cubicle, a sheet of white butcher's paper, yellowing with age, laid down and on it an array of waxed-paper packets of postage stamps for collectors, their wrappers fly-specked, their contents curling, the whole covered with a film of dust. There was failure, pathos, in that long-undisturbed display, which repelled rather than attracted: a giving up of hope. He imagined the shopkeeper waiting through the long days for the customers that never came, too discouraged now even to dust; then he raised his head and saw the man himself inside his shop, and he fit the image perfectly. Perched on a stool behind a counter, he seemed to doze, his completely bald head glinting beneath a single weak yellow bulb dangling from a wire. On impulse Condon went to the shop's door, tried it. He might even buy a package of stamps he didn't need, just for the hell of it.

The door was locked; he rattled it. The man jerked awake, confused, looked fearfully around. Lan knocked on the glass. Craning his neck, the man stared for a pair of seconds; then, with a frightened swiftness, he cut off the light.

"Sorry," Lan said aloud, shook his head, walked on.

Presently, down a side street, he saw a glitter of brighter lights, a flow of heavier traffic, some distance away. Turning, after a block he reached a long flight of steps going down, where the street ended, and descended into a vast open space that separated him from the lights. Paved, perhaps a half mile in width, stretching endlessly into darkness in both lengthwise directions, it was lined with rows of shuttered, empty booths and stalls; there was the fruity tang of vegetables gone overripe, a taint of spoiled meat; it was a monster of an open-air market. He walked across it toward the lights, passing among the closed buildings.

Something small, a cat, or maybe a cat-sized rat, scrabbled away in darkness. A blob that was a human figure straightened up from its delving in a box or can: a scavenger in garbage. Lan moved on, warily, for there was no lighting here; and he did not miss the other scavengers in the deeper shadows behind the stalls, nor the locked figures that were unmistakably men embracing and kissing here in secret. After a year on the road, that was no novelty either; and he was not shocked. But his head swiveled constantly, he turned frequently to look behind himself, and he carried his body in a certain tough, defiant way, not quite a swagger, that combined with his height and width of shoulders was useful in a place like this, as experience had taught him. Even a minimal show of hardness usually deterred human predators, who sought the easiest, most harmless prey.

No one bothered him, and he reached the market's other edge and the well-lit street that ran beside it. Light spilled from the plate-glass window of a tavern; a sign in Gothic letters overhead said GASTHAUS NASCHMARKT. He knew where he was now; the city's biggest food market was only a short walk from the Ring. Opening the tavern door, he went in.

These places, he thought, were the same no matter where you went. The room was large, its peeling plastered walls painted a dirt-hiding tan brightened by signs and calendars. There was a bar, some tables, warmth, the animal male smell of unwashed bodies; the air was thick with taints of stale alcohol, harsh tobacco smoke, and garlic-flavored grease.

He took the only vacant table, near the door, and managed to make the paunchy waiter in a dirty apron understand his order for a *Viertel* of white wine. Then he lit a cigarette and covertly scrutinized the other patrons.

Workingmen, mostly, in shabby clothes or blue coveralls, and drinking steadily to ease the aches of the day's labor or the worse pain of having none, arguing in hoarse gutturals or staring morosely into their glasses. In the far corner a quartet played cards, slamming down each one furiously, cursing or crowing, while a few kibitzers watched and bantered.

Only three customers were of a different pattern. Sitting at a table before the bar, they were younger, cleaner, better dressed than the others, wearing what he took to be a folk costume of some kind—cocky little narrow-brimmed hats with small colorful feathers in the bands, sweaters over white ties, leather knickers, white knee stockings, and heavy walking shoes. Since their clothes were nearly identical, he supposed they'd stopped in for a beer on their way home from a club meeting of some kind. One met his appraising gaze, raised his beer mug, smiled, and nodded. Lan nodded back, and then the wine came, cold, but bitter, acid.

Strong, too, and he felt it send its message through his body almost immediately, its emphasis in his loins. Yes, he was coming alive again, all right. His mind shifted naturally to Christa Helmer and began to build a fantasy. Then he remembered something and took out his wallet.

Yes, he still had the slip of paper she'd given him. He returned the wallet to his pocket, looked at the firm bold strokes of her handwriting, in the strange German script: "Gut Christina Hof, Ferndorf, N.Ö."—Nieder Österreich, Lower Austria, the name of the province, she had said. He should have had her add her phone number. No, that was foolish. The girls on the Kärntnerstrasse would do just fine. But he must remember to write about the books, have them sent. He took a sip of wine, slipped the paper in his jacket pocket.

Then the door opened and a small man wearing a heavy frowsy overcoat despite the evening's mildness entered. He paused, looked around, saw no vacant place except at Condon's table, and came over. He spoke in German and Lan nodded somewhat grudgingly. The man hung up his hat and overcoat, sat down, shooting frayed cuffs from the sleeves of a shabby suit jacket. There was something strangely familiar about his baldness and his middle-aged rabbity face. Taking out a little purse, he squinted in it judiciously, then signaled for the waiter, ordering a glass of wine.

When the waiter shambled off on tired flat feet, the small man groped in his pocket with unmistakable purpose and, finding nothing, sighed. Automatically Lan shoved his own pack of Lucky Strikes across the table. "Have one," he said.

To his surprise, the reply was also in English. "Oh, thank you very much. But, no, I couldn't." Nevertheless, longing for the good tobacco trembled in the thin voice.

"I've got plenty. Go ahead."

Now the man accepted, inhaling sensually after Lan had lit it for him. Apparently determined to repay the favor with conversation, he said, "American cigarettes. The best in the world. Are you American?"

"Yes, sir."

"Ah, so! I have a cousin in Milwaukee." He put out a small flaccid hand. "Berger. At your service, sir. My card." His hand flashed into his pocket, brought out a worn leather case. The card itself was faintly yellow with age.

"Julius Berger. *Briefmarken für Sämmler,*" Lan read. "*Briefmarken?*"

"Postage stamps, for collectors. I have a little store across the market."

And now Lan placed him. "Oh, yeah, I know your store. I tried to get in it a few minutes ago."

"You?" Then Berger comprehended. "Ah, so it was *you!*" He looked shattered. "I am so sorry, so terribly sorry, Mr.—"

"Condon. Lan Condon."

"Condon. Please forgive me. I couldn't see well, and I thought— This area here around the Naschmarkt— It was after hours, but I had accounts to do and at this hour of the night one must be careful; there are dangerous people about. Times are hard here, and the young men, especially, run in gangs like wolves. I must confess I was frightened. My apologies."

"Don't let it worry you. I didn't want anything particular. I'm not a stamp collector." Berger's wine came then.

He raised his glass. *"Pros't,* Mr. Condon. Have you been in Vienna long?"

"Only a few days. I'm just a tourist." It was a way of avoiding complications.

"Well, please, if I can help you in any way ... I'm so embarrassed. Perhaps you need a guide or translator; I have much free time at my disposal. Oh, I mean there would be no charge, don't misunderstand me. But anything I can do to make your stay more pleasant ..." There it was again, that quick outflowing hospitality, Lan thought. Maybe it was phony.

"Ihr seid Scheisse!" A thick voice, roaring, drowned him out. Berger jumped, twisting to look; Lan raised his head. A short stocky man in blue coveralls was on his feet in the center of the room, heavy jowls drink-reddened. Swaying, he pointed a stubby finger at the three young men at the table near the bar. *"Scheisse!"* His mustache bristled. The trio stared at him without expression. His two companions at his table seized his coattails, jerked him down, their faces taut with fear. He slumped in his chair mumbling. *"Na, na, na, nein!"* He waved his hand as if shooing flies while they argued with him. The waiter hurried over, growled something. The man's companions nodded, paid, got him to his feet, pushed him toward the door. He went reluctantly, and as he passed the table where the young men sat, he turned rebelliously. *"Mist!"* he snarled. *"Bockmist!"* Then the others propelled him through the door and shut it and they were gone.

There was silence in the room. Julius Berger turned forward quickly, hunching over his glass. Then one of the young trio said something loudly; others in the room laughed and one old man with a drink-blasted face roared approval, slapped the table.

The tension broke. One of the three, dark-haired, dark-eyed, raised his glass. Grinning, he shouted, "Heil Hitler!"

His companions and half a dozen others echoed the words. Lan stared, a cold chill creeping down his back. "Nazis," he whispered.

"Yes," Berger muttered. "I'm afraid so."

"I thought they were illegal here."

"Yes, supposed to be. But still very bold, many of them, and many sympathizers. You see, they wear white stockings, a sign they use sometimes since the *Hakenkreuz*—the swastika—and the brown shirts are forbidden."

"So that's why he yelled at 'em."

"*Ja*. Probably an old Socialist, their deadly enemy. But they're outlawed, too. There's only one party now, the Fatherland Front; everyone is supposed to belong to it, and it's supposed to represent all interests. It's all very confusing and distressing. It was much better when we had a parliament and a real republic. Now one feels . . . danger in the air all the time. Especially if one is Jewish." The last sentence was barely audible. He took another sip of wine and he rose. "Excuse me. I must go to the toilet."

Avoiding the eyes of the three at the table, who paid him no attention, he disappeared through a door marked AUSGANG. Lan looked at the young Nazis with new eyes. They seemed absolutely commonplace, unmonstrous: only jovial, laughing young men with lots of beer in them. One was medium-sized, with dark hair and dark eyes and a mercurial face, a joker, a wit; his sallies sent the others into repeated laughter. Another was big and husky, with the clean look of the young athlete who nevertheless would make good grades in college. The third was skinny, rather saturnine, with lank blond hair, a slow smile. His face was pale; he looked a bookworm and a brooder.

Now the joker said something and the blond man smiled and the big one laughed; and the joker rose and also went through the AUSGANG door, making a big production of fumbling at his fly as if the beer were about to overflow. The big one caught Lan's gaze, nodded civilly, averted his eyes. Lan also turned away, signaling to the waiter, ordering two more glasses of wine. He thought of Steiner's intensity on the terrace that Sunday afternoon; and he remembered Louisiana, and he was not deceived by their good humor. The crowd that had destroyed the *Register* had been great jokers, too. Again he felt a kind of coolness on his spine.

The waiter brought the wine, shuffled away with Lan's empty glass. Condon raised the full one, and at that moment Berger returned. His upper lip was trembling, his face was pale as tallow. "Excuse me, please, I must go," he muttered. He dropped a bill on the table, reached past Condon for his coat.

"Look, I bought another glass of wine—"

"No, I must go." He fumbled with the coat, missed the sleeve, and Lan stood up and helped him. "In there." Berger's voice was a shaky whisper. "In the toilet, he stood beside me and saw that I was circumcised and then he said, 'Hello, little Jew. Would you like us to walk you home?' "

The dark man had come out now, saw the flutter his remark had caused in Berger, laughed, and said something to the others. The blond one smiled; the big one stared with opaque eyes at Lan and Berger.

Once, hunting in a broom-sedge field, Lan had chanced upon a baby rabbit, immobile beside a bush with fear. He had picked it up, cupped it in his palms, and felt its body vibrate with the thudding of its frightened heart. Berger was shaking with the same palpitant fear as he drew on his coat; and suddenly Lan was angry. Maybe it was the wine, but only partly; mostly it was the same rage he had felt over the *Register,* total victim of overwhelming, merciless power. He drew himself up and deliberately let his eyes meet steadily those of the three men at the table, in defiance. "Don't worry," he said. "I'll go out with you."

"No, no." Berger's terror grew instead of lessening. "Please. Please, I shall be quite all right. Thank you, but please don't. Good luck in Vienna. *Wiederseh'n.*" He touched Lan's palm, then scuttled out.

All three men were staring back at Condon now, their whole manner changed, the good humor drained, their faces set, eyes hard. As he sat down again, they rose, slowly, deliberately; and suddenly he knew that he had made a mistake. Somehow he had turned what they might have deemed a harmless joke into a challenge, serious business. The dark one pressed a bill into the waiter's hand, then they came toward Lan.

89

He sat tensely, looking at them. They returned his stare, trying deliberately to intimidate him; he had seen the same look in the eyes of deputies and railroad dicks when he was on the road. He waited, toying with Berger's business card, crushing it into a wad.

Then they passed on by him, each looking at him carefully. *"Wiederseh'n,"* each said, not to him but to the room at large. Behind them came a chorus of answers.

The door swung shut behind them. Condon sat there looking at it, indecisive. Then, fiercely, he threw Berger's wadded card to the floor, dropped some money on the table, followed, knowing it was crazy, foolish; yet all the accumulated tensions of the past weeks were rolling up in him so that he could not help himself.

He was ready for anything when he hit the sidewalk, but there was no trace of either Berger or the Nazis. The clean, cool air felt good. He drew in a long breath, looking to his right and left. Nothing. He stared into the deserted market across the way, caught a flicker of motion. Again. And as his eyes grew accustomed to the darkness, the shapes of three men resolved themselves. Well into the market, backs to Lan, they were spread out, staring at something farther on. Then, like a hound's bay, a loud voice rang out in mockery. *"Halllloooooo . . . lieber Abraham . . . wo bist du?"*

No answer, and they spread out farther, moving forward, laughing and joking among themselves. Then the big one tensed and pointed; and Condon saw it, too: the short figure, too old or dignified to run, quartering across the market at a hurried walk, making for distant streetlights that threw it into silhouette.

"Ah, so!" one said. *"Kinder, komm'! Ooooh, Abraham! Nur wart a bissel!"* And now they were loping across the market, footsteps echoing in the silence.

Berger halted, turned, and saw them. Then he moved on, almost trotting now. They increased their pace. Lan cursed softly. But he had brought it on; he had no choice. He ran across the street and into the market behind them.

The big one moved out to the left to head Berger off; the blond one kept straight ahead; the other moved out to the right. Their figures vanished in the shadows, then resurfaced. *"Hooo-hooo. Abraham. Abraham. hooohooo . . ."* The taunting cries, edged with menace, rang out eerily from everywhere and no-where through the deserted market.

Again Berger halted, confused, head swiveling. He changed direction, stopped after a few uncertain paces, turned again. Lan ran faster, dismayed by this indecision, this paralysis of terror. "Berger!" he roared. "God damn it, run! Run, you idiot!"

The three Nazis stopped—and Berger came to life. Suddenly he was dashing, coat streaming, for the streetlights on the market's other edge. The Austrians made no effort to pursue, only stood and watched. Lan halted, breathing hard, as Berger disappeared behind a row of booths. And then the three men in the market turned and faced him.

They could, he knew, see him silhouetted against the lights. In the distance the pattering footsteps of the scuttling Berger faded. And now, slowly, almost casually, the three young men moved toward Lan.

For an instant he stood there indecisively, with half a mind to face them down or even fight it out. Then rationality re-turned; he felt a heart-kicking jolt of sudden fear. And now it was he who turned and ran, rushing across the market for the sanctuary of the *Gasthaus*. If he could make that, he'd be safe; surely they'd attempt no violence in front of witnesses.

When he broke, they broke, too. He heard one shout in German, then they were clattering after him. With every ounce of speed he had, he fled ahead of them. He made the street, plunged across without stopping; there was no traffic. Ahead now, the tavern doorway. His arm was outstretched to seize its handle when the fat waiter's figure loomed behind the glass. He heard something click and then a shade came down. He slammed against the door, but it was locked.

Panting, he turned. Fanned out, they came off the street up on the sidewalk, closed in. Lan straightened up. Only in the movies did one man have a chance against three, and he was no Gary Cooper or Jimmy Cagney; but he had not, either, missed having to fight in a year of hoboing. They would hurt him; but, he thought grimly, by damn, he would hurt them back, win or lose. His heart was full of hatred then for them and all that they represented.

They were smiling. Their kind always smiled when they had you trapped, had the power. They ringed him in, up close, the big one's eyes level with his own. The big one's teeth were very white. *"Grüss Gott,"* he said almost pleasantly.

"Bin Amerikaner. Nick verstay," Lan said.

"Amerikaner? So?" For an instant, he thought that had its effect; they looked curious and interested. Then the joker said something terse, and the big man moved. Lan turned to meet him, and the little blond one hit him hard above the kidneys. He rocked off balance, and the big one caught his outflung arm, twisted with tremendous strength, pivoting. Then he was in a hammerlock, arm twisted up behind his back, the cartilage in its joints almost on the verge of ripping. He groaned with pain, and the joker hit him in the solar plexus, and the wind went out of him. The faces of the smaller ones blurred in his vision; he saw their eyes, mean and cold, dancing crazily. "Now," the big one said in his ear in English. "We talk, *ja?*" His grip merciless, he frog-marched Lan down the deserted sidewalk.

"God damn you," Lan husked. "God damn you, all you bastards."

"Goosh," or something like it, the big one said. *"Halt Maul."* Then he twisted, forcing Lan into a narrow Stygian alley. Suddenly he let go. As Lan turned, panting, trying to raise his hands, a fist smashed into his face, knocking him back against a wall. His ears rang, lights danced behind his eyes, he felt his knees give way. Another blow into his belly, and then he was on his back on dank cobblestones, and someone laughed. A shoe toe caught him with agonizing force in the ribs and he felt something give. Good God, he thought. They are going to kill me. They're really going to kill me! He tried to raise his hands, but he had no strength. Another kick, another, and he screamed or thought he did. "Help! Help!" His whole body flamed with pain. He made one desperate effort to get up, and then he saw the heavy shoe slashing toward his head. There was no time to draw away; there was only a fraction of a second's fraction in which to feel the terrible impact and the pain. Then blackness took him, deep and absolute.

8 SHE HAD HARDLY SLEPT AT ALL, dropping off finally
around two in the morning, and even that rest was
troubled. Now she awakened completely unrefreshed, and the
minute her eyes were open she was once again completely
wound up, nerves taut. Throwing back the cover, she swung
out of bed, padded to the window, opened the curtains. It was
half past five, and the sun was already up, chickens crowing.
The far hills were flooded with gold, seamed with shadow, and
the Fernbach, running along the valley floor, was a glittering
silver thread, half veiled by the giant chestnut trees lining the
road that paralleled its course.

A fine morning, but she took no pleasure in it, lighting a
cigarette though her throat was already scratchy from too many
smoked before finally drifting off to sleep. She coughed, turned
from the window, looked sourly around the pair of rooms of her
apartment. They were wholly feminine but, to the despair of
Aunt Alma and Traudi, never really orderly. Pacing from the
bedroom to the sitting room, she could view them now with the
eyes of others, read the personality that inhabited them. It was
not an impressive one.

In one corner of the sitting room, by the window, stood her
easel, a disreputable square of rug beneath it to protect the
floor; beside it was a long linoleum-covered table littered with
tubes of paint, palettes, brushes in brightly streaked jars of
turpentine, a fat manila portfolio of sketches untidily overflowing. Books and magazines were everywhere, and stacked
against the wall were some finished canvases and more that
were not. She made a mouth of disgust.

Once she'd flattered herself that she had talent, but, as her
teacher had made her see, it had turned out to be nothing but
a knack—like the writing that she had attempted at the University, not worth pursuing seriously. Nothing she had ever
tried had turned out to be worth pursuing seriously. She lacked
even the ability to keep order in her rooms, much less to manage
a household. When you came down to it, she thought, she was
completely useless, her only proven ability that of attracting
proposals from the wrong men.

Oh, damn! She strode back to the bedroom, lit another

93

cigarette. She had been like this ever since leaving Josef's apartment yesterday—excited, confused, and somehow angry, mostly at herself. It would almost have been preferable for him to have gone ahead and initiated her. She had been mentally prepared for that, but not for this. She had taken him and herself lightly; but he had unexpectedly taken her with utter seriousness, and suddenly she was forced to be serious about herself as well.

Because a proposal from Robert Schellhammer was one thing, the prospect of marriage with Josef Steiner was quite another. That was not something to be dismissed out of hand. And by its very magnitude it forced her to look harder at herself—Christa Helmer and who she was and what she wanted out of life—than she ever had before.

What she had seen had not pleased her. She could admit without false modesty her own beauty and the possession of some strange magnetism, or sex appeal as it was called in the women's magazines, but she could take no credit for it, no more than she could claim credit for the color of her eyes and hair. That was Mama's bequest to her—no more, no less. She could take credit, she hoped, for a certain kindheartedness and a sense of self-respect, which, until meeting Josef Steiner, had remained unflawed. Beyond that she could see no special virtues to recommend her to anyone.

But Josef must have seen something in her—challenges, riches, he had said—which he yearned to develop and exploit. Was it possible that he meant more than just her sexuality, that he, with all his experience and cold brilliance, could hand her the key to unlock herself and set free the things she had always felt within her, but which, when she looked for them, she had never found? Or did he mean it simply in a sexual sense—to teach her his own voluptuous sensuality, develop in her a perverse decadence to match that which she could feel in him? That, too, had its own attractiveness.

All that money; it was like having a magic wand. Bored with Vienna, tomorrow you could be in Paris by chartered plane, or in Calcutta or Bombay; bored with a palace like Schwarzgipfel, you could buy another. The prospect was unreal, staggering, fascinating—and yet it existed. Aschenbrödel—Cinderella —must have felt this way when the glass slipper slid snugly on; had she ever asked herself if she really loved the Prince? So far as she knew, the question had never even really come up.

But neither had the Prince been Jewish. And yet even that, considered soberly, might not be the obstacle that she thought it was. Perhaps really she was totally misjudging the way Papa would react. After all, the Steiners were German Jews, as Viennese, as Austrian, as anyone, as Josef had said; and she would not be the first gentile woman to marry into such a family. There was a respectability about them, a cachet, wholly lacking in the Eastern Jews from the parts of the old Empire now in Polish or Russian hands, who had flocked to Vienna after the war seeking refuge from Slavic pogroms. Even the German Jews despised and held themselves aloof from that breed. Their religion aside, which she would not have to embrace, the Steiners' blood-lines were impeccable.

And again the money—and the whole network of the Steiner family's business and political connections. What would all that mean to Papa? This was something *he* must be given a chance to consider.

She brought herself up short. *Hold on. You're pleading Josef's case, aren't you? But you've forgotten one thing—love.*

Again she stared out the window. Love. Drawn as she was to him, excited as she was, did she love him? Slowly she shook her head.

No, there was the rub. Love was what she had seen between her parents, what she had known that Mama had felt for Papa —a continuing exquisite happiness enduring through and com-pensating for even the excruciating pain of illness, a marvelous and magnificent emotion of the kind poets wrote about and heroines of operas died for. A poet's device, true, but it existed and she knew it, for she had grown up with proof of that before her eyes every day, had lived her life warmed by its radiance. And she, perhaps spoiled by her exposure to it, had never planned to settle for anything less herself. Sometimes she had imagined that she felt it, but always it had vanished before it resulted in anything of seriousness; but, hopelessly romantic, she had still awaited it, confident that it would come someday.

But she was twenty-one, and it had not. And she was not Mama, either. A great love demanded greatness in the lovers, and she lacked Mama's greatness and surely would never find a man like Papa. If such love were common, it would not be so celebrated. Most people she knew seemed to have taken what they could get in the way of love and made do with it, and to have been contented. And when what you could get was a man like Josef Steiner and a life of the sort he offered . . .

She did not know. All she knew right now was that she was groggy from lack of sleep, tension, excitement, and apprehension. She needed to confide in someone, and there was no one—not even Luisa. Well, she would think about it later. There was time. Hoping it would clear her mind, she went to bathe and dress.

At half past six she joined the General and her brother Ernst on the terrace. Helmer had long since had his breakfast, been about his work, but he always came to drink another cup of coffee with his son before the boy went off to the Gymnasium in Altkreuzburg, not burdening the still groggy youth with conversation, only being there.

Ernst in some ways, Christa thought, was more like Mama than she herself. He had her blue-eyed blondness, her regularity of features; he would, when grown, be a handsome young man indeed. But he also had her—and Papa's—inner discipline, and Mama's unconscious sweetness as well, her gentleness. Only occasionally did he show the temper, willfulness, and streak of iron inherited from his father. Otherwise quiet, docile, loving, abridge his sense of fair play and justice and he would become a tiger.

In some respects, she knew, he was a disappointment to the General, and yet Helmer took pride in the very qualities that made him so. He had no interest in hunting or in the management of the land; he was active, roaming fields and woods, but almost always alone or with one friend, never with a gang. His overwhelming obsession was music, and his piano teacher in Altkreuzburg assessed him as having talent close to genius. Soon he would have to be sent to the Musikgymnasium in Vienna to embark on a course that would lead to the Academy or the Conservatory and, presumably, after that the concert stage. Helmer, Christa knew, would make any sacrifice to see that his talent had its fullest chance. She herself envied Ernst —his vocation plain, his life built around a central certainty. Already he knew who he intended to be.

Now, gangling in short lederhosen, he stood up. "Papa, I've got to run." He kissed the General on the cheek.

Helmer patted his narrow leather-clad rump. "You have all your books, everything you need?"

"Everything, Papa. Christa—" He kissed her, too, then loped into the house to get his rucksack full of books. Helmer could have sent him down the long driveway to the postbus stop in the valley in the car, but did so only on the roughest days. The morning walk and the steep afternoon climb back were good for Ernst; an Austrian should be tough, able to walk and climb, with muscles developed as well as sensibilities. She had received the same treatment in her younger days.

As Ernst left, Mitzi brought Christa's breakfast, more coffee for the General. He yielded Christa the same boon of silence he had granted Ernst; but as she ate, she could feel his eyes, warm with affection, on her. And suddenly she made her decision. She had to tell him everything. Only he could help her clear her mind, reach a decision. She would not hold back on her meetings with Josef, but, thank God, she could face Papa squarely and say she was intact. She would not tell him she'd been to that secret apartment, but she would describe the enormous marriage settlement, and— If he were favorable or even did not immediately forbid it, she would look at Josef seriously; if he said no, then that would end it. Already she had learned something: that she was not so fascinated by Josef Steiner that she would trade her father's love for his. She drained her cup, seeking the proper opening in her mind.

"Krems," he said. "Would you like to go to Krems this Friday, Christa?"

"Krems? What for?" She tried to bring her thoughts to focus. The picturesque old city was on the Danube, the gateway to the splendid valley of the Wachau. Indeed, Josef's *Schloss* was only twenty kilometers or so upstream from there.

"The Nieder Österreich wine fair. Producers from all over the state will have wines there for sampling, and Max and I are entered, too. Actually, we'll be going up Thursday night, he and Robert and I, staying at the Park Hotel, and we thought you might want to go too. There'll be a carnival—a *Volkfest*— and we'll drive up through the Wachau later on. Why don't you come along?"

97

Christa was half sardonically amused, half angry. Poor Papa, so transparent. He and Uncle Max would tend the exhibition booths, leave her fair game for Robert. Well, at least she had her opening now. The sentence was on her tongue: *Before I answer, Papa, there's something I must discuss with you.*

Before she could speak, though, there was another presence on the terrace. "Excuse me, Herr General, Miss Christa," Traudi, the servant girl, said, voice flustered. "There are gentlemen here to see Miss Christa."

"Gentlemen? At this time of the morning?" Helmer was astonished, and Christa's mind was wholly blank.

"Police," said Traudi. "Revierinspektor Leichter from Ferndorf and an officer from Vienna."

Helmer stared at Christa. Her heart skipped a beat as she searched futilely for any reason for this. *"I* don't know," she whispered.

"Of course," Helmer said. "Please show them in."

"Yes, sir." Traudi disappeared.

A frown plowed Helmer's face. "Daughter, have you had an accident with your car?"

"Papa, I swear to you—" Then they were there, and Helmer rose to meet them: the local inspector in his iron-gray uniform, the Viennese officer in dark green.

"Morgen, Grüss Gott, Herr Revierinspektor!" Helmer shook hands with the head of the local post, who returned the greeting, clicking his heels, saying "May I introduce Oberleutnant Marz from the Vienna Police?"

"Herr General. Fräulein Helmer, *küss' die Hand."* Marz was a squat man with a dark, ruddy face.

"Sit down, gentlemen, have some coffee and some breakfast," Helmer said. "To what do we owe the honor of this visit?"

"No need to be alarmed," said Marz, dropping into a chair. "We seek your help; we only want some information. Early this morning a young man was found lying unconscious in an alley near the Naschmarkt. He had been badly beaten—several cracked or broken ribs, at least a skull concussion, so the doctors say. He's been taken to the General Hospital, in a serious condition, and apparently will not recover consciousness for some time. He had also been robbed; his wallet and all identification were missing. However"—he looked at Christa—"the malefactors overlooked a slip of paper in his coat pocket. Perhaps you recognize this, Miss Helmer?" From a billfold he took out a sheet from a small notepad, handed it to her.

She stared at it, her name and address in her own handwriting. For a moment her mind was frozen, and she shook her head confusedly. Not Josef, surely, she thought, heart nearly stopping. Then she remembered, and suddenly she went weak with relief. Again she saw him, leaning on the terrace rail, heard that strangely accented English. "My God," she heard herself say. "It's the American."

9 FOR A LONG TIME he floated in darkness, aware occasionally of intense pain when he breathed in, but then someone would come with a needle and that would cease, yielding to dreams occasionally weird and often voluptuous. Once he was conscious of being moved. The voices that came to him from time to time spoke no language that he could understand. He had no way of measuring how long he drifted thus; and once he thought Phyllis was in the room, standing by his bed, and he wondered where Ross was. Away, he hoped, because the sheer physical lust he felt for her was enormous. But then she was gone, without touching him; and he thought, I must get back to work on the script. We're running late already.

Gradually, however, the confusion and darkness receded, like flood waters falling, and he awakened to find himself in a small tan-painted room, lying between crisp sheets. He comprehended that he was in a hospital but was not sure where. He discovered that head and torso both were wrapped with stiff bandages, and that his face was swollen, painful. Obviously, he decided, he had damaged ribs and maybe internal injuries, and from the bandages on his head, perhaps a fractured skull, at least a concussion. He felt a stab of fear. Suppose his brain was damaged? Suppose he could no longer write?

A nun, short, gentle, with a face like an aged chipmunk's, fed him breakfast, a viscous buttery porridge; but again the fact that she spoke only German balked all communication. She patted his hand reassuringly and left; and as she went out, he found himself strangely content. All power of decision, all capability of action, had been taken from him, and for the first time since early childhood he bore not one iota of responsibility for himself or his eventual fate. It was the first time he had ever found helplessness a luxurious sensation. It was almost like being in the womb again, and the first chance he'd had to think abstractly, dispassionately, in years.

He had, he realized now, known not one moment of peace or repose since the acceptance of *Sup with the Devil*. From that day on, he had lived with disaster, like the victim of a witch's curse. Not from any weakness in himself, but because unremittingly he had been a victim of a system. One system. Though it had been administered differently, he saw, by the Long regime, by the manipulators who had brought on the Depression, by deputy sheriffs and railroad bulls, by the heads of the studio who ruled by fear and cruelty—they were all part of a whole; and the system had hounded him until his nerves gave out, he had gone into a tailspin, and had sought a hiding place wherever he could find it: in that case in Ross's wife's bed. Now he'd been caught up by three Nazis in an alley. It was all part of the whole.

Well, anyhow, his brain had not been damaged, or he would not have been able to think like that. But it was good to be able to think that he was not a monster, only a victim. And, almost, he could be grateful to the three Nazis. It occurred to him that perhaps he had been seeking subconsciously what Ross should have given him in the first place—a damned good beating. And maybe they had been Ross's surrogates. Perhaps everyone needed to expiate guilt in pain; and maybe the three Nazis had shriven him . . . something had been paid on account.

Anyhow, lying there, he sensed that he had reached a dividing line. Tranquility. Almost a kind of regained innocence. He had mental, moral elbow room. And now he was in an ideal position to make the decisions he had tried to reach that night he had tried to be William S. Hart in the Naschmarkt. Or he would be when his head was clearer.

There was a discreet knock at the door. "Come in," he said, and then the chipmunk-nun ushered in another woman who was not a nun. She wore a huge-brimmed straw summer hat with flowers on it, and a sleek blue summer dress; she was young, blond, very beautiful, and surely familiar. With her was a squat red-faced man in uniform. When the girl smiled, he immediately placed her: that terrace in the Vienna Woods on Sunday afternoon. Helmer. Christa Helmer. "I'm sorry," he said promptly. "I never got around to sending for your books."

She looked blank, then smiled. "Never mind the books. You know me then: Christa Helmer. Good morning, Mr. Condon. How are you feeling?"

"Fair, all things considered."

The blue-gray eyes were concerned and sympathetic. "You're very lucky. You had a bad concussion of the brain and some cracked ribs. But Dr. Kleinmann says you will be perfectly all right."

"Good. Maybe you could tell me where I am and how I got here?"

"Of course. You're in the Altkreuzburg Krankenhaus—hospital. Four days ago you were found in a side street near the Naschmarkt very badly beaten. The police were called, and you were taken to the General Hospital in Vienna. Whoever attacked you took your billfold and passport and all identification. But . . . speaking of your books. Do you remember the slip of paper I gave you with my address? Well, it was in your jacket pocket, and so the police came to us."

The uniformed man fidgeted impatiently, taking out notebook and pencil. "They requested that we come to Vienna and identify you, and, of course, we did. After which we reported the incident to the American Legation; but they needed all sorts of forms from the police and the Vienna government, and that moves so slowly. And we were quite concerned, Papa and I. The Vienna General Hospital is so crowded, and you were in a ward with all sorts of people, and Papa and I decided you would be much better off here in the Altkreuzburg Spital. It's small, but it's very good, and Dr. Kleinmann, the Primarius, is a dear friend of ours and a fine doctor. So you mustn't worry about anything but getting well. You're in good hands, and if there is anything you need, we shall see to it."

The sunlight raying in the single window struck her face, bringing out its high-cheekboned elegance, the sensuality of the full red mouth, and the magnificence of her eyes, despite the shading hat brim. Condon let his eyes range lower, along the graceful slender neck, down to the breasts sensuously draped by the light summer fabric, to the slender waist, the curving yet narrow hips, and the long legs outlined by the skirt. Her calves were smooth and silken, and, yes, she shaved her legs. Her feet were rather large but graceful in the open shoes with low heels. He let his eyes move back up along her body, and now, devoid of the tension that had gripped him on that Sunday, he thought he had never in his life seen a girl more lovely. And yet, strangely, she had none of the hard arrogance of a great beauty.

"That," he said, "is a lot of trouble to go to for a stranger."

"Well, I suppose that's just the point. You *are* a stranger, which means you know no one to help you. So if we don't, who will? And—" She broke off as the uniformed man said something in German. She answered briefly and turned again to Condon. "Now I must ask if you're too tired to answer questions for the police. Oberleutnant Marz from Vienna must have a statement from you. If you feel up to it, I'll translate."

The policeman put the questions gruffly, almost with hostility. Once he barked something and Christa's brows went up. "He wants to know how you could be sure they were National Socialists."

Condon looked at the beefy face, the little eyes set with professional distrust and intimidation, as if he were on trial. "One," he said, "they gave the salute and heiled Hitler. Two, they wore white stockings. And three, they chased that poor Jew all across the market to beat him up. He was lucky he got away."

"How do you know that was their intention?" Marz snapped at Christa.

"If what they did to me's any indication," Lan said, "they didn't want to kiss him."

Christa grinned, translated verbatim. Marz snorted. "And this man Berger. Do you know his given name and address?"

They were all the same, Lan thought, cops, Viennese or American. *You sonofabitch, you're on their side.* "No. Berger is all I can remember. That, and . . . he had bushy black hair."

"So." Marz snapped his book shut, put away the pencil, clicked his heels, saluted briskly, shook hands with Christa, and strode away. The girl waited until his footsteps had faded; the door remained decorously open. There was disgust on her face.

"Papa said not to count on their being caught. Nobody in the *Gasthaus* will have seen a thing. Nobody wants trouble with the police or *them*. Besides, he says, many Vienna police are Party members, too, or sympathizers."

"And that was one of them. I've met his kind before."

She said, "You must be very tired. I should leave now."

"No. No, please stay, if you can."

"Only for a minute." She sat down on the only chair in the little room.

"I want to thank you," Lan said, "for all you've done. You and your father."

"But it was nothing."

"A lot, I think, from my viewpoint."

Christa crossed her legs. "Mr. Condon, it's only what anybody with decency would do. Look at it from our point of view. We are Austrians and proud of our country. Now you, a visitor from a great country like America, come here and this happens to you. You will go home and say all Austrians are Nazis and bad people, brutes and thieves. Now truly, could we let you do that? And it was really no trouble. Dr. Martinus said you were staying at the Sacher, and we went there and closed out your account and had them store your baggage—"

"And I owe you money, for the hotel bill and this hospital and ... I had a letter of credit for two thousand dollars in the Sacher safe. Thank God I wasn't carrying it. So, look, I don't want you and your father to worry about the money. I can pay my way."

She shrugged. "Money was not the question. Only that after what happened everything be right for you. Such matters can be settled later, Papa says. Now—" He was surprised when she touched his hand briefly, reassuringly. "You are not to worry about anything. There are two visiting times a day, but I imagine Dr. Kleinmann will let me see you more often, under the circumstances. So someone will look in on you often, and if there is anything you need, you must ask. Mr. Condon, I am *so* sorry about all this."

"It could happen anywhere." He was surprised at the weakness of his voice.

"You are tired, you must rest. I'll be back later; when you are stronger, Papa and Dr. Martinus will come, too. You will be here perhaps ten more days, Dr. Kleinmann says. After that, for perhaps three more weeks, you must rest and live very quietly." She paused. "Really. It was a brave thing you did."

Condon grinned wryly. "It was a stupid thing."

"I think it was admirable. Here everyone minds his own business very, very closely, and there are not many who would have done what you did."

"Next time I won't either," Condon said, but he no longer felt like such a fool.

"Let us hope there won't be a next time. Now please don't get overtired. *Wiederseh'n*, Mr. Condon."

"*Wiederseh'n*," he said. She went out and closed the door.

In common with most men, he found it embarrassing for an attractive woman to see him helpless. But the visit from Christa Helmer left him with a sense of well-being, a strange satisfaction. She was so damned beautiful, he thought, strange emotions he had not felt since adolescence stirring in him. The kind of girl a man's imagination might conjure with ... and his imagination was still working; and, indeed, lying here like this, it was all he had.

Good as her word, she returned that night, bringing flowers, candy, and a few old magazines in English, mostly of British origin. From beneath his bandages, he watched her move around the room with brisk unconscious grace, arranging the roses in their vase, straightening a crooked picture that had jarred his nerves. Then, sitting on the only chair, she opened her handbag and took out a notebook and fountain pen. "It occurred to me that there must be people in the United States you'd want to notify. If you'll speak very slowly, I'll try to write any letters you wish to send. But you must help me with the spelling." Her smile made something move within him. "My spelling of English is absolutely dreadful."

"There's only my agent in California." He explained what an agent was.

Her brows went up. "No other people? No wife?"

"My parents are dead, and I was an only child. And I've never been married. A cable to the agent will do. I'll pay you for it later."

"Very well." He dictated it and she read it back. "I'll send it first thing tomorrow morning. The post office is closed now, of course. California. I should like to see California someday. Isn't it a very exciting place, Mr. Condon?"

"Lan," he said.

"What?"

"My first name. Or what everybody calls me. In California everybody calls everybody by first names."

"Really? So soon after meeting? Here it is just the opposite. One has to know someone for a very long time before one says *du* and uses a given name. But"—her nose and forehead wrinkled slightly, charmingly, as she considered—"but I rather think I like the California way. Lan. So you must call me Christa. My full name, which I never use, is Christa Maria Helmer-von Weidenau. Isn't that a mouthful?" She giggled slightly, then was serious. "When you're stronger, I hope you will tell me all about America."

"Sure," he said. "I—" But then the nurse stuck her head in and said something cautionary, and Christa rose.

"Oh, dear. Now I must leave. May I come tomorrow?"

"You'd better. You're my only link with the outside world. Without you, I'm stranded."

"Then I shall be here." She took his hand, shook it gently.

At this time of year it was not dark until nearly nine, and there was still daylight left as Christa drove slowly back to the Ferntal. "Lan," she said aloud, aware of pleasure and excitement within her. Something was happening to her, something nice, delicious. She did not dare try to analyze it for fear that, like a bubble, it would pop and vanish under too heavy a touch. For the moment she only savored it. But she thought she discerned the outlines of a miracle, of destiny at work. Why else should he have had that slip of paper in his pocket, why else should the police have come just minutes before she was going to tip her hand about Josef Steiner to Papa? Why else had she conceived the idea, persuaded Papa, to have him moved to Altkreuzburg? She had not at that time even known that he was single, or that he was so nice. It had been, she supposed, more an impulse to find an excuse to keep from going to Krems with Papa and Robert, or for making a decision about Josef, something purely selfish and expedient. But now . . .

But now she had something else in mind; and that might

105

take more cleverness on her part, for Papa might offer more resistance. Still, she thought confidently, I can manage it. It shouldn't be too difficult, especially if . . . Yes, that's it. I must be very nice to Robert. Divert attention until . . .

She turned up the long winding road to the Christina Hof. Despite the precariousness of the way, she drove instinctively, from long practice, handling her gears expertly. But, she thought, that still left Josef Steiner. What about Josef?

Josef, she decided, she did not want to think about right now. She would think about Josef later. Right now what she wanted was to cherish this strange excitement whose source was Lan Condon, and to make sure it did not escape her until she had a chance to understand it; she was not entirely certain, but almost, that she was falling in love, and in quite a different way than she had ever loved before.

The house rippled with the music of Bach's Two-Part Inventions, Ernst completely rapt and absorbed at the piano in the drawing room. As Christa went down the hall, she heard the sound of voices from her father's office and knocked on the door. "Come in," the General said.

All three men stood up as she entered: Max Schellhammer, Robert, and her father.

"Uncle Max." She went to him first. He was short, blocky, hard as a chunk of oak, in white shirt, sweater, short lederhosen, and knee socks. As always, when she embraced and kissed him, he smelled of schnapps, tobacco, and an ineradicable tinge of cow dung.

"Christa, *Schatzi!*" His voice was hoarse, raspy, as he patted her back uncle-fashion. His hair was short, salt-and-pepper, his face seemingly covered with old wrinkled leather, his eyes bright blue, lively, his mouth like a trap, and his chin like a clenched fist.

She patted his cheek. "I heard you won all the prizes at the wine fair!"

"Not I," he crowed, voice resonant with pride. "The expert there." He jerked his thumb toward Robert. "There must be something to his newfangled ways after all."

Christa turned to him. The adoration in his eyes made her uncomfortable, but she masked that. "My congratulations," she said and went to him and kissed him briefly on the lips.

"Now, that's the real prize!" Uncle Max exclaimed.

Robert glowed. "Well," Christa said, "I know how hard you've worked to make Uncle Max see the light. And," she taunted the old man obliquely, fondly, "it's not easy with somebody whose idea of pressing grapes is to get the whole family barefooted and jump in."

Robert laughed. "Oh, he's not that bad. But thank you very much. I really was quite pleased." Dressed like his father in leather, and with his strong bare legs, he was almost breathtakingly masculine; that she had to acknowledge. He smelled of the wine they'd been drinking and of soap and shaving lotion. She turned away from him, kissed her father. "May I join you for a glass of wine, or is this all male, all business?"

"Nothing special. Sit down." He found an *Achtel* glass for her and poured. "We were just congratulating ourselves on the way the wild boar have come back on our hunting grounds."

"A sign that times are getting better," Max said, lighting his pipe. "Oh, the poaching in those years after the war! The Viennese were thick in the woods as fleas and shot everything that moved and took it home and stewed it. They nearly wiped out all the game. And what could you do? They were starving. The judges wouldn't even convict 'em. And the wild pigs suffered the most. It's been a long hard job bringing them back. By the way, speaking of that, how's the American?"

"Improving," she said. "Did you know he's a *writer?*"

"Not a very smart one, or he wouldn't be so crazy about Jews," Uncle Max said. "But I guess that's the way Americans are. After all, they've got a Jewish president, that Rosenfeld." He belched loudly and took another drink of wine. Then his face went hard. "It was the Americans, don't forget, *Schatzi,* who destroyed Austria. Their Wilson could have stopped Clemenceau and Lloyd George from tearing us apart in 1919."

"Well, you can't make one American responsible for his government's mistakes," Robert said, surprising her. "They just don't understand the world, that's all. They hide behind their oceans and they don't really know what's going on anywhere else. The real Americans I rather admire and respect—the ones of English or German or Scandinavian heritage. After all, a lot of them are on our side. It's not the English or the Americans who're our enemies; it's the French and the Russians. The French want to get even for their defeat in the 1870s, and the

Bolsheviks want to take over all of Europe, the whole world. One of these days the Americans and English are going to see the light and make common cause with us against the Reds, and the world will be a decent place again." He held out his glass. "Incidentally, Christa, he's quite wrong, this American. It couldn't possibly have been Party members who did that to him. He just got mixed up with some of those thugs who hang around the Naschmarkt. He should have used better judgment."

Christa thought, I must not lose sight of my objective, and she nodded. "The whole thing is rather hazy to him. Anyway, he's coming along nicely. Papa, I think in a day or two you should drop in on him. He'll want to talk about the business of all this with you."

"Yes, I'll find the time," the General said in a neutral voice.

"Good." Christa held out her glass and he replenished the inch or so she had drunk. Then she stood up. "It's an absolutely lovely night and I'm going out and walk in the park." She glanced at Robert. "Maybe someone would like to come along and tell me all about the wine fair."

Max Schellhammer grinned. "It was your show, boy, not mine. I don't think she means me."

Robert stood up, pleased. "No, *Vati,* I don't think she means you. General, you will excuse us?"

Darkness had settled over the Vienna Woods; a crescent moon rode high above a distant ridge. The air was perfumed with the smell of forests, meadows, grass, and flowers. Robert and Christa walked under the old lindens on the dew-wet lawn.

"I'm very pleased about your prizes at the wine fair," she said. "And awfully sorry this thing about the American came up. But what's one to do in such a case?"

"You're too softhearted for your own good," Robert said, but his voice was easy, loving. "Still, I guess you did the right thing. Only . . . I did miss you. It was all a little spoiled because you weren't there."

She found that touching, and she wondered, Why can't you just be friends with a man? Why do they always have to fall in love with you? Why couldn't he stay eleven and I eight? I would love for it to be just as it used to be back then. And she steeled herself for what she had to do, because it was going to be fairly ugly. She took his hand in hers, squeezing it. "I'm sorry. I truly am. Tell me all about it."

And he did, relating a tale of triumph that was, she knew, the culmination of much striving over a long time, battering down the opposition of his father and all his father's friends to the innovations in wine making he had instituted at the Schellhammer Hof.

"I am very proud of you," she said quietly, and meant it.

"Thanks," he said.

She leaned back against a great old linden, raised one foot, slipped off her shoe. There were still the silk stockings, but she wanted if possible to feel her bare feet in the wet grass. "Turn your back," she said.

He did. She slipped off the other shoe, unlatched the supporters, peeled off the stockings, then was barelegged and barefooted, with shoes and stockings under her arm. Robert turned around again grinning.

"I remember once," he said, "fishing you out of the Fernbach on an October day and building a fire and drying you off. And you were as naked as a potato. And we never told our parents."

"But I was only nine then," she said.

"It seems like yesterday," he said, and he moved in on her, not much taller than she, but so much wider and stronger; and it suddenly struck her that at Krems he must have analyzed what he had been doing wrong and had decided that he had not been aggressive enough. He was aggressive now—bracing one hand against the tree trunk, putting out the other, cupping her chin, bending forward, kissing her.

She accepted the kiss, but it was with secret amusement. Hard and forceful as it was, it was also so naive as to be absurd. His lips were closed and reverent, and indeed it was as if she were eight and he eleven.

When he raised his head, he looked at her with love. "Christa—"

"Let's walk," she said, and took his hand and went barefoot through the grass.

"Look out for snails," Robert said, and that spoiled it all.

"Ugh," she said, "why'd you have to tell me that?" And she pulled on her shoes. But it was true, there were lots of snails, their shells as big as small dumplings.

"Well, I didn't want you to step on one."

"Thank you."

They walked to the wall, climbed up on a step, and looked out at the sparse lights twinkling in the Ferntal. Robert put his arm around her. "There's a Garbo film coming to the *Kino* in Altkreuzburg on Monday. Will you go with me? I know you worship Garbo."

"But you said she bores you."

"I can stand her if it will make you happy."

"Thank you," she said. "I'd love to go." Then, deliberately, she shivered. "Let's go in, it's getting chilly."

"I thought it was very warm."

"Men never feel the cold."

"Here, take my sweater."

"Thank you, but really we should go in."

He draped the sweater, warm with his body heat, about her shoulders. "In a minute," he said. "But first—" Emboldened, he kissed her again, more roughly this time; and she sensed the hunger and yearning in him, felt pity and that old affection, and she gave a little of herself. When he raised his head, she tried not to look at his eyes.

"Now," he said and put his arm around her. "Now we'll go in. I don't want you catching cold." And holding her to him, he led her into the house.

10   BY THE END OF HIS FIRST WEEK in the hospital at Altkreuzburg, Lan Condon had begun to realize what was happening to him, but he did not know what to do about it. At first he was sardonic, amused. After all, he knew all about love. Love was the girl in the Baton Rouge hotel, dressing to go to the next customer. Love was his own stock in trade, the very bricks and mortar on which the movie industry was built: the cute meeting, the attraction-repulsion leading up to the happy final clinch. For two years he and Ross had devoted every working day to plotting love stories by formulas as well-established as Newton's laws of motion. And love, too, was Phyllis—face

raised, staring in horror at Ross poised there in the bedroom door.

But what was happening between himself and Christa Helmer bore no relation to any of that, and cynicism was no armor against it. It had a force and strength of its own that overrode cynicism. She came to see him at least twice a day, and for him those hours were luminescent. He tried to rationalize; for her it was probably only a gesture of kindness to a stranger. And yet she *was* always on time and stayed the very limit and seemed to hate to leave. And there was a certain way she looked at him, and more and more she found occasion to touch him, and sometimes the little room was so full of a strange tension it nearly crackled as they talked.

She was different, she had a mind as good as Phyll's, he thought, and less calloused by the constant need for wit and put-down. The cheap wisecrack, the slashing remark, the reducing of every emotion to a witty phrase: that was the conversational coin around the swimming pools and at the cocktail parties; genuine emotion was what you tried to arouse in the audience, and the audience, of course, had a twelve-year-old mind. So every seriousness was handled briefly by a crowd, reduced to a tarnished penny and a bitter laugh. It was strange, refreshing, to find a woman who matter-of-factly betrayed a sense of values without embarrassment, even if the values were not always his. And, of course, to give Phyll her due, Christa was thirteen years younger and, as he had learned, far more sheltered. But that was part, too, of what fascinated him: the fact that she was waiting to learn, to be taught, and the idea that he could teach her to suit himself, that, to use a cliché, she was a blank slate on which he could write whatever pleased him.

But that made her sound like a nonentity, and she was not. He was startled by the workings of her mind revealed so far —her insight into people and the world, and especially herself. And dumbfounded, too, by her range of knowledge—of literature and music and art and the world—which, he supposed, was what was meant by a European education. Withal, she could be earthy, too, and pungent at times, but never really unkind; he, of all people, had reason to know her innate kindness.

But overpowering all the rest was the fact that she was young and lovely and desirable, and he wanted her, wanted possession in every possible way, carnal and spiritual, and could not now imagine, if he had her, ever wanting anybody else.

They knew a great deal about each other now. The way they talked, an hour and a half could slide by like a minute. She was hungry to know about him and about America, and in telling her, he saw his own life and the land that had shaped him with new eyes: hers. He was amazed at what a strange and wild and brawling country, full of marvels and outsized wonders and mean hatefulnesses and flashes of glory, he came from, and how much pride in it he felt, for all its failings. And it dawned on him that she, as a European, had almost no frame of reference by which she could comprehend it.

He was a figure moving against that landscape, and he told her about himself, the house on Cypress Street, the *Register,* and what he had caused to happen to it and Ewell. She was appalled at his softened version of what it was to be a hobo, a migrant worker, and would have been more so if he had described the full bitterness of that interlude. But mostly she wanted to know about his writing (she, like everyone, had tried herself to write), and he quickly realized that in her eyes that was what set him apart from ordinary mortals and made him someone of importance. It must be fairly hard for a woman to imagine herself as the inspiration of a hardware dealer or an insurance salesman. For the female mind he was the stuff that dreams were made on, and that was an advantage he did not now hesitate to use.

And, having come to terms with what he felt, yesterday he had asked Dr. Martinus, who had come laden with books in English, "What do you have to do to be a Catholic?"

"I beg your pardon?" Martinus said.

"To join the Catholic Church," Lan said. "Become a member in good standing."

Behind his thick-lensed glasses, the priest's eyes gleamed. "When one draws back from the edge of eternity . . . Yes. It gives one an appreciation of—"

"I mean the technical things. Instruction and all. How long does it take?"

He liked Martinus, profoundly; the man was brilliant. He

had his blind spots, but he had presented Lan with a book of his own poetry, and it was superb. Deep inside the little priest there were reservoirs of wisdom and well-disguised sensuality, and an appreciation for the English language that could only be felt by one approaching it from afar. One did not talk down to Martinus.

"About two months," Martinus said. "The instruction is rigorous, and there is much to learn."

"Who gives the instruction?"

"Well, any priest is empowered, but preferably—"

"Considering the fact that I don't speak German, could you do it?"

Martinus smiled broadly. "Of course. Mr. Condon, I would be delighted." He leaned forward. "When would you like to start? We could begin here and now."

"No," Condon said, "it's something I need to think about. I was just asking. Anyhow, it shouldn't take me long. I grew up in Catholic territory, even though we were Presbyterians. I've got a head start."

"Mr. Condon, I am completely at your service." Lan listened as Martinus outlined the course of instruction he would have to take. The prospect filled him with ineffable boredom, but it might be necessary, since her family was Catholic. It would have made no difference if they had been Buddhists; he would have as willingly and as meaninglessly made the conversion. "All right," he said at last. "We'll see."

"Excellent," Martinus said. "And . . . there is one thing I would remind you of, Mr. Condon. Your church in America is dominated by the Irish, and they have always been a self-scarifying, guilt-ridden people. Here in Europe there is a different, ah, emphasis. Worship must not be without its joys and its glories. Let us say that here we are inclined to take all the elbow room that God allows us." He smiled, almost wickedly. Then he rose. "Mr. Condon," he said, putting out his hand, "I shall pray that you will make the right decision."

"You mean," Christa asked, incredulous, "that you could insult a government official to his face and not be taken into court?"

"Of course."

"But to insult an official is to insult the government."

"It insults us, we insult it back."

"But that's *Amtbeleidigung!* To insult the Emperor's man in office is to insult the Emperor!"

"We don't have an emperor. Neither do you."

"Yes, but we still have the law. One could go to jail for being rude to an official."

He thought about what had happened to the *Register*. "It can be dangerous in America, too. But they can't jail you for it—not directly. I could call President Roosevelt a bastard to his face and there'd be nothing he could do about it."

She considered this, sitting on the chair in the room as he lay on the bed. As always, the door was discreetly left slightly open, a precaution insisted upon by the *Krankenschwestern.* "How very odd. And if anyone may do that, how can you keep order?"

"We don't."

"But there must be order."

He grinned. "Not the way we run things. Ever watch beans boiling in a pot? Some of the beans rise to the top and fall back and then others rise. Every bean has its chance—but only because the pot is boiling."

Christa laughed in a deep husky way that moved something inside him. "So. Now you have explained America to me. Americans are beans."

"Right. Pinto, string, lima, red, and some black-eyed peas."

She tapped a cigarette on her case. "Sometimes I wonder why I come here every day, but now I know. Nobody talks like you. Nobody even thinks like you. What a strange people you are, with your cowboys and gangsters and your Wall Street."

"No stranger than you and your wine and music and dancing."

"We are not like that at all," she said stiffly. "We are very serious and industrious."

"Then how come Willi Orlik told me that the philosophy of Austria is 'Elsewhere the situation may be serious, but it is not hopeless. In Austria it is hopeless, but it is never serious'?"

She laughed. "He told you that, eh? Your friend?"

"The impression I got from him, that we all have at home, is that you're living in a Germanic fairyland."

"Not a fairyland," she said. "And you must understand that we are not Germans, either. I have German, Austrian, Rumanian, English, Hungarian, Serbian, and Italian blood in my veins. So I think you could hardly call me German." She shrugged. "I am what I am."

"And I," said Lan, "am pure Anglo-Saxon, both sides. One ancestor hightailed it after Culloden and another just before a scheduled hanging at Highgate."

And then he heard himself say, "What extraordinary children we'll have with all those strains."

"I—" She sat up straight, and he was as unprepared for the change in her face as he had been for his own statement. Her eyes widened, and her lower lip trembled as she stared at him, and the cigarette was frozen halfway to her mouth. "Pardon," she whispered.

"I said, what extraordinary children we'll produce." Clad in his robe, he swung off the bed, stood up. Her eyes followed him as if she were hypnotized. He went to the door, closed it.

"That is not allowed," she whispered. "The sisters—"

"Damn the sisters." He was full of courage now, and heard himself rushing on. "Christa, I love you and I intend to marry you." And he came to her and took her hand.

She dropped her cigarette case. It clattered on the floor.

"And we *will* produce some extraordinary children," he said and pulled her to her feet and kissed her.

He felt the slenderness of her against him, her body sensuous under the fabric of the summer dress, and smelled her perfume and found her lips to be very soft. And for just one instant her body was rigid. Then it slackened, and then it pressed against him, and her arms went about him, and he felt a great surge of triumph and happiness and fear. When finally they broke apart, she moved only a little distance away, keeping her hands on him. Her eyes were awed, enormous, shining. "How did you *know?*" she whispered.

"I don't know. I just knew."

"So did I. I did. Oh, Lan—"

"God, I love you," he said, and they kissed again.

Just after they broke apart that time, the door opened, and a young nun said something threatening. Christa replied, and the sister went away, lips pursed. Christa turned back to him. "Oh," she said, "I wish you understood German. It would be so much easier to say it now."

"I understand *Ich liebe dich.*"

"Then I'll say that, anyhow. *Ich liebe dich."* She shook her head wonderingly. *"So viel. Furchtbar. Ich liebe dich so viel, es ist furchtbar."*

"I hope that means what I think it does."

"It does."

He let go her hands, turned toward the table, picked up an envelope. "I've already written my agent. I did it even before I found the courage to say— Because I knew I would stay here as long as it took. I'm not going back to America, Hollywood. I'm going to stay here. For a while, anyhow. A year, maybe more, and they can sue me if they want to, the studio, but I don't think they will. It won't be worth their while, really. Anyhow, I'd already made up my mind. To stay in Austria, write another book—and marry you. And as for the rest of it, we'll see." He grinned. "You see, I plan ahead. I even asked Martinus about joining the Church, in case your father made an issue of it."

Christa laughed, then came to him, pressed herself against him, head against his chest, regardless of the open door. He stroked her hair. "You planned . . . How delightful." She drew back. "Because I have also planned."

She closed the door. Her smile was wicked. "After all, you must have three weeks to regain your health somewhere. And where else but the Christina Hof? I could not allow you to go anywhere else. But there was Papa to deal with and . . . other considerations. But now I have everything *in Ordnung.* But you must not be jealous of it if . . ." And then she told him about Robert Schellhammer.

"Poor Robert," she finished. "I feel badly about it, but I simply don't love him. But Papa thinks it would be a good marriage, and if he thought you would spoil it, he would not consent to your coming to our house. So for the last few days, I have given Robert—and Papa—much encouragement. But it's necessary, you see? I must put up a"—she waved her hand, searching for a word under stress—"smokescreen. So I will go to the *Kino* with Robert and *am Heurigen,* enough to divert Papa's attention. And then you will come to the Christina Hof for three weeks to rest and let me take care of you. And Papa will come to know you and fall in love with you like I did, and after that it will be easy. Except," she said, a little sadly, "for Robert. But maybe he deserves it."

116

"Christa, I don't *need* to come there. I have money enough to take an apartment in Vienna."

"But then I could only see you two or three times a week. At the Christina Hof we could be together every day."

"Sold," he said.

"I am a terrible woman," she said. "I know it. But I love you, and I will do anything for you. You are the first man I ever loved so much that I didn't care what I did to anybody else."

"I'd better be the last one, too."

"Listen," she said. "I know how my father loved my mother. All my life I've dreamed of finding someone to love that much. Now I have him. I will never leave you. And please"—she trembled, as if in sudden fear—"you must not ever leave me."

"Never," he said, and took her in his arms. He held her so tightly that it made his wounded ribs ache. "Never, never, never."

"Then," she murmured, "everything will be all right."

Much later the nurse came again to push the door wider. "And now," Christa whispered, "I must go." In defiance of the watching nun, she kissed him briefly on the lips. "Tonight I shall finish all the arrangements with Papa. And in only a few more days you'll be at the Christina Hof."

"I don't care where," he said. "Just where you are." They looked at each other again, and they both laughed; and then she went out. He did not sleep that night, but sat up writing a letter to his agent. Presently he realized it was not to his agent at all, but to Ewell. He wadded it up, threw it in the wastebasket. And now he no longer hated the dead Kingfish who had set in train the events that had led him here; and even Ross's sacrifice had been worthwhile.

11 CLIMBING THE STAIRS of the building off the Gürtel, Christa felt armored against anything that could happen. She would have preferred not to be here at all, but there was no way she could snap her fingers and make Josef Steiner vanish. And until they had talked, he was a threat. No one was supposed to read anybody else's mail at the Christina

Hof, but you could never trust Aunt Alma; anything the least out of the ordinary, especially letters with no return address, heated her curiosity to the boiling point. Anyhow, she had been lax. She should have seen Josef or called him from the post office before now and put an end to all of it. Well, today she would do that.

In the corridor, she rang the bell beneath the nameplate SCHMIDT. Almost at once Josef himself opened the door, and relief and something more lit his long pale face. "You! Thank God you've finally come! I've been going mad, brain cell by brain cell." He pulled her in and closed the door. Then he tried to kiss her. Only lightly she brushed his lips, and then she moved away. He stared at her, stricken. "So," he said. Then: "Let's go into the living room."

"Yes," Christa said, and went ahead of him. Entering it, she paused, and this time the impact of its lavish black and scarlet decor was wholly different. Why, she thought, it's just kitsch! Kitsch for bored little *Hausfrauen* and servant girls! She stifled a strange need to laugh.

"Please sit down," Josef said, motioning her to the sofa. He stood above her like a desperate waiter in a place dying for lack of business, long fingers intertwined. "What would you like to drink?"

"Nothing, thank you."

There was silence in the room. Then he said, "Before you say anything, I want you to know that I have handled all this very badly. From the very beginning. But it was something new to me, something I'd never had to face before. And I have repeated in my mind every word that I said last time, and . . . I must have sounded like an idiot, and looked like one, too, here in this place." He turned, gestured. "This"—his lip curling—"absurd, overdone, musty den of iniquity."

He turned to face her. "I did nothing right—nothing. First, the marriage settlement, as if I'd tried to buy you. And how you must have laughed at that—what a Hebrew trick, thinking that everyone has her price! How cynical I must have sounded, how cold-blooded. But . . . in a way, perhaps that is my biggest failing. I suppress my real feelings. I talk only about the things I don't value and never about the things I do. Somehow, I can't reveal that much of myself. Oh, I made a great show of explaining how industrious and serious I am, working at my genetic experiments and making my land pay, which is true. But that is only window dressing and is not important. Deliberately I withheld from you the one thing that *is* important. For two reasons. The first was that my trust of you was imperfect. I see that now and see, too, that if I cannot trust you"—his face darkened—"and I mean with my very life, then you would be right to reject me for lack of faith in you. Also, it would be the most important thing, the dominating factor of our life together, and it is wrong and dishonest of me not to tell you beforehand. And when I do so, you will know more about me than my own mother did, more than any other person in Austria; and"—his face turned somber—"from then on my life will be in your hands. But willingly I place it there. I have nothing more precious to offer to attest my love and need."

Christa stared at him.

Josef drew in a breath like a diver going off a high board. "I am many things," he said. "And one of them is a Jew. And because of that, I am a member, a leader, of an organization with two purposes to which I have determined to dedicate my life and fortune. The first is to rescue as many Jews from Germany as possible. The second is to overthrow Adolf Hitler and, with luck, restore Germany to sanity."

Whatever she had expected, it was not this. The two of them were silent for half a minute, frozen in a tableau, staring at each other. Then Josef went to the cabinet, took out brandy and a glass, poured himself a drink. "That's not the real secret," he said raggedly. "The real secret is that Josef Steiner can feel. If you prick him, he hurts. He can feel rage and pain and sorrow; he can suffer not only for himself but for others. And, believe me, no one was more surprised to learn that than Josef Steiner."

He took a swallow of the brandy, faced her. "It grew on me slowly. For a long time I paid no attention to what happened in Germany; I was working with my brothers and was preoccupied with business and also . . . pleasure. The Nazis were a silly minority that soon would fade away. But then Hitler became Chancellor of Germany and . . . it began."

His eyes were lambent above the dark circles beneath them. "It began through secret business channels. Inside information that was horrifying, unbelievable. And then the pleas for help; begging letters by the dozens, then by the dozen dozens, that would break your heart. We were Jews and we were rich and powerful and, best of all, outside the Third Reich. And where else should the poor devils inside Germany turn but to us? So, bit by bit, I began to comprehend. And although I fought against it, my shell of indifference cracked and broke, and then I could feel the pain—others' pain. And when it was too much to bear, I begged and pleaded with my brothers to throw the whole weight of the firm behind helping those poor people. But they refused. Business is business, and one must not rock the boat. One must not damage the profits. The German government's bonds were a substantial part of our investments." His voice went harsh. "That, not my profligate sexual habits, is why I finally broke with them, took my share of the family fortune, and went on my own. I had to promise, though, not to embarrass them publicly in that respect. Adultery, you see, or debauchery does not embarrass a banker so much as betraying a measure of humanity. Anyway, my reputation as a dissolute rogue was fortunate; it gave us a reason for the break and provided me with a fair disguise. Who would think that Josef Steiner, that ineffable libertine, had a serious thought in his depraved head?"

"Josef, this is incredible," Christa whispered.

"But true. Look, Christa, what the *Pifkas* practice on the Jews is extortion, pure and simple. The whole idea is to force them to get out of Germany—all of them. But they're not allowed to take anything with them, everything they own is confiscated by the state when they leave. So, while the Nazis allow them to emigrate, emigration takes money, and the Nazis seize all their money. So they're caught up in a devil's circle."

He finished his brandy. "I do my best to break that. Through certain channels, I pay passage—or ransom—for as many as possible. But there are hundreds of thousands, and the number I can help is only a drop in the bucket. There really is only one way to save them all—change Germany. And the only way to change Germany is to destroy Adolf Hitler. In the long run, that's my aim."

Christa stood up. "Josef, please don't tell me any more. I don't know much about such things, but I do know that such talk is dangerous, and it scares me. Even here in Austria, if it got out—"

"My darling," Josef said, "I know all that. And obviously, if you speak a word outside these walls, I am destroyed. But don't you understand? The truth about myself is the gift of love I bring to you."

"Josef, I think I'd better go."

"No." He interposed himself between her and the door. "Not until I finish. Please."

Resignedly she nodded.

"Of course, if word leaked, the government here would drop on me like a ton of stone. There are delicate negotiations under way just now with Hitler, and I would be a profound embarrassment. Because while what I'm saying may sound mad to you, I assure you that it is not."

He wagged his finger, almost like a classroom lecturer. "To the outside world, Christa, Hitler looks to be firmly in the saddle. All powerful. But he's not, far from it. Right now his throne is shaky, shakier than anyone might believe. There is a good chance, given cleverness and luck, of bringing off what we hope to do—simply disposing of him and his gang. I can't tell you how or when; but he has enemies with power that equals his own, if they can only be brought to use it. Anyhow, while the chance exists, it must be taken. Not for the sake of Germany, as I tried to make my brothers see, but for the sake of Austria— and our own necks. Because if he does take Austria, it's the same thing for us: my brothers, myself, for every Jew in Europe."

He spread his hands. "So there you have it. The secret life of Josef Steiner. I lay it at your feet."

Christa swallowed hard. She read the truth, the need, on his face; and if two weeks ago he had told her this, laid himself bare like this, she might well have said yes on the spot and faced the music with her father. But there was no question of that now. Lan, the thought of Lan, her love for him, possessed her wholly. "Josef," she heard herself say in a tone that left no room for doubt.

His face went bleak. "So I've frightened you. But listen, you must understand. Things will be arranged. Never will you be in jeopardy—"

"That's not it."

For a moment he was silent. Then: "Is there someone else?"

"Yes. Yes, there is."

He dragged the back of his hand across his mouth wearily. "Not the American?"

"How did you know about him?"

His smile was weary. "I know almost everything. Far more than I should like to." He closed his eyes a moment, leaned against the door; then he straightened up. "Christa, isn't that rather silly? You can only have known him a few days, and that only in the hospital. Don't let the wounded-bird syndrome deceive you. His need for you is temporary; mine is deep and permanent. And"—he laughed brassily—"if getting beaten by the Nazis is what it takes, that's absurdly easy for me to arrange."

"Josef, stop it, please."

"But it's not fair."

"I know it isn't," she answered finally. "Everything you say is true. I hardly know him, and yet I feel I know him better than anyone I have ever known. And . . . it's happened, and there's nothing I can do about it. Just like it happened to Mama, she said, when she first saw Papa at that ball in Bucharest. And—" She raised a hand, dropped it.

"So. And when he's well and goes back to America. What then?"

"He won't be going back. He'll be staying here, for a while, at least. But if he does go— Well, I'll go wherever he goes."

Josef's mouth twisted. "Well, as long as it's he, I still have hope. Because it may not work out as you have planned. He may hurt you, Christa. For your sake, I hope he doesn't. For mine, I hope he does, because if so, I'll be waiting. Thank God it's not that Schellhammer."

Her brows went up. "You know about him, too?"

"Yes. He's a Nazi, of small consequence right now, but likely of much more later on, if there's *Anschluss*. It's necessary for me to know about all such; they are my enemies." His eyes met hers. "You need only repeat a fraction of what I've told you to Robert Schellhammer and I'm a dead man."

She stared at him, touched by a chill. "Robert wouldn't—"

"Robert would—and leap at the chance. He's a fanatic, and as dangerous as a loaded pistol. Don't ever deceive yourself about him. You've seen what his Party comrades did to the American, from what I've heard, a thorough job. In the end he's not one jot different from them. And— Christa, I may have been mad to confide in you; but there's a method in it. It's necessary and far past time for you to think and grow. And I risk my own safety in the hope that doing so will bring you to that. Now you must look around and become aware of what is going on; you must examine people like Robert Schellhammer in a different light, with new eyes. Your innocence must end. And I think, when it does, when you understand much more about yourself, about me, about Austria—then I hope that you will let your American go and come to me and join and help me. So I have laid a burden on you, maybe a curse, if you wish. But remember this: When you find yourself about to talk, remember that *what you say could kill Josef Steiner*. Then, in your own mind, you will automatically question everyone you meet, his opinions, what sort of person he is. You will see the world with new eyes. Because this is no joke, no game to be shared with your friend Luisa. *This is life or death.*"

Suddenly she could bear being here and subject to his intensity no longer. She had not asked him to share his secrets with her, put responsibility on her for his survival. It was not fair; and she felt abused, almost raped by this forcing of her.

"I shall do my best to guard your secret, Josef," she said levelly. "Everything I can. But remember, I didn't ask to know it, and—"

"And if you slip . . . Yes, that's a risk I've made up my mind to take. Because I know you, Christa, and I don't think you will slip."

"I want to go."

He moved away from the door. "Surely. Well, I suppose neither of us will sleep soundly for a while. But, then, I haven't anyhow, not for a long time. Do you have your car?"

"Yes, it's downstairs."

"Then . . . be careful. Not just on the way home. But all the time. In what you say and do. And look around you. *For God's sake, look around you.*" Then, at the door, very formally he kissed her hand and said *auf Wiedersehen*.

12 THE COLD WIND BLEW across the wide Galician plain, stirring the red dust, rustling the dead stalks of the endless fields of sunflowers. Overhead, against a gunmetal sky, carrion crows swooped and circled like flakes of charred paper floating in chimney heat. Helmer's big gelding moved restlessly between his thighs, made nervous by the scent of death. As a warhorse, that scent was something to which it should have been accustomed; but this was different. Three of the men were still alive, past screaming now, but pleading in hoarse whispers for an end to their irremediable agony.

A sour scalding liquid rose in Helmer's throat. Refusing to display weakness before his men, he somehow forced it back into his vitals and then made himself look once more at the unspeakable.

The fourteen Austrian infantrymen had been cut off from their unit in the first phase of the swift, unexpected Czarist attack, and it had been their misfortune to be captured by a troop of Kuban Cossacks, those fierce clannish horsemen who lived only for combat, and to whom anyone not of their brotherhood was both enemy and less than human. There were rules for the treatment of prisoners of war, but the Cossacks made their own rules. They had driven fourteen strong wooden stakes into the cold red earth, with sharp ends pointed upwards. Had dragged the uniform trousers and underclothes off each man, had bound hands behind their backs, ankles together, and then they had impaled each Austrian through the anus by forcing him down on a stake, ramming the wood brutally up through the bowels. After which, the Cossacks retreated before the counterattack, leaving their victims to die with agonizing slowness as their own weight forced the points upward through the vitals.

The moment the advance troops had found them, Helmer, always near the forefront, had been sent for. At first he had not believed his eyes; vaguely he had heard of this infamous Eastern style of execution, practiced by Turks, Huns, and ancient Magyars, but this was 1915, and, as a man of his time, he found it beyond his comprehension. But it was fact, and all at once something blew up in his skull, making his brain an incandescent white flare of total rage.

The surgeon moved unsteadily as he strode to where Helmer sat his horse. His face was pale, and he was trembling. "Colonel, there is no hope. I have given morphine. If the stakes are removed, hemorrhage will kill them immediately. No, not immediately, in minutes. My God, I don't know what to do."

"You certify that medically there is no hope?"

"I swear it."

"Then there is only one thing we can do," said Helmer, and he passed his horse's reins to an aide. Dismounting, he un-snapped the flap of his pistol holster. He felt as if everything within him had turned to solid ice. The drug had taken hold now, and their moaning and screaming had turned to whimper-ing, not unlike the sound so many hurt puppies might have made. "My boys," Helmer said, his voice hoarse, "God will bless you, and among your countrymen you will be immortal." One of them only looked at him dully. He walked behind them, drew his gun, and then, stepping from one to the other, shot each of the three quickly in the back of the head. It was not something he could have commanded any other man to do. His horse jumped when, returning to it, he slammed one fist fero-ciously against the saddle. Then he mounted and addressed the surgeon.

"You will have a photographer brought up and pictures made of this from every angle before the bodies are disturbed. Then they are to be removed with the stakes still intact, in place. Secure fourteen large casks from the monastery in that last town, put them as they are in the wine, and seal the casks. Have them taken to the railroad and sent by special sealed car, under guard, to the chief garrison hospital at the Van Swietengasse in Vienna with a full description of the incident, for autopsy and verification." He turned to his aide. "You will also see that affidavits are taken from the men who discovered this atrocity. You will prepare a letter for my signature describing the inci-dent and all actions taken in their entirety, and leaving space for my designation of the appropriate posthumous decorations I shall recommend. As to the pictures, I want them printed immediately and copies of them distributed with the order which I shall now dictate to all units of the regiment."

"*Jawohl.*" Captain Ropertz turned a page, pencil poised above a fresh sheet of paper on the writing board balanced on his saddle pommel. Helmer began to dictate, voice toneless throughout. Once Ropertz' busy hand paused. Then he said with grim satisfaction, "Yes, by God!" and went on writing. When he was through, Helmer said, "Distribution in addition to the regiment: copy to division, corps and Army headquarters, and to the Chief of General Staff. See to it at once and send Lieutenant Paulus to me to take your place; I shall be riding with the advance." His skull was still full of that cold yet white-hot crackling dazzle. He touched his horse with spurs, rode on.

And then they had him, the Cossacks. He did not know how they had captured him, but he knew what they would do with him. He felt their rough hands stripping him. The sky above was gray, the wind cold. Voices chanted, "The Butcher of Galicia! The Butcher of Galicia!" Fur-hatted men, with bandoliers of cartridges, animal faces... and then their faces were grinning skulls. He saw the long thick stake set in the ground, its sharpened point fresh-wood white and gleaming. His arms and legs were not bound, but they were paralyzed. He could not move a muscle of his naked body. They were all around him, hundreds of them, thousands, and crows circled in the sky. A mighty roar went up: "The Butcher of Galicia!" Horror, mortal fear, surged up in Helmer; he tried to scream, but his jaws were locked, paralyzed. Hands lifted him, locked him in a seated position, high above the stake. "The Butcher of Galicia!" The roar came again and suddenly his body was rammed downward, and this time his jaws unlocked and he could scream.

As always, he had awakened with the sound reverberating in the bedroom, his body shaking uncontrollably, his nightshirt plastered to his torso with cold sweat. And, as always, the nightmare left him momentarily disoriented in space and time. Instinctively his hand had slid to the far side of the bed where, in years past, she would have been, waiting to hold and comfort him, but that space was empty now and he'd had to fight his way out of the terror by himself. That was not easy. Though the dream came far less frequently now, only a few times a year, its effect on him had not diminished with time. It would, he knew, leave him depressed and shaken the whole day long. The

Russians, he thought, skin goose-pimpling with fear and horror. It was absurd to nurse this secret terror of them still, after more than twenty years. And yet it lingered, ineradicable by reason, his private abhorrence, like another man's fear of snakes or a woman's fear of mice or rats, only stronger.

The reward was still on his head. Because, after all, as he had learned through channels of his own, Kerensky had not lifted it, nor Lenin, nor Stalin; he had verified that through channels of his own. In 1934, in fact, when Dollfuss had crushed the Socialists, *Izvestia* and *Pravda* had trotted out the Butcher of Galicia as a previous example of Austrian brutality toward the Russian people and their ideological allies. Through tortured reasoning, he remained as much an enemy of the Communists as he had been of the Czarists.

Because it was only the second part of the dream that was false; the first part was true. The impalement of the fourteen men was something forever branded on Helmer's brain. Nor did he regret the order dictated that day at white heat to Ropertz— that while prisoners of war from other Russian units should continue to be given normal treatment in accordance with international law, no member of his regiment was to give quarter to any captured Cossack, Don, Kuban, or any of the other clans. None was to be allowed to surrender, none taken alive.

The order had, of course, been revoked by Army headquarters, despite its outrageous supporting documents—but not before, during Helmer's counterattack against the Russian salient, it had been carried out enthusiastically by his own regiment, and others that had heard the news. And it was not only Cossacks who died trying to surrender or who were slaughtered where they lay wounded. But Helmer had no regrets. By then the Eastern front was one great slaughter pen, and he no longer considered Russians, any Russians, human. He wanted only to wipe out them all, as dreadful Oriental vermin.

Meanwhile, a copy of his order had fallen into Russian hands, and the Czar, reeling from the defeat at Tannenberg, seeking any propaganda advantage to divert the masses, made a cause célèbre of it, placing a reward on Helmer's head—ten thousand rubles for his capture: *alive*. Wind of that had gotten to the Emperor, who, after reprimanding, decorating, and promoting Helmer, sent him to the Italian front. "We do not know what they would do with you if they should take you," the old man had told him personally at a brief imperial audience. "But you are too dear and valuable to Us to risk that happening. Therefore, We are sending you to a command in the Trentino." For an instant the steel-gray eyes, rheumy now with age, flashed fire; and though, with his white muttonchops and basset-hound face, he looked like everyone's favorite great-uncle, Helmer sensed the man beneath the benign legends, the steel-hardness of him, which had cost him the love of his Empress, driven his son to suicide and murder. "As a regimental commander, I would have done precisely what you did." Then he turned away, hobbling to the window, looking out in silence, traditional sign the audience had ended; and Helmer, in the traditional way, backed out.

He was still depressed after breakfast, in his office glancing through the latest copy of the weekly veterans' newspaper and leftover mail from yesterday, much of it pleas for help from old comrades. Captain Ropertz, for example, now managed a Pebeco toothpaste factory in Hungary, but dental hygiene was not a high priority across the Leitha, and it was on the verge of bankruptcy. Could the General perhaps...? To Ropertz it was a crucial sum, to Helmer a modest one, and the General could, in this case, though not in all. Presently he laid the letters aside, leaned back, lit a cigarette. Maybe Max was right; maybe he was too softhearted. Yet he liked people, was intensely interested in them, and, knowing his own strength and luck, felt a responsibility for the less fortunate that he could not dodge.

Anyhow, there was more method in his generosity than Max understood. While helping others pleasured him, it had also been a tactic vital to his survival—and that of his family and his property.

Christina had been right, of course; with conditions as they had been, purchase of the Christina Hof had been a dangerous gamble. In the past thirteen years, life in Austria had been like a whip-cracking ride on an enormous roller coaster, one wave of turmoil following another; and, just when it seemed things could not get worse, the roller coaster would dive even lower.

In all the turmoil, it had taken more than strength, more than luck, to survive; and Helmer had known that from the beginning. Only by staying at least one step ahead of events could he cope with them, and that required sound advance information, which could come only from a network of reliable informants. A rumor here, a scrap of hard fact there, it all came back to Helmer; and painstakingly, intelligently, he separated chaff from grain. To be informed was to be ready to act in time. His system worked and he was proud of it; and it was cheap at what it cost him, which was mostly kindness, Christian charity, and human understanding—qualities in perpetually short supply.

But now, he thought, rising from his desk, it had failed him in one large respect, one that might be fatal; and he had not realized it until this spring, when Hitler had marched into the Rhineland, the industrial region of Germany occupied by France since the Great War.

It was inevitable, he saw now, it had to come—the Nazification of Austria—and he had taken no steps to prepare for it. For all his artful dodging, he was caught short, one flank exposed. And, for that matter, his own feelings had become ambivalent.

Through the freshness of early summer morning, Helmer walked across the courtyard, passed through the arch in its wall, and, a couple of hundred yards farther on, entered the heart of the Christina Hof—the pressing house and bottling works. He passed through the pressing house, its machinery idle now, unlocked a massive door, switched on a light. He descended ancient steps of stone, dank with mold and moisture, into the first of a labyrinth of cellars honeycombing the interior of the mountain. They had been hewn out one by one over centuries, from the days of the castle that had once stood here.

The only ranks he commanded now, he thought, were these ranks of oaken casks, cradled in lines along each wall, with choice vintages maturing in them. He walked down the aisle between them slowly, thoughtfully, pausing here and there to stare at the head of one or another. These were the ones whose ends bore intricate carved bas-reliefs, some decades, even centuries old, which would have done credit to any museum, and some newer, commissioned by himself, executed by a master craftsman at the cooperage in Ferndorf.

There was one to commemorate his purchase of the Christina Hof, with her name and a view of the house itself scrolled and wrought in the dark wood. And a row of others, one for each wedding anniversary, until—

Until, he thought, and braced himself against that other remembered horror. Cancer of the female organs, and a long courageous time in dying, longer and more agonized than any of those impaled men and no way he could end her misery. But he knew one thing for certain: he'd had his woman, and he would never have another one. He could discipline himself to continence until age finished the job, and he had to; there would be no way that he could make love to another female without a whole range of memories and associations rising—not fair to him or any woman either. But he missed her. God knows, he missed her. Not a day went by that he did not feel the emptiness in his life her going had left. And just now, because of Christa, he missed her more than ever.

He could, he thought, manage an estate, stalk a wild boar, kill a man, maneuver a regiment, command a division; but his inability to handle one young girl seemed total. With Ernst he could meet on level terms and communicate, and although Ernst had no desire to follow in his own footsteps, as soldier, business-man, or farmer, but yearned only to be a musician, fortunately this was a country in which a musician outranked all three, so Helmer could accept that. But he could not find out what Christa wanted or determine what was good for her. It was as if they spoke two languages that sounded exactly the same but in which each word had contrary meaning. Alma was no help, and he was worried.

She had tried so much by the age of twenty-one and still had no idea of what she really wanted. The University—given up. Her painting—given up. Men in swarms around her, and none she seemed to want, which, he admitted, had at first been a relief to him. But more and more it appeared to Helmer that Christa was tending to skate on thin ice. That minor scandal, the picture in *Die Bühne,* had been a symptom; soon something must be done, a choice made.

If necessary, for her own good, he would make it for her, he'd concluded; and he had. Robert Schellhammer.

If Christina were alive, she'd have put an end to that at once. To her it would have been unthinkable, marriage of Christa to a farmer's son. But in this era no rules held—and

Robert was no ordinary *Bauer*. He was educated, would some-day inherit holdings and a fortune at least as large as and maybe bigger than Helmer's own, and he was upright, strong, capable of exerting the firm hand she so badly needed. When Helmer himself was dead, Robert had the knowledge and ability to manage both estates and make them pay. Until this spring, Helmer's only objection to him had been his Nazi politics.

But now that had become an advantage. The handwriting was on the wall. Helmer knew the Nazis. If you were not with them, their philosophy ran, you were against them. He had not been with them. But if he had a son-in-law, one assuredly des-tined to rise when the Nazis gained control, that would be enough. Robert was perfect protection for that dangerously exposed flank.

And then when Helmer had heard the rumors, his resolve had hardened. They had drifted back like the taint from a bordello, and they had shocked and sickened him. Christa—and Josef Steiner.

He would not believe it, could not believe it, and yet he had to admit it might be possible. Indeed, some part of himself knew that it was all too possible. And he'd made his mind up firmly then, lending overt support to Robert, praying only that Robert didn't hear the rumors. To know that Christa had been going with that decadent Jew, had kissed him, maybe more than kissed him ... It would have sickened Robert as much as it sickened the General, and it would have made her repugnant to him. No time must be lost.

And then she had suddenly kicked all his careful plans to flinders! Helmer grimaced, but the grimace changed to a smile of almost fond admiration. He should have expected it, been on guard. If nothing else, she had at any rate inherited his genius for strategy; and the way she had outflanked him in the matter of the American had been smooth and expert.

He walked down the rows of casks, paused before the one commissioned for her most recent name day. He had one carved for each name day in the family, and it had become the most eagerly awaited surprise of all. And, of course, there would be one for her marriage, but damn it! Helmer thought.

Still, there was no way he could have known that morning when the police came what would happen. And Christa had been right—it was something that, as Austrians, they owed the man. Alone and friendless in Vienna, his own legation seemingly indifferent, he had badly needed what charity they could offer; and arranging to have him moved to Altkreuzburg had been simple.

Nor had there been anything untoward about Christa seeing him every day—he did need a translator and a link with the outside world. He simply could not be left there in isolation. For that matter, Helmer had dropped in on him twice himself, had found him likable, appreciative, and interesting. He was intelligent, which was natural for a writer, and his manners were good; and he was respectful to his elders, which was less natural for a writer. Martinus had been there during one of his visits and they had left together. Sharing a glass of wine later at an outdoor cafe, Helmer had asked, "What do you think of this Condon?"

"A very decent chap," Martinus said. "Not at all loud and pushy the way I thought Americans were. And in my estimation, extremely talented. As a matter of fact . . ." He opened the briefcase he carried with him everywhere. "I have one of his books here, if you'd care to take it with you and read it. In English, of course. He just autographed it for me."

"So." The General leafed through it. "Well, I'm not much for novels, but . . . yes. Since I know him, I'd like to glance at it. I'll take good care of it."

"And there's another thing," Martinus said. "I suppose you know more about this than I do, but it's really amazing how his brush with death has turned his mind toward spiritual matters. He wants to receive instruction for conversion to the Holy Mother Church."

And that, Helmer thought now, was when he had smelled a rat. A kind of faint warning bell had rung in the back of his head, but, at the moment, not quite loud enough to alarm him. And it was true, a narrow escape did make men consider the condition of their souls.

He had read the book and found it gripping, and his respect for Condon soared. Though obviously the work of a man quite young, it was—and Helmer appreciated this—direct and to the point, and the characters rang true, were flesh and blood. At least there was none of the experimental maundering or outright obscenity one found now in so much one picked up.

The bell sounded louder in his brain as he watched Christa closely. He had thought he'd seen something in her eyes, her manner, her smile, after each visit to the hospital. His suspicion and misgivings grew—until she disarmed them. Her visits tapered off and suddenly she was paying attention to Robert Schellhammer. Several nights in a row she'd gone out with him, to the *Kino,* to a *Heuriger.* By the time her real assault was mounted, he had been distracted by the diversion that she'd created. Otherwise he would under no circumstances have agreed to Lan Condon coming to the Christina Hof to recuperate.

He had protested slightly. "Christa, I really think it would be better if he went to a spa. Why not Baden? The waters would be good for him. And he can easily afford it."

"But, Papa, I've as much as promised—"

"Oh? Don't you think you should have asked me first?"

"It never occurred to me that you would mind. I mean that I didn't say yes, but I led him to believe . . . I never heard of you refusing anyone before." She looked at him strangely. "Why him?"

"Well, I . . ." He groped. She was right; it was rare for him to refuse anyone in such a pass, and he was caught short for an answer.

Christa shrugged. "So, if you think we have done our duty by him as Austrians . . . Although it seems to me we've done little enough. Being a stranger, not knowing the language, they'll fleece him at a spa; and it will be uncomfortable for him anyhow, alone at such a place. But maybe he won't take too sour a taste home with him. He seems to be a forgiving sort of person. I'll tell him tomorrow I was wrong and that he must make other arrangements. Now, if you'll excuse me, Robert and I . . ." She went out, leaving him feeling guilty.

And even now, to Helmer, much of how she'd managed it remained a mystery. But by noon the next day she'd overcome his reservations, obtained his consent, and set to work arranging a room for Condon on the first floor, so he'd have as few stairs to climb as possible.

The day after that she brought him home to the Christina Hof. Two days later, when he noticed that Robert had not appeared or called, he asked her about it. "Robert?" she replied offhandedly. "Oh, we had a quarrel. Really, Papa, he can be so stupid—"

"A quarrel about what?"

"Oh, just things." She shrugged; and then, seeing her complete indifference, the General sighed. But by now it was too late, and there was nothing he could do about it. In any event, he was sure, Condon was blameless; the whole affair was Christa through and through—or Christina, for that matter.

And now Condon had been a guest here for nearly three weeks, and even a blind man could have seen it. Max Schellhammer was not blind.

Together, walking over their *Jagdpacht*—their hunting grounds—one afternoon, they paused to rest on a fallen log. Max tamped his pipe. "Well, Herr General, we have trouble."

Helmer looked at him keenly. "What kind of trouble?"

"Girl trouble, boy trouble. Christa and Robert. She's hurt the boy, hurt him as bad as anything I've ever seen."

"Max, I'm sorry. What—?"

"Well, she led him on for a week, built up his hopes; then she threw him over. Now he's angry at the whole damn world, slinks around like a cat with diarrhea, off his feed, ready to claw anybody who gets too close." Max shook his head. "Oh, I don't blame you. But that American, he's a mistake."

"Yes."

Max turned, fixed him with keen blue eyes. "What'll you do if he marries her and takes her off across the ocean?"

"Max—"

"It could happen. *Gott im Himmel,* Herr General. Don't you see the way they look at one another? It's a case, a bad case if I ever saw one. And you know what I hoped and what you hoped. What about that now?"

"It's not going to happen. He's not going to marry her and take her anywhere."

"Good. For my boy's sake, I hope you're firm about that."

Helmer then was suddenly rankled. As if, he thought, Robert were all that counted. He stood up. "Of course, Max, in the long run the main thing is for her to be happy. What she wants must be considered."

"Excuse me," said Max, "but what she wants and what is good for her may be two different things."

"Yes, but that's something that only she and I together can decide." There was an edge to Helmer's voice. It was one thing for him to dictate his daughter's future, quite another for an outsider to attempt that.

Max looked at him obliquely, then took the schnapps flask and cup from his rucksack and poured a drink. Tossing it off, noisily smacking his lips, he also rose. "Happiness," he said. "Young people think of nothing else these days. In my day and yours, it was different. We were serious. A woman picked a man —or her parents did—because he was a good provider, by God, he could get the kronen and hold on to 'em. And a man picked a woman who could give him plenty of strong kids and keep his house the way it ought to be. If the man can make the money and the woman bear the kids, the happiness comes soon enough. But now they got it all the other way around. They think life's a fairy tale—or one of those moving pictures at the *Kino*." He spat into the leaves. "Me and you, we know better." He took another drink, offered the flask to Helmer, who shook his head. "But, excuse me, Herr General, what she did to Robert was not nice."

"No," Helmer said. "I'm sorry."

"And when you think," Max said, and something almost shuddered in his raspy voice, a kind of eagerness, "what it could be here in the Ferntal someday if those two got together . . . You and I could sit back and take it easy then."

"Yes, we could take it easy," Helmer said. Greed, he thought, that was what he'd heard in Schellhammer's voice; and suddenly he looked at the stumpy, leathery farmer with new eyes. Almost he felt himself a fool. All this time, he thought, while I was using him, or thought I was, he was, of course, using me as well. And . . . I almost played right into his hands on this. Something within him rebelled. He could nearly hear Christina saying, *No. Absolutely not.* And he saw himself, too, in a new light. But his voice was mild when he said, "Well, we'll see how it all works out. Come, Max, we'd best be getting on."

Helmer glanced at his watch: nearly eight. Soon time to confer with Hans, his major-domo. He left the cellar, switching out the light. In the pens and buildings of the farm, chickens crowed and hogs grunted. A pheasant cackled in the orchard.

The American, Helmer thought... The fact was, the more he'd seen of Condon, the more he liked him. Older than Christa, true, but she of all people needed a husband with maturity and judgment. The man was well-spoken and had a quick, clear mind; he was learning German with amazing speed. And as for money—people who wrote motion pictures raked it in. Sixty thousand American dollars a year, Christa had mentioned offhandedly. My God! And the General himself had seen the documents by which Condon had transferred over fifteen thousand to the Steiner bank: a fortune for a man so young! He had courage, too, and apparently a quality of gallantry rare nowadays, or he would not have tried to help that Jew against the Nazis. A misguided attempt, certainly, but then he was a stranger, could not have foreseen the consequences. He drank a bit heavily, yes, but then who didn't hereabouts? He seemed to come from a good family, judging from his manners.

Helmer had always pictured Americans as boorish—spitting, slapping loudmouthed nature children, a species of Cro-Magnon —but Condon could almost have been a well-bred Austrian. And apparently he was no indoor man, no hothouse flower. He had talked with fair knowledgeability of guns and hunting with the General, had stories of his own of hunting in America, which weighed strongly with Helmer. But— In God's name, what was he trying to do? Make a case for Condon as a son-in-law? A foreigner, a man whose family and origins were still unknown, uncheckable? A writer, a breed notoriously neurotic and unstable? One who might take Christa thousands of miles away, leaving an emptiness in his life he was not sure that he could bear?

And yet... Helmer remembered a girl in white across a seething ballroom, a girl so young, so lovely in the muted light; and he remembered, too, a soldier already in his middle thirties, from a foreign land and his parents simple people of the back country, and no guarantee with the tensions pulling Europe taut just then that he would be alive next year...

Max was wrong, he thought. Happiness must come first. Joseph and Mary, but what if he had not been able to convince Christina's parents? Suppose she had not used all her wiles, played mercilessly on their love for her?

And he had seen the way their eyes met, and the way, in secret,

they touched each other when they thought nobody saw, and—
He halted in the middle of the farmyard.

They would, he was sure, present him with the necessity of
decision soon. But he knew, entering the house, turning toward
his office where he must confer with Hans, the decision was
already made, not by him, not even by Condon and his daughter,
but by Christina.

13 IN CHRISTA'S STEYR, they had driven deep into the
Wienerwald along narrow unpaved roads with
obscene, irrational curves and switchbacks springing out with
unexpectedness, forested cliffs falling dangerously away on the
vergeless outside, or, the land more gentle, great meadows and
cultivated fields rolling off and down. Their journey yielded
one flawless lovely landscape after another, Condon thought,
like turning the pages of a cheap calendar that was almost
tasteless in its repeated scenes of beauty; yet this was reality.
Still, it had a dreamlike quality that captured him.

And Christa's presence made it perfect. They had, in the past
three weeks, had so little privacy that being alone together
now was an unexpected, exquisite boon; and every moment must
be savored. Sometimes where there was a turnoff and the road
deserted she pulled off, and for a few moments they would hold
and kiss each other, and search each other's bodies lovingly and
without violation. Then, a little guiltily, since she was aware that
her Aunt Alma would question them if they were gone over-
long, they drove on.

But presently, coming down a forested mountain, Christa
pulled off the main road onto what appeared to be a logging
trail, its entrance marked by a small gilded wayside crucifix,
with a little roof built over it and a shelf beneath on which sat
small jars of freshly picked wildflowers. She drove a hundred
yards over ruts, the beeches towering over them, and parked.
"Lan, I think we still have something like an hour."

"Yes," Condon said, and he was already folding up the lap
robe.

Through the beech woods, feet scuffling in fallen leaves, they went down a hillside to a level beside a little stream, where small brush screened them. There Condon spread the robe and they lay down together and held each other and began to kiss hungrily. After a while, trembling, breathing hard, Christa said, "Wait," and she rolled away and sat up. Somewhere nearby a woodpecker drummed as she stripped herself naked to the waist. It was the first time Condon had seen her that way. She offered that much of herself to him proudly, her skin ivory white, her nipples small and pinkish-brown. "Kiss me," she whispered. "Please."

His mouth ranged up and down her torso, and her lips were all over his neck and ears and face, and he knew now that he could take her, that she wanted him to take her; and there was nothing more on earth that he wanted than to do so. Yet he held back. He was thinking, What if something happens and we can't get married? Suppose something comes between us and I never have her? I'll regret it the rest of my life.

But he knew it was a chance he had to take. Because this had to be different. It must in no way be anything like the thing with Phyllis; it must be a wholly new departure, handled entirely right from the beginning, with nothing to mar it, not even the faintest risk of marring it. And if she was generous enough to offer him her body, he could be generous enough to offer her his restraint. He was on strange ground, surrounded by strange customs, and he must take no chance of violating them and spoiling everything. It was one of the most difficult things he had ever done; but he felt, too, a sense of pride, of self-reward, in finally breaking away. "Look," he said, "we've got to talk."

He lit a cigarette. "I think it's time to talk to your father. Today. This afternoon. We have to lay all the cards on the table. I don't know about you, but I want everything cleared up, to know exactly where we stand."

"Lan, must we so soon?"

"Yes," he said, "we must."

She was silent. Then: "What will you tell him?"

"Exactly what we've already planned. Just as soon as this rigmarole with the Church is over, we'll be married. But there's no need for him to get agitated; I don't intend to take you away. We'll stay on here in Austria until I finish another novel and it's published—that'll be about a year and a half. Oh, we'll go to the United States for a month or two when I deliver it to the publisher, but we'll come back. After that, we'll see. But meanwhile we'll take a place in Vienna where I can work, so he won't be losing you right away. And later on, if we do live in America, I'll try to send you back or we'll both come every year. Or he can come to visit us; hell, he can afford it. There's no reason to lose touch. We can take a ship or a zeppelin, and they say before much longer there'll be airliners making transatlantic crossings. Anyhow, it's all got to be laid on the line. If it isn't, soon I'll be moving to Vienna and you'll be at the Christina Hof and— Maybe it'll work out that way for another few weeks anyhow, until I'm finished with Martinus and his instruction. But I want my claim staked on you if it does."

"Your claim staked." She mused over the strange words a moment. "Lan, you know we don't have to wait. We could have a marriage outside the Church, at the *Rathaus*. Right away, and nobody could stop us."

"I don't want it like that. I've talked to your daddy and Martinus enough to know that the Catholic Church cracks the whip and calls the tune here. And it would embarrass him, maybe cause him trouble, if we did something like that."

"Yes, it would. But..." Her voice softened and she touched his hand, and then she smiled. "You know that if we're married in the Church, we can never be divorced?"

He stared at her and touched her cheek. "Who wants to be?"

"Never me. But I only wanted to make sure you knew that." Then she stood up, very serious and, he thought, a little frightened, and he did not blame her. But she simply said, "All right, darling. This afternoon?"

"This afternoon."

They drove back in a communion of nearly total silence, each pondering the significance of what they were committed to, and Condon planning how best to approach the General. He had no idea what to expect. There was a quality of unreality about everything that had happened to him; it was all outside his previous experience, and he had no rules to follow.

Now they were in the Ferntal, passing through Ferndorf, no

different from those other little towns, only a bit larger than most. Christa slowed, following its winding, cobbled *Hauptstrasse*. Once, just outside town, she stopped while a herd of cows moved across the road.

Her hand shook a little as she took the cigarette he offered. "I think I'd better talk to him first."

"No. No, I think we should go in together. Let me do the talking. Then you can have your time with him later. But I think I'm the one who ought to lay it on the line with him."

She licked her lips. "All right. Whatever you think is best." The cows had passed and she drove on. Lan looked at her covertly, and suddenly he was aware of the difference in their ages. To him the General was a man to be confronted, formidable, perhaps, and older, but since he himself was mature, to be met on level ground; but Christa was still young enough so that her father was divided from her by the gap between youth and old age, which made him a towering, almost Godlike presence. That added to the amount of courage she would have to muster. Feeling almost fatherly himself, he put out his hand, took hers. "It will be all right," he said.

She smiled at him faintly, nervously. "Yes, of course it will."

When they had finished, silence hung thickly in the office of General Helmer. The *Auerhahn*—the black mountain cock—mounted on the wall, wings spread, mouth open to call, almost seemed itself to shriek silently with the tension. Helmer had listened carefully for fifteen minutes, as first Condon had spoken and then Christa. Lan had kept his voice steady, confident, displaying neither arrogance nor humility; Christa's had trembled with passion and hope, mixed with fear. And now there was nothing more for them to say until the General spoke.

Which he did not do. Instead, his eyes went from one of them to the other, probingly, and he ground out his cigarette in the ashtray and rose, neat, imposing in his gray suit; and he stood there wordlessly looking out. Christa and Lan stared at his back and then at each other. She opened her mouth, but Condon gestured her to silence.

After a pair of minutes stretching to infinity, the General turned. "I give my consent," he said. "With conditions."

"Oh, Papa!" Christa stood up, voice full of relief and tears.

Helmer smiled at her a little wanly. "These conditions. The marriage will take place within the Church, in the usual way. And in no case within less than sixty days. During that time, Mr. Condon, I shall ask you to remain as our guest here at the Christina Hof. I think the sixty-day limit is fair. The two of you have not known each other very long—"

"You and Mama hadn't either," Christa said, but she was laughing.

"No. But her family saw to it, also, that the wedding was postponed until we did. And, here together every day, you'll know each other well enough to be sure of your decision when the time has come." He turned to Condon. "You will also give your word that you and Christa will remain in Austria for at least a year after the wedding. Partly because it will take some time to become accustomed to . . . the prospect that you might take her away. That is wholly selfish on my part. But also . . . It is necessary for a man to understand his wife. You will never understand Christa without understanding Austria, and a year will hardly be time enough for that. Someday you will ask her to become American, I imagine. But first I think you should become at least a little European; common ground is necessary in any marriage of this sort. You will be happier for it. Mr. Condon, do you agree?"

Lan stood up jubilantly, admiration for Helmer's insight swirling in him. "Yes, sir; you're being very fair."

"Then good. I congratulate you both on your choice of a woman and being chosen by such a woman, and I hope the two of you will be entirely happy." And as Christa cried out and ran to him, he put out his hand to Condon.

When, much later, the two of them were gone, Helmer went once more to the window. Suddenly he felt old, tired, drained. "I think I did the right thing," he said aloud, not addressing himself. "They were so much like the two of us." He sighed faintly. Well, her happiness came first, but now the fat was in the fire. No more Robert Schellhammer, and Max would be just as unhappy; and he wondered if even his diplomacy could smooth it over. No doubt his flank was still exposed, and he must move swiftly, rearrange his affairs to cover it. Well, he could do that somehow. He could manage. He always had.

141

14 ROCKETING OUT OF THE BRUSH, the cock pheasant climbed straight up, wings blurring, long tail streaming. For a half second before it leveled off, it seemed hung, pasted, against the cold gray sky. Condon's shotgun roared, spread wings folded, and heavily it plummeted to earth.

"*Waidmann's Glück!*" Robert exclaimed, lowering his own weapon. "Good shot!"

"*Waidmann's Danke,*" Condon said. He broke the gun, replaced the spent shell, and then descended into the wooded gully from which the bird had come, to help the dog find its body.

Standing there in the beet field at the gully's edge, Robert Schellhammer watched Condon's back, clad in green loden, disappear among the trees; and when it vanished, he consciously relaxed the clamped grip of his hands on the gun. How easy it would have been, he thought, how simple, at that moment of the bird's rising. An accident, of course, and he would have to pay his fine, lose the right to hunt ... But at that range the charge of birdshot would have torn the American's head apart, and who to dispute that he had become confused, fired prematurely as Condon had moved in front of him. His father, General Helmer, and the two men from Vienna were across the gully or down inside it, and they could not have seen.

Schellhammer let out a shuddering breath, shook his head, lit a cigarette with hands that trembled slightly. I must be going mad, he thought. And yet, in that moment, when Condon, wholly absorbed, had raised his gun to aim at the upward spiraling bird, the temptation had been nearly irresistible. Robert thought of the old legend of the Spartan boy, the fox concealed inside his toga, gnawing at his vitals. And that, he told himself, was what his hatred for Lanier Condon was, an animal, ripping at his entrails, eating him alive; and yet, like the boy of legend, he dared betray no trace of what he felt.

The cold wind blew across the field; the sky, like a graphite smudge, darkened. For eighteen months, he thought, he had lived with that agony; and it had never lessened, indeed had become more intense with every passing day. Beginning on that summer morning when—a rare occurrence—Christa's Steyr had pulled into the driveway of the Schellhammer Hof.

He had been supervising the loading of a truck with crates of two-liter bottles for the wholesaler in Vienna when he had seen the car stop and Christa get out, lovely in a summer dirndl, her apron red, the white blouse cut low enough to show the upper slopes of her breasts. Something leaped within him; he felt a glow of satisfaction. All those nights together recently, and now she was coming to him in the daytime and— He plucked at the blue workshirt plastered to his torso with sweat, strode across the courtyard to her. *"Du! Grüss Gott!"*

"Grüss dich." She touched her hair with one hand, nervously; the morning breeze had unfurled a tiny banner of it. Robert's mouth was dry with love, desire. Then, as he took her hand, reached for her to pull her to him, give her a brief kiss of greeting, he sensed something wrong. Her body was stiff; she did not respond. "Robert," she said. "Robert, dear, I must talk to you."

"Surely. Come in the house." But already something like a huge knot of undigested food was forming in his belly.

"No. Over there will be all right." She gestured to a table with wooden benches near the back door, where his family ate its midday meal on pretty days. He tried to smile as she sat down. "What about a cup of coffee?"

"No, thank you." Her hands clasped and unclasped on the table before her; her eyes were grave. "Robert—" And then she told him.

A chicken, dust-bathing, chirred somewhere. Pigeons on the cow-stall roof cooed softly. Robert felt as if the ground had simply fallen away beneath his feet. He could not believe it; it could not be true. "You must be joking," he heard himself say, and his voice seemed to come from very far away.

"No, I am not. Oh, Robert!" She jumped up and ran to him, embracing him, laying her head against his chest. He could feel the softness of her hair against his chin, its perfume in his nostrils, her breasts soft and warm against him. He raised his arms to embrace her, then let them drop. "Oh, Robert," and her voice was strangled. "I do hate so hurting you. I am so sorry, but . . ."

I will not permit it! he wanted to bellow. He wanted to seize and shake her. I will not permit it! He mastered that impulse, and the one to cry. Men did not cry; he had not since the age of seven. Instead, he stood there motionless until she pulled away, and pride came in a saving surge. By the time she had backed away, staring at him white-faced, he was in possession of himself again. "I'm sorry," she whispered once more.

"Sorry?" His voice was steady. "Why should you be sorry? What is there to be sorry for?" He managed the mixture of indifference and curiosity nicely, he thought. Inside him, his belly was knotted like a fist.

"Because . . . I know it hurts you."

"Hurts me? Why should it hurt me? I'd think it's the General who'd be hurt. Your choosing to marry a foreigner, a stranger. But if you have his consent, you certainly don't need mine." He found that he had lit a cigarette without offering her one.

"You don't mind?" she asked wonderingly.

"Of course I mind. I don't want to see you throw yourself away on some . . . some mongrel *Auslander*. Still, if that's what it takes to make you happy . . ." He looked at her opaquely. "My congratulations," he heard himself say, putting out his hand. Numbly she took it for an instant.

Then he let hers drop. "Now, if you will excuse me for just a moment. The driver is waiting for instructions." He turned away.

"Robert," she called after him.

"Excuse me, this business is quite important." He could not face her for another instant. It was with relief that he heard the Steyr come to life, its engine's sound fading down the mountain.

When the truck had also left, Robert went to a huge wooden door built into a kind of earthen bunker at the corner of the courtyard. He unlocked it and descended into the wine cellar; there he took the glass used for sampling and a length of rubber hose, went to a cask of Veltliner, opened it, siphoned out a *Viertel,* and drained the quarter liter in two swallows. Then, leaning against the cask, he struck its oaken side a half dozen times with his clenched fist. He remained like that for perhaps ten minutes, leaning on the cask, breathing hard. Presently the wine took a strong grip on him and he straightened up, wiping the back of his mouth with his hand. The worst part would be telling his parents, facing their pity. Well, he did not want their pity. He did not want or need the pity of anyone.

Because it did not matter anyhow. She was nothing, compared to his work, his cause, the future. Really, he was better off without her. Now, without distraction, he was free to throw himself wholly, totally, into that cause and, by his efforts, bring the day of victory that much nearer. He rinsed the glass and hose, restored them carefully to their proper places, and went back up into the sunlight.

At lunch that day he told his parents in an almost offhand way. "Christa was here this morning. She says she's going to marry that American staying at the Christina Hof. General Helmer's already given his consent. The wedding's to be two months from now."

Max Schellhammer, mouth full of black bread, sat up straight, jaws ceasing to work. Beneath his tan, he was pale, then red. "Are you serious?"

"I tell you what she told me." Robert went on eating; although he had no appetite, it was important to show that he did.

His father swallowed audibly. "I was afraid of this!" His voice rasped with anger; he struck the table so the dishes rattled. "Helmer must have lost his senses! Well!" He stood up, a gamecock figure in old sweater and baggy grease-blackened leather knickers. "I think I'd better go straight over and have a word with him!"

"No!" Robert almost roared. "It's none of our affair!" Robert snapped.

Max only stood there wordlessly. "It is," he said at last, quietly. "It truly is. It changes everything we'd planned for the Ferntal. But..." He came around the table and—it was not with him a usual gesture—laid one rough hand on Robert's shoulder. "All right."

"I shall take care of the Ferntal," Robert said firmly, but with no more anger in him. "I ... we. You won't need him anyhow."

"That's not the point. He is ... I'd hoped ... I know he'd hoped ... But that scatterbrained little piece of fluff could always wrap him around her little finger. He's a great man, but when it comes to her he's blind, absolutely blind."

Robert's mother said stoutly, "Frankly, I'm relieved. What do you need with a girl like that anyhow? She's useless, she can't cook, can't clean, all she knows how to do is drive around in that

145

car of hers with her fancy clothes and her nose up in the air. There are plenty of nice girls in Ferndorf and Altkreuzburg. Just the other day I met Lisl Köhler on the *Hauptstrasse,* and there's a fine young miss! And she asked about you and—"

"Bertha," Max growled.

"It's all right," Robert said. "It's nothing." He got up and, on impulse, kissed his mother on the temple. "Now. I'm going over to Professor Busch's. I've got some paper work to do before the meeting tomorrow."

They all came up out of the gully: Condon, the General, Robert's father, and the two wine buyers from Vienna. The light was fading fast now, and Max, the appointed leader of the hunt, gave the command to unload guns. It had not been a formal affair, but still the rules had to be observed, and now there was the time-honored ceremony of *die Strecke,* laying out the cumulative bag of pheasants and hares and the one fox Robert had shot in the prescribed manner. Helmer's pride in Condon's marksmanship was obvious: six shots—four pheasants, two hares. "He doesn't waste ammunition, that one! They teach them to shoot out there in the Wild West!"

Robert dropped the butt of his cigarette, ground it out. Lugging the game, they walked toward the car parked on a nearby farm road. Condon fell in beside him. "I enjoyed this," he said. "It was a fine day. I don't get out of the city often enough."

"You must come for the Big Hunt at the end of the season," Robert said, with automatic courtesy. He envisioned it, then: the great circle of huntsmen and beaters closing across the high plateau; there would be a lot of shooting, and . . . No, he thought. No. And yet, as they walked on in silence, never having had much to say to each other, it was a thought that lingered in his mind. Eighteen months, he thought. A year and a half he had been living with this. Damn it, he thought brutally, callously, I should have heated up the bitch and screwed her years ago and then let *him* have the leavings! He sighed, so deeply that Condon looked at him curiously. The thought that he would never have Christa now, never make her yield to him, had missed his chance, was intolerable. No, he thought. Used or not, someday I will have her. Somehow . . . One day I will make a fool and cuckold of him. After we have won.

He took consolation in that thought. When they had won, he

would be a man of power, consequence, and he would be different in Christa's eyes. Maybe a vice-*Gauleiter*, in due time a full *Gauleiter*. At any rate, a high Party and government official. And then this foreign fool with his crazy scribbling would shrink to true perspective alongside him. Once the Party ruled and ruled completely, he could do anything he wanted, to anyone he wanted; and she would feel his power then. And that day was coming soon, only a few months away; he could feel it in his bones. Until then, he must be cool and careful, mask his feelings and intentions. He must do nothing to frighten Condon out of Austria, taking Christa with him, beyond his reach.

At the parked cars, a servant waited to leash the dogs and take them to the Christina Hof. "Where to for the last drive?" Condon asked.

Max said, "I think Gördeler's. He's *ausg'steckt* and his wine's good."

"Ride with me?" Condon asked.

"Sure," Robert said, and while the rest got in the Mercedes, he got into the Steyr with Condon.

The American made no attempt to break the silence as he drove back to the main road running through the Ferntal and turned in the direction of Ferndorf, and that suited Schellhammer. He had only one recourse against the emotions surging in him, and he took it, savoring in his mind the imminent triumph of the Party.

How masterly, he thought, der Führer had played his cards! His stroke in July of last year had helped, to some extent, offset the shock of Christa's betrayal. In that month Hitler and von Schuschnigg had signed a treaty. At first the Austrian government had gloated and Robert and the Austrian Nazis had felt confused, betrayed. In the clauses at first made public, Germany had promised to respect Austria's sovereignty, not interfere in its internal affairs. In return, von Schuschnigg had promised to conduct Austrian policy, especially that toward Germany, with the full recognition that Austria was a German state and that a special bond existed between the countries. With Hitler's virtual guarantee of Austrian independence and hands off its internal politics, the Austrian Nazis had felt left high and dry—until they learned the secret provisions of the pact. Then they realized that their long struggle was nearly won.

Secretly, von Schuschnigg had agreed that Nazi organizations could exist in Austria provided they did not propagandize. A cultural agreement was reached in which each state promised to lift restrictions on circulation of books, films, news, and plays of the other, and restrict the criticism of the other. Thus, at one stroke, the banned *Mein Kampf* reappeared inside Austria.

More important, the Austrian government had agreed to allow five German newspapers to circulate—including one that was the mouthpiece of Hermann Göring. Thus Nazi propaganda once more circulated freely, although occasionally the Austrian government confiscated individual issues.

But those were almost minor considerations. More major ones were the promise of an amnesty for imprisoned Nazis, except those guilty of the gravest crimes, the sanction of the use of the swastika, and the singing of the "Horst Wessel Lied" in public.

And then the greatest coup of all. Von Schuschnigg had agreed to take Nazis into his cabinet. Oh, they were not overt National Socialists. "Pronounced Nationalists," they called themselves. But Dr. Guido Schmidt, now Foreign Minister, and Glaise-Horstenau, Minister without Portfolio, were staunch adherents of der Führer.

And so, almost immediately, though still illegal, the Party had surfaced. Robert remembered the great wave of exaltation he'd felt that night in the Heldenplatz in Vienna, on the twenty-ninth of July. The Olympic torch, on its way to Berlin, arrived in Vienna that night, and a huge crowd had assembled for the ceremony in the vast mall behind the Hofburg, and the Ringstrasse for blocks around was packed. Robert had been there, too, and his men from the Ferntal, like the others seeded in groups throughout the mob wearing their white stockings as identification. There was an air of tension, of expectation. And then it began, the chanting of one group, taken up by another, and then another and another, rising and swelling out of the crowd. *"Sieg Heil! Sieg Heil! Sieg Heil!"* Robert, shouting, arm outstretched, felt a surge of mystic power, the short hair rising on his neck's nape. And now the shouting was thunderous, coming from thousands of throats: *"SIEG HEIL! SIEG HEIL! SIEG HEIL!"*

Someone near Robert, an old man wearing gold-rimmed glasses, turned. "Shut your dirty mouths!" he yelled. Robert saw the small Habsburg crown on his hat: a Monarchist. "Shut your dirty mouths!" Fritz Adam, Schellhammer's second in command, a hulking baker from Ferndorf, turned. *"SIEG HEIL!"* he roared in the old man's face, gave him a rough shove with one huge hand that sent him staggering into the crowd.

The police, hemming in the throng, looked at one another. Some of them were grinning; one or two were also yelling. The Austrian national anthem broke from the loudspeakers. It was drowned by the voices singing "Deutschland über Alles" to Haydn's fine old music. Someone yelled: "It's coming! The Olympic torch is coming!" *"Heil! HEIL!* HEIL HITLER! HEIL HITLER! HEIL HITLER!"

But there was other shouting, too. "HEIL AUSTRIA! HEIL SCHUSCHNIGG!" The contending voices mingled. Now the police went into action, shoving through the crowd, breaking up the shouters. "That's enough!" Robert snapped at Fritz. "Fade out! Fade out!" But, he saw, grinning as they dispersed, they had nothing to fear. Mostly the police were snapping up the Reds who'd dared appear, the Communists and Revolutionary Socialists passing out propaganda on the sidewalks.

And from then on they were on the streets, demonstrating, fighting the counterdemonstrators of the Schuschnigg government. The amnesty was suspended, the police cracked down halfheartedly, but the damage was done, The great wave, building so far out at sea, was coming inshore now, cresting, towering, about to break and smash, destroying an old world, washing in a new one. This month, next, the month after—it could not be much longer, Robert was sure.

His men could hardly wait. He felt contempt and sympathy for them. His own motives were the purest, wholly unselfish, but then he could afford unselfishness. They could not. Bitterly poor, they lived for the day when they could get their hands on wealth, the day when all the money and property of the Jews was forfeit to the Party; and they were the Party and they would get their share. They itched to be unleashed, to march into those sealed mysterious houses, villas, seize their treasures, seek out the hidden vaults: to loot. And they would loot, Robert promised himself and them; they would have their chance. They had earned it.

Let them have the loot. He would take the power. He was already high in the province's shadow council: the Gauleiter knew him. Power, and then ... He looked at the man beside him in the car. And then he would decide. Maybe he would not even want her then.

But he knew he would. As the car sped on through gathering darkness, he knew that there would never be a time when he did not want her.

15 THE BIG ROOM WAS CEILED, walled, and floored with gleaming pine, its rows of wooden tables crowded. Two dirndled daughters of the farmer sweated as they rushed back and forth with trays of glasses full of potent, sparkling new wine. There was laughter, raucous conversation, in voices masculine and feminine, occasional singing, and the air was thick with the rank smoke of cheap cigarettes, damp wool, and a taint of barnyard. *Gemütlichkeit,* Lan Condon thought, grinning; the place overflowed with it—that mood of boozy, good-natured well-being for which Austrians had invented a term untranslatable.

And, of course, hunters always wound up in such a place to rehash the day and dissolve their fatigue in wine; the "last drive" it was called. He would have been enjoying himself right now if it had not been for Robert Schellhammer.

The specter at the feast, he thought. Maybe he was uncharitable, but he detested that handsome bastard. He had tried, God knows, to get along with him for Christa and the General's sake; and when they met, they managed to maintain a strained civility. But leaving Robert's obvious jealousy aside—he did not blame him for that—the man represented everything that set Condon's teeth on edge. After a year and a half in central Europe, he knew all about the Nazis, more than he wanted to know. In damp weather sometimes his ribs still ached from the stomping at the Naschmarkt. But that was not the origin of his disgust for them. The fact was, he thought, sipping his wine, he had come to love this little country and it was for him a sort of second homeland. Indeed, he had found here the closest thing to a home he'd known since Ewell's death and more happiness than he had known anywhere, ever; and *Auslander* or not, he had a stake in Austria's fate, a vital one. This man, either blindly or knowingly, was dedicated to its destruction, a traitor to his own country.

"They're fools," Josef Steiner had said. "Pawns. Do they really think the Hitler gang will let them run things their own way when it takes over? Why, the *Anschluss* people from Berlin will sweep them aside like ants off a table. Hitler wants the Austrian economy at his disposal, the Austrian base of power for his drive to the East—not a clutch of Austrian administrators running things with typical Austrian *Schlamperei*. Do you know what the Germans call the Austrians? *Schlappschwänze*. Limp penises. A Nazi Austria will be a German Austria; and when Hitler has no more use for these poor fools, they'll be disposed of! But try to make them see it!"

Which, my friend, Lan thought, looking at young Schellhammer, is another reason why you make my gorge rise. I can abide a lot of things, but stupidity is not one of them. He drained his glass, glanced at his watch. Fortunately, he'd bought the last round; now he could gracefully escape. "Gentlemen," he announced, taking a grim pleasure in the flicker evoked in Robert's eyes by the words, "I have a wife at home wondering if I've been mistaken for a hare. I'm afraid I have to go." He shook hands all around, and to a chorus of *Wiedersehen*'s and *Waidmann's Heil*'s departed.

Outside, the green light burned above the pine bough of the *Heuriger* sign. The night air flowing down the village street smelled of forest, wet cobblestones, defective sewage systems, meadows, barnyards. It was the usual odor of a small central European village. Lan started the Steyr and wheeled it through the narrow lanes until he reached the *Hauptstrasse* and there picked up speed, bound for Vienna. He hardly needed to concentrate on the route; he was totally at home here. Not only in the Ferntal and in Vienna, but the country as a whole. He and Christa had spent their *Flitterwoche*—their honeymoon—making a vast circle of it.

They had been married in August 1936 in the *Pfarrkirche*, the ancient Baroque parish church attached to the monastery of

Altkreuzburg. Christa, sitting, kneeling, standing beside him during the various phases of the ceremony, had seemed to float in a mist of white, the veiled pearl-seeded dress that had belonged to her mother. Afterwards there had been a reception where *Sekt* and wine flowed freely at the largest *Gasthaus* in the town. Jammed with the Helmers' friends, it had held for Lan only a few familiar faces: the Schellhammers, Dr. Martinus, Christa's pert, dark, pretty friend Luisa. He knew enough German by then to understand the congratulations and make the responses, but not much more. Finally, heads buzzing, they had escaped in the General's flower- and ribbon-decked Mercedes, leaving the party to roar on without them. Christa leaned against him as he drove, and Lan held her tightly. His wife, he thought, with disbelief. He was amazed to find himself so full of primitive emotions at the age of thirty-three, but even the Observer, cold and dispassionate as it was, jubilated and kept its silence. And he was glad that they had waited, that it was all starting as it should, and that they had, for all their exploration of each other, saved the ultimate for tonight, when it could be achieved without the slightest taint of guilt or sordidness.

Helmer, he saw now, had been wise. Those sixty days had not only given the General a chance to appraise him closely, but they had given Lan time to know the country, make his decision about Austria. Helmer had been testing him for backlash, revulsion, about what had happened in the Naschmarkt, and for any incompatibility with his daughter's country and style of life. Well, there had been no need for the man to worry; with Christa as guide and interpreter, and once released by Dr. Kleinmann, he had explored and tested all of it within a day's driving range and found it good. They had roamed Vienna together, attending concerts and the Opera and a few private parties, had explored the Wienerwald, swum at Baden, and listened to concerts in the park. Martinus conducted them on a tour of the Stift at Altkreuzburg, a vast, cold labyrinth full of treasures and the relics of saints. To Lan the countryside had seemed a treasure trove, or, more aptly, a kind of jewel box, packed with unexpected, exquisite bijou pleasures. But Christa was the real treasure trove, the unending source of surprise to him. She wore, always, her emotions on her sleeve, delighting unashamedly in small things, awed by great ones, seemingly naive, yet often earthy and caustic, with a range of sensibilities that astonished and delighted him.

Anyhow, those two months had sped by; and then the marriage was accomplished and they had driven up the Danube to Tulln, crossed the great bridge there, and struck the road to Krems. "I will not take you to the Wachau," she had told him previously. "The Wachau I have always thought I would save for the beginning of my *Flitterwoche*." And so it had been arranged; their first night was to be spent in a town called Dürnstein.

"Dürnstein," Christa said. "The castle there was built by the Babenbergers, who ruled Austria before the Habsburgs. There, in the twelfth century, the English king, Richard the Lionhearted, was captured and held prisoner returning from the Crusades. That's the castle where they say the minstrel Blondel found him by singing his favorite songs underneath his window."

It was possible, Lan thought. Anything was possible here in this wild, romantic mountain valley. They drove into the little town, its streets wide enough for only one car at a time, and that barely; and at an inn perched on a cliff above the river they spent their first night.

The rooms had no baths. While Christa bathed down the hall, Lan waited, staring at the mighty river winding through the mountains. Then Christa returned, in robe, and he drained his glass of champagne and went to bathe.

When he came back and entered the room, she was waiting, standing by the bed in the lampglow, and she was naked, a glass in her hand. He closed the door and halted, and she smiled. "I hope you like me."

"Like you—" Lan said hoarsely.

She came to him, holding up her mouth, and her hand unfastened his robe. "Finally," she said, and then she kissed him and pressed her nakedness against his. After a while they were on the bed together. "Don't worry about hurting me," she whispered. "I don't think it will hurt very much. Nothing that anybody wants as much as I do this can possibly hurt." But she did cry out once, only briefly. But then her body arched beneath his. "Don't stop," she said. "Please, don't stop."

It seemed they could never get enough of each other. She was not, of course, experienced like Phyllis or as sophisticated,

153

but her concern was for his happiness, his ecstasy, not her own, and somehow that made everything more exquisite. And she learned quickly, the passion within her natural, not calculating. The next morning she lay exhausted beside him, their bodies seeming to meld. "Now," she said, "I think I have found where my talent really lies." She smiled. "They say everybody is cut out for one thing in life."

"Yeah. It's a shame you wasted yourself on marriage. You could have been one of the world's great courtesans."

"Only one small trouble. I could never be this way with anyone but you."

"You'd damned well better not," he growled and pulled her to him again.

The next day they drove on up the river, where each coign of rock was crowned with a castle's remnants, like grim, tattered skeletal eagles on their perches. Their destination was Melk, a town built around a monastery on the Danube; but in Spitz, a town at a valley's mouth, they paused for lunch in a restaurant's garden on the riverbank. There they watched strings of barges pushing up and down the stream. A white passenger ship belonging to the Donaudampfschiffgesellschaft, a stately sidewheeler, passed them. Lan was about to comment on it when Christa raised her head, eyes widening, and laid down her fork. "Josef."

"Frau Condon," a quiet voice said. "Herr Condon." The tall lean form in the black suit moved around the table, coming into Lan's vision. The dark eyes were opaque in the long pale face beneath the thick well-oiled hair. "I congratulate you on your happiness," Josef Steiner said in English, kissing Christa's hand. "And you, Mr. Condon. Perhaps you don't remember me, but we met once at the Christina Hof."

"I remember you," Lan said. Christa had told him something of what had gone on between her and Josef Steiner. *But perhaps he is not at all what he seems,* she had said. She had volunteered no more than that and it was not something he cared to press her on. *You came along just in time to save me,* she had added. Steiner had received no invitation and had not been at the wedding.

"May I join you for a moment?" He sat down without waiting for assent, ordered a glass of wine. Lan watched him suspiciously. "So. Beautiful weather for a *Flitterwoche*. How nice you're passing through the Wachau and I have this chance to see you."

"Yes," answered Christa quickly. "We're driving on to Melk after lunch and then to Salzburg. I'm showing Austria to my *husband*. Then the Tyrol and we'll come back through Carinthia and Styria."

"And live in Vienna?"

"Yes," Lan said. "We've sublet an apartment there."

"Delightful. But please, before you move on, can't you let me show you Schloss Schwarzgipfel? It's only twenty minutes in that direction." He gestured up the valley feeding into the Danube.

"That's very kind of you," Christa said at once, "but I'm afraid we simply haven't time today. Another time, perhaps. We'll be coming to the Wachau often."

Steiner nodded. "Yes, of course. Another time." For only an instant a shadow of melancholy crossed his face. His wine came, and he raised his glass. "To your happiness."

"Thanks," Lan said, sensing in the man a curious vulnerability.

"I was just passing, saw you sitting in the garden, couldn't resist intruding. Now ..." He took another swallow of wine and rose. "I shall be getting along. Again, Mr. Condon, my congratulations and best wishes. And to you, Christa, my dear." He kissed her hand. "Perhaps ..." He looked from one to the other. "Perhaps I may call on you in Vienna when you are settled? I should very much like to talk to you some more about the United States, Mr. Condon."

Lan felt as if he were being appraised, and not necessarily as the victorious rival. There was something speculative, yet practical, in the way Steiner looked at him, something having nothing to do with either love or sexual rivalry. Instinctively, Lan sensed that there was something Steiner wanted of him, a proposition to be broached at a later date. Curiosity aroused, he said, "Sure. We'd be glad to see you." And he gave Steiner the address of the apartment.

When Josef was gone, Christa looked at Condon oddly. "I'm not sure I want—"

"Don't worry. I'll protect your honor. But there's something about him that makes me want to know him better. He's up to something, and I'm wondering what. It won't cost anything to see him a time or two and find out what it is. I—" Then, at the expression on her face, he broke off. "You already know."

Christa licked her lips. "I—"

"What is it?"

"I promised not to tell. Not ever. Not to anyone."

He stared at her, and he felt a sudden roil of fierce, possessive jealousy. But, no. Steiner had not had her. Their first night together the pain and genuine, if minimal, bleeding were proof of that. Despite his curiosity, he forced himself to say, "Well, if you're honor-bound not to tell me . . ."

But when she saw that he would not press her, immediately she reversed herself. "On the other hand, I don't know why I couldn't tell *you*. Surely . . ."

"All right. Tell me then. And I'll guarantee that nobody else ever hears."

"Yes. I think you're entitled to know. Then if I ever slip, you can catch me." She looked around the garden. "But not here. Wait until we're in the car."

Driving on up the river, she told him. "I don't know whether it's true or only to impress me. But if it's true, of course, he's not as bad as everyone thinks he is."

Lan considered. "I'm pretty sure it's true. Well, at least he's doing *something*, which is more than a hell of a lot of other people can say. But—overthrow Hitler! He's sure as hell playing in the big leagues." He said no more about Steiner, but was doubly intrigued now and hoped the man had meant it about seeing them in Vienna. Then he forgot Steiner, and he and Christa traveled deeper into Austria.

They swung back through Carinthia and Styria and presently moved into their apartment on the Argentinierstrasse, almost in the heart of the city. It and its furnishings had been leased from the ruined son of a formerly prosperous family, and because it was all he had left, he was jealous of every square inch of wall, every coat hanger or dustcloth. At least twice a month he appeared to inspect the place, a lean bald man with staring blue eyes and a small sour mouth, heel-clicking and hand-kissing like a Prussian. Lan sensed a touch of madness in him, perhaps brought on by the shock of his family's fall, and was irritated profoundly by these arrogant inspections, as if he suspected they might abuse, pawn, or sell his remaining treasures. Christa, however, accepted them as a matter of course. In fact, Lan began to see, there were a great many things these people accepted that few Americans would have tolerated.

She could not, for instance, understand his disgust and anger at having to turn over their passports for registration with the police at every overnight stop. "What the hell business of theirs is it where we go or where we stay?" And the endless forms and stamps necessary for even the slightest official transaction appalled him.

What shocked him most, though, was going to the neighborhood tobacco store or news kiosk to buy a paper, only to find that the government had confiscated the entire edition or that great white spaces were left where stories had been censored. Remembering the *Register*, he would go into a rage that was nearly irrational. Still, he had to remind himself, this was—for all the courtesy and smoothness, the gaiety and cultivation of the flow of everyday life—a dictatorship, a Fascist dictatorship. And most of the rebellion against it, whatever opposition there was, came not from freedom-loving rebels seeking the return of a republic, a democracy, but simply from opposing factions like the Nazis, Reds, and Monarchists, who sought to install their own system of totalitarianism.

Even in Christa he saw it: not so much an indifference to political freedom as an ignorance of it. It was simply something about which there was no tradition. This had always been a society built from the top down, structured for the favored few, and less than a decade and a half of tentative, abortive democracy had made no dent in the customs of centuries. This acceptance, this passivity before authority, sometimes infuriated Lan and always made him subtly uncomfortable. But for the moment it was only an almost imperceptible taint of uneasiness in what was otherwise sheer happiness.

He passed Franz Josef Bahnhof, the gray pile of railroad station named for the old Emperor, headed up the Porzellangasse, toward the city's center. Vienna, he thought, as the Steyr rattled over trolley tracks, was as much a part of what they had as each other. Perhaps only here could two such different people have so truly mingled. This magnificent, absurd city was designed for the complete intermingling of humanity—races, cultures, and the sexes—and he loved it, as he loved Christa, for its unending fascinating variousness and its grace.

Willi Orlik had been right. His money was adequate to support them in almost princely fashion, provided Christa did not journey too often to the fiercely expensive salons on the Kärntnerstrasse. With any money at all it was impossible to be bored here. Perhaps after twenty years or thirty or a hundred, one might exhaust the possibilities of Vienna, but not in a year or so. As in New York, simply to go out into the streets was an entertainment in itself, to see and be seen a fascinating pastime.

He had lived through all the seasons here now at least once: spring, with the delicate blooming drapery and scent of chestnut blossoms, the brilliant explosions of flowers in the city gardens, the restaurants and hotels unfolding their sidewalk cafes, and the populace, like groundhogs blinking at the sunlight, emerging to take their places at the tables or promenade up and down the Kärntnerstrasse; the brief, hot summers, with the sky at last dependably blue, the sunlight on old stone and marble, on old gilt and ivory, rich, luxurious, the long lazy evenings drinking wine in the gardens of the *Heurigen* in Grinzing; and then the autumn, September and October glorious, and the stirring excitement of a new season at the operas and theaters and concert halls, November gray and drab, fog and mist and rain and wet, heavy snow; December with a sky like steel, white blanketing the gardens, the stores full now of images of stately St. Nicholas, and Krampus, the frightening devil who visited children on the night of December fifth to fill their shoes with presents or with ashes; the great city Christmas tree before the old gray Gothic Rathaus with its upthrusting towers; the candle-glimmering masses in the chill of St. Stephen's Cathedral or the Votive Church; then Silvester—New Year's—with the great crowd packed before the cathedral in the square in the city's heart, fireworks exploding high above the spires, chimney sweeps, the New Year symbol, capering in their dark suits and top hats, with coils of wire and rope around their shoulders; the formal balls, public and private, on New Year's Eve, and the champagne; gaudily dressed children on Three Kings Day; and then, before one's breath was quite recovered, Fasching, the joyful, exhausting blaze of pre-Lenten carnival, with balls and masquerades and wild parties; the celebration of Easter and the rebirth of spring, and the cycle wheeling around again.

He had by now heard the greatest orchestras and singers of Europe, perhaps the world, in the richest surroundings; and, facile in German now, he had savored the classic plays at the Burgtheater. He had sampled the whole spectrum of middle-European cuisine available in the city and on brief vacation trips had explored the sister cities of Prague and Budapest, almost as lovely, almost as fascinating; and he had spent hours simply roaming on foot through the byways and labyrinths of Vienna, finding always some new arresting splendor or some drama. And, of course, it was impossible to exhaust the galleries, museums, or not to be caught up in the omnipresent music.

The Helmer connections had gained him entree into many levels of society, and every day he came in contact with the ordinary people of the city; and, high and low, they all seemed friendly, warmhearted, easygoing. The Viennese "Heart of Gold," that was a motto for the attitude of all toward life in this strange place where the laws of time were no longer in force, where every hardship and unpleasantness was ignored or plastered over with wine and courtesy, grace and religious festival, and the dancing and parading seemed never to stop.

That was one view of it, Condon thought, turning into the web of streets behind the Karlskirche. Another was that it was a volcano. The twin wolves, Depression and Germany, would not go away. Poverty was as much an omnipresence as the music, desperate drunkenness as much a product of the wine as gaiety. Every day the papers were full of the shocking and sensational, the ugly boil-over of the seething that went on in the gray Bassena tenements, where a single basin and faucet supplied water to an entire floor, where families were jammed together in tiny rooms, their breadwinners unemployed, their wives and mothers no sooner delivered of child than pregnant again, to the glory of the Church. Husbands murdered wives, mothers strangled children, robbers beat to death old women, prostitution and petty thievery were commonplace. Beggars and war-wounded were very much in evidence; and in many stores there were bowls into which customers were asked to drop their spare *Groschen*—small change worth fractions of a cent—for distribution every Friday to the neighborhood poor.

There was starvation and desperation, and not only among the lower classes. Usurers thrived, and the broken middle class was in their grip, borrowing to keep up appearance. For appearance in Vienna was something crucial.

And the demonstrations, the near riots; Condon had seen those, too. The Nazis demonstrated at the slightest pretext, showing their massive muscle. The arrival of a dignitary from Hitler's Germany was enough to spark a massive *heiling* greeting, then the police moved in, then counterdemonstrations were sparked by the government; so that, unpredictably, the streets would surge with hardbitten bullyboys of every political persuasion. And the same smiling, obsequious taxi or *Fiaker* driver who bowed and called you Herr Baron and whistled as he drove would be there in a brown shirt or white stockings, using both fists on a Heimwehr man or vice-versa. And, of course, cursing the Jews; for anti-Semitism was another ancient omnipresence in the city, as solid, central, and typical as the Opera.

All of that could be ignored, of course, if one chose to. Christa ignored it because it was something that had never impinged upon her own existence. Condon tried, too, because it was not really his business; as a foreigner, it was obvious that he had no right to have opinions. Besides, he was busy working on his novel, and it was easier to swim in the warm surface water of prosperity and pleasure than to dive into the cold currents of cruelty and unrest beneath. Anyhow, maybe, just maybe, things would get better. Maybe all the problems would go away if properly ignored. That was, after all, the sovereign Viennese remedy—ignore, keep up appearances. Substance was nothing, shadow everything.

But he was finding it harder and harder to do that, now that his understanding of the country and the language was less imperfect. Reality kept intruding, jabbing at him from every side with its bony elbows. And somehow it was all of a pattern, from the destruction of the *Register* to the deputies and railroad bulls harassing the roaming starving bums, to the beating he'd taken in that alley by the Naschmarkt, to the planes and tanks of Italy and Germany in Spain, stamping out there the last flicker of freedom, to the rioting and fighting in the streets of Vienna, and to the chilling stories that came incessantly now out of Germany. The world was tumescent with things dark and ugly seeking birth, and they were things that he hated. He felt a need for action, a fierce desire to stand up, be counted. But he was helpless, really, drifting here in Cloud-Cuckoo-Land; there was nothing that he could do that would count.

He turned into the Argentinierstrasse, then swung through the gates of the courtyard of his apartment building, which would not be closed and locked till ten. Parking the Steyr, he was surprised to see Josef Steiner's black car also there. Usually Josef was meticulous about not calling unless certain he was home, careful to avoid all appearance of evil. Lan grinned faintly. It didn't matter; he supposed he trusted Josef. The main thing was he trusted Christa. With his gun and gamebag, he entered the building, rode the antiquated lift to the third floor. Emerging in the lighted corridor, he saw that blood from hares and pheasants smeared his hand. No, he thought, not blood. That was not hunterly. A German or Austrian hunter never called blood by its right name; it was always "sweat." They had all sorts of terms, evasions, euphemisms, for making killing less repulsive and more sporting. He reached his apartment and, too heavily burdened to find his key, rang the bell, and Christa let him in.

16 SHE HAD SPENT THE AFTERNOON being fitted for the new gown Lan had said she could have for New Year's Eve, and it would be sensational, baring her shoulders, much of her bosom, and nearly backless, in the latest Paris style; and Lan would love it, because he loved her to look sexy, alluring. The gossip of the seamstresses had been titillating and enjoyable, and later she'd had coffee and cake with Luisa at the Sacher. Then back home to make sure Rezi had dinner well in hand: liver-dumpling soup, stuffed veal breast, a green salad, and a fruit compote for dessert. After that she had bathed and made careful preparation for Lan's return. The bath and dressing were a slow, almost erotic ritual; she was in a mood to be made

love to tonight. She had just patted the last strand of hair in place when the bell rang and Josef was there.

"Christa." He kissed her hand. "I hope I'm not intruding. Is Lan home?"

Surprised, she was aware of a tinge of apprehension. His appearance like this, without calling first, was strange, unusual. Then she smiled; of course it would not be anything like that, and anyhow Rezi was here to chaperone. "No, he's hunting in the Ferntal with Papa, but he'll be back in time for dinner. Come in, Josef! Of course you'll dine with us. Rezi, set an extra place."

"If it's no inconvenience."

She handed the roses he had brought to the servant. "Josef, you know they're never like this. Red, not black? Not from Schwarzgipfel?"

"No. I've been in Vienna all week." In the living room he went to the steam radiator, spread his hands to warm them. He had not changed, still lean, pale, wearing a black suit, white linen. And although sexually she was well satisfied, she was aware of a certain tension inspired by his masculine presence in the room. But his behavior toward her had been impeccable, and she was pleased that he and Lan were friends and that she could participate in that friendship, which had allowed her to discover him as a person, not a lover, predator, or suitor. "I've had important business here." His hands flexed, and she saw that he was unusually nervous and excited. "You say Lan won't be long?"

"He should be in any time now."

"Then good." He smiled. "How's his book going?"

"All right, I guess. How should I know? He never lets me read anything while he's writing." For an instant she let resentment tinge her voice. "It's really quite unfair."

Josef smiled. "I suppose. But there's another way to see it. Creation is a very private thing, at least as he's explained it to me. It shows how much power you wield over him."

"Power? Ha."

He laughed. "How much your approval means to him. He explained it quite clearly. He has to keep the book in his head until it's finished. If he let you read it while it's in progress, in bits and pieces every day, he's afraid he'd find himself tailor-

162

ing it to win a smile, a nod, from you and be quite distressed if you didn't like it. So he'd end up not with a novel for a wide audience but a bunch of bits and pieces written for one person only—his wife. And a novel written exclusively for a young Wienerin is not exactly what he has in mind."

She had heard all that, understood it, of course, but it still pleased her to pout and banter. "And what's wrong with a young Wienerin?"

Josef raked his eyes up and down her slowly. "In your case, nothing, absolutely nothing." He was not jocular now, and she felt blood mounting to her cheeks. Then he laughed. "Now if *I* were a novelist, I'd lay every word at your feet every hour. But I'm not. Anyhow, from what I hear about the breed, be glad he's no worse than that. At least he hasn't taken to cocaine or opium, and so far as I know, he doesn't have a mistress. Or does he?"

"No," she said flatly. "He doesn't."

"You see?" But Josef's smile was forced. They both fell silent, the ticking of the clock on the mantel suddenly too loud. "Excuse me," Christa lied, "I must have a word with Rezi."

In the kitchen she perfunctorily checked the cleanliness of the silver, though it was spotless. It was strange, she thought, the way the relationship between Lan and Josef had come about.

Josef, true to his request in the Wachau, had rung them up and asked permission to call. Christa waited with apprehension to see what he had up his sleeve. But when he appeared, he was a Josef she had never seen before, not a lady's man but a man's man, though in an intellectual sort of way. Gone was the hothouse exoticism, and in its place was a more relaxed, straightforward masculinity. After the first stiffness was overcome, she sensed that Lan enjoyed Josef's company. Partly that was because he would have welcomed any man his age who spoke fluent English; but as time passed, she understood that he and Josef had a great deal in common, a vast range of knowledge outside her ken. Now Josef came often, or entertained them at his own luxurious house on the Singerstrasse—not the love nest in the workers' district—and the friendship between the two men had ripened. Sometimes Lan would simply leave his work in the late afternoon and say, "I'm going out to have a drink with Josef."

Their closeness, however, was intermittent. Steiner was gone from Vienna for long periods, sequestered at his *Schloss* in the Wachau. But by then they had other friends, and Lan had discovered the Cafe Louvre.

It was a coffeehouse, that uniquely Viennese institution of which there were hundreds in the city. Less restaurant or cafe than club, each catered to its own specialized clientele—jewelers, perhaps, or politicians, or painters—who could, for the price of a single coffee prepared in any of the countless Viennese ways, linger all day without disturbance, meeting friends, transacting business, carrying on affairs with lovers, or simply reading the latest magazines and newspapers, always provided in profusion. The Louvre, because of its nearness to the National Telegraph Office, was the hangout for foreign newspapermen in Vienna, who filed their stories by wire. There the correspondents gathered with their wives, mistresses, informants, and hangers-on; it actually served as an office for many of them. Among them were several Americans and Englishmen who had formed a loose trade association; and Lan, as a writer and former newspaperman, had found prompt acceptance among them. Now the Condons spent one or two evenings a week at the Louvre, moving in a circle whose business it was to know what was going on, everywhere. The women were as interesting as the men, and Christa enjoyed those evenings and the resulting friendships as much as Lan did.

But Josef was still Lan's closest friend, although Dr. Martinus occasionally visited as well. Strangely, things had worked out so they had never been to Steiner's Wachau *Schloss*. They went up the Danube several times a year, but each time Josef had been away, or he had invited them at times when it was not convenient for them to visit. It had become a joke. "Once I have you at Schwarzgipfel," he would say with a ferocious grimace, "you are in my power." They had all seen Bela Lugosi in *Dracula,* and his imitation was a good one.

"*Gnädige,*" Rezi said now, "will you please get out from under foot? Everything's under control."

Christa laughed. "I'm sorry." Rezi's kitchen was Rezi's kingdom. She returned to the *Wohnzimmer* just as the bell rang. Josef straightened, turning eagerly to the door as Christa opened it, revealing Lan, laden with gun and rucksack with two hares dangling from his hand. "Oh, you had a good hunt!" she exclaimed and kissed him.

"Careful, I'm all bloody." He returned the kiss. *"Grüss di',* Josef. Rezi!" But Rezi was already there, exclaiming over the game and taking it. For a week at least it would hang in the pantry uncleaned, and then at the proper stage of ripeness she would clean and serve it. "Josef," Lan said, shaking hands with his left because of the sticky redness on his right. He was still a little drunk from the "last drive," Christa saw. What a masculine mystery it was, a day of killing and drinking!

"Home is the hunter," Josef said, grinning.

"Yeah, and glad to be here, considering that I was paired with Robert Schellhammer. It always makes me nervous to turn my back on him when he's got a gun."

"Never turn your back on a Nazi," Josef said.

"Actually Robert behaved very well—for him. Look, let me wash up and change. Good wife, what about a whiskey with ice."

"Right away." In the kitchen she poured the whiskey, sent Rezi for one of the trays of water kept on the rear balcony to freeze in winter. Everyone thought Lan mad for drinking iced drinks at all, much less at this season, but it was an Americanism he would not give up. She brought the drink, refilled Josef's wineglass and her own. Lan went off to the bedroom.

Josef sipped his wine. "It's wonderful the way you light up when he enters a room."

"Really? It's something I can't help."

"I know. And I know something else now. We would have been wrong for one another." It was the first time he'd mentioned that old relationship. "Not terribly wrong, but not as right as you and Lan are. While I still feel a twinge of envy, it gives me a certain aesthetic pleasure to see such perfection of happiness. I only hope—" He broke off.

"What is it you only hope?"

"Nothing," he said. "And everything. Christa, you and Lan should seriously consider going to America soon. Very soon."

"We've talked about it," she said, startled by his gravity. "And, of course, I'm dying to see the United States. But he doesn't want to go until the book's finished. Then we shall, for a while at least."

"Maybe longer than a while."

"Well, that depends on Lan. But, of course, we have to come back often, to see Papa and Ernst, and"—she smiled—"you."

"Yes. Well, how are your father and your brother?"

"Excellent, thank you. We had a fine harvest this year and Papa was very pleased. And Ernst— He's grown like a weed! Suddenly he's a foot taller than I, and his teachers say he should go directly into the Academy if special arrangements can be made. Perhaps he'll study there part of the day and at the Musikgymnasium part of the day. But they say he's going to be one of the best pianists Vienna has produced in decades."

"Good. But has he ever considered studying elsewhere?"

"No. Why should he just now?"

Steiner shifted restlessly. "Look, Christa, may I ask a favor? Could you hold dinner for perhaps a half hour? And make sure your girl in there doesn't disturb us. Close off the dining room and leave her in the kitchen so we'll have total privacy. I need to talk to you and Lan. It's . . . quite important."

"Josef. What's wrong?"

"Christa, if it's not too much trouble—"

"Well, of course. I'll see to it right away." Puzzled, she went to the kitchen, gave instructions to Rezi, who was not pleased. "*Gnädige,* what about the *Kalbsbrust?*"

"Just keep it warm." She put cheese and sausage and little biscuits on a tray, more wine. "And under no circumstances disturb us until I call for you."

"Very well." Rezi sighed. When Christa returned to the living room, Lan was there, in slacks, soft shirt, and cardigan. He shot her a puzzled glance as she went to the big wooden doors of the dining room and closed them, sealing off the area from Rezi's ears.

"Now, Josef . . ."

"Thank you." Steiner stood by the radiator smoking, and he was very tense, looking from one of them to the other. "Christa, perhaps you remember one day long ago when I told you a secret about myself and certain of my activities? Which, of course, I am sure you did not for a moment believe."

"I . . . Yes. I remember."

"I asked you to swear not to tell anyone, and you did. But, of course, that was before you married. Have you told Lan?"

"I . . ." Her face began to burn. "Josef—"

"She's told me," Condon said. "If what you mean is this stuff about helping German Jews and"—instinctively he lowered his voice—"overthrowing Hitler. She told me briefly, not in detail. I'm sure she's told no one else, and neither have I."

"Then good," Josef said. "I'm glad she told you. It will save me some time." He paused. "I must ask if you will do me the favor of hearing more. It is important, quite important. Not only to me, but to Austria, to all of Europe, and maybe all the world." He smiled. "That sounds portentous, but I'm convinced it's true. And, Lan, I need—Austria needs—help which you can give it, without undue risk to Christa or yourself, and with very little effort. But I do not want you to agree to anything blind, so to speak, and so first I must tell you the whole story, if you will listen, with only the condition that you will never repeat it."

Christa looked at Lan. He was frowning, eyes searching Josef's face, a wariness in his manner as he lit a cigarette. Then he sat down on the sofa, motioned Josef to a chair.

"All right," he said. "Sure. You have our promises. Nothing you say will go beyond this room. Let's all speak English; Rezi doesn't understand it."

"English then, I think," Josef said with relief. "So—" He took a gold-tipped cigarette from his case, lit it.

"As I recall, Christa, what I told you was this, that I had broken with my brothers and gone on my own in order to do something for the Jews in Germany, and that I had an organization assisting them to emigrate. But I also told you that I could aid only a fraction of those who needed help, and that the only way to help all of them was to get rid of Hitler."

He turned to Lan. "I'm sure Christa thought I was mad, and probably you do, too, another Quixote, tilting at windmills. But really, we're not mad at all, my associates and I. And instead of diminishing, we feel our chances are improving."

He rose, began to pace. "Oh, it's true, Hitler's wiped out nearly every vestige of opposition in his Reich—the Socialists, the labor unions, the churches—almost every faction that could stand against him is broken, its leaders either dead, in prison, or in exile. But there's one force in Germany too big, too powerful, for even Hitler to destroy or bring to heel. One that existed long before he came, will be there long after he has gone. And I mean the German Army—the General Staff and the Officer Corps."

He paused. "You have nothing to compare with them in your country, Lan. Your army's small, totally under civilian control, exists to serve the citizens and the state. Not so in Germany. There, since the days of Frederick the Great, the people, even the state, exist only to serve the Army, for it is the Prussian tradition around which the Officer Corps is built. They're like priests or monks or the knights of old, bound to something greater than themselves by stringent oaths, long tradition, and a code of honor which may be warped, but which may also be the last remaining scrap of honor in the Reich. In any case, political leaders exist only on sufferance of the Officer Corps, and Hitler is no exception."

Lan sat up straight. "You think the German Army might turn against him?"

"I think there's that strong possibility," Josef said. "It's one that, through certain connections, we are exploiting. You see, the officers judge everything by one standard only. Is this good for the Army or is it bad? If it is good, they back it. If it is bad ... well, they dispose of it. As they have disposed of ... how many chancellors since the founding of the Weimar Republic?"

He paused. "Oh, Hitler's wooed them, the officers. He had to, every leader does, but he more than most. After all, what was he? An insignificant corporal, not even a German, much less a Prussian, but a *Schlappschwanz*, a grubby, dubious Austrian rabble-rouser, borne to power by a minority vote. And they have tolerated him so far because he's given them what they've wanted ever since the defeat—carte blanche to rearm. But the gulf between them is still enormous, and he's still on probation. They are afraid of him—not of the power he represents, for in the long run they have much greater power—but because he's wild, erratic, unpredictable, and adventurous. He nearly scared them to death last year when he retook the Rhineland. If France had brought up one division, he'd have been a goner then."

"They don't want war?" Lan asked.

"Of course they do," said Steiner. "War's what they're born and bred for. But they don't want it forced on them prematurely, and perhaps on the wrong front, by an amateur. The German Army retains the right to say when it will and will not fight.

168

And it knows that it is far from ready now, will not be for another half a dozen years. It'll not fight again until it's sure it will win."

He helped himself to more wine. "Be that as it may, I'm connected with certain people in Germany—non-Jewish—who are connected with people in the German Army in a most influential way. My function is to provide certain financing. Beyond that, I can't go into detail. And—" Suddenly his face went hard and he looked drawn and tired. "And something has just happened up there in Berlin. I only got word today." He drank the wine. "Adolf Hitler," he said, "has just signed what will be either Austria's death warrant or his own."

For a moment the room was silent. Christa tried to make sense of that and failed. "Josef," she asked in a low voice, "what do you mean?"

"Last summer," Josef said, "Hitler signed an agreement respecting Austrian independence. That took France, England, Italy off his neck, as you say, Lan. It also took pressure from the German Army off of him. They were frightened that he would move against Austria by force and that would mean a war which they would surely lose. So we had a breathing spell. Now it is ended."

He set down his glass. "Last week, my sources tell me, there was a meeting in Berlin—most secret. Only Hitler and his chief commanders. And he has taken the bit in his teeth. He has laid it to them flatly: they must prepare for war, perhaps as early as next year. Because he intends to take Austria and Czechoslovakia, by force if it comes to that. And if France and England fight, or Italy, or even Russia, then so be it."

Christa stared at him. Deliberately she sought the import of what he had said, and suddenly she felt a coldness in her stomach, in her chest. "War," she whispered. "No. Surely he wouldn't dare."

"He's mad," Steiner said. "He's a genius, but he's also mad as a hatter. He would dare anything."

Lan stood up. "And what do your German generals think about that?" he asked, voice strained.

Josef smiled bitterly. "They're outraged. Which is our only hope." The smile went away. "They know Germany isn't ready. And my hope is that now their hands are forced they'll act.

And ... there must be pressure on them to act. Which is where you come in, Lan. You can help to build those pressures."

"Me?"

"You." Steiner took from his coat pocket a folded sheet of paper. "This is an account in general terms of the meeting I've just described. There can't be many specifics for fear of betraying the source of my information. I would be very grateful if you would turn it over to your friends of the foreign press at the Cafe Louvre. I realize that without confirmation it's little more than a rumor, but the papers are full of rumors nowadays. All the Army needs is a reasonable intimation that Herr Hitler's ambitions will indeed bring on war—a war that will surely ruin them—and there will be a confrontation with him. Once it comes to a test of strength between the National Socialists and the generals, the Nazis will surely lose. At best, Hitler will be overthrown; at worst, his plans for taking Austria will be balked. Can you get this information to the American, French, and British correspondents? You know them all, the right ones, which ones to trust, the ones who'll make best use of it." He paused, eyes glowing. "If you love Austria, it would be the greatest service you could render her."

Christa watched as Lan unfolded the sheet, read it swiftly. "You're right; it's more a rumor than anything else. Not much for them to go on. But"—he grinned—"it'll start some of them checking, asking questions. It might create excitement." Then he was completely grave. "Look, Josef, why don't I put you in touch with these people myself? Bill Dameron with the Associated Press, Mark Gorton, who reports for a syndicate of left-wing papers in England. They're good men, and they know what's going on, too. If you all worked together—"

"We shall work together," Josef said. "But only through you, Lan, if you are willing. I was coming to that. This"—he gestured —"is only the beginning. I can provide your correspondent friends with a constant stream of stories that give the lie to Herr Goebbels' propaganda. But I cannot do it directly. I need a conduit. The Cafe Louvre is out of my usual circle, and it would be noted by certain people if I began to frequent it more than I do."

Something about the way he said that chilled Christa. "Anyhow," he went on, "it's too risky for me; but you could safely bring it off."

Lan toyed with the paper. "So you're being watched," he said harshly. "That means they'll be watching us, too. God knows you come here often enough."

"Yes," Steiner said. "That's true. But I have a good reason for that, which has nothing to do with what they're interested in." He glanced at Christa. "Of course," he said, "I'm still in love with your wife and I'm hoping, eventually, to seduce her."

Christa stood up. "Josef Steiner—"

"Hush," Lan said harshly. Then, to her surprise, he smiled. "God damn you," he said. "You're clever, aren't you? You remind me of the meatpackers in the United States who say they use everything from the pig but the squeal." He put the paper in his sweater pocket. "And now I know why you looked at me that way the first time in the Wachau. You were already figuring out how you could use me."

Josef nodded, his own smile crooked. "Of course. I had no idea then exactly how, but I knew this: as an American, you'd have access to channels I couldn't reach, a freedom of movement I couldn't achieve. And I knew you already had reason to hate the Nazis. So you were no longer a rival, but an instrument. Now you are a friend, and I would not use you as an instrument without your consent. I debated with myself, and then when this news came I knew that I must approach you. You could accept, reject, but you would be in no jeopardy, and neither would Christa. Because everybody knows Josef Steiner and how he operates. Everybody knows that Josef Steiner was laying siege to Christa Helmer. Everybody knows that Josef Steiner never gives up, and never lets a marriage stand in his way. So any contact with you would be presumed to be . . ."

Lan looked at him a moment, then turned away. He went to the table and poured himself a glass of whiskey. Then suddenly he went through the closed doors of the dining room, shutting them behind him. Josef and Christa looked at each other. The clock on the mantel ticked loudly. "Well," Josef whispered, "of course it's true. In a way. I've never stopped loving you."

"Josef—"

He raised a hand. "Don't worry. There's much more at stake now than what Josef Steiner wants."

Lan returned, with ice in his glass. "I think we'd better eat," he said, "and wait until Rezi goes home before we continue this discussion. She was setting the table very close to the dining

171

room doors, and I don't like the way she jumped when I came in."

"Servants are always as curious as hares," Christa said. "Aunt Alma says so."

Rezi had surpassed herself on the *Gefüllte Kalbsbrust*, even though its stuffing had dried a little during the delay. Their conversation at dinner was innocuous, and Christa sent the girl home early. In the living room she shook her head. "To hide from one's servants. Ridiculous."

"My dear," said Josef, "in Germany today one not only distrusts one's servants but one's very children. That's the essence of the blight they want to lay on Austria. Fear, distrust—that's how they govern."

"Look," Lan said, "let's get down to business. Josef, I'll do what I can. I'll pass this along, and anything else you send me; and, of course, I'll keep you out of it. It's little enough for me to do, if you're right about what's happening. Myself, I doubt it'll have any effect. Outsiders always overestimate what a newspaper can do. Generally, I suggest you mail to me whatever you want me to have, in a plain envelope. And"—his face shadowed—"I think that had better be the extent of our contact from now on unless something damned important comes up. I don't think you should come here any more and I don't think we should go to you."

"Lan," Christa said.

"He's right," Josef cut in. "There's no reason to draw any more attention to you two than necessary, or to take the slightest risk of exposing you to danger. So, we will appear simply to cut each other off. Perhaps"—he smiled—"I became a bit too affectionate toward Christa. So the thing between us is over."

Christa's eyes stung. Everything said this evening had depressed her profoundly, and her voice was choked, angry. "Damn them! Why can't they leave us alone?"

"Because Hitler needs the Austrian economy to arm for war. Because he needs the opening to the East. And because"—Josef's mouth thinned—"he wants his revenge on Austria, Vienna."

"Revenge?"

"Yes. He's from the Waldviertel, you know, out in the backwoods, but as a young man he came to Vienna, afire to be a great painter. But they rejected him at the Academy—God, how I wish they'd accepted him! Anyhow, after that he became a drifter, a vagrant. He just sank into the lower depths of Vienna, staying alive God knows how, by what expedients. Life was as hard for the poor and friendless then as it is now. I have taken the trouble to do some research on his activities during that period, and by and large he lived like a pariah dog. He has never lost his bitterness or his hatred of those who abused him in those days. It is a period of his life he would like to obliterate —along with all those who figured in it. And apart from all the rest, I know that's one burning reason he wants control of Austria—so he can get at them. But . . . that's something I'll say no more about just now." He paused.

"Lan, I told Christa before you came. I don't know how long Austria has if he isn't stopped—a few months, maybe a year. Anyhow, I think it would be prudent for you and Christa to be prepared. I'd certainly keep a reserve of money in Switzerland; nobody, not even my own blind brothers, knows what will happen to bank accounts after *Anschluss*. And, frankly, if you and Christa plan to go to America, you'd best watch things carefully and get out of Austria in time. Otherwise, even though you're an American citizen and she's your wife, you're likely to have some trouble with the red tape. Their *Amtschimmel* is every bit as bad as the Austrian kind. And, without revealing from whom you heard it, you might pass along what I've told you to the General."

"Yes," Lan said. "I'll do that."

Josef set down his coffee cup. His face looked drawn, exhausted, and very melancholy. "I am sorry to be the bearer of such bad news. Now I must go. I'm not sure when I'll see either of you again, but I'll be in touch. Good night."

When he had gone, Lan stared at the closed door. *"Scheisse,"* he said after a moment. Then, wearily, "Let's go to bed."

"Yes."

The bedroom was warm, but Christa shivered; she did not take time to remove her makeup, but only quickly shrugged out of her clothes and into a nightgown so thin it was no help. Lan was already in the bed beneath the thick down comforters. Hastily she slid in beside him, seeking his warmth, and he put his arms around her, held her closely. "Oh," she said fiercely, "it's rotten, isn't it? Why don't they let us alone?"

His arms tightened. "Don't worry. Maybe it will never happen. And if it does, I'll look after you. I'll see that nothing ever harms you."

"It's not just me. It's Papa, Ernst, the Christina Hof, everybody there." The fear was like something undigested in her stomach.

Lan laughed softly. "Don't worry about the General. If there's anybody in Austria who can look after himself, it's the General." Then he was serious. "My God, you *are* cold. Let me warm you up." His mouth played along her throat, up her jaw, his tongue caressed her ear. His hand moved gently over her breasts. She felt some of the chill seeping out of her. Turning, she kissed him fiercely, her body moving against his under the comforter. He was both gentle and adept with her, having learned precisely what she liked in these past months, and in a few moments she was not thinking at all. Afterwards they lay together in a pool of warmth, and he murmured, "Oh, God, how much I love you."

"And how much I love you," she whispered. "I would die without you."

"Don't worry, you won't have to," he said, and stroked her hair. But later, when he was asleep, still holding her, despite his closeness and his warmth she grew cold again.

17 IN WELL-DRILLED RANKS, they marched down the Ringstrasse, booted feet clumping on the icy cobblestones. Their banners, with their awkward barred-end crosses, neither Maltese nor swastika, but something halfway in between, were damp and limp, and their bearers had to swirl them to give them any bravery. The wind was icy, whipping drifting flakes of snow, adding a new layer to the six sooty inches already blanketing the Burg Garden. "It's those damned silly crosses that bother me," Lan said. "It's almost as if von Schuschnigg were trying to give them their own version of the swastika. Competing with Hitler, silly symbol against silly symbol."

"Precisely," Mark Gorton said. Short, squat, in his early forties, he had a red weathered face, a long bulb-ended nose.

He was one of the most brilliant newspapermen Lan Condon had ever met; and, having lived in Austria almost uninterruptedly since war's end, he was in many respects more Austrian than the natives. Once he had come here with a British military mission in 1919, he had been totally enchanted, he said, and ever since had felt more at home here than in his native London.

"It's something in their soul that must be appealed to—the love of militarism, and all its trappings. They're not much good at fighting, but they do love to put up a fierce show. And Schuschnigg gives them the chance, to keep them loyal. He's trying to steal the Nazi thunder—and so, of course, he's cutting Austria's throat."

Lan nodded. "All I know is that every time you turn around, somebody's marching. The Front Miliz, the Bauernbund—hell, even the farmers march like soldiers, or the students, or the loyal order of stamp collectors, or whatever. Everybody's got to have his club, and everybody's got to march."

"Yes," Gorton said tersely. The December wind was knife-edged, and they did not speak until they had crossed the Kärntnerstrasse. "Let's pop into the Bristol for something to warm us," Gorton said.

The hotel bar was mellow with the light from crystal chandeliers. They settled into easy chairs, ordered Scotches. Gorton kept his voice low.

"Schuschnigg's committing suicide. That's all it comes to. Dollfuss started it, and he's continuing it. They rang the knell for Austria in February 1934, when they broke the Socialists. All right, so they've alienated half the people from the government. The Nazis have about a third, and who does that leave to follow Schuschnigg? He could reconcile with the Socialists if he weren't so damned proud, and so Catholic. But he won't. He'd rather die for principle than compromise! So he tries to out-Herod Herod with all this pseudo-Nazi, pseudo-Blackshirt militarism, and that turns the stomach of liberal elements in France and England. Why should they worry about saving one Fascist state from another one; why should their young men die for that? And, of course, the conservative elements among the Allies are simply mad about Hitler anyway. He's the brown monkey who's going to pull the red chestnuts out of the fire for capitalism. They're hoping he and Russia will eat each other up." He shook his head. "It's maddening. It's all so stupid."

"The stuff I've been feeding you and Dameron isn't helping?"

"It's good. Keep it coming. It's raw meat, and it's creating discussion. But I'm afraid it's too late to save the Austrian government from its own stupidity." He sipped his drink, shook his head. "Damn it, this ridiculous little country has the worst case of split personality I've ever seen. It makes it awfully hard to know what to think about them. I— Oh, the devil with it. Let them have their *Anschluss*. They wanted to try it just after the Great War, and we wouldn't let them. I wish we had. A united Germany and Austria might have prospered and stayed democratic." His mouth twisted. "Not a very pleasant subject for Christmas Eve, is it?" Then he glanced at his watch. "Blast, I've got to run. Marietta's waiting for me at home." His English wife, far less fascinated with Vienna than he, had divorced him and gone back to London years before; now he lived with an American music student less than half his age.

Lan finished his drink, and they went to the *Garderobe* for their coats and briefcases. *"Wiederseh'n,"* Mark Gorton said. "And greetings to Christa. And a very merry Christmas."

"The same to you." They shook hands and went their separate ways into the snow-swirling afternoon.

There was, Lan thought, walking toward the Argentinier-strasse, something almost magnificent about the monumental bleakness of Vienna on a winter day. After the first of November there was rarely sunshine until March, and the city was a stony massiveness of unrelieved gray narrow streets funneling and accelerating icy winds to brutal sharpness. The warmth of home was good.

Christa was packing; they were spending tonight and tomorrow at the Christina Hof. Lan embraced her; she was as excited by the season as a child. "Your nose is cold." She laughed.

"And that's not all." He plunged his hands inside her dress, against her breasts, and she let out a little scream. "The best hand warmers ever invented," he said, cupping them. She pressed her own hands against his. "Only a wife would allow that," she said. "A mistress never would."

"I don't have a mistress."

"I know. If you ever come home with warm hands, that's when I'll begin to worry."

He withdrew them, kissed her again, poured himself a brandy. "Get to work. It's getting late, and I want to leave in a little while." Then he went into his office.

There he lit a cigarette, sat down behind his typewriter, sipped the brandy, stared sourly at the page in the machine, the stack of manuscript beside it. It was slow, tortuous going, this book, and it got harder every day. Besides, he was caught up in events more urgent than any fiction.

For six weeks now the envelopes had come from Josef Steiner, sometimes by mail, sometimes delivered by a Wiener Dienstmann, one of the licensed messengers who could be trusted utterly with anything from a note to someone else's wife to delivery of the family jewels or a hundred thousand dollars in securities without ever breaking their code of confidentiality. Those mailed were never postmarked from the same station. This caution seemed overly dramatic at first; but when Lan read the contents of those envelopes, he saw that Josef acted wisely. They were full of dynamite, detailing and documenting the ugly lawlessness, large and small, the brutalities and ferocities that had become routine in the Third Reich. Lan read them with horror and disgust, and then took them to Dameron and Gorton at the Cafe Louvre.

So he was, he thought, in a sense drifting, waiting for something to happen, some climax which he could not predict. But he had taken Josef Steiner's warning and had put five thousand dollars in a Swiss bank. If something sudden, shocking, and unexpected happened; if overnight the Nazis came, there would be no way they could tie that money up.

He finished the brandy, shook his head. Well, let it ride. This was Christmas Eve. For thirty-six hours, anyway, they could all pretend that there was such a thing as peace on earth and good will toward men. He left his office and went to help Christa with the packing. He was eager to get to the Christina Hof. Home for Christmas, he thought wryly. Well, when you came down to it, that was his home now, the only one he had; and Christa's family was his family. And so he had to care about these people and their country.

The drawing room of the Christina Hof had been sealed off all afternoon. Most of the preparations had been completed during that interval. Now, after the traditional dinner of fried carp, eaten beneath the burning candles of the Advent wreath suspended from the chandelier, General Helmer and his sister Alma, together with Mitzi, crept into it to apply the finishing touches.

The tree was enormous and absolutely fresh, cut that morning in the Wienerwald, brought in with snow still on its branches. Glistening baubles from Czechoslovakia, chocolate ornaments wrapped in colored foil, straw ornaments and glazed cookies all dangled from its limbs. Beneath it was an enormous pile of gifts. Even now, the General thought, they would all be gathering in the halls and sitting rooms: the families of his people, his tenants and his employees, the children wide-eyed, tense, expectant, and their parents only a little less so. And there would be something for every one of them beneath the tree: he, Alma, and Christa, especially Christa, had shopped Vienna carefully, meticulously, agonizing over what was best and right for each of them. As he watched Alma and Mitzi apply the last of the candles, he felt both satisfaction and a gnawing melancholy. For him there was an emptiness in the room.

Well, it could not be helped. She was grown and married, and Ernst was almost a man now. Meanwhile, Christa was not allowed in here, and neither was Ernst. He allowed himself that much indulgence, anyhow, treating them like children for this one day, and he was grateful to them for going along with him. Soon, he hoped, he would be a grandfather, and then the tree would become the responsibility of Lan and Christa. But he did not blame them for defying the edicts of the Church and using whatever it was they had used to keep them childless this long. The way things were right now, there was no use—what was the term—giving hostages to fate.

A thought he put from his mind; this was Christmas. Stepping back, he listened to Alma shrill at Mitzi, smiling faintly, but concerned. Alma was fading, no doubt of that. She was all humped over with her arthritis now, and in nearly constant pain. Of course, the servants did well and made allowances. Still, it troubled him, and Dr. Kleinmann had said that there was nothing he could do; only a matter of time. Anyhow, now, *Gott sei dank,* there was nothing more to do but light the candles; that was his function.

He did it carefully, and presently the tall fir was a blaze of glory. "All right," he told the women. "Go outside."

When they had, closing the big doors behind them, he waited long enough to smoke a cigarette, letting tension build. Then, picking up the small bell from the table, he rang it vigorously.

A moment, and then Mitzi threw the doors open and everyone crowded in, children at the forefront, eyes wide and shining, and a gasp of awe went up at the magnificence of the tree the Christ Child had just brought and decorated, and at the heap of presents He had left beneath it.

For an hour then there was chaos as Helmer and Alma passed out gifts to all but immediate members of the family. Children laughed and cried, adults exclaimed, and presently Ernst sat down at the piano and began to play. Suddenly the room was quiet, and then two dozen voices lifted in the strains of "Tannenbaum." After it had died, there were handshakes, thanks, drinks all around for the adults, and presently the *Schloss* was empty of all save family.

This was the moment Helmer had waited for, and it was with an almost fierce intensity that he savored having those he loved around him and watching their faces light with pleasure as they opened gifts. Condon included, because he had made Christa happy and in no way had played her false or Helmer's trust in him; an American, yes, but she had herself a *man*, Helmer thought. Christa exclaimed over the pearls and the earrings and the gloves; and Condon was delighted with the superb shotgun from Brünn, light as a feather, beautifully balanced. Helmer was touched by the sweater Christa had knitted, knowing what an ordeal knitting was for her, and by the fine books on hunting in America Condon must have, with forethought, ordered months before. Most of the bounty fell to Ernst, clothes and books and stacks of new records of classical music for his gramophone.

Afterwards they sat talking for an hour over brandy, and by then it was twenty minutes before eleven. Helmer tried to talk Alma out of going to midnight mass, but, as pious as she was testy, she insisted. "Besides," she said, telling him something he had not heard, "Father Mathias is ill, and Dr. Martinus will officiate. He never preaches long sermons, so I shan't get too chilled. And he is a lovely talker."

Helmer himself drove them down the steep icy way to the valley floor in the Mercedes, its low gear growling, its chains gripping. Only once did it fishtail slightly, and he caught it in time, but he was glad when they reached the level road, also coated with a glaze of *Glatteis,* fortunately dampened now by a layer of new snow, which was falling steadily. They passed a number of people on foot or traveling in sleighs, the sturdy Haflingers powdered white, moving at a surefooted trot, bells jingling, all bound for the *Pfarrkirche* in Ferndorf. For Helmer, appearance at mass there was not only piety but politics, binding him that much closer to the people of the valley.

Leafless plum trees set in orchards were like gaunt black soldiers with arms uplifted against the snow as they reached the outskirts of the town. Helmer parked the car in the tiny lot beside the church, a square ancient structure with two flying buttresses on each flank and a steeple rearing high above, and carefully he and Christa helped Alma across the ice. The organ was murmuring softly—it was very old; he and Max had just donated considerable sums for its repair—the wooden benches and prayer rails had been polished to dark gleams by generations of rough cloth. Everyone was bundled to the eyes in heavy clothing against the dank chill in here.

As his family settled down in its accustomed spot, Helmer saw that, as usual, the Schellhammers sat just in front of them. Max turned, smiled, and so did Robert and his mother, and they all shook hands; then the Schellhammers turned forward again. Helmer thoughtfully rubbed his chin.

Well, there was no help for it; Max and Robert were both entitled to their disappointment, to feel as if somehow he had doublecrossed them. In retrospect, he was glad it had worked out as it did; one Lan Condon, he now believed, was worth a handful of Robert Schellhammers. He was disappointed, too, in them, with their readiness to yield Austria to the Germans; and if Christa's marriage had driven the wedge between them, it was not the only thing that had widened the split in the past year. Each had made a fundamental political decision, a philosophical decision. Helmer's had been made alone, Max's, he knew, under Robert's influence. The cleft between the older men was so deep that they no longer even debated the future with each other.

Then the organ pealed. The service had begun, and the General settled back, losing himself in the immemorial celebration.

In the candlelight, Martinus' face had been a sharp blur. His slender form was lent size, dignity, authority by the religious ritual and its trappings; his sermon, though brief, had been truly poetic, Helmer thought, with a musical nobility far beyond the capacity of Father Mathias. But Helmer had not liked its theme: peace, all right. Reconciliation, yes. Brotherhood, certainly. But not the thinly veiled references to pan-Germanism, to the oneness of Austria and Germany. He meant to speak to that young man about that. Meanwhile, with the fine old hymns lingering in his ears and soul, the General led his family from the church.

The parishioners had gathered along the street and in the parking lot, breaths white fluffs in the still, bitter cold, to exchange Christmas greetings, gossip, and wait. It was five minutes until midnight, and the service would not be complete until a custom old here in Ferndorf had been observed. Helmer, surrounded by his family, held court among his people. In years past, the Schellhammers would have joined him. Now they stood aside, surrounded by a clique of their own.

Minutes ticked away, and then it was time. Down the street, the lights in the wing of Birnbaum's tailor shop in which his family lived went out, as if the Jew somehow felt it not fitting to be in evidence at this moment. Beside Lan, Christa said delightedly, "Now," and a hush fell on the crowd.

Then, from the belltower of the church sounded a trumpet's notes, clear and sweet in the icy darkness: "Stille Nacht, Heilige Nacht." The old carol rang out across the town, across the snowclad sleeping valley. Helmer could imagine the deer and the boar in their coverts on the hills raising their heads, wondering. The trumpet sound went on and on and finally died, only the last notes echoing, along with the final words of the refrain, softly sung by a few people in the crowd: ". . . Sleep in heavenly peace."

Helmer put his arm around Alma, whose thin frame was shivering with cold. "Sister, you're about to freeze. Come." He led her to the Mercedes.

He saw it from the corner of his eye before he heard the sound: a giant flare of orange, like a miraculous flower in the darkness, diagonally across the *Hauptstrasse*. The following thunder of explosion was like a fist against his ear. Helmer whirled instinctively, shielding Alma with his body. Women screamed. From somewhere in the alleys behind the *Hauptstrasse* a jeering voice bellowed, "Merry Christmas to the kikes!"

181

There was the patter of falling stone fragments, a roil of dust. Then, raising his head, Helmer saw what had happened; the rear corner of Birnbaum's tailor shop had been blown away.

"In the car," he rasped, and when it seemed to take ages for Alma to manage to dispose herself on the seat, he shouted, "Christa! Mind your aunt!"

"Papa!" She was there at once. Helmer turned, strode across the street, not daring to run because of glare ice on the cobbles. Condon was right behind him, and so were others, now that he'd taken the lead.

"General," Lan said hoarsely, "careful."

"Only the one bomb," Helmer snapped. "Small, controlled. They knew what they were doing." He looked behind himself. Martinus, face a pale blur in darkness, was following, and so was a village policeman, plus half a dozen men trailing more slowly. Going to the front door of Birnbaum's living quarters, Helmer rattled it. No one answered.

The General wasted no time. "Around here," he snapped at Lan, and they circled the house. One corner of the one-story shop had collapsed. Helmer picked his way to the door leading to the living quarters. "Birnbaum! Herr Birnbaum! General Helmer here! Are you safe? Where are you?"

A half minute passed. The other men crowded up behind. Then a key turned and Birnbaum was in the doorway in his nightshirt, a short, dark, hairy man with powerful arms and hands. He stared past Helmer into the wreck of the shop, which the policeman was sweeping with a flashlight. "No," he whispered. "Oh, no. God . . ." Somewhere in the house a child was screaming, a high-pitched braying sound.

"Your family, man! Are they all right?"

Birnbaum shook his head dazedly. "Yes. *Gott sei dank,* we are all right. But look. Look what they have done."

"Yes," the General said and raised and dropped a hand. "I am sorry. We'll catch them," he lied. He patted Birnbaum's shoulder. "Don't worry. It will be all right. Look, I'll get a car brought up. Get your family together and you can come to the Christina Hof for tonight."

"No," Birnbaum said almost absently. "Thank you, no. I must . . . clean up this mess." He rubbed his face. "Who did it? Why me? This is foolish."

"I insist you and your family come to the Christina Hof."

"Please, no, I could not trouble you. We must not leave here. Not now."

Helmer gave up. Undoubtedly the tailor had money, valuables, in the house, and he would not leave them. "Very well," the General said, and he turned to the policeman. "A guard must be kept over this house," he ordered. "There must be no more of this, you understand? There must be no harm to these people."

"Nobody's going to hurt 'em," the policeman answered, almost sullenly; and immediately Helmer knew that he was right. Most probably the officer had been involved in the planning, and this whole affair had been designed not to injure, but to demonstrate purpose, power, to warn and frighten.

"See to it," the General repeated and waited until an obedient, respectful *"Jawohl"* finally came.

"Very well. You will be safe, Herr Birnbaum. I personally guarantee it."

"Thank you. Thank you." The man's teeth chattered with cold. "Now I must get dressed. Excuse me." He closed the door.

Beside Helmer, Lan Condon said thickly in English, "The sonsabitches!" Someone plucked at Helmer's sleeve. It was Dr. Martinus, his eyes wide and face pale.

"General Helmer, this is terrible. This is . . ." He groped for a word. "Absurd."

"No," Helmer said. "It is normal. Perfectly normal for our brothers in the Third Reich with whom you said tonight we should join hands. We have our culture and they have theirs and here it is. As you see, the two are already mingling. This is your brotherhood, Dr. Martinus. Now that you have seen it, perhaps you should go home and prepare another sermon."

Martinus stepped back, and Helmer both regretted having flung it at him that way and having done it in public. Then, angrily, he told himself it didn't matter. There were such things as decency, honor, and an end to patience.

"I'll . . . I'll get the sexton," Martinus said, "and we'll help Herr Birnbaum clean this up."

"Good." Helmer's tone was more gentle. But he was still seized by, rigid with, fury as he said, "Come, Lan." They left the shop and walked across the street. The crowd had completely evanesced; the parking lot was empty save for his car and that of the Schellhammers. Robert and Max stood before the latter, with Frau Schellhammer huddled in her coat inside.

Helmer stopped before them wordlessly. Max's eyes shifted away and he bit on his pipe. But Robert's gaze met the General's directly, unreadable. Helmer did his best to keep his anger from shaking his voice. "I will not," he said, "tolerate this. Do you understand? This will not be tolerated in the Ferntal."

After a few seconds Robert answered very slowly, "I agree, Herr General. It is regrettable. If those who are responsible are found, we must see that they are severely punished. I cannot imagine that any of our people did this." Each word was distinct, so weighted as not only to be devoid of regret, but faintly mocking. Again Helmer knew that in a way Robert was right; no one from the Ferntal had done this. Someone from a different district, Tulln, perhaps, would have been brought in. Then Robert said, "Merry Christmas, General Helmer," and turned away and got in the car.

Max took his pipe from his mouth. "Kurt," he said hoarsely, "I agree. There were children and a woman in there. It was a damned fool thing to do, and on Christmas Eve. Anyhow, why pick on some helpless little yid like Birnbaum when the bigwigs still run loose? The wrong time, the wrong man. Don't worry. I'm going to look into this." He was abashed, and there was something almost pleading in his eyes. He put out his hand. "Merry Christmas, Kurt."

Helmer hesitated, then took it. "Max—"

"Now let's get home before we freeze." Schellhammer turned away.

18 IT HAD BEEN A STRANGE FASCHING, Christa thought. Yearly, almost as soon as they had sobered up from New Year's celebrations, Austrians threw themselves into Carnival, an orgy of gaiety before the austerity of Lent, battling the depression of the final grim months of winter with weeks of

drinking, dancing, partying. But no matter how fiercely they sought the release of pleasure and exhaustion, there was something in the air that tainted all of it, a sense of time running out. It was a sensation Christa had never known before, and one she hated.

She was not alone. For every Austrian there had been one shock after another for the past six weeks.

First, in early February, news of a shake-up in the German Army. In her previous incarnation as a child, the fate of two generals, von Blomberg and von Fritsch, in Berlin would have meant nothing to her. Now, it was like the tolling of a bell. What she did not understand, Lan made clear.

"They were the most powerful generals in the Army, and Hitler's chief opponents. The ones Josef was counting on to overthrow the bastard if he took too great a risk of war. But now, somehow, he's crushed them, and anybody who might block him is gone. He's got a clear track all the way for anything he might want to do. Including marching into Austria. There's nobody left in Germany to stop him from anything."

The first shock. And even while the dancing went on bravely, there were more, like hammer blows. In mid-February the news seeped out that, answering a virtual summons, von Schuschnigg had conferred secretly with Hitler in Berchtesgaden. What had happened there was still unclear, but the results were immediately obvious and visible. The swastika measled out all across the land, unafraid, arrogant; and the Brownshirt legions marched in the streets without fear of reprisal. Nazi propaganda blossomed in the Nazi-supported papers, and every day there was violence of some kind in the capital and in the provinces. Whatever Hitler's terms at Berchtesgaden, von Schuschnigg had apparently caved in completely rather than risk warfare against the ever-stronger German Army.

Vienna's whole climate changed; one sensed a mordant tinge in all the gaiety, an effort to shrug off gut-wrenching fear. Josef and the General, with pipelines that led behind the scenes, plus the reporters at the Cafe Louvre, fed information to Lan Condon, and he in turn made it clear to Christa.

"This is the last act," he said harshly. "Von Schuschnigg's trying desperately to get guarantees of Austrian independence from Britain, France, and Italy. He's getting turned down all around. And—there's no word for it—the man's lost his nerve, his guts, and maybe his common sense."

Lan struck his fist into his open palm. "The heartbreaking thing about it is that the Austrians are clamoring to be united! The Socialists and labor-union leaders—all the outlaws—have come to him and begged to be given the chance to work with him, begged to be armed to fight for Austria. So have the old conservative private armies, the Heimwehr and the Sturm-schären. The Nazis are still a minority. Most Austrians will fight, and fight hard against the common enemy! Otto von Habsburg has written von Schuschnigg asking him to resign and let a Habsburg take over as a national leader. And the man turns a deaf ear to all of them! Why doesn't he resign and let Habsburg try to form a united front? Why doesn't he tell Hitler to go to hell, proclaim that Austria'll fight to the last man! Jesus Christ, no wonder the Germans call Austrians limp dicks! And von Schuschnigg's showing the limpest one of all!"

Once she would have been unable to follow all that. Now she knew all too well what it meant. And she knew what the Nazis were as well—the men who'd kicked her husband when he was down, had blown up Birnbaum's tailor shop on Christmas Eve —they were beasts, she thought. And remembering Robert, who was not a beast, she could make no sense of it at all. And yet, there was no way around it. He and Uncle Max were too power-ful in the Ferntal for such a thing to have happened without their knowledge.

But it was so confusing. Dr. Martinus was convinced that Robert was innocent. On their last weekend visit at the Christina Hof, he had appeared in time for *Jause*. "Arrangements have been made for the damage to be repaired," he said. "Surely you must understand that it was no one from the Fern-tal. Some rowdies from Tulln or Klosterneuburg, more likely. No one in Ferndorf would do such a thing to the Birnbaums, Jews or not."

"Shit," Lan said crassly in English.

"I beg your pardon?"

Lan stood up. Aunt Alma had caught influenza from that night in the cold, and though partly recovered still remained in bed most of the day. Only Lan, Christa, Martinus, and the General were at the table in a parlor of the house.

"I said shit." There was a tone in Lan's voice that she recognized. He had been pushed too far, and it took a lot to push him, to break that Southern courtesy of his. "Martinus, why don't you come out with it? You're a goddamned Nazi."

The priest rose, lean face pale, eyes wide behind his glasses. "I beg your pardon?" he said again, voice trembling.

"You're a fucking Nazi," Lan said in English.

Martinus swallowed. "Lan . . . Mr. Condon—"

"Don't Mr. Condon me. You're one of them. You're just holding your breath until they take over. The first day we met, you were telling me that the Church could live with them. Sure it can. It's the oldest dictatorship in the world. It knows the score. Power. Nobody knows more about that than a cardinal."

"Lan," General Helmer said.

"No. It's time Martinus heard some facts." His voice crackled. "The fact is that the Catholic Church and the Nazis are a lot alike. Everybody who isn't for them is against them. All right, I'm a Catholic too, by conversion, by necessity. I couldn't have married Christa otherwise. But I'm fed up. I'm fed up with Catholics rolling over and playing dead in Germany, and the Lutherans forming the only real opposition. I'm fed up with the hammering of acceptance of authority and infallibility into the heads of all these people. Authority, infallibility, that's the Nazi gambit. All right, you've been raised to accept it. Maybe I can't blame you. Maybe it's what you feel comfortable with. Me, I don't. And I know what you're getting into, and you don't. You think you're going to have a Nazi-Catholic Austria. Nice Catholic Austrian Nazis are going to take over and run everything and stamp out all the other churches and give you a clear field and— Why, you poor idiot, there aren't going to be any nice Catholic Austrian Nazis in charge. Once Austria's in German hands, there'll be a bunch of German thugs here running things. And they have only one God and one religion, and that's Adolf Hitler."

"Sir," Martinus said, and spots of red blazed on his cheekbones. "You don't know what you are talking about. You're an outsider and you don't know. You just don't know—"

"I know about dictatorships. I've lived in Louisiana and worked for a movie studio and been kicked in the head in the Naschmarkt."

Martinus drew in a breath that made his thin chest swell beneath his black clothing. "Yes. Yes, perhaps you know all these things. Now . . . now, suppose I tell you some of the things I know."

"Do that," Lan said harshly.

"Yes. Well, now, some of the things I know are these." Martinus met his gaze unashamedly. "Because I am privileged, and I hear confessions, and I know secrets you will never hear. What I know"—he rubbed his mouth—"I know about despair," he said. "About husbands who can't feed their wives and children because they have no jobs. Men who contemplate suicide because of their shame and pain in such a situation. Families breaking up because of the want of a hundred schillings more a week. Girls going into prostitution. You," he said bitterly, "you are an American and rich. You can afford the luxury of ideology. You can even afford the luxury of a religion of convenience. The people I must deal with every day cannot. I cannot. What do you tell a man who says, 'Father, I have sinned. I walked Vienna the whole day long looking for a job, and I found none. And I begged two schillings, and instead of buying bread for my family, I was so exhausted that I spent one schilling on a glass of wine, and then I spent the other schilling on another glass.' And the man is in agony. What penance do I assign him?

"Or the woman who says, 'I slept with him because he gave me twenty schillings, and my kids were hungry!' And how do you carry that? What, may I ask you, is the answer? It is not a matter of the Pope or authority or anything— It is a matter of people! Germany was like that, too, B.H.—before Hitler—and now it is not! There men have work, and children have food! Thanks to the new regime! And if that is what it takes here to rid me of my burden, then I am for it. I think—"

Again he drew in breath. "I think there are some evil aspects to Nazism. I think one must weigh the good against the bad. I think the good overbalances the bad. I think we can take the German drive and the Austrian compassion and combine them into a New Order that is really new!" His face was hard. "I can stand here before you and say that in good conscience. I say to you that there must be some way to still the anxiety within the human heart and let every man live as a human being. Marxism is no answer, because it denies God, and man cannot live as a human being without God. The Nazis offer both God and bread in sufficient amounts."

"Martinus—" Lan said.

Martinus shook his head violently, as if something buzzed around it. "I seek answers," he said heavily. "You only ask questions. Good day." Then he went out.

There had been a long silence. Lan said, "I'm sorry, General Helmer."

"No." Christa's father stood up. "No, there is right on both sides. But Martinus is correct in this: You are from another world. Your understanding of us is imperfect. You must not judge us by the standards of America. America is so big, there is always somewhere you can go. But in Austria, as it is now in all of Europe, there is no place to run. So we compromise, as Martinus said. Lan, listen. You are afraid of being conquered; we are not. We were conquered by the Romans, the Turks, the French, and finally the English and the Americans. God knows who else in between. This is a hard thing for a soldier to say, and maybe an American could not understand it at all. But we do know how to be conquered and to survive."

He raised his glass, tossed off his wine. "Don't mistake me. If the *Pifka* bastards come, I'll be in the front line if I have to carry a pitchfork. But if they beat us, I'll find another way to survive. I'll save the Christina Hof and everybody dependent on it, no matter what I have to do. I—" He broke off, as if he had said too much. "Oh, we are fighting shadows. I've lived a long time, and this I've learned: that nothing is ever quite as bad as one expects. And we Austrians can always wriggle out."

But later that night, Christa remembered, her father and Lan had sat up talking; and she had been excluded.

But Papa knew what he was about, and he was right: Austrians could always wriggle out somehow. And now it seemed that Kurt von Schuschnigg had found the answer. Yesterday, the ninth of March, he had made a fiery speech in Innsbruck. There would be a plebiscite on the thirteenth of the month. A vote of the people, long demanded by Hitler, to determine whether Austria would remain free or voluntarily become subject to Germany. She and Lan had heard the speech on the radio.

Schuschnigg's voice rose with unwonted passion. "What do the people of Austria want? I must know whether Austrians approve of our proposed path! Now I will know and must know whether the people of Austria want this free and German, independent, social, Christian and united Fatherland!"

Cold chills ran up her spine at the authentic emotion in the voice of the country's leader.

Lan listened to the end and then, as the National Hymn stirringly died away, clicked off the radio. "Well," he said. "At least he's found one way of fighting. If he can bring it off—"

"What?"

"The plebiscite. If he can get a whopping majority for an independent Austria, against German takeover, the country will unite. He will have something to use to face down Hitler, and Britain and France might even stir their stumps. All the same ..." Lan paced their living room. "All the same ..." He turned. "Christa, we've got to make some decisions. How long would it take for you to get ready to go to America?"

"What? Go to— But your book, it's not finished. You've hardly worked on it since New Year's."

"Hell with the book. I want you to pack whatever you'll need and want to leave for the States on short notice. We'll go to Italy and sail from there. You and I and Ernst."

"Lan! I don't understand?"

"Well, you'd better." His voice was crisp. "This is the out that von Schuschnigg's decided to take. A majority vote against the Nazis, and Hitler's left with egg on his face. The Allies may even crack down on him. Me, I don't think he can let this plebiscite take place. I think he'll move in and try to break it up. If he does, that may mean war between now and the thirteenth of the month—five days. And if there's war, the General will be with the Austrian Army and— He and I have already talked. The best thing is to get you and Ernst out of the combat zone. I want you to pack and see that Ernst is packed."

Christa sat there numbly. "Lan, must we really?" What he was describing was the end of the world.

"We must," he said. "Really."

She met his eyes and felt a new surge of courage, and of trust. "All right," she said. "We don't really need a lot. I'll have to get some steamer trunks. Papa has several at the *Hof*."

"Yes. I think he already has Ernst more or less packed. Darling, we didn't want to spring this on you until we could see what was happening."

"But Papa must come, too!"

Lan laughed. "Can you see him leaving with an enemy on the border ready to come in? Do you think he'd run out without a fight?" Then he was serious. "No, he'll stay here and do whatever he thinks he has to. Meanwhile, I'll take you and Ernst out, and then we'll wait and see what happens. If there's luck, if the *Anschluss* is balked somehow, I'll bring you back. But have everything ready to go by Friday. The General will send in the trunks from the *Hof*."

Christa swallowed hard. "Very well."

The next morning the trunks were there and she began to pack.

Then Josef Steiner called.

19 THEY GOT OFF THE TRAIN at a small town called Braunkirchen, where Josef's driver met them. The car wound through the village and up a narrow valley, following a thaw-swollen stream. It was unseasonably warm for the second week of March, and the road they traveled was deep in mud. Presently they crossed the stream on a wooden bridge behind a sawmill; and on a squat peak ahead they saw Schloss Schwarzgipfel, like some huge pale fungoid growth springing from the mountaintop, dead white walls and dead white towers, with tile roofs black as anthracite against the sky.

Reaching the entrance of the palace's enclosing wall, they passed beneath a raised portcullis and entered a labyrinth of scattered yet linked buildings. Then, through another arch, they passed into the main courtyard, where high walls rose about them, devoid of any bright color. The car stopped, and they got out and looked around at the complex of window-ranked walls and soaring towers and turrets on every hand.

"This makes the Christina Hof look like a shanty," Lan said. "Josef—" He broke off as a grating, earsplitting scream from above and behind made them whirl. It came again, high-pitched, squawking, a nightmare sound going straight to the nerves. And then they saw the bird, large, black, and lustrous, on a low roof across the court. Extending its long neck, snakelike head weaving, it screamed again and spread its tail into a luxurious black and violet fan. "Peacock," Lan said. "I never saw a black one before."

"Everything Josef raises here is black."

"Yes. I'd forgotten." Another peacock joined the first one then, and it screamed, too. "I understand they make good watchdogs," Condon said. Then they were led up high steps through a door into the *Schloss;* and when it closed behind them, it shut off the sound.

Josef came to meet them, austere as usual in black and white. A word of dismissal to the servant, and he was silent for several seconds after the door was closed; his face, Christa thought, looked drawn, his mouth grim and weary. "Thank you for coming," he said. "I know it was an inconvenience. But, Lan, as I told you on the phone, it is a matter of utmost urgency, and it's impossible for me to get to Vienna." He smiled faintly. "Anyhow, I've succeeded at last in enticing you to Schwarz-gipfel. You must be absolutely frozen. Let me give you something to drink."

"Thanks," Lan said. "But, Josef, I hope you can make this pretty short. We need to get back; we're packing to go to Italy."

"Yes, you told me. And a wise move." Steiner went to a table, poured schnapps, handed glasses to the Condons. "So I'll not waste your time, never fear; I'll get directly to the point. *Pros't.*" He drank. "Please. If you will bring your glasses and come with me to the library . . ."

Christa and Lan exchanged glances and then rose. Lan had been upset over the interruption in their preparations for leaving and had tried on the telephone to beg off, but Steiner had phrased his summons in terms he could not refuse: *Absolutely imperative. If you have any friendship for me, I implore you.* Now Lan shrugged and nodded, and her own curiosity had reached fever pitch.

Josef led them through double doors into a vast booklined room with a big table in its center. There was an open fire, and he motioned them to the sofa before it. "All right," he said. "I'll waste no time." He went to a shelf and pulled down a pair of outsized volumes bound in black leather. Christa sat up straight. She had seen those before—or their like.

Face expressionless, Josef laid them in Lan's lap. Lan opened the topmost one and blurted something, staring at the vivid mounted photographs. He raised his head. "Josef, for God's sake—"

"Only part of a very extensive collection. I am perhaps the best single customer of the pornographers of Vienna."

Christa felt a thrill of fear, mingled with dismay. He's snapped, she thought. He's lost his mind.

Lan turned another page, closed the album. "What the hell," he asked harshly, "has this got to do with anything? Dirty pictures!"

"Dirty pictures are important," Josef said. "As a matter of fact, pornography and vice may have settled Austria's fate. Hitler has just used them to dispose of the two most powerful officers blocking his way. Von Blomberg, Minister of War, has just been destroyed by him because the old man, a widower, married his secretary. And then the Gestapo learned that her mother had once run a Berlin brothel and she had posed for pornographic pictures. Hitler used this to break him. Then von Fritsch, von Blomberg's most likely successor—and even more opposed to der Führer's war plans. They trumped up charges of homosexuality against him, my sources say . . . and now he's gone, too."

Lan stared at him a moment, nodded. "Go ahead."

Josef looked at them strangely. "What," he asked, "do you know about the early life of Adolf Hitler?"

He waited, and the room was silent. Christa sought to make a connection in her mind and then realized that Lan already had. He was looking at Josef intently. "Not much," he said. "Only what's in *Mein Kampf*."

"Deceptive and self-serving. There's more, much more."

"Suppose you tell us," Lan said quietly.

Visibly, Josef relaxed. "Very well. He's Austrian, of course, from a small town on the German border. His father was a customs official and a holy terror at home, it seems; his mother was half the old man's age, and Hitler was something of a mama's boy. He and his father didn't get along, the home was full of tensions, and as soon as possible he left to study in Linz. There, apparently, he was an indifferent student—not stupid, just idle, dreamy, lazy. He had some talent for art and conceived the idea that he'd be a great painter; and, truth to tell, I've seen some of his early work and it wasn't bad. Be that as it may, when he was not yet twenty, he came to Vienna to apply at the Academy of Arts. His portfolio was reviewed and ... well, only God in His infinite wisdom knows how the cultural bureaucracies in Vienna operate. I am sure many students of lesser talent have been admitted, but perhaps they didn't like the way he brushed his hair or smelled. They turned him down, suggesting that his real talent lay in architecture. But he'd been such a *Lausbub* in school that he lacked the scholastic background to enter the School of Architecture. Which more or less left him stranded."

Now Steiner's manner was that of a classroom lecturer. "Even Hitler in *Mein Kampf* admits that his next four years in Vienna were dreadfully unhappy. Anyhow," he continued, "after four years he went to Germany and when war broke out joined the German Army—completely caught up in primitive pan-German nationalism. After the defeat he drifted, fell in with the National Socialist Movement, took it over, and made it his, having discovered his talent as an orator. He figured in a failed putsch designed to break Bavaria off from Weimar, was imprisoned, but, having stirred sympathies in German breasts with his conservatism, remained there only just long enough to write *Mein Kampf*. You know the rest—his manipulations, rabble-rousing, his rise to power—"

"Yes," Lan said.

"Now, for a moment, let me digress. I want to talk about sex again—its relation to National Socialism. Hitler is the Nazi prophet, and surely you've noticed that Nazism is based, grounded, on a sexual foundation. Its basic philosophy deals with who should be allowed to breed with whom and on the potency of German men and the fruitfulness of German women. It's a very curious mixture of libertinism and prudery, and look how much of its propaganda is sheer pornography. Take Streicher's paper, *Der Stürmer,* which they say Hitler reads avidly. Look at the imposed taste in Nazi art: big-bosomed, complaisant, explicit female nudes and randy naked or half-naked German muscle-men. Look at the men around der Führer: Röhm was a queer; Goebbels has the sexual tendencies of a buck hare; Hess is rumored to like boys as well as women; Ley carries a whip with him everywhere he goes; only Göring seems normal, and he's on drugs and eating himself to death. The whole Nazi inner circle seems more likely to be found hanging around a railroad station men's room late at night than governing a country. And that . . ." He paused. "That brings up the question: Where does Herr Hitler stand in this company of perverts?"

The fire crackled in the grate. Josef, tired of standing, propped one lean haunch on the table, his eyes glowing. After a moment Lan said, "I suppose *you* know."

"I think so," said Josef promptly. "As der Führer, he poses as an ascetic, a man wedded only to the German people, far too busy to have time for sex. The fact is, he's no better than the rest."

"I've heard rumors," Christa said, "that he's impotent, or maybe a 'warm brother' himself."

"What he is," said Josef, "is very complicated. And he has a propaganda machine going full blast to cover his real tendencies, his peculiar transgressions. But my associates and I have done a great deal of digging and spent a lot of money, and we have unearthed information as to his real tendencies." His face grim, he picked up a volume from the table, thumbed through it, found a place, and passed the book to Lan. "I'm sorry, Christa."

She craned her neck to look, and her stomach roiled. "Judas Priest," Lan whispered.

"Not pretty, is it? But you'd be surprised what a market there is here for such pictures, they tell me, and an even better one in Germany. There's something in the German mentality arrested at that stage, it seems. After all, *shit* and *stink* are two of the most-used words in our vocabulary. Never mind. The pictures make clear what I'm driving at. An ultimate, groveling subjugation: that's his fulfillment." He shut the album.

"If you could document that—" Lan began.

"If I could have, I'd have done so long ago. But he's had years to cleanse Germany of incriminating evidence. Nevertheless, at least one girl involved with him has killed herself—or been murdered—and a couple more have tried suicide and failed. Apparently they fall in love with the great leader, the ultimate in masculine power, and then find out that *this* is what he wants. No, Lan. He has purged Germany of all proof. But"—Josef paused and looked at them—"he has not been able to do the same with Austria."

Slowly Lan Condon stood up, and there was a strange quality in his voice as he said, "Go on."

"Four years in Vienna. Four lost years. By his own admission, Hitler was a drifter. Nevertheless, a man doesn't live four years here and not leave tracks. And I have spent a lot of money, Lan, finding those tracks and following them. The trail, my friends, of a tramp, the lowest of the low, with no visible means of support, a few odd jobs here, perhaps a postcard or two painted there for a publisher. He was a man who by all accounts not only sank to the depths but seemed to enjoy it, enjoyed being unwashed and filthy as he went from room to room, doss house to doss house—flophouses, you so aptly called them in your books."

Lan said nothing, but he was looking at Josef in a way that Christa knew: eyes probing, his whole being intent on assessing not only the man's words but his manner, seeking any taint of falsity.

"Barely staying alive," Steiner went on. "And, of course, in such a situation, absolutely at the bottom, one does what one has to in order to survive, and why should he be an exception?"

"If I get you right," Lan murmured, "you're trying to say—"

"A rumor reached me a couple of years ago. Incredible on the face of it, and yet, the more one considered, it had a real kernel of logic, of possibility. Since that time I've become a valued customer of the makers and purveyors of pornography in Vienna. Known"—he smiled coolly—"as a man with extremely special tastes who will pay premium prices for merchandise that suits him. I have, consequently, first refusal of almost everything that turns up in that, ah, special repulsive area of obscenity, particularly photographs made before the war."

"Which would cover the period Hitler spent in Vienna."

"Yes. And eventually I was rewarded. At last I found a single photograph—obviously one of a broken set—and I felt at once there was little doubt of the identity of the young male participant. Here." He unlocked a drawer in the table, took out what seemed to be an ordinary portfolio of stationery. Hidden among the sheets of notepaper was a postcard-size photograph and a number of clippings from magazines and newspapers. He spread them on the table, and Christa rose to look. One glance was enough; she turned away, but Lan and Steiner bent over it with preoccupation. "You see," Josef said, "the face shows quite clearly. And here are photographs, official ones, from his younger days for comparison. In my opinion, there can be no doubt. What do you think?"

Lan straightened up, drawing in a breath. "It may be," he said. "It sure as hell looks like him. But it wouldn't be enough."

"Of course not. But when the picture fell into my hands, I pretended to be enraptured by the woman in it. She's quite ordinary, but—" He shrugged, smiling ironically. "Anyhow, I let it be known that I would pay fantastic prices for more pictures featuring her, and, more than that, if she were still alive—though obviously she'd be quite old now—I'd pay even more handsomely for the privilege of meeting her. I set a trap baited with financial incentives." He paused; his eyes met Lan's. "A week ago it sprang."

Carefully he restored the picture and the clippings to the folder, hiding them among the sheets of paper. "She's still alive," he said. "She lives in Vienna's Second District in poverty. And... she has a complete set of these photographs. And she remembered well the young man who posed for them; his name was Adolf."

Lan Condon made a sound in his throat. Christa said, "Josef, you can't mean—"

"I told you it was incredible. At first even I wondered if I were the victim of some elaborate plot. Especially when I learned that— Well, let me take things in their order."

His voice was steady, but his dark eyes glittered. "The whole matter, of course, was too sensitive to be handled by an intermediary. Still, I am being watched. The Nazis have their agents here, you know, and they're keeping us Steiners under surveillance, to be sure we don't abscond with the bank's funds before they can get their hands on them. So I went to quite elaborate lengths to throw them off my trail and only proceeded to the Second District when I was absolutely certain that I had. I kept up my pose as her admirer, or one of her as she had been. I daresay that was somewhat painful for her; the kind of life she had led took its toll, all right; she has become a hag. I took a bottle as a present, excellent brandy. A few drinks loosened her up quite properly and put her in a reminiscent mood."

Christa had a vivid image of that: the elegant Steiner and some dirty old crone drinking together in a dim, shabby room. She could not help a nervous giggle. Josef looked at her and smiled. "Get on with it," Lan said sharply.

"Yes. As I said, she remembered it all clearly. Adolf was an intense young man who represented himself as a painter, but that was not why he was unforgettable. There were two other reasons. First was the enthusiasm with which he performed—or let himself be performed upon. For most men, what was demanded of him would have been endurable only as a last resort, but for him it was obviously a kind of ecstasy. For her, of course, it was only business. When they had both been paid, it was over as far as she was concerned. Filthy little bastard, she called him. But on his part . . . well, he was captivated. Perhaps, after countless rejections, he had at last found a woman who would give him the fulfillment that he yearned for. And afterwards, for quite some time, he was a nuisance to her. Of course, he had no money, which was all that interested her; but he couldn't seem to understand that. He wrote her letters, which she immediately destroyed, damn her. But then he took another tack. He had procured an extra set of the pictures himself, and every day for twelve days he sent one to her, with a long desperate screed on the back of each, a warped love letter, if you will, the outpourings of a young, deranged, and desperate mind. Unlike the letters, she did not destroy the pictures, which had intrinsic value, could be sold. And . . . you can imagine how I felt when she produced them and what my emotions were as I saw that face and read the filth on the back, signed with a simple *A*."

Christa shook her head. "Only *A?* Not his whole name?"

"Of course not. He was not that demented. But handwriting experts could make confirmation. I myself am already convinced. I am sure others would be as quick to see the resemblance, and that there is too much here to be sheer coincidence. It *cannot* be, it *must* not be."

After a second, Lan said, "Where are the pictures?"

"She still has them. Of course, I asked her to name her price at once. That was a mistake: all the instincts and suspicions of the *Dirne* were at once aroused. Even an old whore is still a whore and thinks like one. So she understood at once that by holding back and tantalizing, she could raise the price. But I am sure that never once in all these years has she made the connection between *that* Adolf and the other one. Be that as it may, I left her with the request to set a price, any price, and notify me. Two days ago I had a letter from her naming a staggering sum for immediate delivery. I sent a Wiener Dienst-mann with an acceptance, but, naturally, considering the gravity of the matter, I would trust no one but myself to pay and take possession of those pictures.

"And I set out to do that, but once again I was followed and I couldn't lose them. Worse, the situation in Vienna, as you know, has become chaotic. Bands of Nazis march boldly in the streets in full cry against the upcoming plebiscite, and they're not gentle with Jews that they encounter. And"—his mouth twisted—"I am a very well known Jew. Not that I'm concerned about myself, but I don't dare risk anything happening to those pictures. And my people, my associates, in Vienna are in the same boat, though some are non-Jewish. And so, Lan, I was stuck, and I tried hard to think what to do. And I kept coming up with only one answer." He paused. Then he said, "An American with the proper documents would have nothing to fear from either the mob or the police. An American could pick up those pictures and deliver them to me. Now do you see why I insisted that you come to Schwarzgipfel? And do you see the magnitude of the favor? You are the only person whom I trust who could do it."

Once more there was silence as he and Lan looked at each other. Then Josef said, "Another drink?"

"No," Lan said. "Josef, this is the damnedest thing I've ever heard."

"I told you it would stretch the bounds of credibility."

"To try to blackmail Adolf Hitler—"

"Not I. I only would get those pictures to certain people. They would have to do the rest—and they would. Lan, in anticipation I've set up a photographic laboratory here, would send on several sets and the originals. Give others to the von

Schuschnigg government for whatever use it might make of them. But Germany would be the scene of the real action."

"What kind of action?"

"I am convinced," Josef said, "that within twenty-four hours of receipt of the pictures and a full explanation of their significance, the leading officers of the German Army and Navy would confront Hitler with them."

"And the outcome?"

"I can't guarantee anything. But I think it would be fair to say that he who lived by the sword would die by it. His use of pornography against von Fritsch and von Blomberg has made him vulnerable. I doubt the Officer Corps would show him any mercy. At the very least the old guard would regain control, clip his wings, and avoid any risk of war. At best there would be a coup. The ideal would be the usual Prussian procedure: they would lock him in a room with a pistol with a single bullet and expect him to do the rest; if he did not, somebody would do it for him. At the least this would give the German Army the means of controlling him and saving itself from the inevitable defeat which would come with another war just at this stage."

Lan stood up. "You think the pictures would do all that?"

"We shall never know until they reach the proper hands."

Lan turned toward the fire. "This," he said, "is a hell of a thing to throw at a man."

Josef said quietly, "I know. But I and my friends have gone as far as we can. Now we need your help. Otherwise it's all wasted, all the years of effort. And the chance of success, Lan, is too great not to be exploited."

Emotions swirled within Christa as she watched Lan stare into the flames. It was incredible, a fantasy. But she had known Josef too long, too well, not to sense that he believed that all he said was true. And if it were . . . Excitement rose within her as she grasped the magnitude of it all. If Josef were right, if it worked, they would not have to flee, and Papa would not have to stay behind and fight; he would be safe, the Christina Hof safe, Austria safe.

And, of course, Lan could do it. He could do anything he undertook, and that American passport of his was as good as armor, a kind of magic. She watched him, wanting to speak herself, but knowing that she must wait; this was a matter for him to decide.

He turned. "It's not all that easy."

"No. And I don't ask it lightly. For me it would be dangerous. For you, not very."

"You say you're watched. I presume you mean by the Nazis. They have agents here, you said. The Gestapo?"

Josef shrugged.

"Well, if you're watched in Vienna, you're watched here, too. Which means that we might be in trouble just from visiting you."

"I don't think so. Not if you will do a little acting. We can provide them with a logical and deceptive reason for your visit: my old interest in Christa. It's served as a smokescreen in the past, remember? All right. You came for what should have been a long weekend. But tomorrow, very early, you'll reappear in Braunkirchen in the Gasthaus Golden Bear, where you'll have breakfast and a frightful argument simultaneously. In English, of course, because it's an intimate matter you don't want the locals to understand. But the *Wirt* of the Golden Bear understands English perfectly, though he doesn't let on, and is a Nazi. He'll spread the word soon enough. You'll be furious at Christa. Obviously I invited you just to get my hands on her. She was far too responsive and you became enraged; we had a confrontation and you dragged her out to catch the first morning train, and the awful Josef Steiner has perhaps broken up another marriage. How does that sound to you?"

"I don't know. But say it works. Suppose they're watching *her*? After all, Hitler, if it is he, can't have forgotten those pictures, and he knows a set of them can ruin him, especially those he wrote on. I'd think, if he has undercover agents here, they'd be looking high and low for her."

"I think not," said Josef. "Put yourself in his place. Given the shifting loyalties and the crosscurrents in his regime right now, whom would he dare tell about the pictures, entrust finding them to? Whoever got his hands on them—Himmler, Göring—might seize the opportunity to use them against him. Would he risk that? If I were he, I would tell myself that after twenty years they were bound to have disappeared, and that it was safer not to rouse a sleeping dog. I would pray my luck would hold and that she and the pictures both were dead and gone. Later, *after* I had got my hands on Austria, I would make inquiries, but surely not before. Anyhow, as to finding her, she was, is, of the underworld. They are birds of passage. She used a false name then, probably uses another now. She bears no resemblance to the woman she once was and has lived at a dozen different addresses since then in a dozen incarnations—"

"But you found her."

"After two years and the expenditure of vast sums of money. Believe me, she's well buried. She's safe, Lan, as long as no one leads them to her. And, of course, if you should be followed, you must turn back at once."

Lan was silent. Then: "How would I get the pictures to you?"

"Once you have them, take the train from Franz Josef Bahnhof to Horn in the Waldviertel. From three o'clock tomorrow on, my black Mercedes—I'll give you the plate number and the keys—will be parked near the Bahnhof. There is a young lady in Horn whom I occasionally visit in the afternoon while her husband is away. I always park at the Bahnhof. Anyone watching me will naturally follow me and ignore the car. You merely unlock it, get in as if it belonged to you, slide the pictures behind the seat, get out, and lock it again. After which you catch the next train to Vienna."

"You make it sound like buying candy in a *Konditorei*," Lan said acidly.

"For you it should be no more difficult. What do you say?"

"I say nothing. Not yet. It's all too fast, there are too many angles. I need to think about it."

"Certainly. I realize that. You and Christa will want to talk. But please, Lan, take everything I have said with the utmost seriousness. And you, my dear"—turning to Christa—"it is your country as well as mine."

Then he smiled in a way that made some of the tension dissipate. "Let it go for now. Finally I have you at Schloss Schwarzgipfel, and I insist that you must see it, and my experiments with animals and plants as well. Let me show you around. Then, before dinner, you and Christa may retire and talk, and over the meal we can settle any further details. But for the time being let's put it from our minds and pretend the last year never happened. We may never have the chance to so deceive ourselves again."

20 COMING INTO HEILIGENSTADT, the locomotive blew its piping whistle. Christa, nervous and excited, saw her dim reflection in the window of the coach and realized she had gnawed off all her lipstick; she fumbled in her bag for her compact. Her mind was not working well at all today; last night's sleeplessness had left it groggy, and besides there was the tension of what lay ahead for Lan. Maybe, she thought, we were wrong, maybe . . .

Josef had given them a partial tour of the *Schloss;* a full exhausting day would have been required to see it all. He himself used only a fraction of it, and the rest was as it had been when he had purchased it—colorful, exquisite, full of treasures. But there was something disturbing, jarring, about the section he had redecorated, where, save for stark whites and blacks and an occasional sudden touch of scarlet, all color had been obliterated. Instead, here and there geometrical designs of black and white produced strange, hallucinatory optical effects, for which he apologized. "They are my substitute for color, the only visual satisfaction within my reach." Nevertheless, Christa found it oppressive, and that held, too, for the blackness of the animals in their spotless buildings, the birds in aviaries, and the plants in a vast greenhouse, their blossoms leached perversely of all brilliance satisfying to normal vision. By the time Josef excused himself and they were alone in the conventionally colorful suite alloted them, her nerves were on edge, and, she sensed, Lan's as well.

Kicking off their shoes, they sprawled on the huge double bed. Lan slid his arm beneath her head. "Well, what do you think?"

"I don't know what to think." She paused. "At first I was excited. Then I saw this house and all those black creatures and flowers and . . . Lan, do you think Josef is . . . all right?"

Lan was silent for a moment. "I've been asking myself that. He's weird, no doubt about it. On the other hand, it would take somebody with a weird cast of mind to figure out an angle like that and follow through on it."

Christa rose, went to the window, looked out into the courtyard, watching two black peacocks strut along a wall. "How much real danger is there?"

"That's what I don't know. For Josef, there's danger in just being out on the street in Vienna right now. But for me . . . I don't know. I don't have much experience at this E. Phillips Oppenheim sort of stuff."

"Maybe you should talk to Papa."

"I can't. No time. And besides . . . You know."

"Yes," she said, "I know."

"It's just, damn it, that I hate to get mixed up in anything that might delay us if we have to pull out in a hurry. It's another complication at a time when we've got too many already. For myself, I don't mind. But if it made it hard for you and Ernst to get out and there was a war . . ."

Christa drew in breath. "Well, today is Friday. The plebiscite's on Sunday. We have until the votes are counted anyhow, don't we?"

"I hope so."

She turned. "Lan, what do *you* want to do?"

He looked at her. After a moment he said, "I want to go ahead and try it." He paused, seeking words. "It's wild, yes, but suppose it *would* work, suppose . . . You know, this is a peculiar little country. To an American, nothing ever quite makes sense here. But it's my country, too. I have been happy here and I don't want to see it go down the drain if there is any way I can help it. It's only you and Ernst I worry about."

"Then stop worrying," she said, and she came to him, feeling love and fear and a strange kind of exaltation all intermingled; and she stood before him. "Tell Josef you'll do it."

He looked at her a moment, half smiling. "You want me to?"

"I insist on it. I am glad you feel that Austria's your country. But far more than yours, it's mine."

"Yeah," he said. He stood up, put his arm around her. "Okay. It's settled, then. We'll tell Josef at dinner. And . . . don't worry." He grinned. "Like Mark Gorton sometimes says, it'll be a piece of cake."

At dinner, when he heard their decision, Josef said quietly but with a thickness of relief in his voice, "Thank you. Thank you, Lan; thank you, Christa." And for another hour they had talked, discussing ways and means, examining every possibility of mishap. Truly, the risk did not seem overwhelming.

Later, she and Lan lay together beneath their comforter,

holding each other, immersed in the warmth of each other's bodies. She felt the taut-strung tenseness of him against her, and her hand moved to caress him; she knew how to relieve it. "Lan—" Then she broke off as from outside there came a thin, grating shriek, muffled by the closed double casements. "My God, what's that?"

Lan slipped out of bed, went to the window, and after a second Christa followed. The cry came again, still sharp enough to make her feel as if a blade had cleft the fibers of a nerve and twisted, dividing them. She put her arm around Lan's waist. Below, in moonlight, four black birds stalked the lower roofs around the courtyard. One snaked out its neck, craned its head, shrieked again.

"Damned peacocks," Lan said. "Something must have frightened 'em. Hell, you're shivering. Come on back to bed."

Again beneath the cover, a wave of hunger, need, swept over her with sudden force, desire to be united with him wholly. He felt it, too, and responded instantly, mouth coming down on hers. Outside, below their window, the birds kept on shrieking, disturbed by something in the night, walking the roofs, spreading their fans.

Franz Josef Bahnhof was a sooty concrete cave echoing with train whistles and the shouts and cries of arrivals and departures. Today it was crowded with people traveling in groups and bands. Some wore the uniforms of units of the Front Miliz, the government's private army; others flaunted swastikas and white stockings. Christa even caught a glimpse of the long-outlawed Socialist badge with the three red arrows. Red-white-red Austrian flags waved in the crowd, and there were jeers and shouts: "Heil Hitler!" "Heil Schuschnigg!" "Österreich!" Something dank and violent seemed to hang in the air; and as they jostled through the crowd and left the station to find a cab, a plane flew low overhead, unloosing a snowstorm of propaganda pamphlets. Lan caught one out of the air: *JA! With Schuschnigg on Sunday for a Free Austria!* But the gray walls of the building were smeared with huge red swastikas and Nazi slogans. Somewhere in the distance a sound truck nattered: Christa caught tags and bits of its hoarse urgings: "Austrian workers, free Austria needs your support. . . ."

They caught a taxi, told the driver to take them to their

apartment. Vienna seemed different. Yesterday there had been activity in the streets, but nothing like today's. Police and soldiers in helmets and battle gear were everywhere, and the streets were clogged with marchers. A steady stream, many of schoolboy age, headed toward the Inner City wearing Nazi armbands. On the corners more swastika wearers boldly peddled the *Volksruf,* a violently anti-Semitic Nazi paper that had appeared from nowhere only a few days before. Every wall and kiosk was plastered with posters for and against the *Anschluss.* Even the hammer and sickle had come out of hiding to join the symbols of the other illegal factions.

Christa's misgivings returned with greater force. Today was no time for anyone to be on the streets. She clutched his thigh. "Lan. Look at it. It wasn't this way yesterday. Maybe you'd better not—"

"It won't be bad. I'll stick in a cab. See, we're safe in this one. But first we get you home, and you stay inside, you hear? Don't you go out, and don't let anybody in unless you know them. It looks like every thug in Austria's on the loose right now."

"I don't want you to go! We didn't know it would be like this when we said—"

The driver's head was cocked. "Hush," Lan said.

"Ho," said the driver in thick Viennese dialect as he waited for a channel through the square. "A big mess, hah? You can bet all the dirty kikes are hidin' under their beds today!" Then he turned forward to growl a curse at a car trying to ease in front of them, and the cab crept on, halting once more for a howling, shrieking platoon of teenage girls, each wearing a swastika. When, shouting *"Ein Reich, ein Volk, ein Führer!"* they had passed, the cab was able to reach the Argentinier-strasse.

Lan told the driver to wait and carried their luggage upstairs himself. Outside the door, he took Christa's hands. "Now, one more time. Do *not* worry. I'm not going to stick my neck out. Just get the packing finished and plan on a late supper tonight. Okay?" He pulled her to him, kissed her. "I'll take the same cab," he said, releasing her, and he touched her cheek. *"Wiederseh'n.* I love you."

She watched him start down the stairs. One landing, then

another, and still she stood as motionless as if paralyzed. Then her numbness broke and she rang the bell. Rezi could bring in the bags. And then she too was running.

"Lan!" she called as she made the stairs. Below at the main entrance, he halted.

Once she stumbled, caught herself on the railing; since he was waiting now, she slowed. "Lan," she said, reaching the bottom, "I'm going with you."

"The hell you are."

"Yes. I insist. We're in this together and—"

"You've got to get us packed."

"Rezi will have done some of it. I can finish the rest tonight. I don't intend to go with you to Horn, but I'm going . . . there. To *her* place. And see you safely off at Franz Josef."

He looked down at her, and she braced herself for more argument, which she was determined not to lose. But, after a moment, he smiled faintly and slowly nodded. "Okay. Come along. Maybe I can use an extra pair of eyes. I don't much trust that cab driver; he's a Nazi bastard if I ever saw one. I think we'll let him take us to the Praterstrasse and walk from there." He took her hand. "Come on, let's go."

It took the cab half an hour to reach the Schwedenbrücke over the Danube Canal, and each time they halted for a group of marching Nazis the driver chortled. Once, unabashed, he leaned out the window, arm raised. "Heil Hitler! Good luck, comrades!"

"You're for *Anschluss,* eh?" Lan asked in a carefully neutral voice as the man settled back.

"Absolutely, Herr Baron. Things have got to change, and der Führer is the man to change 'em! Look, I've got a wife and three kids and I was out of work for two years before I got this job. How we lived? Don't ask me! My wife scrubbed floors for a rich lady; I pinched a schilling here, a schilling there. We went hungry plenty of times, us and the kids, and we still do some-times."

Anger vibrated in his voice. "I got debts you wouldn't believe! Had to borrow—and from a dirty Jew! Nobody else may ever have any, but they're always *stuffed* with money! And this one, he can hardly even speak German! A Galizier, you know? And when the Poles took over his town, he and all the other kikes poured into Vienna—and imagine, it was allowed because they were Austrian citizens! Now the city's overflowin' with 'em, and they've got all the money! But do they try to become good Germans like the rest of us? No, they all stick together like mice in an attic trunk, with their own government and laws and all that black magic in their temples, and do nothin' but suck our blood. When I think of all I've paid in interest—

"And it ain't only in this country, either. It's everywhere. All over the world. You look at all the banks and stock markets. Who runs 'em? People like the Rothschilds and the Steiners— the lousy Jews! They got all the strings in their hands, and honest Christians got no chance at all!"

He hawked, spat out the window. "But it'll be different after Sunday. I tell you, when Hitler comes, I'm moving fast. I got my eye on a damned nice flat full of Jews, and just as soon as der Führer takes over, me and my brother are gonna throw the whole bunch out and take it, like it or not! When Austria's National Socialist, there won't be a damned thing they can do about it! Then it'll be *our* turn!" Spotting an opening, he put the car in motion.

Lan had known it for a long time. When a man was desperate enough, especially if he had a family, he would steal and even kill to survive. Certainly a man like this driver would, and even the best and strongest of men broke under desperation endured too long without hope. It was hope that made all the difference. Roosevelt had offered it in America, Hitler offered it here; and desperate men would seize any hope. "If," Lan had said once, "we hadn't had a Roosevelt, then we, too, would surely have had a Hitler. Candidates were already lining up for the job."

"Here," Lan said. "We'll get out here." They were in the Leopoldstadt now, the district across the Danube Canal, where the Jewish population was the heaviest. Strangely, there were no demonstrators here and very little traffic. "Here," Lan said. The driver pulled over to the curb, and Lan paid and tipped him. The man bowed low. *"Danke schön. Grüss Gott, Frau Baronin, Herr Baron. Wiederseh'n."* The courtesy was instinctive, not ironic.

After he had pulled away, they stood on the curb warily looking around. Here the sidewalks were deserted. In the distance the *Riesenrad*—the giant ferris wheel of the Prater—made its leisurely revolutions against the sky; apparently not everyone was demonstrating, if the amusement park was still in business.

Lan led her into a little sweetshop, where they were the only customers. He ordered two coffees and a couple of slices of chocolate cake, and took a table where they could look out the plate-glass window. She remembered then the possibility of their being followed, but it seemed unlikely anyone could have done so through that moil of activity in the heart of town. In silence they ate the cake and drank the coffee and saw nothing to alarm them. "Well, let's go," Lan said, and as they went out on the street, he added, "We're going to just wander until we make sure the coast is clear. Stop and look in windows from time to time, but don't turn and look behind you. Okay."

"Okay."

"Come on," he said, and they crossed the Praterstrasse.

Christa had driven through the Second District often, but basically it was unfamiliar to her, and she looked around curiously as Lan led her through narrow winding streets away from the Praterstrasse.

Vienna had no ghetto as such, and Jews and their synagogues were sprinkled all across the city, in every sort of dwelling from Bassena tenement to villa or even palace. Despite Vienna's tradition of anti-Semitism, Jews held high positions in government and were the yeast, the driving force, in the cultural, medical, and financial life of the capital. Those mostly were the old Austro-German Jews like Josef Steiner, who more than once had sounded almost like the cab driver.

"You realize, of course," Josef had told them one night at their apartment, "they, the immigrants from the provinces, we could do without. People like my brothers despise them almost as much as the Christians do. They are like lightning rods that draw down the fury on us. We, the Steiners and our ilk, reformed, even atheistic, have acclimated and accommodated over the years. We think of ourselves as Austrians first and Jews later. Quite the opposite with the Galiziern and the others. They remain so resolutely Jewish that they rouse all the animosity we have worked so hard to still.

"It is, of course, to be expected—a hundred thousand strangers, speaking different languages, wearing different garb, with a different religion, pouring in in only twenty years. The city simply can't digest them. Anyhow, if you want to find the fiercest anti-Semites in Germany or Austria, look among the old German-Jewish families. Most, if they had the power, would gladly send the others back where they came from in a minute." He'd smiled crookedly. "I myself, naturally, must be perverse. Lately I often even go to the Second District to *Shul,* but what I'm seeking I'm still not sure."

If there were power and prosperity here, she saw, it was not visible on the surface. Most of the stores were small used-furniture and clothing shops, or tiny groceries or butcher shops with Hebrew characters on their signs; and just now virtually all were closed. It was, she thought, as if this were a warren of small animals, which, scenting predators, had all popped deep into their holes, hoping the killers would pass by.

In an alley so narrow she could almost have spanned it with her outstretched arms, Lan halted and lit a cigarette, his eyes moving covertly. Then, dropping the extinguished match, he let out breath and smoke simultaneously. "We're clean," he said decisively. "I've seen nobody, have you?"

"Only those policemen at the bridge."

"They were just guards on duty there. Well, I think we can get down to business now. It should be up this next street about a block. Let's go."

She followed him around the corner, heart beginning to pound, but a look up and down the street revealed no one else abroad. In a moment Lan halted before a three-story house, its plastered walls peeling, revealing the brick beneath. He checked the number, nodded. "This is it." Looking dubiously at the big wooden entrance doors, both shut, he added, "I doubt we'll even be able to get inside." He tried the right-hand door, and to the surprise of both it swung open.

The entry was small and dank, and there was no directory. Stairs, worn concave by generations of shuffling feet, led upward on their right. "Second floor, room seven," Lan said, and they began to climb, presently emerging into a dank, peeling hall. It was even colder here than outside. They found a plain wooden door with a 7 on it. There was no bell, so Lan knocked.

No one answered. "You see?" he murmured. Almost reluctantly, he knocked again. Christa held her breath, hoping there would be no response and they could go home to safety. But then she heard the sound of footsteps within.

The door opened, and not a woman but a man stood there, in a neat blue suit. His face was broad and Slavic, his eyes small jet dots. "Yes?"

"I—" Lan broke off. "I'm sorry. I have made a mistake."

"Are you looking for Frau Charim?"

Lan did not answer.

The man's face relaxed. "I'm her brother. I think she's expecting you. Please come in."

"Expecting me?"

"If you are from a certain gentleman in the Wachau." He stood aside, and his voice was urgent. "Please. Quickly. Before someone—"

"All right," Lan said and entered, and Christa followed. They were in a tiny room curtained off from a larger one by dingy patterned fabric.

The man closed the door, turned a key in the lock. "Now," he said loudly, and through the curtain came two more men.

Christa stifled a cry of surprise, and Lan said harshly, "Oh, Christ."

"Don't move," the man with the dark eyes said. "You are both under investigatory arrest: Vienna Security Police." With one hand he drew a revolver and with the other brought out identification, holding it before their eyes.

Christa's heart lurched and her knees went weak. She heard Lan's indrawn breath. Then he asked sharply, "What's the meaning of this? What's going on here? Where's Frau Charim?"

"She is . . . unavailable. What do you want with her?"

"I came to pay a debt owing her." His voice was steady now, outraged. And Christa remembered the three thousand schillings cash he carried, which Josef had given him, and realized he had concocted an explanation for that; she herself must not speak.

"On whose behalf?"

"A friend who's an American newspaperman. He bought some merchandise from Frau Charim."

"What sort of merchandise?"

Lan licked his lips. "Pictures of a certain sort. He collects them."

"His name?"

211

"I'll not tell you that. Now, look here, I'm an American citizen and my wife's an Austrian citizen and we'll not have this. I don't know what's going on, but I want to telephone the American Legation and my wife's father, General Kurt Helmer, at once. I can assure you that there'll be trouble if—"

The dark-eyed man's voice snipped off his words coldly. "Your papers, please. Yours, too, *gnädige Frau*."

Christa found her courage. "First, I want an explanation—"

"Your papers," he said in a metallic voice.

"Give them to him," Lan said quietly, taking out his own.

"Search them, please," the dark-eyed man said to another, who was blond and lean. He did so, whistling softly as he pulled the three thousand schillings from Lan's billfold, then put it back. He touched Christa lightly, respectfully, and emptied the contents of her handbag, then replaced them and returned it to her. The dark-eyed man had put their identification papers and their passports in his pocket.

"Give me back my papers," Christa said angrily. "You have no right—"

"In due time," the dark-eyed man said. "Come in now." He pushed them through the curtain.

They were in a tiny squalid room containing a bed, a dresser with a mirror, and several large portrait photographs on the wall of a young dark girl in old-fashioned deep decolletage. There was one ancient tintype of a family—father and mother in black, several stiff, staring children, all unmistakably Jewish —on the dresser next to a brush containing a number of stiff gray hairs. The room smelled faintly of perfume and powder, but there was no sign of any woman.

"Where is Frau Charim?" Lan demanded.

"She is away," the dark-eyed man said. "Please. Make yourself comfortable. Would you like some tea?"

"To hell with tea! I demand to be allowed to telephone my legation!"

"In due time," the man said. "Now"—his voice roughened— "sit down and be quiet. Wolf, turn on the radio again."

Rage welled up in Christa, generated by fear, not so much for herself as for Lan. "Now listen here, I insist—"

"Madam, you may insist on nothing," the dark-eyed man said. *"Sit down!"*

"Christa," Lan said, "do as he says."

Furious and frightened, she dropped into the single chair by the dresser. Her hands were cold as ice. She could not comprehend this. Had something happened to Frau Charim and they were suspected? Had Hitler's men got to her first? Then the knowledge hit her, sure and sickening. *These were Hitler's men!* She glanced at Lan. He was pale, taut, but he tried to smile reassuringly. She knew, though, that the same realization had come to him.

And yet, she thought, calming slightly, we mustn't be afraid. They won't dare harm him, an American. And I'm his wife, under his protection. And when Papa learns of this . . .

The radio was on now, spilling music. Christa took out cigarettes, lit one, and then she smiled back at Lan. It was important to reassure him, to show him that she was not afraid either. "You gentlemen have certainly made a mistake you'll regret," she said quietly. "I hope you realize that."

Nobody answered. The dark-eyed man went out and a door closed behind him. The blond man and the other, who had a round red face, sat on the bed opposite Lan, watching him. The blond man had a revolver in his hand, though he did not point it at either of them. The news came on the radio: first an optimistic outburst about the prospects of an overwhelming government victory in the vote on Sunday, then other items completely ordinary and reassuring: "The Minister of Agriculture has refused a request from farmers for higher meat prices. This will keep the cost of food to its present low level. . . . Four passengers were slightly injured when a tram was derailed on the Wallensteinstrasse early this morning. . . . Now a lecture on the Austrian heritage from Herr Professor Doktor Anton Schönau."

"Dear Austrian friends and listeners. Today we discuss the condition of the Romans in Austria. As I am sure you all know, our beloved country was once the Roman province of Pannonia, the last barrier against the *barbarians* north of the Danube . . ."

Suddenly there was an interruption. *"Achtung, achtung!* Official announcement! All unmarried reservists of the class of 1915 with at least ten months' service will report immediately to their units for active duty. Repeat, all unmarried . . ."

The men on the bed stood up, looking at each other. "This

indicates no emergency," the voice went on. "The purpose of this call-up is to insure an orderly election on Sunday."

"*Scheisse*," one of the men said.

"We repeat, this indicates no emergency. We now return you to Dr. Anton Schönau."

"The Emperor Septimus Severus himself commanded at Carnuntum, headquarters of the Roman Seventh Legion . . . At that time Vienna was a fortified camp, known as Vindobona. It is presumed that its name came from the excellence of the wine produced from the vines introduced by the Romans to that part of Austria. . . ."

"Lan," Christa said, "you understand that if we're not home tonight, my father will take drastic measures—"

"You will not talk with one another," the blond man said. "Please be still."

"You can't stop me," Christa said. "If I want to talk to my husband . . ." The anger had risen in her now, and all caution had ebbed. "If I choose to—"

"My dear lady, we can't stop you. But we can take your husband elsewhere."

"Be quiet, Christa," Lan said heavily.

"But—"

"It's better if you're quiet."

The lecture droned on. Then there was an interlude of *Schrammelmusik*. Cheerful voices sang old songs: "Vienna Is Always Vienna," "My Mother Was a Viennese," "Out There in Grinzing" . . .

Time crawled by. I will not cry unless it will serve some purpose, Christa thought. But by midafternoon she broke down, whether purposefully or involuntarily she did not know. But she soon saw that it had no effect on anyone but Lan and choked it off.

The dark-eyed man returned, bringing with him a huge bag of sausage rolls, some pickles, and a *Doppler* of cheap wine. Although she'd had nothing since breakfast in the Wachau, Christa could barely force down a sandwich. An *Achtel* of wine went down more easily, calming her. The room was full of the feculent odor of the cheap cigarettes the three men smoked.

No one asked them even a single question. Later she and Lan

were taken, separately and under guard, down the hall to the toilet. The announcement about reservists had been repeated several times; then there was nothing but music on the radio. The dark-eyed man came in and went out repeatedly, as if he were very busy. Lan seemed perfectly calm, except for his chain-smoking. She knew that was a show for her benefit; inside he must be seething. But Papa, she thought. Papa will take care of everything.

And now it was dark outside. She and Lan were offered more sandwiches, but both refused. The blond man paced the little room impatiently. Bells tolled around the city; they could hear the Pummerin of St. Stephen's: vespers. Another couple of hours crawled by. Twice she tried to speak to Lan, each time she was cut off. Then the dark-eyed man ran back into the little room. He was grinning broadly, eyes shining, as he went to the radio, turned it up. "Listen!" he said. He faced Lan, then Christa, and there was triumph and relief in his voice. "Both of you listen!"

The radio was silent. Then a voice said, shakily, "Please stand by. Please stand by."

Another silence. Then: "Chancellor Dr. Kurt von Schuschnigg."

A pause. Then the voice that came from the speaker was one she recognized, though it trembled slightly now, lacking its former authoritarian certainty. No more now of the imitation-Hitler shouting, which had always sounded tinny.

She leaned forward, straining to catch every syllable.

"The German government has today handed to President Miklas an ultimatum with a time limit, requiring him to designate as chancellor a person designated by the German government. Otherwise German troops will invade Austria . . ."

"Hell," Lan whispered.

"I deny before the world," von Schuschnigg said, "the reports from Germany that the workers are in disorder, that the government has shed Austrian blood, that we are no longer in control of the situation. These are lies from A to Z. And at the request of President Miklas, I now tell the people of Austria that we have yielded to force, since we are not prepared even in this awful hour to shed German blood. We have ordered our troops to withdraw without resistance.

"And so"—he drew in a long, audible breath—"I take leave of the Austrian people with a German word of farewell and the single wish from the depths of my heart: *God save Austria!*"

For a moment the radio buzzed with a silence she would always remember as terrible and profound; suddenly it was broken by a ghostly voice remote from the microphone: "Long live Austria! Today I am ashamed to be a German!" Then there was an audible click as something was disconnected.

Christa wrestled with the significance of what she had heard. "Lan—"

"It's over," he said harshly. "Don't you understand? The Germans are coming in."

"Yes!" the dark-eyed man snapped. "That's absolutely right. It is settled now, after all these years." He turned to his companion, raised his arm. Almost reverently he shouted, "Heil Hitler!"

"*Heil!*" they shouted back. "*Sieg Heil!*" Then, faces glowing, they shook hands all around among themselves.

Lan Condon got stiffly to his feet. "All right," he said. "It's settled now. There'll be no war, right? You've won, you have nothing to fear from us. Will you please give us back our documents? I suggest you take us to the American Legation at once."

The three men looked at him as if seeing him for the first time, and slowly the dark-eyed man nodded. "Yes," he said. "It's time for us to go now. Please, madam—" He took Christa's hand and helped her up.

She was numb and dazed. She felt as if the world had collapsed around her. "Are you going to take us home now? You had better take us home."

"Please come with us," the dark-eyed man said. He took Lan by one arm, and the blond man took her. They were kept far apart as they were led down the stairs. Outside on the deserted street a black Mercedes was parked, a driver behind the wheel. They were shoved into the rear, and the dark-eyed man got in beside them, the blond one in the front. Lan put his arm around her. "Don't worry," he said.

She leaned against him desperately. Her hand squeezed his thigh; she was not only seeking reassurance but giving it. Together they were stronger than either separately. Divided, anything could happen; united, they could overcome every challenge.

The streets of the Leopoldstadt reeled by. Lan said, "This isn't the way—"

"Be quiet, Mr. Condon," the dark-eyed man said, speaking English for the first time. Christa was startled. Somehow that made him seem far more sinister.

They rolled on through streets suddenly packed with jubilant people. Swastikas had appeared by magic, hanging from windows along the way. A brass band marched along a sidewalk playing the "Horst Wessel Lied." The car turned into a parking lot. Christa sat up straight, recognizing the massive bulk of the East Station. "What—?"

The driver parked the car. "Get out," the dark-eyed man ordered. The blond man seized Christa, and the dark-eyed man locked his hand around Lan's arm. His other hand was in his pocket. "Come with us."

They entered the great echoing station. It was bedlam, jammed with people. The man shoved ruthlessly through the crowd, dragging Lan and Christa. Somebody shrieked, "But I must get to Prague! Don't you understand? Who has a ticket? I'll pay any price for a ticket! Who'll sell me a ticket to Prague?" Desperate faces swirled around Christa, faces contorted with the rat's expression of self-preservation. Hands clawed at her. "*Gnäd-ige Frau,* have you a ticket to sell?"

The dark-eyed man hit a clawing gray-haired man across the face. "Get away!" he shouted.

They were dragged through to a concourse where a train waited, and now they had an escort of police, hard-rubber clubs raised. They reached a third-class carriage. Lan jerked his arm free. "I demand—!" he roared. The dark-eyed man seized him, pulled out his gun and shoved it in his belly. Somehow, even in the echoing uproar, Christa heard every word distinctly.

He spoke in English. "You demand nothing, Mr. Condon. You are not going home nor to the American Legation. You have been declared *persona non grata* by the Austrian government, by Dr. Seyss-Inquart, Minister of Interior and Police, and now to be the Chancellor of Austria. The decision was made personally by him. If you do not resist, you will not be harmed. If you have representations to make to your government, they can be made in Prague as well as here."

"Prague!" Lan flared.

"You are being expelled, Mr. Condon, to Czechoslovakia.

You..." The piping of the train whistle, a blast of steam, drowned the rest.

She saw Lan tense, go pale. She tried to lunge toward him, and the blond man jerked her back. Two policemen seized him by the arms, shoved him toward the steps of the nearest car. The train piped again. Lan grabbed a handrail, twisted his head, tried to turn to look at her.

She fought the blond man. He locked an arm around her neck. The dark-eyed man shoved Lan into the car and followed. A crowd surged in after him, like dirt into a vacuum cleaner, and he was lost from view.

"Lan!" she screamed, and she kicked the blond man in the shins. He might as well have been made of marble, his arms around her were like bands of iron. The train screamed again. People clung to the sides of cars, then fell away as it picked up speed, moving from the station. Christa shrieked, "I want my husband! Let me go with him! Let me...Let me...!" But now, in a rush of steam and smoke and a final blast of whistle, the train was gone.

A great collective sigh of disappointment filled the huge hall as the train rushed out into the night. "Lan," Christa whispered, and she sagged back against the blond man.

His hands brushed her breasts insolently. Then he took her arm. "He is gone. It will do you no good to create a disturbance. Come with me. You belong here. He is American, but you are not."

She hardly heard. She only stared into darkness, head craning at the emptiness along the track, as he led her roughly back toward the car.

BOOK TWO
The Golden Pheasants
1938–1941

1 HE DID NOT EVEN HAVE A CHANCE to kiss her, touch her. He could still see her standing there, face pale, stricken, as the man with the gun shoved him toward the train. He heard her scream. Then they were in the carriage, jostled by the crowd that fought for every inch of space; he turned to look, but a fat woman's head blocked the window. Suddenly the train lurched and began to roll.

Despite the mob, they had a compartment to themselves, blinds drawn, door locked. The man with the gun sat across from him, refusing to speak or let Lan speak. Totally alert, he gave Condon no chance to jump him or take the gun. In a couple of hours they reached the Czech border; and there it was Judgment Day, the Austrian and Czech officials like avenging angels separating the saved from the damned. The lucky ones were allowed to enter Czechoslovakia; the doomed ones, shouting and protesting, crying and struggling, or accepting their fate in stunned silence, were forced back to Austria. Once in Czechoslovakia, the man with the gun rose, speaking for the first time. "Goodbye, Mr. Condon. For your sake and your wife's, do not try to enter Austria again, ever." He went out, leaving Lan to deal with the Czech officials alone.

His American passport cleared him quickly. And by now he knew what he would do. He would go on to Prague, work from there, and, by God, he would turn the American Legation upside down to get Christa out. But, in the meantime, what would they do with her? Arrest, a concentration camp...? God damn Josef Steiner! God damn himself for playing cat's paw in such a hare-brained scheme! Then relieved, exultant people were jamming his compartment; the Czech stationmaster saluted from beside the tracks, and the train rolled on.

After two hours of competing with other desperate people at the great gray railroad station, he found a cab to take him to the American Legation. It was a madhouse, swarming with Austrians with American relatives or connections. A weary clerk listened to him for thirty seconds, checked his documents, told him to find a hotel and come back tomorrow. Two hours later he was in a clean, cheap pension where everyone spoke German, and then reaction hit him. In shock and exhaustion, he simply passed out, fully clad, on the bed.

Mercifully, his memory of the next two weeks was fragmentary. He finally got an interview at the Legation; they promised to do whatever possible to learn Christa's fate, secure an exit permit for her. He haunted the place every day, but it was like beating his head against a wall; nothing was ever done.

Frantically Lan tried to get through by telephone to the Christina Hof or their apartment in Vienna; it was hopeless. But finally the operator reached the Cafe Louvre, and something unclenched within him as he heard Mark Gorton's voice: "Yes, I heard about it. Christa seems to be all right for now. She's at her father's house in the country. I know that much at least."

A few seconds passed before Lan could speak. "You're sure? Not in a *KZ-Lager*?"

"No, I'm certain she's safe and well. Look, where are you staying?"

Lan gave him the name and address of the pension.

"Don't leave for another two weeks at least. That's all I can say just now. I'll be in touch, but I suggest you not phone again. And for God's sake, don't try to phone her. Don't worry. Maybe I can do something. Goodbye, Lan."

"Mark, wait—"

"Goodbye," Mark said firmly and hung up.

Ten days later Gorton was in Prague. They met in a coffee-house near the old City Hall.

"First," Mark said, "here's a letter for you." He handed Lan an envelope, smiled. "Nature calls," he said and discreetly vanished. Lan's hands shook so that he could hardly get the flap unsealed.

My darling [she had written]. *I love you, love you, a hundred times, a thousand, much more. I am well and so is everyone. They brought me from the station to the Christina Hof, but then they arrested Papa. However, he was released, and he and Robert say that we have nothing more to fear if we are careful and correct.*

You must not write me directly or try to call; as things are now, it is too dangerous. When our friend told me that you were safe and well in Prague, I cried, and then I lit several candles at the Stift in gratitude.

Papa and our friend both say, please, don't do anything on our behalf just now, it could be dangerous. We must wait and see what happens and be very careful meanwhile.

It is terrible, not having you here. I am lonely all the time. The bed is so enormous and empty without you to lie against. But we must manage somehow for a while. All at the Christina Hof are well, except poor Aunt Alma, who is very sick. We really have no hope for her. I'm doing my best to take her place, but it is very hard, as you know what kind of housekeeper I am. I work from morning to night, and that is good because it leaves less time to think.

We must only be patient and love each other very much until we are again together. I love you another thousand times and more. Your C.

Below, there was a lipstick print, firm, red, vivid, open-mouthed.

"Mark, I don't know how to thank you," Lan said when Gorton returned.

"Don't bother. You've supplied me with enough inside stuff for me to be in your debt. Besides, I'd do anything to confound those bastards. Now listen. My days in Austria are pretty well numbered. I'm bound to be expelled soon; but as long as I can, I'll serve as go-between. I don't know why all this happened, but I suppose it had to do with the information you were feeding to the Louvre. Anyhow, here's what I can do."

He sipped his coffee. "I've a good friend in the British Ministry here in Prague and another one in ours in Vienna. Here's the Prague man's name and address. Take your letters to Christa to him, and they'll go to Vienna by diplomatic pouch, where I'll pick them up and dispatch hers to you. You can be as frank in those letters as you care to; no one else will see them. But for God's sake, don't try to write by ordinary mail or call her. It's a damned sure bet the Helmer's mail and phone are monitored by the Gestapo. And the way things are down there, nobody knows what will set them off. But as long as you're in Prague and I'm still in Vienna, you'll have mail once a week. All right?"

"All right? My God . . . Mark, you've seen her?"

"We met at the Stift. She looked pale and rather thin, but fine otherwise. She'd had a rough time for a while, though. Those Gestapo agents who picked you up . . . They had them salted all through Vienna, and the minute Schuschnigg capitulated, they went into action. After they put you on the train, they took Christa back to the Christina Hof and in the same swoop arrested General Helmer. They kept him for some time and then released him, mostly, I understand, through the intervention of a man named Robert Schellhammer. Now he's back in the Ferntal, operating as usual. But, without knowing precisely what the bunch of you were up to, it must have been a very close thing."

Gorton's eyes were sad and angry. "Here's the big picture of what happened. Hitler knew the Austrians would vote overwhelmingly against him in the plebiscite, and he didn't dare let that happen. So on Friday, the day you had all your troubles, he issued an ultimatum: Schuschnigg was to resign in favor of Seyss-Inquart, who was to form an Austrian Nazi government. At first Schuschnigg resisted. He sought help from France, Britain, Italy. And everybody waffled; nobody would move. So it boiled down to Austria fighting alone."

Mark's voice was bitter. "Von Schuschnigg had five thousand troops on the frontier against the whole German Army; he might have, in a week, raised another twenty-five thousand, but he didn't have a week. His air force consisted of perhaps thirty planes; and as for armor, he had exactly two serviceable tanks. He couldn't bring himself to see Austrians—or Germans for that matter—slaughtered hopelessly, so he yielded."

Mark's voice roughened. "And yet I blame him for not fighting. Austrians would have made a stand if he'd given them the chance. And any show of resistance might have forced France and England to act decisively. But he simply caved in." Mark sighed. "Did you hear that strange voice after his final speech, off microphone? *Long live Austria! Today I am ashamed to be a German!* That was old Baron Hammerstein-Equord, Minister of Culture. He was there when Schuschnigg spoke; sick, on crutches. But Schuschnigg's surrender was too much for him. He staggered up and yelled his battle cry before they could turn off the microphone. I suppose it's earned him a berth in a concentration camp."

He spread his hands. "You've read the Prague papers, the London *Times,* the Paris *Herald.* It was ... Walpurgisnacht. I thought I knew the Viennese, the Austrians. I lived there by choice for nearly twenty years, because they were the finest, the most graceful people I'd ever encountered. Well, I suppose every city has its mob, its scum, but— My God, little children, women, old men—the Jews—harassed like hares before the hounds. Unspeakably abused, humiliated in public, made to dance and jig, scrub the Schuschnigg slogans off the walls and sidewalks, spat on and beaten, robbed and evicted ... And decent people not daring to cry shame because of fear. I've fought for and believed in the common man. But seeing the common man in action then was enough to make you puke. It really makes you fear for democracy. Maybe it all comes down to leadership. If the leadership enforces decency, people are decent; if it gives them free rein, they become animals. Maybe civilization is really only fear of being punished. I tell you, I've got rethinking to do. I always thought the people unleashed would be a force for good, but ... ."

He shook his head. "Never mind. But to get back to the Helmers. Temporarily, they've squirmed free and are safe, but nobody is really safe from one day to the next. You must be very careful not to rock their boat. For the time being, there's no hope of Christa getting out or you back in. And if you try to force things, there could be real trouble."

Lan nodded.

"For the time being, work through me. Maybe things will get better by and by."

"Yeah," Lan said. "Mark, thanks again—"

"*F'Gornix,*" Mark said in Viennese dialect. "For nothing. Now, go write a letter and I'll take it back with me. Meanwhile, I've got to see my stringers here." They shook hands, and Gorton left. Later Lan stood on the Charles Bridge, with its strange tortured statues, over the Vltava and read and reread the letter. Then he climbed Castle Hill and in the Cathedral of St. Vitus lit candles.

He stayed in Prague and traded the letters as Mark had arranged for another month. Then, as predicted, Mark himself was expelled. "I'm sorry, old chap," he told Lan. "But now that Hitler's had his own plebiscite and got nearly a hundred per cent *Ja* vote, they're even more firmly in the saddle and I'm *persona non grata*. However, all is not lost. I've made inquiries and pulled strings. I still wouldn't call her, but it should be fairly safe for the two of you to write to each other directly now if—"

"If—?"

"If you keep your letters innocuous. You shouldn't—and I've told her this—put in anything that will embarrass the Helmers. Nothing about any plans to get her out, no criticism of the regime. She mustn't write you about her desire to leave, and she ought to lard her letters about how well everything is going, how everyone's so happy that even the birds sing the 'Horst Wessel Lied.' Put in all the passion you've a mind to, but no indication that you bear any resentment against the Third Reich. Understand?"

"Right. But . . . You're sure I can't call her?"

Mark looked at him, then grinned. "Obviously you will, anyhow. But if you do, watch what you say. A letter can be reviewed and edited until its harmless, but on the phone even a casual remark could be used against her or the General. If she so much as says, 'I wish I were there with you' . . . Understand?"

"Yes," Lan said glumly.

"See here," Mark said. "I know a little bit more about what you were up to than I did before. I had a rumor from a friend of Josef Steiner's; and, Lan, you were dealing in dynamite."

"Where is Josef?"

"Who knows? He's vanished and his property's been confiscated. Anyhow, if what I've heard is true, it makes things more explicable. If you'd been Austrian, both of you would have been killed out of hand. But since you were American and the situation was still in doubt, they didn't dare that. So they expelled you, and they kept Christa as hostage, insurance that you wouldn't spread any ugly rumors about their noble leader once you were in the clear. As long as they've got her, you don't dare talk. On the other hand, you're *her* insurance. If they hurt her and you find out, you *will* talk. So it's a stalemate. You keep silent, she'll be fine. But they're certainly not going to release her and free you to spill the beans. Incidentally, a special Gestapo team currycombed Vienna immediately after the *Anschluss* and picked up anybody and everybody who might remember anything about Hitler's Vienna period. Most have simply disappeared without a trace. You can thank your American passport for saving you and Christa, but sleeping dogs must be let lie."

"You're saying I'll never get her back."

"*Never* is a long word. I'm saying that for now the two of you must play your cards very close to your chest, be discreet." His face relaxed a little. "He won't last forever, Lan. The ice he skates on is always thin. Sooner or later he'll be tripped up. All you can do is wait."

Mark and Marietta had then left for England. Lan remained in Prague, double-checking the possibility of getting Christa out, but with no success. For her Austria was a dungeon, locked and guarded. Prague crawled with shady characters guaranteeing to smuggle out anyone if the price was right, but he backed away from them. That was no solution, even if they could have been trusted. As she was hostage for his silence, Ernst and Helmer were hostages for her good behavior; to spirit her out illegally would destroy them.

Twice, despite Mark's warning, he called her. "*Du!*" Her voice broke when she heard his. "*Du!* Oh, God—"

"Listen. I know you are very happy there. And I'm well here in Prague. But I had to call to say how much I love you."

"And, oh, I love you, my darling. . . ." They exchanged endearments for minutes. For Lan—it would be the same for her —it was like water falling on a thirsty plain. Then she said, "Oh, I do miss you."

A kind of warning bell rang in his head. "Of course you do. But we must accept reality. Do you understand? Do you see what I'm driving at?"

As if to emphasize his words, there was a faint, amorphous disturbance on the line. There was a pause before Christa answered in a different voice. "Yes, of course I understand, and you are exactly right. And naturally we are all well and happy here. Everything is quite exciting, and we are proud of being German." Another pause. "If you see your friend Sweeney, be sure to tell him that."

Lan blinked, then grinned. A fragment of American slang, already obsolete; he had picked it up riding freight trains. Must have used it in her presence and explained it—*Tell it to Sweeney,* and that meant *bullshit!* He was surprised she had remembered. "Oh, I will," he said.

"Good. Lan, darling, I love you so much—" and then the connection was broken and the Prague operator could not restore it.

That was the first time; the second, they had hardly said hello to one another before the line went dead. A chill walked down his spine; this was too dangerous a game. He never called again, but every day he wrote her. Without the freedom of the diplomatic pouch, though, the letters were only affirmations, not communications. *I love you. The weather is good/bad/terrible.* And from her the same, plus shameless propaganda as insurance. *Things are much better now; everybody has work. My darling, I think of you all night long. Do you remember . . . ?* All they could do was rehash harmless memories, relive what happiness they had known. It was better than nothing, and it was also agony. So was the knowledge that they were separated only by a few hours' travel. But she might as well have been on the moon.

As the summer dwindled, history began to repeat itself with appalling inexorability. Obviously Hitler intended to rebuild the whole former Habsburg Empire—Austria first, now Czechoslovakia with all its heavy industry. By the time autumn turned the lovely old city of Prague and its rolling countryside into burnished bronze, he knew he must get out.

"You won't," he wrote, "hear from me for several weeks. I'm going back to America. Write me in care of Matthews . . ."

He fled from Prague just in time and took a ship from Belgium. He paused only briefly in New York; with the book still unwritten, he could not face his publisher. Looking at America from the window of a westbound Pullman, it seemed as if the whole country was drying up, blowing away. A dust storm slowed them in Oklahoma; all through the Midwest he saw whole families in rickety Fords and Chevies with everything they owned: refugees, like himself, bound for California. Out there, someone told him, they called them Okies.

Matthews, his agent, was a tall, still-handsome man in his sixties who chose his clients as a father might choose a child for adoption, and thereafter remained unshakably loyal—as long as they produced. Professionally sympathetic, he listened to Lan's story. "So the book isn't finished. And you want the studio to take you back?"

"They've got to. Matt, I've got to have some money. I left five thousand in the Swiss account in case she needs it in a hurry, but otherwise I'm broke. And if things change, if I can get the cash, maybe I can buy her out."

"Yeah." The agent nodded. "A lot of people are doing that. There's a regular trade in Jews now. Only—"

"Only what?"

"I'll find you something. But Lan, you've got to understand. It won't be like it was before. Austria's not the only place where you're on a blacklist. Hitler's not the only dictator who can make or break you."

"But they know what I can do."

"What you and Ross could do. But Ross is gone now. They also know you had a contract and you broke it. I had a hell of a time blocking a lawsuit. You promised them the film rights to your book, and now you have no book. So you're starting from behind the line. Pride will be something you can't afford. You might as well know now, they'll make you eat a lot of crow before they take you back."

Lan stared at him, then nodded. "All right. I'll eat shit if that's what they want. God damn it, Matt, I'll do anything that might help me get Christa back. Crawl on my belly, lick their boots. They don't count. She does." He rose, paced the room. "Look, with my firsthand experience, I could give 'em an anti-Nazi script that would knock their eyes out."

"Are you kidding? Forget it."

"Forget—?"

"They wouldn't touch it with a ten-foot pole. Not even when their own relatives are disappearing or being held for ransom. Germany's still a primary market, it represents a lot of money. Chaplin's the only one who's dared to make an anti-Nazi picture, but he's big enough to get away with it. The rest don't dare; and even if they did, the Hays Office wouldn't approve a script. We're neutral and we stay that way. So don't even mention it."

Lan stared at him. "You mean they don't care? Nobody out here cares?"

"A lot of people care. But the money's the first consideration. There's an old saying, Lan: *Don't eat where you shit and—*"

"*Don't shit where you eat.*" Condon drew in breath. "Yeah, I've heard that before."

"The first law of the jungle." Matthews stood up. "Don't worry. We'll work it out. Just be patient, and I'll be in touch. Where're you staying?"

Lan told him and Matthews grimaced. "Can't you do better than that? Look, would five hundred help? I could go five hundred."

"We'll wait and see. If you'll just hurry and I can get back to work, I can manage."

"I'll do my best. Just hang on." He knuckled Lan's shoulder. Then: "Oh, yeah, Lan. Phyll O'Donnell."

It was a name he had not wanted to mention, and he had hoped he would get out of there without hearing it. "What about her?"

"She's still around, you know. Went East for a little while after Ross . . . But she's back and I still hear from her, wanting news of you. I've played dumb, by and large, but I did tell her that you were married. It seemed to hit her pretty hard."

"Yeah," Lan said.

"She's still got the house—Ross had lots of insurance—and she's picked up a few parts here and there, character stuff. And . . . she hasn't given up on you."

"That's her problem."

Matthews turned away, toying with a paperweight on his desk. "Well, it hit her pretty hard. Ross . . . and then you running out. I'm not making excuses for her—"

"There's no way to make excuses for either one of us," Lan said tautly. "You know that, Matt. What happened is something we both had to get over the best way we could. I have, and I've got other things on my mind. If she hasn't, I'm sorry. But all that's done and finished and I'm not dragging it back up. My one concern is for my wife. Maybe it sounds like a line from a lousy script, but I happen to love her."

"Sure. Well, you're my client and you're both my friends, but I'm out of it, except to pass on the warning, or tip, or whatever. One way or the other, she'll know you're back." Then Matthews shrugged. "Never mind. You sit loose and phone me tomorrow late, after I've had time to nose around." He put out his hand. "Lan, I'm glad you've come back to the fold."

2 BEGRUDGING EVERY SECOND of the long drive to Willi Orlik's house in Brentwood, he pushed the rickety Graham-Paige as hard as it would go. Five minutes now, maybe eight, he thought. All right. You've waited nearly a year and a half; you can hold out that long. But, damn it, why couldn't he have told me on the phone?

Obviously the news Willi had brought back from Switzerland was not all good. But maybe, he told himself, it was not all bad either. Hell, it couldn't be. Twenty-five thousand, a fortune in hard American dollars; surely they wouldn't turn that down. So maybe they wanted even more; all right, he could raise another five, even ten, somewhere, somehow. But it must be fast. He had to get her out before there was war. And there would be one this time. Hitler had got Austria without a fight, been handed Czechoslovakia, and had swallowed Memel and other bits and pieces without opposition. But both France and England had pledged to fight for Poland, and if Germany did not draw back . . . Well, August 1939 was not March 1938.

The car's valves chattered as he swung around a truck. Anyhow, he thought, there will be a decision. At least I won't be living in limbo any longer. Because I can't go on like this. And if it's like this for me, what's it like for her?

Condon parked behind a wood-paneled station wagon in Willi Orlik's drive and got out. The August heat boiled sweat from him as he stood by the car for a moment, bracing himself for whatever lay ahead. Willi had made no promises except to do the best he could. Now the verdict was in and it must be accepted. Lan's mouth was dry, his heart hammering, as he strode up the drive.

Matt had got him a job, all right, and Matt had been correct: he'd had to crawl for it, cower meekly before all the little dictators at the studio, hating it, but reminding himself that it was for Christa, that on her behalf he could endure anything. Six months at five hundred a week, half his former salary, but it would do. He would not be living in the old way, no four-hundred-a-month bungalow at the Garden of Allah, no high-stakes poker games, no expensive starlet tarts. He could live on five hundred a month if he was careful and save the other fifteen hundred. That, plus the reserve in Switzerland, might do it.

Willi had been hopeful. "It's possible. Hell, they're nothing but a band of kidnappers. Bruno Hauptmann came by it naturally."

"Do you know how to do it?"

"I've brought out three cousins already. It's not really complicated. The Nazis want hard currency; that's mostly what's behind the whole Jewish business. Force 'em out, confiscate their estates, demand ransom from their relatives. And it works that way for *goyim*, too. I've helped a couple already. But it's a delicate business.

"What you need to do," he went on, "is put, say, twenty thousand dollars in a Swiss account over which she's got authority."

"There's one already set up."

"Fine. Anyhow, she applies for an exit visa. When she does that, she has to list all her assets, so she puts down that twenty thousand. But since it's in Switzerland, they can't touch it without a release from her. Usually, in return for signing over an account of that size, they'll issue the exit permit. That leaves her broke, of course, but that's part of their game, too. You pay for her passage in hard money, and they collect a little extra. It depends on how badly they want to keep her, but usually twenty thousand will buy almost anybody out."

"Her father could put up twenty thousand right away."

"No good. Him they've already got; they can take everything he has any time they want to. No, this has to be extra. That's what makes the deal attractive to them. Anyhow, once the cash is there, she proceeds either through the Swedes or Quakers, who've set up special offices to help people emigrate; or I can work it for her through the IKG—Israelitischen Kultusgemeinde, the organization the Nazis have designated to be responsible for governing the Jews in Austria. The IKG is really cleverer and more efficient. You see, there are lots of forces working to help the Jews. Gentiles are a stickier matter. Nobody really seems to care about them. You say the State Department won't help—"

"Got nowhere with them. Nowhere. Everything they try hits a blank wall."

"It's the money. They won't let her go unless they make a profit. Look, you get the money up, and the next time I go to Switzerland—"

"I'll have it," Lan said. "Somehow."

And he had raised it—scrimping, saving, and currying favor with the studio, regaining lost ground. No more arguing in script conferences, no more foolishness about art. He knew what they wanted, liked, and he gave it to them, grinding it out quickly and professionally, as a butcher grinds out sausage. His option had been picked up for a hundred a week more, and he saved every cent of that, too. He worked on scripts at night, too, alone in his apartment, to keep from going crazy. But it was impossible to forget. Unbidden memories would harass him: the sunlight on green hills, the sound of bells across a valley, the thunder of an overture at the Opera ... He remembered the old woman they had met one day while walking on a country road, who had kissed them both and given each a rose from her garden, because they were so young and happy. Remembered the pink and white angel-food-cake aspect of Vienna at sunset; the smell of lilacs in the spring; rooks circling the crumbling tower of a ruined castle; and an elderly couple, faces seamed and withered, both lame with arthritis, who ran a *Heuriger* in the Wienerwald and, when they thought no one was looking, held hands or rubbed their cheeks together. *I would like for us to love one another that much when we are old*, Christa had said. *Aren't they like a pair of monuments, built to honor love?*

233

When Lan had the money, he gave it to Willi, and Willi had been to Switzerland, and . . . He strode on toward the big white house. But Willi's voice came from one side. "Hello, Lan. This way!"

Condon turned. Willi rose from a chair beside the swimming pool. Seeing weariness in Orlik's thin, pale torso and haggard eyes, Condon knew.

"Lan," Willi said bluntly as they shook hands, "I'm sorry. It's impossible."

"Willi," said Lan desperately, "you don't mean that."

"I do, and I won't keep you on the string. Here, have a drink." He poured a martini from a shaker as he spoke. "She's one of the impossibles. The kind there is no price on. Believe me, I explored every avenue, but nothing worked. Finally I understood that I might actually be putting her in danger and I had to draw back. But a travel ban's been imposed on her and her whole family from the beginning. You might as well face it. They are not going to let her out of Austria for any reason whatsoever. Not alive."

Lan drank the whole martini in two swallows, not even feeling the burn of gin. "Why didn't you tell me that?" he whispered. "On the phone? Why did you—?"

"Put you through the extra hell?" Willi's face was regretful, grave. "Because what I had to say is not what a man should hear alone in such a grubby place as yours. He should hear it with a friend at hand. Lan, I brought out seven people on this trip. I did every turn I knew. But they will not let Christa go." He shook his head. "F.D.R. himself couldn't get her. She's in a special category. I brought back your draft for the twenty thousand; it's in the house. I'll give it to you before you go."

"I don't care about the money," Lan said numbly. His throat was clogged; tears burned in his eyes. "All I care about is— Damn it, Willi, they can't do this! They can't do this to me and her!"

"They can do anything they want to," said Orlik quietly.

"Then I'll go back! I'll get in somehow and I'll—"

"Get yourself killed. They'd rub you out in a minute and make it look like an accident. Besides, you couldn't get there before war breaks out. There's going to be one this time, you know; everybody in Europe says so. He can't get away with taking

Poland, nonaggression treaty with the Russians or no. It's only a matter of days until the balloon goes up. And with wartime security in force, you'd have even less of a chance."

Lan stared at the shimmering abstract refraction of sunlight on the pool. "Oh, Christ," he said thinly; in the two words were all the despair he felt.

"I know," Willi murmured. "But look at it this way. If there is war, it can't last forever. Sooner or later it will end—and they can't win, not even with Italy on their side. So when it's over, maybe in a year or two—"

"A year or two," Lan said. "It's already been so long."

"But it can be borne if you stay busy. Somehow you can bear it." He gripped Lan's arm. "Yes, old friend, it's bitter medicine to swallow. And you must stay with us now, today, and we'll talk about it. I'll tell you everything I know, and I made a special effort to get the news. Lan, please. Sit down and have another drink and we will talk. . . ."

He had a lot of drinks with Willi, and more when he got home, sitting there at the table in his apartment, the letters, every one she'd written, in an untidy pile before him. He reread the latest:

The wine harvest will be very good this year. You must tell Sweeney how much Ernst enjoys the Hitler Youth. But for us only is my secret. I too have written a book—but only in my mind. At night before I go to sleep, I always read a chapter. There's a Jochberg chapter, and a Graz chapter, and many more . . .

It was a shorthand way of communicating passion: Jochberg in the Tyrol, Graz, the capital of Styria—these had been the erotic peaks of their honeymoon.

He picked up the other letters. They were all cut to a pattern. A paragraph of love, a paragraph of praise for the Third Reich, another one of innocuous news, and a final one of hinted private desire. No change, every one the same.

Suddenly he knocked them all fluttering to the floor. He had failed her. She had counted on him and now he had failed and what was he to tell her; how could he write her, go on scribbling

235

banalities, torturing himself and her, when there was no hope?

He poured another drink, blurred visions tormenting him. Jochberg, Graz, all that passion, that desire—and it still gnawed at her as it gnawed at him. But he found occasional relief at least; twenty minutes with a cheap paid girl would purge him temporarily. But Christa had a carnal appetite matching his. And now how did she manage it? She was not in jail, not in a vacuum either. There were other men around her. Maybe she had waited this long, but for another year, two, three? Impossible! He could not ask it or expect it! Yet the thought of her with someone else — He had a quick obscene image of Robert Schellhammer lying between his wife's spread thighs, pumping hard . . . He groaned, and raw alcohol welled up nauseatingly in his throat. No, he told himself, he would not wait! Let there be a war! Good, then he would go to Canada or England and join it. He would kill Germans, Austrians if it came to that, fighting his way back to her with a gun! He would— He whirled as someone knocked on the apartment door. He blinked, cocked his head. The knock came again.

He cleared his throat. "Who is it?"

A woman's voice said, "Phyllis."

Condon stood motionless. She knocked again. "Lan?"

Heavily he lumbered to the door. As soon as it was open just enough, she pushed through. Several paces into the room she halted, facing him, a slender figure in trim black, dark hair falling to her shoulders in a gleaming pageboy. Uncertainly, she removed her sunglasses. She had never been a great beauty, her features too uneven for that perfection required for stardom, but she had always possessed something better than that: a magnetism that drew men. Now, at thirty-nine, she looked her age, and Lan, fogged by alcohol, waited to feel something, but no reaction came at all.

"Hello." There was uncertainty in her voice. "It's been a long time, hasn't it?"

"Phyll—"

"Oh, I've kept track of you. I know all about it, everything. What Willi was trying, and when I heard that he was back, I called him and he told me. And I made up my mind—this didn't seem precisely the time for you to be alone. Willi thought not, too. Besides, there are some things I want to say."

236

"No. I don't want to talk about it. We made a mistake and—"

"Mistake?" Her brows went up. "It wasn't any mistake. It was what he wanted. He set us up, Lan, and did it beautifully."

"You're not talking sense," he mumbled.

"You think not? Friend, we were *had*. In the dirtiest way possible by that dear sweet man who was everybody's friend and wouldn't hurt a fly. Your Ross and mine and everybody's. Only the truth is, Lan, there wasn't just one Ross O'Donnell, or maybe there wasn't any Ross at all. Maybe what there really was was just a bag full of psychological broken glass. I know. It took me a long time to figure it out. But now I understand. It was what he wanted, Lan, and he maneuvered us into giving it to him—the excuse he needed to kill himself."

"Oh, for God's sake, Phyll—"

"Yes. He had a death wish a mile wide—always guilty about something, punishing himself, inching toward it. That's why he drank too much, smoked too much, gambled and always lost, and threw away a fine career as a playwright to do crap for the studio. I don't know where it came from, it was there when we first met; maybe it was part of the attraction. He was young and slim and it was all romantic then—the beautiful and the damned. But it's not romantic when you get past forty and you're not beautiful and you've made all the wrong turns. Anyhow, he was Catholic, and that kept balking him. He didn't have the guts to do it by his own choice, free will. He had to be pushed into it, have an excuse so shattering and overwhelming that it justified it—and that's where you and I came in."

She paused, looking at him intently. "Looking back, I can see where he tried and failed with at least two others before you. Pimping for them—maybe unconsciously. Only I wouldn't go along. Back then I believed in love and marriage vows, and I tried to play it straight. Then you came along, and you were the answer to his prayer. You struck the chord in me the others never did. More important, you struck it in him, too. He loved you, he really did, and so in that poor drink-and-guilt-fogged brain of his, it made perfect sense. Do you understand?"

It was penetrating now. "Go on," he said.

"Another neat little tactic," she said bitterly. "One you never knew about. Before *it* happened, he hadn't laid a finger on me sexually in months. No explanation, no reason that I could see,

237

just left me to stew in my own juice. And..." She shrugged. "Finally it worked. I can see now that when he went East he was counting on it. And it was no accident that he came home early; it was on purpose, if only subconsciously. And there we were... and now he could do it."

For the first time, her voice broke. "W-when I got all this w-worked out, I thought, My God, how he must have hated us. And t-then I saw that he couldn't have, he had to l-love us or it wouldn't have worked. And it made it even worse to know that." She went to the bottle and the glass on the table, helped herself with a hand that shook. "So there it is. Believe it or not, that's what happened."

Lan rubbed his face. The truth of it struck even through the drunkenness. He turned away.

"Anyhow, you need somebody now," she said. "Will you come to Willi's with me?"

"No. Just leave me alone."

Her voice was soft. "Is there no hope, really?"

"Willi says not. It depends on if there's a war."

"Maybe there won't be a war."

He switched on the little radio on the table. The voice of H. V. Kaltenborn, strained and tense, said: "The Polish government has rejected..." Lan clicked it off. "There'll be a war." He took a swallow from the bottle, gagged.

"I think I'd better make some coffee," Phyllis said. She put down her bag and started toward the kitchen.

"No," he grunted.

She turned. "What do you want, then?"

He shook his head. He wanted her to leave, yet now dreaded being left alone. "I don't know," he mumbled.

Phyllis shrugged. "In that case, I'll make some coffee."

He no longer protested. It was a good feeling to have someone taking care of him again—and a better one to have another person in bed with him that night.

238

3 WAR OR NO WAR, the grapes would not wait; the
Weinlese—the harvest—must go on. The invasion of
Poland and the reaction of France and England had all come
so quickly that everything had been thrown into turmoil. Just
when needed most, workers who were in the military reserves
were called to duty, and inexperienced Hitler Youth laboring
on the land could not fill the gap. Now the *Weinlese* was simply
one knotty problem after another, everyone doing double duty
seven days a week from dawn to dusk. Vineyards swarmed with
pickers lugging huge wooden pails strapped to their backs, big
wagons rumbled into the courtyard piled high with grapes to be
cleaned and sent to the press, manned now by inexperienced
youngsters; and the General had driven himself furiously, from
first light till last. Even Ernst had been out among the vines,
and for Christa there was no rest either, with hordes of people
to be fed, cleaned up after, and some of them quartered at
the *Hof* as well.

Tonight it was after nine before she had a chance to rest.
Exhausted as she was, there was no possibility yet of sleep, and
so she bathed, changed clothes, and savored the luxury of being
alone with a glass of wine on the terrace. Above the Wienerwald
the moon was high and rich, a hammered blob of silver; a couple
of bats swooped and darted over the lawn. In the house only
Mitzi and Traudi were still awake. Christa sighed, leaning back
in her chair, kicking off her shoes.

How, she wondered, had Aunt Alma done it, old and crippled
as she was? Even after more than a year of filling her shoes,
managing the household still stretched Christa to the limit.
Which was a blessing, she supposed, for it left her no time for
grieving or remembering.

The recollection of that dreadful night had softened a little;
its outlines were no longer so brutally sharp and gouging. Still,
sometimes it rushed back unbidden, vivid, agonizing, and she
could hear again the piping of the whistle, feel the iron grip
clamp her arm as Lan was hustled through the crowd. She remembered screaming, fighting. Then . . . She had never fainted in
her life before, but for seconds there had been a blank and when
she was once more conscious the train was gone.

After that, a blur, she in shock as they dragged her to the car and took her to the Christina Hof. Then she was home, they were helping her up the steps. Her father opened the door, wearing his smoking jacket, tieless. She had flung herself in his arms, sobbing, trying to tell him and unable to form the words.

There had been no time to tell him anyhow. "Generalmajor Kurt Helmer?" "Yes." "Staatsgeheimepolizei. You will come with us please." "What? This is—" But they were pulling him away. "One minute! I insist!" "There is no time. Come." He was dragged down the steps. Christa watched blankly as they shoved him into the car. "No," she whispered as it roared through the gate and down the hill. "No!" Then Traudi was there, and she sagged against her.

Next she was in bed, Aunt Alma bending over her. "Child, where's your father? What's going on?"

Somehow she must have managed to gasp out an account. Then, after an enormous drink of rum, she slept. Sleeping, she dreamed that she had dreamed all this and had awakened to find Lan beside her and that it was all right; then she had truly wakened and reality had hit her like a fist, and she began to scream.

Eventually she calmed somewhat, but the whole house seethed with fear and dismay. The radio blared bulletins. Austria was firmly in Nazi hands. Aunt Alma gave orders to keep the gate locked, admit no one but the General without her permission. Ernst was pale, confused, and frightened; and it was his need of her that brought Christa out of shock. Simultaneously she tried to reassure him and herself. "They can't do this. I'll call Dr. Faber, Papa's lawyer. He'll straighten all this out in a hurry." But, of course, Dr. Faber could do nothing; no one could. Then she remembered Robert Schellhammer; almost she called him, but she drew back. He was one of *them*—the enemy. They were alone, helpless, and there was nothing for it but to wait and pray and trust Papa to be stronger than *they* were, and smarter, and come back to them.

Aunt Alma, drained, collapsed, was put to bed again. Ernst played the piano endlessly, trying to drown his anxiety in music; Christa moved numbly around the house giving servants necessary orders, as much reassurance as she could. But everything within her was frozen with fear for her husband and father. Hours dragged by, prolonged by the wan expectation that at any instant the phone would ring, or the gate bell, and Papa or Lan would be there.

When she could get a circuit, she called the apartment in Vienna, but no one answered. Rezi was not there.

She thought of Josef Steiner. What of him? Rage and hatred broke briefly through her numbness. He had ruined her, ruined all of them, with his mad schemes. Then even that faded, and she could not hate him. He had been right in everything, and it was not his fault that time had run out on all of them. And if the Gestapo had taken him, he would not be merely expelled; he would be doomed.

The first day passed in a blur of fear and tension; the second, a Sunday, was a duplicate. By Monday her head was clearing slightly. Surely they had not dared hurt Lan, and he would find a way to get in touch with her. Surely Papa would be released before long; he had done nothing to harm them. And later she could get out to Czechoslovakia, meet Lan there ... or somewhere. But hard as she made herself hope, fear and loss were still forces that almost paralyzed her. Then Robert Schellhammer came.

As Mitzi showed him in, Christa stared. This was a Robert she had never seen, erect and military in crisp brown uniform, visored cap, shining boots, golden leather shoulder belt, a pistol at his waist.

"Christa!"

"Robert, what—"

"Kreisleiter Schellhammer, NSDAP, at your service, Frau Condon." His smile was faint.

"Kreisleiter?" It was, she knew vaguely, a fairly high Party rank.

"Yes. I'm the senior Party officer in this district. Surely that's no surprise to you."

"No," she said heavily. "No, it isn't."

"I would have been here sooner, but I've been so damned busy, Christa." Now his face was grave. "What in God's name were you and Lan mixed up in? He's been expelled, your father's been arrested, you almost were. As soon as I heard, I went to the Gestapo, but they won't tell me anything; they say the entire matter is absolutely and completely secret. What kind of danger have you managed to expose yourself to—or let Lan expose you to?"

Christa hesitated. Suddenly her mind worked swiftly, clearly. So Robert didn't know about Steiner and the pictures. Of course not. The Gestapo would let no one know about the pictures. She could lie. "I don't know, really. Lan was working with some foreign correspondent in Vienna, I don't know which one. On a story, something about the reaction of Jews to the *Anschluss* or ... I'm not sure what. All I know is I went to the Second District with him and then we were arrested and dragged to the station and ... and he was sent away. They brought me home and took Papa and ... and that was Friday night and we've heard nothing since." The tears coming then were genuine, as was her desperation, but the move was calculated when suddenly she ran to him, threw her arms around him, pressed her face against his chest. "Oh, Robert, you've got to help us. I'm so frightened."

She felt his body stiffen as she began to sob, everything pent up within her breaking loose. His arms encircled her and his hand stroked her back, soothing her as if she were a frightened child. "All right, Christa," he kept whispering. "All right, now, my girl." When finally she reached the end of tears, he gently pushed her away and took out a crisp, clean handkerchief. "Here." He wiped her cheeks and nose. "Now, steady. We must talk. Your father. Did he know anything about whatever it was that Lan was doing?"

"Nothing, absolutely nothing, I swear it."

Robert nodded. Thoughtfully he began to pace. She waited tensely, daring now to hope. Abruptly he halted, turned. "Very well. Perhaps there is something I can do. I shall certainly try. You understand, of course, there is nothing I can do about Lan's expulsion, even if I would. But ... General Helmer is a patriot, whatever our misunderstandings; and next to der Führer and my own father, there's no man I love more. It's not a simple matter for an ordinary Party man to mix in Gestapo affairs, but ... On your word that he's innocent of any activities against the Party or der Führer, I'll go the limit for him."

"You have my word."

"You must not, however, expect any results for several days; probably not until after der Führer has come to Vienna and gone again and things are more orderly, better channels established.

These matters require a little time. But I will do my best to make sure he suffers no undue hardship meanwhile."

"Oh, thank you." And she meant it this time when she embraced him, kissed him.

She felt him draw in a deep breath, and as she moved away his eyes met hers, and they were swirling with emotion. "One should help his friends," he said quietly, "and show no mercy to his enemies. Now, I must leave for the city." His eyes flared. "There's a chance der Führer will arrive this evening. You realize, Christa, this is the fulfillment of my dream! Not just for myself, but for Austria."

"I congratulate you." Her voice was toneless.

"You'll see. We'll get this settled and five years from now you'll bless the date of March eleventh, 1938!" He picked up his hat. "Now, some advice. Neither you nor your family should leave the Christina Hof until you hear from me. Just stay quietly here and wait, and if you have any trouble, ring up my father; he's not going to Vienna. You know how he despises crowds." He started toward the door, halted, turned. "And Christa—"

"Yes?"

"I suggest you not try to get in touch with Lan. Certainly not until your father is released. And if he should communicate with you, by phone, by mail, be careful of every word. Don't say anything that might be misconstrued in any way. Understand? Your name is on the Gestapo's list and, bluntly, your mail will be read and your telephone tapped. Do you understand?"

"Yes."

He smiled. "Now don't look so glum. All will come well. *Wiederseh'n*. Heil Hitler!"

"*Wiederseh'n*, Robert," she answered numbly.

He seemed about to speak, thought better of it, and went out. When he had gone, she leaned against the doorjamb, weakened by relief. Then slowly some strength ebbed back into her. She was not as alone and powerless as she had thought; she had a certain power of her own, which she had just used to good effect. Heart lifting, she ran to find Ernst and share with him the scrap of encouragement Robert had offered.

No triumphant Caesar entering Rome could have been more jubilantly received than Adolf Hitler in Vienna. The Army that preceded him had been welcomed by thousands along its route as a band of heroes and saviors; he was greeted like a god. To witness his arrival, hear his speech from a balcony of the Hofburg, men and women flocked to Vienna from every corner of the country. The trains were jammed; some rural folk from the outskirts walked miles to reach the Heldenplatz, the great courtyard park behind the palace. Tens of thousands cheered and shrieked his name and slogans, and Christa, listening to the radio, found it awesome, terrifying. None of them—not Papa, Lan, herself, or Josef—had realized how hungry, avid, the crowd was for a leader of real strength and decisiveness, one who could capture their imagination with both pomp and action, satisfying some deep-seated need for a father figure that had gone unsatisfied since Franz Josef's death. It was shameful, almost blasphemous, Christa thought, for one man to be worshiped so intensely, and yet . . . and yet . . .

Even through the speaker of the radio, there was something in that strange voice, its rise and fall, its timbre, cadence, that stirred even her involuntarily, wholly apart from the words he spoke, a quality not mental but physical, a familiar rhythm which at first she could not identify. Then she realized that it was the rhythm of sexual intercourse: the gentle seductive foreplay, the increase in excitement, the sudden driving earthy power, and then the shrieking mindless climax. Even armored against it by hatred, disgust, and sophistication, she felt its impact; and the servant women, also listening, were wholly rapt. Waldi, at the climax, had both hands on her own breasts, squeezing. And when it was done, they were all silent, empty, with glowing eyes. She dared not imagine what, out of her hearing, they said among themselves later on.

Other news followed, so fast, so complicated, she could hardly absorb it. Austria was, in due time, to become wholly a part of the Third Reich, part and parcel of Germany, a decision to be ratified by a plebiscite on the tenth of April. Seyss-Inquart would not be Chancellor after all, but something amorphous called *Reichsstatthalter;* Schuschnigg had been arrested, and so had many other enemies of the state. Later she learned that thousands had been taken up by the Gestapo without warning, precisely as it had snapped up Papa.

Robert Schellhammer phoned twice, reassuringly. "Your father is well and matters seem to be in hand. Don't worry." As if in a besieged fortress, the Helmer family waited in the Christina Hof. And finally, eight days after his first visit, Robert reappeared, this time with General Helmer beside him in the car.

He still wore the velvet smoking jacket and the slippers he'd had on that night; his eyes were deeply sunken in a haggard face unshaved for more than a week. But his shoulders were straight, his voice firm and steady, his smile quick as Christa and Ernst rushed to him. He held them both at once, tightly. "Yes. Yes, I am quite all right. No trouble at all. How is your Aunt Alma? I must go up and see her at once. Christa, will you have a hot bath drawn? And I'd like a *Schnitzel* and, for God's sake, some decent coffee." He kissed them both hungrily, squeezed them, released them, and turned. "Robert, I am deeply grateful."

Robert smiled, glowing with pride. "Herr General, I'm glad to have been of service. And I deplore the inconvenience you've suffered. Now, I know you and your family want to be alone . . ."

Christa could not help it; she ran to him, kissed him. "Robert, thank you. Thank you so much."

He looked down at her, surprised, then nodded slowly. "I told you I would do what I could. Now"—he raised his arm—"Heil Hitler!"

Christa was startled when the General briskly returned the salute. "Heil Hitler! My greetings to your parents."

Robert got into the car, waved, and drove away. Christa and Ernst stared at the General. "Papa," Ernst said, "you—"

"Yes," Helmer said. "I'm afraid it's something we'll all have to learn to do as if we meant it." He turned to Christa. "Have you heard from Lan?"

"No." Her voice shook. "Not a word."

Helmer sighed, and what she saw in his eyes made her despair, especially when he offered her no word of hope and comfort. "Well . . . there's a lot we must talk about. But first, daughter, please, the bath and food." He put his arm around the shoulders of his son. "Ernst, come along with me while I see Auntie; maybe my coming home will make her feel better."

He had lost nearly four kilos weight, and he ate hungrily, but moderately. At the table he spoke only briefly of what had hap-

pened to him: the Gestapo had taken him first to the Alte
Liesl, the ugly castellated brick jail near the Danube Canal.
He spent one day there in a tiny cell, alone, fed soup, bread, and
vile black coffee the jailers called "nigger sweat." Then he'd
been taken in a "Green Henry," a police van, to Gestapo headquarters on the Herrengasse. There, for ten days, he had been
questioned by the police; finally, this morning, he had been
released. "And now," he said, "I think, if we are careful, all will
go well and there will be no more trouble." That was reassurance
enough for Ernst. His world once more intact, he drifted to the
piano, crashed out some triumphant chords. The General cocked
his head, listened, smiled, and looked down at his plate. Then
he drained his cup and stood up. "In my office, Christa, please."

When they entered it, he looked around as if years had passed
since he was last here. Then he eased himself into his chair;
she sat down opposite. He lit a cigar and looked at her through
the smoke for several seconds.

"When they took me to the Gestapo," he said, "I was questioned in a most peculiar way. There was something they wanted
to know, but seemed reluctant to ask me directly for fear of
revealing knowledge to me that I might not already have. That
part of the interrogation, the worst part, dealt with the activities of you and Lan and, of all people, Josef Steiner." His eyes
held her, his fingers drummed on the table. "I, of course, was
at a loss to know why you and Lan should be involved with a
man like Steiner."

Christa felt blood mount to her face. "He and Lan were
friends."

"So," the General said. "He and Lan."

"Papa—"

"No." He held up a hand. "I know nothing about it and I
do not want to know anything about it, do you understand? Nor
is anyone else to know, not one breath or whisper. It is something that must be forgotten."

He rose, went to the window, looked out. "Even the Gestapo
seems to want it forgotten," he said. "And that perhaps is the
only reason why we are still alive and free. With Robert's help,
the police and I have reached a rather delicate understanding."

He turned. "At first, you understand, my interrogators were
three young men, all Prussians, who were not gentle with me.
But when I understood that there was more to the whole affair

than showed on the surface, I allowed myself a display of force. I lost my temper and gave them a thorough dressing down. I pointed out that I was a Generalmajor of the Imperial and Royal Army, held highest honors for bravery and devotion to duty, including those awarded by their own Emperor Wilhelm, that I had defended German people against the Russians while they were still in swaddling clothes, and that I declined to be treated so by upstarts who had never heard a shot fired in anger!" He smiled grimly. "Well, I know Prussians. Authority they respond to; and once I took the initiative, they lost their confidence. Presently there were apologies, and the interrogation was continued by a colonel who had also served on the Eastern front. Then everything was different. Finally I convinced him that I was wholly ignorant of your and Lan's activities, and fortunately I have been careful to have my affairs in order in that regard. Still, I'm not certain how things would have fallen out if Robert Schellhammer hadn't intervened with higher Party officials. Eventually we reached the following tacit understanding."

She had never seen his face so grave. "First, Lan has been expelled and he will never be allowed to return. Second, under no circumstances will you or I be allowed to travel outside the country. Apparently what Lan knows is explosive; we are the insurance of his silence. You are hostage for him, I for you. If you should ever speak of the matter, whatever it was, it would mean my destruction."

"Papa—"

His mouth twisted. "They're not joking, Christa. Only Lan's American citizenship and the fact that any sort of formal proceedings might have brought out more than they wished to have on any sort of record have saved us as it is. One word, one wrong word and—" He made a sharp cutting gesture with his hand.

Christa stared at him, then turned away. Words came hard, through a thickness in her throat. "You're saying," she whispered, "that I'll never see Lan again."

His voice softened; he came to her, put a hand on her shoulder. "Things change, matters are forgotten. Maybe even this government will not last forever. I don't say never. But neither must I give you false hope. It will be a long time, and you must understand that and accept it."

She laid her cheek against his hand.

"Believe me, I would change it if I could. But . . . you and I, from now on our primary concern must be for ourselves, Ernst, the Christina Hof. We are in mortal danger, Christa, and we must work our way out of it, with all our cleverness and courage. You must understand."

She raised her head, swallowed hard, looked at him. "I understand," she managed.

"Good. You are your mother's daughter; I knew you would." He backed away, continued, tone more businesslike.

"That is part of the agreement I have reached with them. Beyond that, I will also join the Party and use my influence to further its affairs. Further—and this was not an inconsiderable factor—I am to put myself at their disposal in matters of propaganda. I am remembered for certain actions I took against the Russians in Galicia and the fact that the Russians still despise me. In some way, the Nazis think this will someday be useful to them. And, of course, I have no objection to that. When it comes to hating Russians, I'm with them a hundred per cent. Anyhow, from now on we must make a great show of Party loyalty, no matter what we feel inside. The lives of all of us depend on it. We are in the hands of Germans now, and they are always serious. That is something we must always keep in mind."

"Yes, Papa."

"Beyond that, we owe a great debt to Robert Schellhammer. He went to some risk, used up some credit, so to speak, on our behalf. We must continue to have his good will. In the past you have sometimes dealt rather shabbily with Robert. In the future we must deal with him correctly at all times. As, I am sure, he will deal with us. Now, let me make myself clear. You are a married woman, and all of us must understand and respect that, most especially Robert. I am sure he will. And— Oh, the devil, your mother could put this to you properly, but I can't find the words. Robert still loves you. With Lan gone, that could create an embarrassing situation. And somehow . . ."

Christa looked at her father with a kind of pity and somehow managed a smile as she stood up. "Yes, Papa," she said. "Don't worry. I know what you mean. Robert and I will continue to be friends. I shall do nothing to damage his love for me, but I won't give him false encouragement that might disappoint him later. I will not be petty with him in any way, or hold him responsible for what happened to Lan. But beyond that, we

248

should all be clear. I *am* a married woman. And I love my husband and always will, even if I never see him again. He is the only man I will ever really love, I think."

The General did not meet her eyes. "Yes," he said. "I understand how you feel."

She took his hand. "Anyhow," she said, "leave Robert to me. Believe me, I know very well how to manage that."

He looked at her strangely, as if seeing her anew. "Yes, I think you would. Very well, I leave that to you. But you must tell me if there is . . . trouble, anything serious. Then I shall talk to Robert."

"You won't have to," she said. "That's one thing you needn't worry about."

"Good." After a few seconds' silence, he went on briskly. "Well, we shall dispose of your apartment in Vienna. You will live here from now on, for the Christina Hof will need you. Your aunt will not be with us much longer, and there must be someone to take her place."

"Yes, Papa."

He put his arms around her. "So," he said. "From now on, we shall do the best we can, and the main thing is that we must not, under any circumstances, ever despair."

"Yes, Papa," Christa said.

4   THE WINE HAD RELAXED HER, but it was also making her think and remember too much. Uneasily she refilled her glass, lit a cigarette. There had been no letter from him for two weeks now. Of course that was understandable; everything was upside down, delayed. Still . . . He could not have given up; he must not give up! Because she would not, never.

Two weeks, that was nothing to be alarmed about. All the same . . . She put that thought from her mind. Instead, settling back, she picked up the thread of memory.

Five days after her father's release from prison, Aunt Alma had died in her sleep. Normally, hundreds would have attended her funeral; in fact, as her body was carried from the church to the open grave, the bells ringing out their savage, discordant requiem as if challenging the power of Death, there were hardly more than two dozen mourners. Word had spread: for the time being the Helmers were tainted, association with them dangerous.

Christa had thrown herself into managing the household, determined to think of nothing else—but that was impossible. There was no word from Lan, and she sank into depression, the wound of loneliness too deep and raw to heal.

Then, three weeks after his expulsion, the mail brought a ticket to a concert at the Konzerthaus in Vienna, the debut of Fräulein Marietta Duncan singing a program of Schubert Lieder. Enclosed was a terse note: *"Please attend."*

Something clicked in Christa's mind. Marietta was Mark Gorton's young American mistress. Of course, it could be only an effort on Mark's part to insure a full house for his protégée's first performance, but—

Helmer did not want her to go into the city; she overrode his objections, and she was surprised to see that life went on as usual. "Wien bleibt Wien," the old song went, and it was true: Vienna was always Vienna. The coffeehouses were full; lovers strolled in the spring-greened parks; nearing curtain time, the same well-dressed people left the Sacher and the Bristol and the Grand, bound for the Opera or the concert halls or theaters. Only the posters, the omnipresent swastika flags, and the spicing of uniforms in the crowd certified the change that had taken place. Soldiers in field gray, SS men in sleek black, and Nazi Party officials in their brown and gold regalia, with medals, armbands, pistols, and daggers, were everywhere. Already the Austrians had found a term of mockery for the resplendent Party functionaries: Golden Pheasants they were called behind their backs.

The Schubertsaal of the Konzerthaus was filled, the crowd sprinkled with military men and Golden Pheasants. Mark Gorton sat in the front row; Christa's ticket was for a seat at the rear. On her left was a girl her own age who claimed to be French and chatted in abysmal German, a classmate of Marietta's. When the lights went down and the applause began, she pressed an envelope into Christa's hand.

Marietta sang superbly, but Christa did not hear. At the

intermission, in the privacy of a restroom stall, she opened the envelope with hands that shook.

Our friend is safe and well in Prague. We have spoken and he misses you terribly, and sends all his love. Be in the main courtyard of the Stift at Altkreuzburg and bring a letter for him at 1500 Saturday afternoon.   MG.

The monastery at Altkreuzburg had been founded in the Babenberg era at the beginning of the Middle Ages, and had expanded ever since. On its high hill above the Danube it was a massive gray complex covering a full twenty acres. Its winery was one of the best in Lower Austria; and over the centuries it had amassed treasures of painting, sculpture, and manuscripts of a richness no single mind could inventory or comprehend. Like the abbeys of Klosterneuburg, Melk, and Heiligenkreuz, a prime tourist attraction on this pleasant Saturday afternoon, the Stift swarmed with sightseers, mostly Germans, in uniform and out. Meticulously they scoured the whole monastery for culture, each laden with his camera.

The center of the main courtyard was dominated by a huge crucifix erected to the memory of the town citizens who had fallen in the war. There were other memorials to pious ancient noblemen set in the weathered wall of the church and main building itself. Inscriptions hundreds of years old in Latinized German or Germanized Latin were set in panels, now barely readable. Christa, at three o'clock, pretended to be preoccupied surveying these.

Then Mark was there, only another tourist standing by her. He told her of Lan's phone call, took her letter, and promised to hand deliver it to Prague and bring one back. When she met him the next Saturday in the same place, he had one for her, and after giving him hers, she fled into a smaller deserted courtyard, where, beneath an enormous decaying sundial set on a high wall, she leaned against the stones and read. And suddenly everything had changed; the depression lifted; she could have sung, danced. She hurried to her car, drove out on an empty road, and read the letter over and over, until she had memorized every word.

After that Mark never failed to meet her, usually at the Stift, picking up and delivering letters. She lived for Saturday afternoons; then, one day, in the *Pfarrkirche,* he told her, "I'm being kicked out, too, and Mari's going with me." Christa's heart sank, but he went on quickly. "Listen, I've made inquiries. I think now it's safe for the two of you to write each other directly, *if*—" And he told her what he would tell Lan: the letters would undoubtedly be opened and read. "So don't even write about getting together again. You can say how much you love him, but nothing to indicate you want to leave the country, even to be with him. Throw in as much guff as possible about how much better everything's getting, pour on the praise for the New Order. He'll know it's phony, but it's insurance that you'll be able to stay in touch. I know it will be like kissing through a handkerchief, but it's the best you can manage for the time being. Anyhow, just remember, nothing lasts forever and tyrants always overreach. Just hang on. Do what you people always do so well: survive. And someday it will be all right."

She looked at him, this stumpy red-faced man who had selflessly run so many risks for her. She knew that he loved Austria as much as she, maybe more, for he had chosen it as his country in the wisdom of maturity, and had not been born here. Then, suddenly, regardless of the risk, she hugged and kissed him.

His red face turned even redder. "It will be all right," he repeated. *"Wiederseh'n,* Christa."

"Wiederseh'n," she whispered and watched him walk out through a vast gray arch and disappear behind a buttress.

It had worked, but the letters were no longer the same. In the diplomatic pouch they had been inviolable; now lack of privacy leached all the passion from them. She never tired of the words *I love you always,* in his handwriting, but there was hardly more than that; and her replies were not much better. She could only hope he comprehended what longing lay behind the simple phrases, what a void there was in her life and in her bed. Beyond that, she wrote what news seemed safe, tricking it up in a way he would understand:

Ernst has joined the Hitler Youth. He says it is very stimulating. We had sixteen guests last Sunday—imagine! Most were important Party officials. I send you my heart. Your Christa.

Truth and fiction. Ernst had indeed joined the Hitler Jugend, and he hated it. But Papa had said it was necessary to strengthen their position, his portion of the sacrifice. And now that the General had joined the Party, the Golden Pheasants, the Wehrmacht, and SS officers had begun to show up at the Christina Hof. Some were old Austrian comrades of the General, others friends of Robert Schellhammer; the word spread, not only about the food and the view but, Christa suspected, about the General's blond daughter. Anyhow, the quarantine had slowly been lifted, a measure of their increasing safety.

She herself performed like a monkey on a stick at those affairs, she thought bitterly, always careful to be charming, not quite flirtatious, still armored by her status as a married woman but using her sex appeal to dazzle Austrians and Germans alike. And sometimes she realized with dismay that she even enjoyed it. Not usually, but there were afternoons when some officer wittier and more cultivated than the others would seek her out; and she'd had some wine and the sun was warm, the breeze from the woods cool, and suddenly she would realize, *I'm having a good time!* And then, full of self-reproach, she would draw back inwardly if not outwardly. Besides, even if she had wanted to relax, let herself go with someone, she could not; there was always Robert Schellhammer to consider.

She had promised Papa that she would manage him, and as time passed, she realized how all-important that was. He, not General Helmer, was now the real power in the Ferntal, and their lives and property were in his hands. Robert had to come first, before all others.

They saw a great deal of each other. There were local functions—some social, some political—that the Helmers were expected to attend. Robert tacitly moved into position as her escort when one was needed and was almost always present in the background when one was not; hawkishly he watched her; no old-maid chaperone could have been more zealous. In a sense, she was grateful; he fended off not only a lot of unwelcome advances but some genuine temptations as well. If he could not have her, no one else would.

And yet, with her he was always absolutely correct, careful never to go beyond the bounds of the friendly intimacy they had always shared. Underneath, she knew, he seethed, and she under-

253

stood the effort it took to hold himself in check; no one knew better than she the agony of loving someone unattainable. But his correctness was also the reason she could feel nothing for him but respect and gratitude; it was what had made him dull; it had also made him a Nazi. There was something both corrupt and frightening in his increasing stodginess; she had a vague feeling that once someone had convinced him, or he had convinced himself, that a course of action was correct, he would follow it no matter how monstrous its results. His correctness could be counted on to the limit, but she wondered if the same could be said of his humanity.

So she herself was meticulously proper, careful to neither tantalize him nor arouse his jealousy. And she considered herself fortunate that she had him, who did not excite or stir her, as a shield against the others who did.

Because, as the shock had worn off, the sheer carnal need which had so delighted Lan with its intensity reasserted itself. But that intensity was no joke now; more and more it was sheer torment. Hard work and fatigue helped suppress it; yet sometimes in the night she would awaken feverish and moaning with it, and of necessity had learned to give herself a sordid counterfeit of relief. She was not, the knowledge grew in her, made of iron; if it had not been for Robert and the threat he represented, she might not always have won in her struggle against the quick unbidden desire occasionally aroused in her by some young attractive officer with a sense of humor, a good body, and an invitation in his eyes.

But Robert protected her against that, and the letters from Lan—and Robert's own personality—protected her from Robert; and so she had struck a strange and delicate balance with which so far it had been possible to live. Now, though—

Inside the house a bell rang.

Christa jumped in sudden fear. It was so late, and everyone knew too well by now what the appearance of someone at the gate at such an hour could mean. The only servant up, she saw, hurrying inside, was Mitzi. "See who's out there," she commanded tensely.

Her heart pounded until the girl reappeared. "It's only Herr Schellhammer," she said a little shakily, as relieved as Christa.

Christa steadied, handed Mitzi a key. "Go let him in." But her apprehension had not completely subsided as she waited in the entry. Then she heard his car enter the courtyard, its door slam, and he was coming up the steps.

"So. Christa, I hope I'm not intruding."

She masked a frown. His uniform, usually so natty, was rumpled, sweat stains beneath the arms. His hair was tousled, and there was a kind of wildness in his eyes, a faint unsteadiness in his movements as he took her hand and kissed it. He had, she saw at once, drunk a lot of wine.

"No, certainly not." At all costs he must be welcomed.

"Good." He stood there motionless.

"*Gnädige,*" Mitzi broke the silence, "will you be wanting something?"

"Perhaps a little wine," said Robert before she could answer. "May I have a little wine?"

"Of course. I was just on the terrace with an *Achtel*. Mitzi, bring another glass and a liter of Müller-Thurgau."

"Good. The General's Müller Thurgau is superb." Robert fell in beside her as they walked through the drawing room to the terrace. "I am truly sorry to disturb you at this hour—"

"Don't give it a thought. Is something wrong?"

"I don't know." He shook his head as if something buzzed around it. "There are things . . ." He broke off. On the terrace he dropped heavily into a chair, patted his pockets, said disgustedly, "I left my cigarettes in the car."

"Here." She offered him her pack, then snapped her lighter into flame. His eyes met hers as she bent over him, and she saw in them distress, maybe even pain and anger. Then Mitzi came with the wine, opened it, and poured him a glass.

"Thank you," he said, tersely. "We won't need you any more. Go to bed."

When she was gone and Christa had taken a chair opposite him, he took a long swallow from the glass, drew savagely at his cigarette.

"Robert, what's wrong?"

"Well, for one thing, they took Professor Busch today." His voice was rasping, bitter. "Without consulting me, they just came and took him."

No need to ask who *they* were; she felt a pang of pity for the strange old man. "But why?"

"Old Busch...Never a man more dedicated to the German soul and spirit. We met in his place for years when we were illegal. He had dedicated his life to his German heritage and now...But he's nonproductive, you see? And with a war on we can't afford nonproductive mouths to feed. And he wouldn't work in a factory or even on a farm with modern implements, he simply couldn't grasp—" Robert gestured. "Never mind. No matter. They took him."

"And you couldn't stop them?"

He drained his glass. "No," he said harshly. "I couldn't stop them. How could I? I'm just an Austrian, and it's the *Pifkas* who rule the roost now and call the tune. *We're* the ones who risked everything to bring Austria into the Reich, but now it seems we're not competent to manage our own country. They send people from Berlin and Karlsruhe and Dresden down here to show us how—" His voice clanged with bitterness as he reached for the bottle.

Christa said, "It's not just Busch? Something else has happened?"

"Well, there was more to it than Busch." He rose, went to the wall, stared out at the woods. "It was a blow at me, a deliberate blow at me. No need to go into detail. There was a post coming open, a promotion. I was, am, due for it. I've *earned* it, was entitled— Of course there was somebody else who wanted it, too; there's always somebody else. Naturally, a German, and—"

"And he got it?"

Robert let out a long rasping breath. "It's his. He just proved that to me. Busch was a test of strength. He won."

"I'm sorry," Christa said.

"Just now," he said bitterly. "Just now when the war opens up so much opportunity within the Party, and I am balked. As things now look, I'll never get past where I am now, and—" He turned. "You know, of course, you're part of the reason."

"I?"

"You. If I hadn't stuck my neck out for you and the General ...When one has enemies there are so many things they can use against one, so many ways they can cast reflections on your loyalty. I knew even then I was taking a chance, but I hadn't expected it to be *this* costly."

Christa said nothing. She had never seen his reserve break;

whatever had happened must have been shattering. Then he said, commandingly, "Come here."

"Robert—"

"Come here. I've got some things to say to you."

She found herself rising, moving toward him. When she was in reach, he took her hand with a traplike grip, pulled her very close, looking down at her, his face strangely twisted in the moonlight. Her nostrils filled with the male smell of sweat and wine.

"Some things to say . . ." The emotion naked in his voice was as unexpected as a glimpse of a strange dark landscape in a lightning flash. "I did it because I love you, you know. I always have. That was one reason I worked so hard in the Party, meant to rise, so no one could say I was beneath you, no one would dare joke. After all, I have my pride, you know? Only it back-fired on me, didn't it? But maybe it doesn't matter; maybe it's all for the best. I can hold my own here, anyhow; nobody's going to take the Ferntal away from me. And now it doesn't matter. There's no more damage they can do to me if I marry you."

"Marry?" she whispered.

"Hell yes, why not? I—"

"Lan," she said. "Remember."

"Lan is gone," he said thickly. "And you might as well understand that. He's gone and he's not coming back and you're not going to him. You'll never see him again."

"No!" she cried, stepping back. "That's not true."

"It's true. You two are finished. It's as if he's dead. You're not a wife, you're a widow!"

"I am not!"

"You are! You have to face it! Maybe there was a chance until the war, but not any more, thank God! It's over, ended, and you've got to make a new life for yourself. Well, I'll help you do that. We'll get married and—"

Christa backed away. "Robert, you're drunk. Or mad, or— We were married in the Church. We'll always be married until one or the other dies. And—"

He laughed. "Oh, no. No, no, no. You're only married until you decide not to be." He took a step toward her. "Christa, I've already checked. It's dead easy! The Church is crawling on its belly to the Party! All you have to do is sign the papers and there'll be an annulment. Oh, it'll take a month or two, but that's nothing! Then we both start fresh. It's what I've had in mind all along, but the time wasn't right, it would have hurt my chances of promotion. But since I have no chances left, it doesn't matter any longer." He snorted. "Hell, he never even gave you a child. But I'll give you kids, lots of 'em; we'll have sons and daughters and put these two estates together and—"

"You'd better go," Christa said flatly.

But he was on her then, had locked her tightly in his arms, his face close to hers. "Listen, you'd better see the light! You and your father both, you're not in the clear with the Gestapo by a long shot! Without me to stand between you and them... But you marry me, it wipes the slate clean." His arms tightened. "Besides, it's what you need. A real husband in bed with you, to make you happy and give you kids. I'll make you happier than he ever did." And then his mouth came down on hers.

She felt the inthrust of his tongue, the solidity of muscular flesh, even the hard bulge in his groin. For a moment she was frozen with fear, surprise, and anger; then she jerked her face aside, began to fight. "Let me go!" she said. "I tell you, let me go!"

To her surprise he did. She dodged back as he straightened up, panting. "Christa—"

"Listen," she heard herself fling at him, "I'm sorry, I don't want to hurt you. But I can't, I never will."

"You have to!"

"No! I'll never ask for any annulment, I'll never sign anything, not for you, not for anybody! I love Lan, I—" Her voice broke. It all came out of her then, all the loneliness and grief and fear and discouragement, pouring out in sobs like vomit. She could not help it, that convulsion of a nervous system that had borne more than it could take and at last rebelled. She turned away.

He touched her shoulder. "Now, listen, Christa—"

She whirled on him in fury, this symbol of all the disasters of the past two years. "Just leave me alone! I hate you, I hate all of you!" She could barely force the words from a closed-up throat. "Oh, God, you and your crooked crosses, I hate..." And then no more would come and she turned to the wall, face buried in her hands.

He was still there, in silence. After a while, he said, "Christa."

She could not have answered if she had wanted to.

"Christa, you didn't mean that."

Still she could not speak, just shook her head, hands clamped tightly over her face, breath coming in painful gasps. She knew that she had destroyed too much in that outburst, that for her father's sake, Ernst's, the sake of all of them, she had to turn, make it right somehow. But she seemed to have no power to speak or move.

"All right," Robert said presently. "Well, I will tell you now, for your own good, I did not hear what you said. Not about the Party symbol, not— You are distraught. I did not hear it. But you must not speak like that again, ever." His voice was harsh and stern now, the pleading gone. "But, thank you for being honest with me. I wish you had been so much earlier. Don't worry. I won't bother you again. I have some pride of my own, you know."

Still she did not turn or answer.

"*Auf Wiederseh'n,* Frau Condon. Heil Hitler!"

Two weeks later the engagement of Kreisleiter Robert Schellhammer to Charlotte Richter, the plump, blond daughter of the owner of the largest butcher shop in Altkreuzburg, was announced.

5   INTERMITTENTLY, because of the regular priest's poor health, Martinus continued to serve the church in Ferndorf, and it was in his office there that Frau Sattler came to him. Her husband had been the town's leading livestock dealer, a wealthy man according to the standards of the Ferntal, and a member of the Reichsbund der Österreicher, a Monarchist organization. Ten days after the *Umbruch* he had been taken by the Gestapo. Now, a month later, Frau Sattler, entering the church office, carried between quaking hands a curious utilitarian ceramic canister. A lean, dynamic woman in her early forties, she had been a moving force in the Church. Her whole body trembled, her voice was a dull whisper as she held out the urn to Martinus.

"This," she managed, "came in the mail today."

"I am afraid I don't understand."

She opened the canister. The gray substance within it was curious. He touched it with a finger. "What—?"

"This is my husband. Ludwig Sattler. His ashes. He is dead and they have burnt him."

Martinus gaped, rubbing his finger vigorously against his trousers.

"In the mail," she repeated. "With this." She fumbled in her reticule, brought out a folded paper. The official letterhead was that of the Dachau concentration camp.

The government regrets to inform you that subject individual died on April 17 of a sudden illness. His remains have been cremated and are dispatched to you herewith. The enclosed reckoning for cremation charges must be paid within one week. Heil Hitler!

Numbly Martinus handed back the letter, looked at the urn, seeing in his mind the tall good-humored horseman.

"They killed him," Frau Sattler rasped. "That dear good man —they killed him. My Ludwig, the strongest man in the Ferntal, never sick a day in his life, and they say . . ." Her voice broke. "The children. They're at school this morning. What am I to tell them when they come home? What am I— Ashes. Only ashes." Her voice was low, terrible. "I can't show them this."

"Frau Sattler." Martinus' knees were weak, his body cold as he put his arm around her, held her close, trying to stop her trembling. His brain seemed to have stopped, frozen by horror.

"Father, you must come with me, be there when the children come. I can't—"

"Yes," he said, stroking her hair. "Yes, I will come."

Mercifully, he could no longer remember how he had got through that day. If he had known how many more like it there would be, his words of comfort would have stuck crosswise in his throat. But Sattler's was only one of many; soon all over Austria the mail carriers were delivering urns.

Meanwhile, Austrians were pried from the last vestige of

260

control over their own destinies; the name Austria was obliterated, replaced by "Ostmark," and soon even that was to go. Nothing was as Martinus had imagined; and as the dimensions of the catastrophe became clear to him, he saw how dreadfully mistaken he had been. The disaster touched even the classes he taught at the Gymnasium. Those he conducted in English literature were virtually gutted, any work of even potentially controversial content thrown out, with finally nothing left but maundering second-rate banalities or works showing the decadence of the British. The classes in religion were worse; contortions were necessary to square what he had always believed and taught with what was happening, to give Hitler primacy over Christ. But, as Cardinal Innitzer had said in his pastoral letter, it was the duty of the Church to pray for the objectives of the Party.

In distress and indignation, Martinus, who despite his reputation as a writer, was a small fish in an enormous pond, went to the *Propst*—the Prior of the monastery—seeking guidance.

The *Propst* could give him none. Around his neck was hung the enormous weight of the huge and varied enterprise he managed, its economic stake in reconciliation with the government. Stift Altkreuzburg was the largest landowner in the district, and the biggest vintner, merchandising its wine all across central and eastern Europe. It was also one of the largest lumbering businesses, harvesting timber from the vast woodlands it owned. Its bowels were full of treasure: gold and silver artifacts uncounted, gifts and donations accumulated over centuries, its collection of medieval, Renaissance, and Baroque art one of the finest east of the Rhine. It controlled the parishes of villages for a radius of thirty miles.

Moreover, the Cardinal had spoken. After the *Anschluss*, in negotiations with the Nazis, who were desperately eager to have the Catholics support the new plebiscite decreed by Hitler, all problems had been resolved by the ancient formula concerning those things which were Caesar's and those which were God's. And Cardinal Innitzer had signed his letter of capitulation "Heil Hitler!"

It was hoped, the Prior explained, that acquiescence and cooperation by Austrian Catholics would secure better treatment, too, for the Church in the old Reich—Germany. That, anyhow,

261

had been Hitler's promise. So, one must go along, and one must pray.

Martinus tried; he mouthed the words he was supposed to and tried to blank his mind to his own revulsion. And then came the nightmare of the ninth of November 1938.

They had called it *Kristallnacht*—Crystal Night—because of all the broken glass—a poetic name for a brutality that indeed extended from the North Sea to the Italian border. All across the Reich, synagogues and prayer houses were desecrated, looted, or destroyed, and everywhere Jews were rounded up and shipped off to concentration camps. Assuming the end had come, whole Jewish families committed suicide. And yet Goebbels had announced to the world at large that the fact that not a hair of a single Jew's head had been harmed, despite the rage of the folk, was proof of the forbearance of the German people.

Martinus, though, knew what he had seen, and something in him grew, rough and jagged as a swallowed stone. It would not let him eat or drink or sleep in peace. He grew taut and listless, racked by shame made worse by a rumor from Berlin: the ferocious reaction of the Viennese against the Jews in the days of the *Anschluss* had made this possible. Until then, the Nazi regime had not realized how far it was possible to go; Austria had shown them how much violence the people would accept.

Flake by flake, Martinus' mind shed its sophistication. More and more he came to embrace the Manichean heresy: evil existed as an absolute, unexplainable by any psychological or sociological theory. The powers of darkness, led by Satan, opposed the powers of light, led by God, as concretely and resolutely as two sides opposed each other across the Maginot and Siegfried lines. Simple wickedness was the enemy, and it did not matter what was said by anyone, *Propst* or Bishop, Cardinal or Pope, or Goebbels or der Führer himself. He spent long nights awake in his room, wondering what that meant for him. Some responsibility was imposed on him, but he could not see it clearly. He tried to clarify his thinking by writing poems, but he crumpled and threw them aside in disgust; poetry now was mockery, evasion. Deeds were required.

First, he must do something about Dr. Kleinmann. He had seen him on Crystal Night, in tieless shirt, beltless pants, house slippers, standing helpless in the street and in the hands of the SS at what they called a "collecting point."

Kleinmann's face haunted him. He went to the Christina Hof to see General Helmer. But the General himself was a changed man; he looked old, really old, for the first time, and tired, and his eyes no longer met those of Martinus frankly. "There is nothing I can do," he said. "Nothing. You know our situation. We are ourselves vulnerable."

"But Dr. Kleinmann— He was Frau Helmer's doctor."

"Do you think I have forgotten that?" He saw the pain that crossed Helmer's face. "All the same, there is nothing I can do." He gestured. "Try Robert Schellhammer."

"I have."

Helmer leaned back in his chair, stared at the mounted *Auerhahn* above Martinus' head. "Then try his father," Helmer said.

Thoughtfully, Martinus left the Christina Hof. Two days later he saw Max Schellhammer stumping through Altkreuzburg, dressed in loden and leather, manure clinging to his rubber boots. Martinus overtook him on the street. "Herr Schellhammer!"

"Dr. Martinus?" Schellhammer's leathery face creased in surprise.

"If I could have a few moments of your time . . ."

"Why not? Something for the Poor Relief, I bet."

"Not exactly." They took a table in a coffeehouse, and Martinus sought words, making the case for Kleinmann.

Schellhammer listened, nodding. Martinus would have gone on, but the old farmer raised his hand. "All right," he said. "You don't have to tell me about Kleinmann. I know what you're saying. You're right. Kleinmann is different. My God, I remember when Robert was a kid and had a bellyache in the middle of the night in February and the snow was a meter deep; it was bellyache like we'd never seen before and I got down the hill and into Altkreuzburg, and Kleinmann came back with me. We had to walk up together and it was cold enough to freeze the balls off a bear, and the snow worse all the time—and it was appendicitis. And Kleinmann operated then and there. I couldn't watch it, my wife helped him, after we put him on the kitchen table in the lamplight." Schellhammer drained his coffee cup.

"So, I've no love for Jews, but... Sure. I didn't know that they'd done that to Kleinmann. I didn't know that Robert had let 'em do it. I'll speak to him."

Martinus relaxed. "Thank you, Herr Schellhammer."

"I'm not saying it'll do any good. Robert's always had a mind of his own. Sometimes I don't even know what he's driving at, but he's a good boy and we'll see what we can do. All right?"

"I can ask no more," Martinus said.

"I'll pay for the coffee," said Max Schellhammer.

Kleinmann was released. But so were most of the wealthier Jews, upon their promise to emigrate. And Kleinmann, like all the others, had to crawl before various bureaus for the multiplicity of permits necessary. But Kleinmann and his family got out to Palestine.

Still that jagged stone was heavy in Martinus' belly. This evil could not be merely tolerated; it must be fought. And he was not alone.

The brighter tenth of his classes resented what was happening —the abridgment of their academic freedom—and they had the raw courage of youth, its disdain for consequences. They assaulted Martinus with demands for explanations of what was happening to their education; and finally in self-defense he began teaching special secret classes in literature and religion in a room deep underground in the Stift. The response was startling; not only students but their parents came. Among them were Dr. Frick and Hubertus Hollander. He sensed in them a kinetic energy. In secret sessions after class, the Organization for Austrian Freedom was born. Hardly realizing what was happening, he found himself its leader, converted from a man of words into a man of action.

The organization had touched a nerve. Now, in and around Altkreuzburg, there were three groups of more than thirty, each ignorant of the membership of the other as a precaution, and an attached women's group, and they were in touch with similar groups that had sprung up independently.

And yet, Martinus thought, there was so little concrete that any of them could do. Only circulate newsletters compiled from listening to illegal radios, scatter in secret anti-Nazi slogans printed on cheap paper. Now, after a Sunday afternoon meeting, he waited at the postbus stop in Dornau, a small town a few miles from the Stift. He was taut, nervous, as always these days, felt naked, exposed. . . .

"Dr. Martinus!"

He looked up, snapping back to the present. From the Steyr that had just pulled over to the curb, Christa Condon beckoned to him, smiling.

Martinus went to the car and took her outstretched hand.

"Dr. Martinus, where have you been? It's so long since we've seen you!" She patted the seat. "Get in, I'll take you wherever you are going."

"Thank you, no," Martinus said. "I'm waiting for a friend. He should be along directly."

"Oh." She looked disappointed. Martinus appraised her covertly. She had refused, he saw, to yield to the Nazi decree of dowdiness for women or to cease the use of makeup. Hat, scarf, trench coat, leather driving gloves—these were all the height of insouciant fashion. Her mouth was red with lipstick, her eyes bright. She was still a stunning woman, but he thought he saw the marks of strain around her eyes, her mouth, and there was something mechanical, almost opaque, in her smiling charm, as if it were a mask she wore. "Well, if you're sure . . ."

"I am. Again, thanks very much."

"Oh, you're welcome. You must come to see us. Papa and I often talk about you."

"I've been very busy. You know how it is."

"Oh, yes," she sighed, "everyone is always so busy, busy. Well . . ." Behind her a car honked; she had blocked passage through the narrow street. "*Auf Wiederseh'n,* Dr. Martinus. Heil Hitler."

"Heil Hitler," he said automatically, attaching no importance to her use of the words than to his; one used them without thinking, and really they meant nothing.

She put the car in motion and he watched it go, stepping into the alcove of a shop door. It had been for her sake that he had refused to ride; the Helmers had troubles enough with the regime without being linked to him if anything should happen. Of course, that worked two ways. Presumably she was still under Gestapo observation and he did not want her to draw undue attention to him. Once Frau Pollack had suggested recruiting her—"Heaven knows, after what happened to her husband, she ought to have plenty of motivation"—but it was precisely for that reason that Martinus had vetoed the idea. He did not want people in the organization who had any obvious motive for working against the Nazis.

Still, he pitied Christa. And Lan—what had become of him? Why had he not written? Martinus tried to think of some charitable explanation, could find none. Lan obviously had simply given up. And yet Martinus could not blame him, either. He could not blame anyone who, achieving freedom, tried to forget this nightmare. And Hollywood and all those starlets ... Martinus allowed himself a series of deplorable, lascivious visions to keep him company in the cold and rain. Human flesh was so frail.

He felt depressed. And, for all their organization, their dreams, they were so helpless, he and the others like him. Really, he could no longer see what they might truly accomplish hemmed off from the outside world as they were.

Then, as the postbus roared up the street, he berated himself for such negative thinking, for having so little faith. If Peter had thought like that, where would the Church be now? He got on the bus, savoring the warmth. It made him drowsy, and for a while he hardly thought at all as it roared down the Danube valley, into Altkreuzburg, stopping rarely, for no one was abroad today. It climbed the hill to the high market square near the Stift, pulled over to the curb there, and its doors cranked open. Martinus waited until the two thick-ankled women returning from an afternoon of tea and chatter somewhere got off, and then he descended, briefcase under his arm, opening his umbrella as he did so.

It popped up and rain splattered on it. He started to turn to cross the street. Then, also carrying umbrellas, the two men who seemed to come from nowhere fell in beside him. As he started to step off the curb, one spoke his name.

Martinus turned, throat suddenly tight and something in his stomach fluttering like a big wounded bird. He looked into the polite, grave, ruthless faces and knew it would do no good to run. A few drops of urine ran down his leg, and he could hardly breathe and found it impossible to speak; all he could do was clutch the briefcase more fiercely to him, as if he would lock it forever with his arms.

6 AT FIRST she had blamed the disruption of transatlantic mail by the war; when it became obvious that communications with the United States were only minimally disrupted, she was certain the Gestapo was appropriating her incoming mail. Discreetly, the General checked with postal authorities. By the beginning of 1940 it was clear that nobody was stealing the letters; Lan Condon simply was not sending any.

Still she kept on writing. Her own letters became more frantic. Was he well? What had happened to him? Please, please, let her know. The ones she mailed were not returned; they were merely unanswered. She had the address of his agent; in desperation she wrote to him.

That one evoked a reply. "Thank you for your letter. I've already turned it over to Lan, who I'm sure will be in touch with you to straighten out the problems in your correspondence." Then, with at least a touch of compassion: "He is well and very successful in his work, which, of course, means that he has been very busy. All best wishes. . . ."

So he was well, successful. That much knowledge anyhow filled her with a shuddering relief. She wrote more desperately without results. And eventually she had to face up to the realization she had tried to keep where it would touch neither mind nor heart. He had given up.

That was the kindest way to put it. There were others. He was disgusted with her country and so with her. He had ceased to love her. He had found someone else. There were so many beautiful women where he was—women he could hold and kiss and take to bed. How could letters, vapid letters, compete with them? It was over.

And yet all too graphically she could see him in bed with another woman, and the rage would hit her, fierce and suffocating. Her mind filled with images of brutal, obscene clarity; they were sometimes so unbearable she struck at herself with clawed nails. That sort of jealous rage would leave her gasping, panting, physically sick.

Eventually the rages became rarer. Presently they ceased altogether, to be replaced by despair, like grief at a loved one's death. With time's passage, that grew less profound; but it was always there like a lingering low-grade infection that left its victim functioning but never truly healthy. She gradually accepted that there was only one cure for it, and that impossible, and that she would never be quite well again. Sometimes she was startled to realize that she was only twenty-five; most of the time she felt like an old woman—listless, joyless, only getting from one day to another as best she could.

And, possessed of pride herself, she sent no more letters to America.

There was, as the months wheeled by, a great deal else to occupy her mind, inside and out of the Christina Hof.

If, she told herself, she had known at the time what she knew now, she would never have resisted Robert that night on the terrace. Resisted? She would have thrown herself wide open to him, let him take her then and there on the cold stone floor, married him as soon as possible. But by the time she understood, it was too late.

She did not, at first, tell her father about what had happened that night on the terrace. That was a mistake; it left him dangling in air. Robert's good will had been the key factor in the intricate scheme of survival Helmer had worked out for the Christina Hof. And suddenly it had been withdrawn, leaving him confused and vulnerable. He had not truly realized what was happening until Robert's engagement to the butcher's daughter was made public. Then he had called Christa to his office.

He himself was strained and nervous, and suddenly she was struck by how *old* he looked and realized with a shock that he was now past sixty. He showed her the item in the Altkreuzburg weekly paper. "Christa, I don't understand this. Do you?"

"Papa, I'm afraid I do," she said, and then she told him.

He had, she noticed, developed a nervous habit of biting his underlip, and he did that as he listened. But when she was through, he only nodded. "I see. Well, at least now it all makes sense." He drew in a deep breath, let it out.

"Papa, I'm so sorry. But I didn't know, and . . . I just couldn't."

He rose, smiling faintly, came to her, held her tightly to him. "Of course you couldn't," he said quietly. "Of course you couldn't."

"Maybe I was a fool. Maybe . . . I know it means more trouble for you."

Helmer let her go, stepped back. "Forget that. That's not the point. The point is . . ." He hesitated, groped for words. "Look," he said quietly. "In 1914 I went off to war. I was gone for months, years, at a time. Your mother waited, never knowing from one minute to the next whether I was alive or dead, what news the post would bring next. She was lonely and she was frightened, but she never gave up. There were plenty of temptations in her way, too, plenty of stay-at-home officers in fancy uniforms and all a lot younger and richer than I was. We had our own Golden Pheasants, you know, who had pull enough never to hear a shot fired in anger. Anyhow, she went through all that, and she never faltered, never lost faith and . . . She was a *woman,* one in millions. Do you expect me to criticize you for being her daughter?" He found no more words, but she knew what he meant, and she loved him fiercely and went to him again and they held each other.

Still, it *had* made a difference, and a drastic one. Papa rarely spoke to her of finances, but she knew the *Anschluss* had changed their situation radically. The whole financial structure of the country had changed overnight; and connections were necessary, graft and bribes required to bring off a transaction of any size. There was now a whole new group of insiders to whom one must have access.

Slowly, carefully, adroitly, Helmer had gained access, through his own sly diplomacy—but also through the good offices of Robert Schellhammer. Now, with Robert's support withdrawn and new wartime restrictions in effect, Helmer had to struggle for the financing that he needed and, failing to get it, dip into his ever-diminishing capital.

In the past the Christina Hof had been profitable enough to make such considerations minor ones. In part, though, its profits had been founded on cooperation, not competition, with Max and Robert Schellhammer.

Now the Schellhammers, without conscience, went after Helmer's markets; and a buyer, faced with a choice between a high Party official and one who was not, could make only one decision: quality and price were not even secondary considerations. Overnight the General had to rebuild his business almost from scratch. That would have been a challenge to a younger man; it was very possibly more than Christa's father, she began to understand, could handle.

Somehow, he had so far brought it off, using all of his shrewdness and reputation. Yet, with the signing of the nonaggression pact with Russia, even his title of the Butcher of Galicia diminished in worth. What kept him afloat was his connections in the Wehrmacht, as high as the General Staff. There were Austrians and Germans, too, on active duty who had not forgotten his exploits in Galicia, and he played those for all they were worth.

He had to, for suddenly catastrophe hit the Ferntal. Like angels of death one winter weekend the Gestapo swept through the valley and the town. Nearly two hundred people, most from leading families, were taken unexpectedly, people the Helmers had known for years. And among them was Dr. Martinus. Newspapers blared triumphantly the destruction of a traitorous spy ring for the British, its leader a renegade priest from Altkreuzburg. And as gossip spread the details, Christa realized with horror that Martinus had been taken the very afternoon that she had offered him a ride. If he'd not declined, he would have been in her car when the arrest was made—and that would have been the end of the family Helmer. The narrow margin by which they had averted destruction left her sick and shaken.

A fear-sick silent tension settled over the whole area. By now everyone knew how the Gestapo operated and that anything arousing suspicion could mean destruction; there were eavesdroppers and denouncers everywhere. The "Hitler Look" had become a part of life—the quick, apprehensive twist of the head to see who was watching, listening, before one spoke. Now there were means at hand for the vindictive and the deranged to settle old scores; even an anonymous letter was all the Gestapo needed. And, of course, already tainted, the Helmers were doubly vulnerable.

Thus, Christa knew, her father was entangled in a spiderweb

of problems, and it was necessary to consider and judge every move. Without the cachet Robert had lent them, only rarely now did Party officials appear at the Christina Hof on weekends, and their invitations dwindled. There was even chilling gossip that Charlotte Richter Schellhammer was pressing her husband to acquire the Christina Hof; she was impatient at sharing the plainer Schellhammer Hof with Robert's parents and already imagining herself as the mistress of a grander house. And Christa and the General both knew that any time Robert wanted the Christina Hof, he could have it almost for a snap of his fingers. The Party owed him that much.

There was nothing she herself could do about any of this except manage the house and its people as best she could and minimize the strain of petty annoyances on her father. Into that she threw herself wholeheartedly, letting it blank out everything else; Ernst, her father, and the Christina Hof became all there was in life.

But despite her efforts, she could see the toll all this took on General Helmer. He had begun to drink now to relieve the pressure, and not just wine, but potent brandy and cognac and slivovitz. His body seemed to shrink, except for his face and belly, and these grew strangely fat and bloated. But even that did not worry her so much as the headaches.

Her first intimation of these was one day when, at the height of the harvest in 1940, instead of going out to the vineyards or taking station in the pressing house, he sat down to his *Gabelfrühstück* at ten-thirty in the morning and then shoved his plate aside. Eyes watering, he put a hand to his temple. "Papa?" Christa, across the table, straightened up. "Papa, what's wrong?"

Helmer shook his head, but she did not miss his wince of pain. "Nothing," he said thickly. "Nothing. Just a headache. I've been on the telephone all morning. They didn't send us half the labor troops they promised. I'm just a little tense. I think I'll go lie down for a while. Do we have any aspirin?"

Aspirin? Lie down? Before eleven in the morning? Christa could not have been more startled if her father had suddenly confessed to some awful vice. Indeed, for him weakness had always been one. "Papa—" She got the aspirin, saw him take not two but three. "Just for an hour," he said, and he left the table and went to his room. But he did not re-emerge until after two.

When Christa looked in on him at the noonday meal, he was asleep.

The rest of that week he seemed himself again. She had no intimation that the headaches had become chronic until, on a routine check of medical supplies before a shopping trip, she found a big flask of aspirin that had been emptied in a third of the usual time. And somehow she knew at once who had taken it.

That was when she tried to get him to the doctor in Altkreuzburg. He resisted, and she could not move him. For that matter, she did not blame him. The man who had taken over Kleinmann's practice was little more than a quack; but he was a devoted Party member from Bavaria. She bought more aspirin, made sure the supply was replenished as it dwindled. There was nothing else she could do.

Ernst demanded her attention as well. He was old enough now for the harsh paramilitary training of the Hitler Youth, and there seemed to be no way to get him exempted. At seventeen he faced a dreadful schedule, trying to cope with the academics necessary for his *Matura,* working part time at the Music Academy in Vienna, and meeting his training obligations with the Hitler Jugend. There was ambition, aggression, masculine drive in him, but it all centered on his music; otherwise he was the tenderest and gentlest of boys. The Blood and Iron philosophy of the HJ revolted him, but he dared not protest. Dragging in at night, trying to practice, sometimes he put his head down on the piano and cried out of sheer frustration. There was little that Christa could do to console him. He and Lan both had taught her the intricacies, unreachable by others, of the artistic personality, which curled up like a hedgehog and showed its spines the moment it was touched by another species.

She did her best to minimize the strain on him, lend what support she could. Her father and her brother kept her hands full, and for her that was a blessing. She drew around herself a closed and narrow circle, leaving it only when a little mild seductiveness might help to soften the attitude of some Nazi *Bonz,* the term for a Buddhist high priest used sardonically by the Austrians. Then she did not begrudge a pat on the rump, a fleeting hand across the breasts, and she could look up, wide-eyed, smiling, breathless as well as any whore. But she hated him, she hated them with a cold hatred she dared not show; they had robbed her of everything.

7 HELMER WASHED THE THREE ASPIRINS down with brandy and buried his face in his hands, waiting for the pain to go away. Sometimes it did, sometimes not; and when it did not, it took all his will and strength to mask it.

Outside, summer was on the land, vineyards in full June leaf, meadows and forests lush. Bees buzzed in the clematis around the window of his office; but the buzzing in his skull overrode the sound they made.

Slowly the headache faded, but it did not cease entirely. Finally Helmer took another drink of brandy, a measure of his desperation. If it did not end the pain, it would diminish the fear. Something, he knew, was badly wrong with him. He needed a doctor, but he dared not go to one. He would be immediately sent to a hospital; and once he was helpless, the wolves would pounce. He had no margin left for illness.

He was not afraid of it, nor of death, but of leaving the Christina Hof unprotected; only he stood between it and destruction. Financially, politically, he dared not falter or show any weakness. So the pain must be endured. If the harvest was very good this year, if England finally surrendered, it was barely possible that he could organize things so he could rest; until then he must hang on.

There was one thing, though, that always helped, distracting his mind from its worries: the battle map pinned on the wall. It was clipped from the *Völkische Beobachter,* and he marked it every day with crayons. This morning there was little to change on it. But surveying it relaxed him, for it was triumphant, to him a true work of art. And it made up for a great deal of what the Nazis had cost him. If one blamed Hitler for domestic difficulties and increasingly ugly problems, one had as well to give him credit for the victories. As a professional soldier, Helmer could feel nothing but admiration.

It had all been done so beautifully and with the fewest possible casualties. The armored sweeps across the Low Countries, the outflanking of the Maginot line, and the delightful totality of the French defeat, at which he could only gloat. He could take less satisfaction in the plight of the English, and yet there had been something deeply satisfying in the way their noses had been wiped at Dunkirk. All the lands of the old Empire of his youth were back under German domination. Every campaign a victory, all the old shames had been erased. And, with superb cleverness, all of that had been accomplished without arousing the sullen bear of Russia; a few bits and pieces here and there thrown to its jaws and it was content—and frightened.

So it had to end soon, Helmer thought, feeling better. Not even Churchill, not even the illegal help Roosevelt was giving the English, could save Great Britain much longer. Which was why, he convinced himself, he need not worry about Ernst.

"I swear by God this holy oath, that I will serve the leader of the German Reich and Folk, Adolf Hitler, the Supreme Commander of the Army, with absolute obedience, and, as a brave soldier, will be prepared at any time to risk my life for this oath."

When, a month ago, Ernst had spoken those words, he had become a German soldier. And never in Helmer's life had any event stirred such mixed emotions in him. As a professional himself, there was the pride he felt in seeing his only son in uniform, even though, strictly speaking, it was not the one he himself had worn. But as a father—and one who knew war all too well—something within him quailed. If anything happened to Ernst, he had no idea how he himself would survive.

But the idea of obtaining exemption for the boy ran cross-grained to everything he himself believed about manhood. And no matter what his talents, however his career ran in the future, first of all Ernst Helmer must be a man. It would be no service to him in the long run to deny him an experience fundamental to every real man—the chance to wear his country's uniform in war. Later it would be something he would treasure, something that would strengthen and sustain his pride as long as he lived.

Still, Ernst was no *Landser*—no doughboy—and never would be, and it would be no service either to the Army or to him to

try to make him into one. There was room in the Wehrmacht
for many talents; and he could best serve as a musician. He
could entertain the troops, giving concerts for them, and still be
exposed to no real danger. Helmer pulled a few strings to make
sure that assignment was certain—his old friends were accom-
modating—and, when Ernst's class was called for the Army,
everything had been set in order. And the boy's reaction to what
awaited him had surprised Helmer with its insight and maturity.
The General had begun to explain why he did not feel justified
in pushing for an exemption, but Ernst had cut him off.

"Papa, don't let it bother you. I understand. Anyhow, you're
right. It's better that I go. This is my country, my people. And
besides, how would it look if the son of General Helmer dodged
serving?"

"That's not the point."

"I know it isn't. You're not thinking of yourself; you never
do. But do you mind if other people think of you a little bit?
You've got troubles enough without a lot of gossip about my
staying home and being bombproof. I know that things aren't
so good with us right now, and I hope my wearing the uniform
will make 'em easier for you. In the long run it'll probably make
it easier for me, too." He paced the room, unbelievably tall,
sprouting almost overnight, it seemed, higher than his father,
though very thin. "Oh, I've given it a lot of thought from all
the angles. In the first place, obviously, as a musician I can't
get hurt. In the second, the war can't last much longer; and
when I'm mustered out and pick up my career, I'll need all the
backing from the state I can get. You know there's terrible
competition among real concert pianists. It surely won't do me
any harm if I've pulled my hitch. And who knows? I might
like it. After all, there's a little matter of heredity. Anyhow,
don't worry. I can take care of myself, and I'd much rather be
playing for the troops than picking those damned grapes." He
grinned broadly and came to Helmer. "So you don't have to make
apologies." And he put his arm around his father and kissed
him, something he did less and less as he had grown older.

Helmer held him for a moment, and then stepped away.
Looking at Ernst with new eyes, he felt a rich, deep surge of
happiness. He had achieved the aim of every decent father: he
had sired a *man*. Something closed his throat; to mask it he

275

turned away. "Let's have a drink together," he had said, as if somehow that would seal a compact, establish a new relationship.

Now Ernst was taking basic combat training at a *Kaserne* in Swabia, and there was an emptiness and stillness in the house. But, Helmer thought, the pain wholly gone now as he surveyed the map, Ernst would never have to use that training. And when the war ended, he could come home, go on with his career, and that in a country prosperous and powerful and proud, once more part of the greatest empire of Europe. Helmer had to hope for that, anyhow, and believe that, and hang on as long as possible, until it was achieved. And, he thought, feeling much better, his old strength returning, he would. Somehow he would.

Now his head was clear and he could tackle the problems on his desk—the need for priorities for new stocks of bottles and new equipment. They had changed the damned rationing system again and there were new forms, opaque with legalese, to be deciphered. These Golden Pheasants, clogging the pipelines with their papers, were worse than Jews. Maybe when the war was over, they would all be shipped east to Poland, too, like the Jews.

The Jews. Helmer lit a cigarette. Well, that had been pretty rough. And yet, there again, maybe the Draconian method was justified. How else to uproot them, break their power? What was the difference, anyway, between a Chosen People and a Master Race? They'd had the idea first and had pursued it single-mindedly, so why not send them back to where they had come from originally—and give the German people a chance to function without them? And really, especially in wartime, it made sense; you could not have a nation within a nation, loyal only to itself. Maybe if they had thought a little more about the country that had taken them in and made so many of them rich, and a little less about their Chosen-ness, they might have been treated differently. Anyhow, they were lucky. The Russians would simply have exterminated them. As it was, they were only being relocated to where they could all live together in one vast Jewish enclave, which was what, anyhow, they seemed to prefer to do wherever they settled.

Still, it was strange not having them around. Kleinmann—there was one Jew he really missed. He could have sat down with Alex, discussed not only his symptoms but his problems, and they could have worked out something. But that stupid swine who had taken Kleinmann's place at the *Spital* in Altkreuzburg, he knew a lot of Nazi doctrine but damned little medicine. Damn it, he did miss Alex. And he hadn't been able to find a decent tailor since the entire Birnbaum family had been resettled.

Well, let that go for now. All these papers to be filled out... Start at the beginning, be methodical and orderly. He wrote in the date on a priority application, 22 June 1941, and went on from there meticulously, losing track of time. He was only vaguely aware of the ringing of the gate bell until Christa knocked on his door, then opened it. He turned, faintly irritated. "Yes, what is it?"

"Papa, there is a gentleman here to see you. A writer for the Propaganda Ministry." She passed him a card.

"Dr. Abelard Hossbach," he read aloud. "What does he want?"

Christa shrugged. "An interview. Something about Russia in the last war."

Helmer frowned, but he could not help being vaguely flattered. So they had not forgotten him. Still, they had been soft-pedaling Russia and it was certainly better that way. Probably Christa was confused; likely they wanted his views on the strategic situation in North Africa. He had been consulted several times by the press on such matters, though his views had rarely seen print.

Anyhow, this was a vital aspect of his connections. "Show him in," he said.

Dr. Hossbach was a towering man in his late forties, with a graying beard and a substantial corporation. His manner was jovial, his eyes twinkling, and in bishop's robe and miter he would have made an excellent St. Nicholas. "Herr Generalmajor Helmer. How nice of you to receive me." His palm was soft, slightly clammy.

"Not at all." Helmer handed him a brandy, which Hossbach tossed off briskly. Smacking his lips, he set down the glass and opened his briefcase, taking out notebook and pencils.

"What can I do for you?" the General asked.

"I am here by direct order from Berlin, at the specific request of Dr. Otto Dietrich, of the Press Department of the Propaganda Ministry. You will remember that in the First War you figured in exposing Russian atrocities, which led to your famous order of no quarter against the Cossacks and the Russians dubbing you the Butcher of Galicia and placing a reward on your head—which, incidentally, has never been revoked. We should like and you are requested to give us your personal memories of the incident—in short, an interview which will be widely published in the press."

Helmer stared at him.

Hossbach lit a cigarette. The twinkle in his eyes had died now. "You have a rare knowledge of the Russian soldier, the, ah, depths of bestiality of which the Slavic mind is capable. I've reviewed the old press archives and photos myself." He made a face of revulsion. "Ghastly. Inhuman. Unbelievable."

Outside, the bees buzzed steadily in the clematis, or perhaps it was the buzzing in his head again. Helmer thought of the sound that wind made in endless fields of dry sunflower stalks. A vein throbbed in his temple, and his entrails stirred with an old familiar sickness. "I beg your pardon," he heard himself answer. "But to be honest, it is something I would prefer not to discuss."

"Understandably. Nevertheless, I must ask you to."

Helmer bit his underlip. Suddenly he craved another brandy. Pouring for himself and Hossbach, he asked, "Are you sure? We're at peace with Russia." Of course, he could see it, every detail, just as it still reappeared in dreams. The decanter's neck chattered faintly against the glasses with a chiming sound. "I can't possibly see any use in—"

"My dear Generalmajor Helmer, the Propaganda Ministry has a reason for everything it does. Believe me, we understand that even the mere recall of such an incident must be extremely painful. Still, I am told it is necessary—not merely the facts, but your own most personal subjective reactions to the atrocity. Surely you have no love for the Russians—"

"I hate the bastards!" Helmer blurted. He dropped into his chair, hands clenching and unclenching on the desk before him. "I loathe and despise them! But—" His heart was pounding with a reflexive, formless fear. His left eye began to water; that meant the pain would soon be coming back. "But we must not anger them!" he snapped. "Strategically it would be a disaster, arousing them against us. What purpose would be served?" He leaned

278

forward confidentially. "Look," he said. "Until the nonaggression pact, the *rapprochement,* they were still using me in their propaganda, the Bolsheviks. And they're not all that far away, you know, and if I revive this now— Really, Herr Doktor Hossbach..."

Hossbach sighed. "My dear Generalmajor, this is, for all practical purposes, a *Führerbefehl*—an order from our leader himself. As a good Party member, I trust you'll offer no more objections. Besides, the matter is fairly urgent. Now, with your permission, shall we get on with it? An hour should suffice, and by the time we're through, there'll be an official photographer here."

"Thank you, Herr General," the photographer said, returning his camera to its case.

"You're welcome," Helmer managed. His head felt as if his brain were growing like a mushroom, expanding, battering against the confining limits of his skull. His face felt flushed, his spine chilled and cold; and he knew his hands trembled and that the last quarter hour of the interview had been disjointed, partly from pain, partly from the brandy that he had used to quench it. "You will, of course, stay and eat."

"Sorry, no. We have a deadline. But thank you for your courtesy. Now perhaps I can repay it and explain it all. Yes, it is exactly noon." Hossbach went to the *Volksempfänger*—the cheap government-made radio set on a shelf near Helmer's desk —and switched it on. It buzzed and crackled.

"Please listen, General Helmer," Hossbach said, holding up a hand. Wagnerian music faded. Then a voice, which Helmer recognized as the deep, rich one of Dr. Goebbels himself, began to speak. Helmer listened, the words blurred by the veil of pain. "No," he heard himself say. "No, that is impossible."

"But true." Hossbach smiled. "Now do you understand? This morning at half past three our armies invaded the Soviet Union on a tremendous front. Already we're smashing forward without opposition, and their air force has been destroyed on the ground. As Dr. Goebbels said, der Führer is disgusted with Russian provocations and is determined to settle the problem of Russia once and for all, for a thousand years. It has all, of course, been kept very secret until now. But"—his eyes shone—"with the

Russ disposed of, we are masters of all of Europe! And—"

"The fool!" Helmer heard himself roar. "The fool, the idiot!" The pain lanced through his skull and flared. "Doesn't he know? He had it won! But, my God, now— Russia? Russia? Oh, the fool!"

"General, you can't mean der Führer!"

"I—" The rage, despair, within Helmer was almost too great to contain. Tears of pain ran down his cheeks; he was sure his left temple bubbled out from the pressure. "Napoleon," he said huskily. "For God's sake. It was on this same date that Napoleon crossed the Niemen. Now war on both flanks?"

"General, you are overwrought," Hossbach said.

"It's madness," Helmer said. "Absolute madness. And so . . . useless."

"Herr Generalmajor—" Then Hossbach nodded. "Yes, you're overwrought. In Christ's name, what you've just relived would be enough to overstretch the nerves of anyone." He touched Helmer's shoulder. "We shan't report this. But please get a grip on yourself. And remember, you must have faith. Der Führer knows what he is doing, and the German soldier is invincible."

"Yes," Helmer said. "Yes. I am sorry. Only . . . Yes. Thank you."

"Come on, Sepp, let's go," Hossbach said. "General—" They shook hands. The radio droned on with news of victories. Helmer did not see them to the door; when they had left his office, he slumped down in his chair. Russia: Napoleon, Moscow. A three-front war, counting the Mediterranean—and those great reaches, those limitless depths of the East, which Hitler had never seen; oh, it was madness, sheer madness, and Ernst—

They must not send him there. If the Russians ever learned that he was the son of the Butcher of Galicia . . . The image that filled Helmer's mind was unbearable. Something must be done. It must be arranged. He reached for the phone. There was someone he must call about it, someone who . . . He would go straight to the Emperor if necessary. . . . No, that was not right. Whom was he to call? He could not remember, but it would come back in a minute.

The bees out there beyond the window, that buzzing in his ears. No, that was the wind; it always made that sound in the fields of sunflowers in the autumn. And those damned ravens circling . . . Well, there is no help for it, he thought. I cannot ask someone else to do it. It is something I must do myself. Those poor boys. Those poor, poor boys. My head hurts.

There was a flare of pain in his left temple, as if he had been wounded. Then it died completely and at last he was all right again. He could do what he had to do. He could—

Behind him the door opened and he turned. For a moment he stared at the person standing there; the wind was stronger in the sunflowers. Helmer sighed. It could not be postponed; not one second longer must they suffer.

"Captain Ropertz," he said, "hold my horse."

8   THE MASSIVE OAK stood in the center of a clearing deep in the Wienerwald, racks to hold hay as winter feed for deer around its base. Crude wooden cabinets encircled its thick trunk five feet above the ground, fitted with shelves and glass doors, and crammed with cheap pictures of the Virgin, crucifixes, and the like, and numerous little jars and vases containing fresh or artificial flowers. A *Waldandacht*—a place of devotion in the woods—and nothing in it could have been worth more than a few pfennigs; yet to Christa its surroundings and the very simplicity of its contents, placed there by devout villagers and peasants, had always transcended its essential tawdriness. Here, far more easily than in a church, she could pray, and often had. Yet today, standing alone before the oak, autumn sunlight slanting through the forest, she could find no words—not even here. All her prayers, all her faith had been used up; she was exhausted.

Had been ever since that shattering day when she had entered Papa's office to tell him of the announcement that Russia had been invaded, and he had said to her, "Captain Ropertz, hold my horse."

At first she had thought it was a joke. "Papa—"

"They must not be allowed to suffer any longer," he said. "I shall undertake what is necessary."

"Papa—" Christa summoned a weak smile, but there was something in his eyes that made her stomach twist. "Listen, Papa, the radio just said—"

He was fumbling at his waist. "My pistol. I seem to have mislaid it. Captain Ropertz, I will thank you for your pistol."

"Papa." She took his hand. "Papa, listen."

Then his eyes met hers. All at once she felt a brutal nausea. There was no recognition on his face; he did not know her. Something was fantastically, dreadfully wrong.

"I must have a gun," he said. "I must have a gun to shoot them with."

Her eyes flickered to the weapons in the cabinet. "Yes," she heard herself say. "Yes, Herr Generalmajor. Come with me. We shall find a gun." She pulled his hand, leading him toward the door, and to her relief, he came.

"Afterwards," he said, "I shall write an order . . ."

She led him to his room. He went readily, as if his mind were somewhere else, wholly occupied. "Herr Generalmajor, you must lie down."

"Lie down? Are you mad? I have no time for—"

She did not know what inspired it. She stroked his cheek, smoothed his hair, managed somehow to keep her voice soft and steady. "Kurt, this is . . . Christina. The campaign is over. You must lie down and rest."

To her relief, subtly, his eyes changed. There was even the beginning of a smile. "Christina. Darling."

"Yes. I'm here. Christina's here. Now please lie down. You've been in Russia, but now you're safe at home. Now, my love—" She pushed him to the bed.

He sank down, then sprawled with a sigh, arm across his eyes. "Home. Thank God. I am tired, so tired. It was . . . bad. If they had caught me, you know, they would have put me in a cage. But now . . . Darling, we've been apart so long."

"Yes, I know. But now it's all all right. Just rest, just sleep. I'll be back in one minute." She pulled off his shoes, then stroked his forehead. It was clammy to her touch. She waited a few seconds; he did not stir. Quietly, watching him, she edged from the room. In the corridor she leaned against the wall, knees suddenly weak, heart seemingly about to wrench itself from its moorings. "Oh, my God," she whispered. *"Oh, my God!"* Then she ran to the telephone.

Christa had given up going to the Party hack who had taken Kleinmann's place. Instead she went to a certain Dr. Walzer, who, while impeccably Aryan, was a strange and prickly character of some independent mind. He was not a Party member, and that, combined with his personality, had reduced his practice to almost nothing. But that did not disturb him; nothing ever seemed to disturb Matthias Walzer except the stupidity of mankind. And, unlike the quack, he had never lectured her on her lack of fruitfulness and never touched her in an unprofessional way.

It had been two hours before he could get there; by the time he arrived, Christa was fighting hysteria. As soon as she had called him, she had run back to Helmer's bedroom, to find him sleeping. She kept vigil over him; in a half hour he awakened. To her relief, he knew her now, but he was still far from normal. Aware of his surroundings, he nevertheless rambled. Most of what he said was disjointed and senseless, but fortunately he was wholly docile in an almost childlike way and she had no difficulty keeping him in bed. He knew Walzer, too, when the doctor finally arrived, but was puzzled. "Where is Kleinmann? If I'm sick, Alex Kleinmann should see to me."

"Dr. Kleinmann couldn't come, Papa," Christa said. "He sent Dr. Walzer." She tried not to cry as her eyes met those of the doctor. He was smooth and reassuring as he wrapped the blood pressure cuff on her father's arm.

"That's right, Herr General. Alex is very busy these days. I'm helping him with his practice. Now . . ."

In a half hour it was over. Helmer obediently took the pills Walzer gave him, lay back, and almost instantly was sound asleep. In the corridor the doctor said, "I think he will sleep for several hours, but someone should be with him all the time. It's not likely, but it's possible he'll need some restraint." He sighed. "Your father, Frau Condon, as you've probably guessed, has had a stroke, fortunately one comparatively minor, I believe. He doesn't seem impaired physically, but as to his mind . . . Well, only time will tell."

283

"Shouldn't he be in the hospital?" Christa tried to wrestle with the implications of all this.

Walzer lit a cigarette. "Under normal circumstances, I'd say yes. But—" He looked at her through smoke. "Of course, it's something I'm not competent to judge, but one hears rumors and . . . The affairs of a man of your father's stature are always complex. And they could suffer if word spread prematurely that his mental competence had been affected. I've known substantial businessmen to be, well, ruined quite needlessly because word had got about that temporarily they could not control their own affairs. Now, it may be that General Helmer is invulnerable, perhaps you or his son can manage—"

"We can't," Christa said, and she saw exactly what he meant. She thought of the rumors Walzer must have heard—Charlotte Schellhammer and her longing for the Christina Hof; she thought of the Gestapo and her father's magical staving off of its pressures. The coldness within her grew. "All the same, his health is what counts. If he can get better care in the *Krankenhaus*—"

"He can't," Walzer said bluntly. "Not under the, ah, present administration of the *Spital*. In fact, I think remaining in familiar surroundings would hasten his recovery."

Christa drew in a deep breath. "Then you think he'll recover?"

"To some extent. Only time will tell. These things are completely unpredictable. But his confusion was already lessening as I examined him and . . . I am hopeful that in a few days he'll be wholly rational once again."

"Thank God," Christa whispered. "I was afraid . . . Then you do think he'll soon be back to normal?"

"Rational, I said. Normal—that I can't guarantee. I only meant that I hope he'll be aware of his surroundings again, recognize everyone in the usual way, be capable of a routine pattern of daily living. But we have to face the fact there's been some brain damage—maybe more, maybe less. To be honest, it's unlikely that he'll ever be completely the man he was before. Even under the best circumstances, there's usually a fall-off in drive, alertness, shrewdness. You or someone had better be prepared to familiarize yourself with his business affairs and to help him with them. In fact, he shouldn't be allowed to manage them at all until he's recovered as fully as possible. And, of course, there may be a repetition; there often is. But I'll prescribe a diet that will bring down his blood pressure; he'll need rest and quiet, and I'll provide you with sedatives and relaxants. For the moment, that's all I can tell you. I'll see him again tonight and tomorrow." His grim face softened. "It could be worse, much worse. And I still recommend that you keep all this strictly within the family if possible." Then, briskly, he had shaken her hand and left.

Christa hurried back to Helmer's room. He slept soundly; and looking down at him, she found the courage of necessity and made her decision. The doctor had been right. Until she knew how things stood, she must not let word of this get around. Fortunately she had told the servants only that their master was not feeling well; she would pass it off as summer flu. For the time being, anyhow, not even Ernst would know. Later she would see.

She had a cot moved into his room and remained with him day and night. In twenty-four hours he was already returning to a semblance of normality, recognizing her, oriented in his world once more. "But I don't understand," he said. "What happened? I remember there were some journalists. Russia. And . . . Why am I in bed?"

"Papa," Christa said gently, "you had a small temporary collapse. Too much work, too much strain, at your age. Nothing serious, but you need rest."

A few days before, Helmer would have snorted, *Rest? Nonsense! I've better things to do than loll in bed all day!* Now he only blinked vaguely, face strangely wan and old. "I see," he murmured.

Walzer, when he came, judged that he was ready to know the truth and explained it. "Rest, proper diet, a course of medicine I shall prescribe. Then you'll come around, Herr General."

"I'm sure. Thank you," Helmer said and asked no real questions of him, accepting all with strange passivity. Though he remembered that Russia had been invaded, he asked no questions about the progress of the war and raised no objections when Christa would not let him have a radio. When she explained that she had thought it better not to worry Ernst, he agreed.

A few more days in bed and then he was up and around, and seemingly as physically as strong as before. But to Christa, who knew him so well, what was left was only a mockery of the man he had been before. All the drive, all the force, was gone; the mind once lightning-swift now worked tortuously, seemingly incapable of protracted concentration, its attention span short as a child's. Yet, an outsider meeting him only briefly would have seen no change; only those who lived with him could measure its extent.

Now a new weight bore down on Christa; it fell to her not only to manage the house itself but every aspect of the Christina Hof and its holdings. It was, after all, an ongoing business and decisions were demanded. And for a while, at least, Helmer was incapable of making them.

Long into the night she pored over his records and correspondence, trying to comprehend the place's finances—receivables and payables, production, sales, taxes, labor, equipment—the entire intricate network spun by Helmer for their survival and prosperity.

Nothing in her life had prepared her for this, and much was incomprehensible. Sometimes she could get clarification from Helmer and sometimes not. All she could do was blunder through, and slowly an eerie, nerve-racking pattern evolved. Her father became a straw man behind which she hid, a puppet whose strings she pulled. It was desperately necessary that the world at large continue to believe in his undiminished strength and capability; perils lurked everywhere. She had to foster that illusion while learning to manage the Christina Hof herself.

For ninety days now she had managed to keep up the facade, but only at great cost. Like a good child, Helmer said and did what she told him to. He made phone calls, went to business meetings with her at his side under the pretense of serving as his secretary and assistant; together they dealt with the labor on the place, preparing for the forthcoming harvest.

Ernst came home on leave, taller, filling out, in the process of metamorphosis from adolescent to man. When she told him what had happened, he took it more calmly than she had expected, and with more maturity. His army training had taught him to withstand catastrophe, and she was bolstered. They discussed whether it would be feasible for him to seek a discharge and come home to help her, and they decided against that. All the circumstances would have to be set forth officially, the General's weakness revealed. So at leave's end Ernst returned to Poland with a special unit to entertain the troops in the East. At least she did not have to worry about his being exposed to combat; and while he had been home, Helmer's mind had seemed sharper, more alert.

But now it had lapsed back into its former foggy, passive state, and not even the activity of the *Weinlese* had aroused him. He required more pushing, not less, and the burden on her during harvest had trebled. Combined with running the house, it was almost more than she could bear; she herself was physically, mentally, spiritually exhausted.

Too tired to pray, she crossed herself and turned from the *Waldandacht*. And, she thought, walking on into the woods, it could not go on like this. Ah, God, what a mess she had made of her life! Lan, Josef Steiner, Robert, now Papa—every man she had been close to stricken by one disaster or another. What had she done, how had she sinned to earn such punishment? For a moment she halted, leaning against a beech. How alone she felt, how utterly alone!

But she had learned this much from all she had endured: self-pity was the most destructive enemy of all. Only yield to it for a moment and you were lost, and too much depended on her for her to risk that luxury. No, she would manage somehow, she would think of something.

The path led her down into a ravine. The clean simple exercise of walking was good, restful. Nimbly she followed the trail up the other side, along a hill beneath the yellow canopy of the huge old beeches; and then, at the crest, she came into a clearing. Here she halted, looking at the curious loaf-shaped house and its adjacent smaller sheds, wattled structures of sticks and mud and thatch.

Professor Busch, she thought, poor mad old man. And he was gone now, too. And— It was strange, but not until this moment had she considered that Busch had been the most important factor in her life. If, on that day that seemed now like a half-forgotten dream, he had not confronted Lan, turned him back to meet Martinus, everything would have, for better or for worse, been different—and how much joy she would have missed! And how much pain, she thought, too, bitterly, and wondered if it had been worthwhile. Then she thought of Busch's woman, that poor, grubby, workworn infatuated girl. And where was she now, and did it seem like a dream to her, that weird idyll in the woods, tending goats for her old demented lover? Christa pitied her. Absently, she went to the house, still sound, undamaged by time or vandalism, and touched the rough wooden door. To her surprise it swung open promptly on its leather hinges. Automatically she entered. It was dim in here and musty-smelling and—

She gave a startled, formless cry as the man sitting at the table in the dirt-floored room jumped up and whirled. "What—?" he blurted. "Christa—"

Her eyes strained against the gloom. Then the swift beat of her heart slowed a little as she recognized that wide-shouldered shape. "Oh," she said. "Excuse me, Robert."

He stood there in the light streaming through the door, neatly dressed in his full regalia, his face unsmiling, something almost guilty in his bearing. For a moment there was silence in the hut. Then he said hoarsely, "Come in." With one hand he closed the file that had been open on the table. Beside it was a *Doppler* of wine a quarter empty and a glass.

"I don't think . . ." she began, not knowing what she would say.

"Come in."

It was still rank in here with the smell of goats and ashes. Christa hesitated, then found herself moving toward him, her body taut with wariness. "I didn't know anyone was here," she said. "I was just walking and—"

"I come here sometimes. It's a good place to . . . to work and think in peace and quiet. There's not much of either at my office in Altkreuzburg or the Schellhammer Hof. Besides"—he gestured—"it brings back memories. This is where we started. In the old days when we were illegal." He looked around the room. "It's well built," he said. "Busch did a good job."

"Poor old man," Christa heard herself say.

"Yes. Poor old man. Well. Would you like a glass of wine?"

She did not answer. Tensely they faced each other. Then Robert smiled. "Oh, come and have a glass of wine." Without waiting for an answer, he threw out what was in the glass, refilled it, held it out.

"Thank you," Christa said and took it.

"I'm afraid it's a little warm."

"It doesn't matter. But it's your only glass."

"No. Wait a minute." He stepped to one of the windows. A cow's horn lay on its hand-hewn sill. With his handkerchief he cleaned the dust from its hollowed-out interior. "Busch's. For his mead. It will serve."

She held hers untouched as he filled the horn, then faced her, raising it. "*Pros't,* Frau Condon," he said quietly.

"*Pros't,*" Christa said and drank. It was the best Schellhammer Veltliner.

Robert shoved the file to one end of the table. He gestured to the bench made of a split log. "Sit down. Would you like a cigarette?" She was surprised to see his hand shake a little as he worked two from a pack. "Decent ones. Gauloises. French. Though very strong."

"Thank you." She took it, sat on the end of the bench. He struck a match, bent to light it for her; the flame wavered, his hand still trembling. Looking up at him, she saw the dark circles beneath his eyes, the lines at the corners of his mouth. And with a flash of insight she guessed why he was alone out here this Sunday afternoon, why Busch's house was a refuge for him, and she felt a stab of pity. She had not meant to do that to him.

He lit his own cigarette. Somewhere in the clearing a woodpecker drummed. Robert, standing well away from her, let out a gusty puff of smoke. "Well," he said in an oddly tinny voice. "Well. Almost like old times."

She thought of what it would have been like. He would have been decent to her, probably even indulgent. There would have been no flame, no excitement, but neither would there have been the grief, uncertainty, and fear. She would have been cared for and protected. There was something to be said for security, comfort, shelter. As she felt now, being cared for and sheltered, simply *secure,* was all she would ever ask of life again this side of heaven; but, of course, it was too late—for both of them. Suddenly she wanted to be away from him and that new regret, and she took another long swallow of the wine, set down the glass, stood up. "Yes. But now I must be going."

"Oh." One toneless syllable. Then, as she turned toward the door, he was across the room in a pair of strides. "*Du,*" he said fiercely. "Christa." His fingers bit into her arm, pulled her around.

His face was red, contorted; his eyes squinted almost as if in pain as she stared up at him. *"Du!"* he said again, hoarsely, and pulled her to him. Startled, she reflexively tried to pull away, but he had both her upper arms clamped hurtingly in his big hands, and then he was kissing her, mouth smashing down on hers, bruising lips against her teeth. She tried to wrench her head aside; this was too quick, too jarring. She was angry, frightened, not because of the assault but because control of the situation was not hers. But his face and mouth followed hers, and then he was dragging her across the room. She knew to what, had noticed it when she came in, the rude bed that had been Busch's and the woman's, spread with a clean blanket that Robert must have put there so he could stretch out. Again she tried to pull away and this time her mouth came free. "Robert, stop! Are you mad!"

"Absolutely!" he said, and he twisted her and bore her down and fell on top of her. Straw-filled mattress bags crackled, the bed of poles and lashings and pegs creaked and groaned. He was heavy, his body hard on top of hers, and she felt the jab against her of his erection. "Absolutely!" he panted. "By God . . . have waited long enough. Mine by right! Now—" His mouth was all over her face and neck; he had her pinned with one arm; his other hand went up beneath the sweater to her breasts. Her tweed walking skirt rucked up as his knee shoved her thighs apart. She was wholly captive to a strength greater than her own, completely helpless, beyond choice, guiltless, and suddenly something flared in her, aroused by the hard rutting, humping motion of his weight, by his mouth and hands, and all at once desire was there, strong and urgent, rushing through her in waves of a deliciousness nearly forgotten; and something in her mind disengaged. Now, instead of pushing him away, her arm went around him, holding him closer, and she moved her head, looking for his mouth with her own. He sensed the change in her, the surrender, and she heard him grunt with satisfaction, and their mouths met, and hers opened, and she sighed, and now she was almost past thought. She only wanted him on top of her and in her, wanted that maleness so long denied, and he clawed at her clothes. Then she heard herself rasp, "Wait. Wait, Robert. You'll tear my clothes. The door—"

He understood. Suddenly he was off her. He barred the door, turned to face her, chest heaving under a shirt dark-blotched with sweat beneath the arms. He watched as she, standing by the bed, fumbled herself out of her clothes, shivering with the need for haste, body screaming at even this brief postponement. Then, unbuckling leather, he was coming toward her.

In the clearing the woodpecker kept on drumming. Bathed in sweat, sticky with each other, they lay on the crude bed, drained, exhausted. Christa's head was on his arm, her eyes closed. She could think again. Examining her own feelings, she felt no exaltation, but no shame, no regret—only a tremendous relief, a sense of comfort after pain, safety after fear, like a cramped, exhausted swimmer who had found a rock to cling to. She hardly heard Robert's murmuring in her ear. "Waited so long ... Love you, you know that ... Charlotte—she doesn't count. A bitch, crazy, that one. I never should have ... Oh, this is what I have wanted for so long. Now. Now." His hand on her breast, the palm rough, hard, its touch alternately gentle, then squeezing, painful, with triumph. "Darling." He turned her head to kiss her on the mouth again.

And she let him, returning the kiss, no passion in her now, and no love, not the kind he felt; but that did not matter. For the moment what she had was just as good or better. Because now she knew where the help she had to have would come from; she would not throw away this second chance. She moved closer to him, glad to be no longer alone.

9 IN HIS OFFICE in the writers' building Condon spent most of the next morning after that first night with Phyllis slumped motionless behind his typewriter, staring at the blank paper rolled into it. Not long before noon Willi Orlik entered, drawn and haggard. "Lan, are you okay?"

"I guess so."

"Good. I was worried, but when Phyll answered the phone I felt better. At least you weren't alone." He perched one hip on the corner of Condon's desk.

"Well, anyway war's inevitable. Now the bastards will get what's coming to 'em. And as far as I'm concerned, no more *kiddush hashem*."

"No more what?" Lan stared at him.

"The old Jewish tradition of not fighting back, of accepting martyrdom as bearing witness to God. Fuck that. I renounce it. My mind's made up. I'm striking back." He lit a cigarette. "I want you to help me. We can organize support for the Allies inside the Guild. Oh, most of the Reds will fight us, of course, on account of the nonaggression pact, but there's only so much twisting and turning even they can do to follow the Party line. We'll want to put pressure on the studios, all of them, to take a stand—so far no one's done it but Warners, with *Confessions of a Nazi Spy*—and raise all the money we can for England, too. There'll be opposition, lots of it, and a lot of people will try to slap us down, but what the hell. The time has come to stand up and be counted. There's an excuse for people who know no better, but you and I have seen and felt and touched the evil; we *know* what it is. We've got to get off our duffs and fight it. Maybe we can't carry guns, but—"

"Why can't we?" Lan sat up straight.

Willi broke off. Then he said, "I'm too old. With too many depending on me."

"I'm not," Lan said, standing up. "And the only one who depends on me is over there."

Something moved in Willi's eyes. "You mean—?"

"Why not?" Excitement was rising in him now; all at once he knew that he had glimpsed the structure his life must take. "Strike back," he said harshly. "That's what I've been waiting to do ever since that bastard shoved me on the train. I wasn't raised in any tradition of martyrdom." He thought of Ewell, of the last weeks of the *Register*. "I was raised to fight back when you're shoved around, with whatever you can lay your hands on. And now—" He let out a gusty breath. "If there's a war, I can sign on with the English."

Willi was silent. "Or the Canadians, yes," he said at last. "Of course, I ought to tell you not to do it. You'd be far more valuable right here where you are, helping me do what I said. Still, I know how satisfying it would be. Well, I should think you'd have no trouble. With your fluent German, you might even get a commission in their Intelligence. Where will you go? To the British Consulate here?"

"To start with, yes." Lan turned, and now every vestige of hangover had fled. "Yes, that's where I'll go first."

Willi was looking at him as if he were a stranger. "I had forgotten," he said. "Where you come from, it is a violent place."

"I'd almost forgotten, too," Lan said.

It was not that easy, of course; the officials at the British Consulate as yet had no instructions on recruiting foreign nationals. Yet when Lan mentioned Mark Gorton's name, he was taken to see the Consul himself. The man asked probing questions, jotted notes, then leaned back in his chair. "Tell me, Mr. Condon, do you think Mr. Gorton would give you a reference?"

"He would if I knew where to find him."

The Consul had a round Dickensian face. "I imagine we could locate him. Would you authorize us to inquire of him?"

"Absolutely."

The Consul drummed his fingers on his desktop. "Hmmm. I can make no promises, of course, but I daresay that if Mr. Gorton supported your statement . . . Of course, we all hope there won't be a war, but if there is, I do think it entirely likely that His Majesty's Government could find use for a volunteer with your qualifications and, er, motivations. May I make a few cable inquiries?"

"By all means."

"Well, we shall know in a few days, shan't we? Meanwhile, I'll start the wheels turning on your behalf. Please don't prejudice any of your personal affairs on my say-so, but of course if the balloon does go up, we possibly might call on you rather quickly. So then you should want things in order, wouldn't you? At any rate, I shall be glad to keep you posted on the matter. Thank you so much for coming in, Mr. Condon."

As a senior writer, he had comparative freedom, and there was no need to return to the studio. Full of a steely joy, he drove straight to the apartment. They were taking him seriously; Mark Gorton's name had impressed them. Mark was obviously up to something. Spying? His imagination rioted: *they* could

293

smuggle him into Austria; he could make contact with Christa ... Anyhow, it was plain that the Consul thought that war was coming, that they would take him; the chance to strike back was real!

He had forgotten Phyllis, was startled when she met him at the door. "You're early," she said. She gave him a kiss of greeting that was almost wifely.

"What are you doing here?"

"It took a while to dispose of the wreckage."

He looked around; the apartment was shining clean. "A drink?" she asked, and there was something proprietorial in her tone.

Lan, rankled, bit back a tart reply. After all, she had been kind to him, and a few more days ... He relaxed. "All right," he said quietly.

They had the drink, supper, another drink, listened to the radio: tensions had reached the breaking point. Dear God, he prayed silently, not another Munich sellout. Then, more than a little drunk, Phyllis took his hand. Her lips, moist and warm, nibbled over his face. "Let's go to bed," she whispered.

Next morning he felt a strange gritty mixture of revulsion and fascination. There had been something desperate and unhealthy in her ferocious search for ecstasy in the night, her determination to put her body at his disposal so he should have all of it. It was reassurance she had to have, sought so desperately. She was thirty-nine in a place where women over twenty-five were as disposable as Kleenex and always being crowded by the torrent of fresh, willing, youthful competition. He felt a kind of sadness. What would happen to her when he left her? Another blow, and what would her desperation drive her to next? Then he put that from his mind; he had enough burdens to carry. Christa was all that counted; Phyll must look out for herself.

Then, remembering, he switched on the radio. The news that blared from it brought him straight up from his chair, and he knocked his cup over. Claiming an attack on German territory by the Poles, Hitler had smashed into Poland, and already trumpeted a string of victories. "God damn!" Lan roared. "At last!" He rushed to the telephone, rang Willi Orlik's number. "Willi! Did you hear?"

"Hell, yes, I heard. I told you, didn't I?" Willi's voice was full of triumph. "England and France have got to fight, now. Either they fight or they're finished as European powers."

"I'll see you at the studio!" Lan plunged into the shower, then shaved and dressed. Phyll was up, staring at him as he started for the door. "War!" he roared and rushed out, slamming it behind him.

Later from his office he called the British Consul; it took a long time to get through. "Yes, of course. We haven't heard from our people yet, the cables are jammed. And, of course, we still don't know for certain. . . . We'll keep you posted. However, if you are still serious, Mr. Condon, you might start setting your affairs in order."

His affairs. Well, there was the script, of course, the second Manly Family thing. The first one had been part of his punishment—a program picture conceived by the head of the studio himself.

Furious, resentful, Lan had deliberately written a parody of American family life, invented a never-never family in a Cloud-Cuckoo-Land of America, certain it would be rejected. To his astonishment, it was made almost exactly as he wrote it. And to everybody's bewilderment except the studio head's, it was a sleeper, exploding into instant popularity, piling up enormous profits. So a sequel had been a natural, to be done by the same team, lest something happen to the magic. Now the second script was only half completed; in all conscience, he owed it to the studio to get it finished.

But, grinning, rolling paper into his typewriter, he gloated over knowing something only writers in the studio knew, a secret they kept carefully from producers, administrators, bureaucrats. Which was that a real professional could grind out a script for a program picture to a formula cut and dried in ten days or two weeks and hardly work up a sweat. It was easy. Now, with the pressure on, Lan knew he could finish this script in less than seven days. Scenes and dialogue flowed magically, mechanically, from his typewriter.

The studio, of course, was charged with excitement all day long; it was possible that Lan was the only one who worked. But throughout all distractions, he kept at it, and that night he took the script home with him. Phyllis was still there, and she had brought clothes with her, a symbol of permanence. She sensed something eerie in his dedication to the script, but he worked on it until well past midnight, telling her nothing. Then, stiff and weary, wanting to continue, but knowing he could go no further, he rose, showered, and made a drink.

It was late now, or, rather, very early on a Sunday morning—nearly five o'clock: in Vienna it would be two P.M.; in London one. He switched on the radio, keeping it turned down low. Most stations had signed off, but he found one still on the air. He sat there for nearly two hours, tired, detached, drinking moderately, shutting out the music, hearing only the news. The sky was lightening with false dawn when it came: a flash.

"London: Prime Minister Neville Chamberlain addressing the House of Commons has stated that Great Britain is now at war with Germany. A similar announcement by the government of France is expected momentarily. We now return you to our regular program pending a special network broadcast. Stay tuned . . ."

Something broke inside Lan Condon. All the webbing strings of tension and frustration suddenly snapped. Now he could strike back. He stood up feeling suddenly whole and clean, and he went to the window and watched dawn break across the city. He had no idea what lay ahead of him, but he felt equal to anything that came. Once more he had hope. He set the glass aside, stood there at the window for a long time, watching the morning sun come up.

Phyllis tried to pretend happiness for his sake and failed miserably; she knew what hopes he had involved in this. But she did not bring it off well at all, and besides, hungover, she began to drink again shortly after breakfast. Willi Orlik called inviting them to his house. There a jubilant group of anti-Fascists had gathered, not only Jews but also many Englishmen and a few Frenchmen. A lot of these were already making plans to go home; the older ones had already served in the Great War—the First War, they called it now—and he listened to them avidly, feeling a kinship with them. Ignored, Phyllis continued drinking.

By late afternoon he could stand it no longer; in Willi's study he dialed and redialed the British Consulate until he was finally put through to the dead-weary Consul. "Oh, yes, Mr. Condon. Well, we've heard from Mr. Gorton; it's quite good. We've a call or two more to make when we can find the time. Could you check back day after tomorrow? We're very busy. Sorry for the delay."

"Of course. I understand." Lan hung up, turned to find Willi there, the door closed behind him. "Well?"

"I think they'll take me," Lan said.

Willi nodded. "Have you told Matt yet? Or the studio?"

"No. I won't until it's final."

"I see. And how's the Manly script?"

"By Tuesday I'll have it finished—turn-key shape, ready to shoot."

"Good," Willi said. Then: "Could you come back out and take Phyll a little bit in hand? She's pretty blue"—it was the Austrian term for drunk—"and these people aren't quite in the mood for her style of celebrating at the moment."

"Sure," Lan said. He found her on the patio, kept her tightly in check as a well-known English star delivered moving passages from *Richard II* and *Henry V;* and then he saw that he had better take her home.

In the apartment she flopped on the bed fully clad. "This blessed plot, this earth, this realm, this England," she declaimed thickly. "This nurse, this teeming womb of royal kings, fear'd by their breed and famous by their birth..." She laughed. "God, they laid it on. I feel sorry for the Germans. If Shakespeare can kill, they don't have a chance." She raised herself on one elbow, blinked at him glazedly. "Have you thought about it, Lan? Has it occurred to you? Your Christa is now the enemy."

Gently he pushed her down. "Go to sleep, Phyll."

"She is the enemy," Phyllis repeated thickly, lying back, eyes closed. "Your Christa is the enemy." Then she began to snore.

For him Monday crawled. In his office he forced himself to work at the final scenes of the Manly script until the phone rang. "Lan? Matthews. Have you talked to George Bernheim?"

"What?"

"Bernheim! He just called me, wanted me to get over there right away for a meeting with you and him. What's going on?"

Bernheim: Lan's mind raced. Son-in-law of the head of the

studio, thirty years old, handsome, oily, feared by everyone, though he had no defined responsibilities. Lan had spoken to him perhaps five times in the past year, never on business. Bernheim, he thought, hand sweating on the receiver, was the hatchet man. "I don't know."

"Well, we're to meet with him at eleven-thirty. I'm leaving now. I'll see you in his office." Matt hesitated. "You're sure you don't know what's going on? You haven't had a run-in with him or anybody?"

"No."

"Is the Manly script going sour?"

"It's ahead of schedule, and it's good."

"Well, damned if I know. Look, I've got to run." Matthews hung up.

At that moment the secretary Lan shared with another senior writer came in. "Mr. Bernheim's secretary called," she said. "Mr. Bernheim wants to see you in his office at eleven-thirty sharp."

Of course he made them wait for twenty minutes in his outer office. That was part of the game. By then Lan was fairly sure what had happened; on the off-chance that he was wrong, he lied to Matt, pretending ignorance. It would not, he thought, make any difference.

Bernheim's approach was simple—get the upper hand and keep it. His eyes were hard, his voice brusque, and there were no preliminaries. "Sit down," he said coldly, his lineless, well-tended face set. Lan felt steel-hard within, determined not to be thrown off balance; deliberately he kept his own eyes and face as set and hostile.

Then it broke from Bernheim. "I want to know what all this shit's about! We get a fucking phone call from the fucking British Consul checking up on you, Condon. A lot of shit about you joining the British Army. British Army, fuck." He threw a sheaf of bound papers on his desk. "You've got a contract with us. It's still got twenty months to run. Would you mind explaining to me how you're gonna write for us while you're in the British Army?"

Matthews stared, then turned to Lan. "You—" he blurted, then recovered. "George, there's been some misunderstanding."

"You bet there's been some misunderstanding. This man"—
he was gesturing at a prisoner in the dock—"broke one contract
with us. We went along because he promised us a book we could
make into a picture at a discount. Book, shit; he's written no
goddamn book. He broke that promise, too. But then he came
back and we stretched a point and took him on and now he's
trying to fuck us all over again. Running down to join the goddamn English Army without a word to us, still working on a
script—"

"You'll have your goddamned script!" Lan flared. "I'll turn
it in by Wednesday!"

"Big fucking deal. And then what? You're off somewhere
that you can't make revisions. What the fuck you think we are,
a bunch of fools? The Manly Family's gonna be the biggest
string of moneymakers we've had for years. Big as Shirley Temple
was with Fox, Durbin with Universal. Besides, it's the Old Man's
pet. We're projecting at least one Manly and maybe two a year.
He's not about to break up a winning team. All right, we got
half the English personnel of the studio pulling out on us this
month. We can't stop 'em or we'll look like a bunch of shits. But
you're no limey. This fucking contract binds you, and you'll
stay here and work it out; or we'll sue your fucking ass off and
tie you up so tight you can't go to Tijuana, much less to
England."

Hardly drawing breath, he turned to Matthews. "You better
talk some sense into this client of yours, or your name's gonna
be fucking mud with us, you understand? We're not gonna stand
still for this kind of fucking shit, and you both better get that
through your heads."

"Listen, George." Matthews' lean face was red. "I need some
time to talk with Lan. But let me tell you now, you can't talk
to me and my client, any client, the way you have. We will not sit
here and be cursed by you in gutter language and—"

"All right. All right, already. I've made my point, and my
point is this. This contract stands. And we've told the British
Consul that. And we'll tell anybody else that calls us up and
asks. We have a valid contract and we'll enforce it. If they sign
Condon on, they do so at their own risk, which means they can
ask no further favors of this studio. That's been made clear.
We've compromised enough already, postponing, putting in

299

abeyance British subjects' contracts. There are still a lot of things they want us to do for them, but war or no war, we've got a studio to run. Now I got another appointment. Good day, gentlemen." He turned his head, picked up his telephone. "Miss Wilson, send in Donald Marshall."

"You goddamned fool!" Matthews had exploded once they were alone. Then he eased. "I'm sorry, Lan. But look at the bind you put me in. Why didn't you level with me? Don't answer. Because you knew from the beginning you couldn't get away with it, that they wouldn't stand for it and neither would I!"

They were in Frenchy's bar. Condon said, "Be quiet, Matt." With no further words, he went to the phone, dialed the number of the British Consulate. By some miracle, he got through to the Consul immediately. "Oh, yes, Mr. Condon. Glad you called. Well, I'm afraid I have bad news. You failed to tell us that you had contractual obligations in the United States. And I've talked to your employers and ... the fact is, there's nothing we can offer you right now."

"Listen," Lan said. "I don't need a commission, no fancy job. I'll carry a rifle—"

"I'm sorry. Nothing at the moment. We have a number of other volunteers to process and the complications in your case are simply overwhelming. But I must convey the appreciation of His Majesty's Government to you for your interest and support. We hope it will continue. Good day, Mr. Condon; I have another call."

Lan hung up, went back to the bar. Matthews read his face. Not without sympathy, he said, "Lan, maybe it's just as well. Look, it may all be over in six months, and the coast will be clear for you; you'll have your cake and eat it, too. In the meantime, hell, if there's any chance to get you a job on an anti-Nazi script, I'll jump at it. And you can work with Willi. I understand he's got all sorts of things going."

"We'll see," Lan said. "After I check with the Canadians and the French."

"All right," Matt said quickly, angrily, "we might as well be honest. I went to bat for you, bailed you out, one time. But this time there's nothing I can do or will do. I'm with *them*. You've got the contract. You're not British or French and you have no valid reason for asking for an abrogation. You break it, they'll tie you up sixty ways from Sunday, and I refuse to be a party to the ensuing mess. If you get in trouble, don't come to me. Now use some judgment." And he squeezed Lan's arm, stalked out.

Instead of returning to the studio, Condon stayed in Frenchy's that afternoon. He called both the Canadian and French consulates and could not get through. It made no difference. He was one man alone, and the studio was the studio. Without even Matt on his side, he was beaten. All he could hope for now was a short war and a quick Allied victory. Well, he had money. He could contribute that and earn more, and if they would just give him a chance to write an anti-Nazi script . . . He was not finished yet.

Late that night he went home to his apartment. In his mail there was a letter from Christa. Just the sight of her handwriting on the envelope pierced him; it was almost with reluctance that he opened it.

The weather was magnificent. She loved him. She had hunted mushrooms and had picked eight kilos of parasols in the meadows in four hours. She loved him. She had attended a gymnastic exhibition staged by the German Girls' League. It had been touching to see all those barefoot young girls in the pink of health united in precision maneuvers honoring the Reich and Führer. She loved him. And so on, carefully and vapidly: she loved him. He realized that he had not written her in over a week.

Phyllis was out somewhere. He sat down at the typewriter, tried to begin a letter to her. Nothing would come. He had too much to say that could not be said; he did not know how to approach it. What had parasol mushrooms and the Bund Deutscher Mädchen to do with Poland and George Bernheim? He tried again in longhand; nothing would come. He made a drink, though he had already had too much. Could he write her about the Manly Family? But how could she understand even that? It was a farce, a joke. He could not get his thoughts organized. The letter must wait until his mind was clearer.

Two years drifted by, and with every Nazi victory Christa became less a reality, more a dream. There was no longer any hope of reaching her, not soon, maybe not forever.

And he could not write her. He no longer had anything at all to say that she would understand within the limits of what she was allowed to read. In the context of things as they were, all else was mockery. He could not get a letter off; and her letters came for a while, and then—by then it was almost a blessed surcease—they stopped coming. You took what you had and relinquished what was unobtainable and cut your losses; and what you dreamed at night did not matter. Christa was a dream; Phyllis was real. And she already knew the route through hell, made a perfect Virgil to his Dante. She knew all the tricks for turning off the mind and quelling conscience.

10 BY ELEVEN, the brunch at Willi Orlik's, really only a continuation of last night's party at Condon's rented beach house, was in full swing, everyone curing Saturday night's katzenjammer with Sunday morning's booze. Lan sought Phyllis, who had been going at it hard, every drink showing like a goldfish in a bowl, failed to find her. It made no difference. He'd had all of this he could take. Out on the cantilevered porch, he stared at the ocean, swallowing a nausea compounded of gin and nicotine and disgust and sucked in great breaths of sea-salted air. It was a fine bright day, warm for December even in California. Beyond the Malibu strand, the Pacific rolled and shifted like some great beast uneasy in its bed. A string of pelicans flapped from nowhere to nowhere across the horizon. A great white yacht moved against the skyline like a swan. Two men emerging from the house took up station near Lan. Holman and Fiedler were both directors. "Flynn's?" asked Holman.

"Looks more like the one Tom Mix used to own," said Fiedler. "Whoever, they'd better look out for Japs."

"Japs!" Holman snorted. "The Japs ain't that stupid. They've got better sense."

"You never can tell. The radio this morning—"

"The radio! Listen, I hate Franklin Roosevelt's crippled guts, but he's not gonna let those Japs make a dime. For Chrissake, Japan! Monkey see, monkey do."

"Don't forget China. And they sank the *Panay*. And they beat Russia years ago."

"Russia! Hell, anybody can beat Russia! Look at Hitler— rolled 'em up like a rug. Listen, that little yellow-bellied ambassador is crawlin' to Cordell Hull right now. The Japs!" Holman spat. "Listen, you seen that new broad in there, the one with the ass like two kittens under a silk handkerchief? Come on, I wanta show you." They went back inside.

Lan watched gulls wheeling across the horizon. They were free to soar as high as they could; he was not. Not even in his writing. The studio was producing mildly anti-Fascist pictures now—just a few—but Lan Condon was not allowed to work on any of them.

Partly that was his punishment; because they knew he yearned to. Partly, too, it was the thundering success of the Manly Family series. Even as war roiled across the oceans, people sought escape in fantasy; the Manly Family furnished that. And Lan was stuck with it; his contract gave him no choice. He took what they assigned him; and while the world crumbled, he tried to write of puppy love and teenage heartbreak in aseptic surroundings. It was sheer agony, endurable only by turning off his mind completely when not at his typewriter. Money flowed in; he donated much of it to England, but that was painless, there was plenty left.

Mostly he followed where Phyllis led. He gave up his apartment, moved in with her, and they never took Ross's picture off the table. But that was only the start. Each time it always seemed to take a little more to shut out memory, but if you gave up squeamishness . . .

A gull swooped down, slashed the ocean, rose with a fish. Well, it worked, he thought; that was the main thing. Once Christa had been a woman, his wife; now she was only a symbol, like a crucifix; and every apostate's drive was to blot the crucifix from his consciousness. There were a lot of ways he knew to do that now.

He watched the bright ocean for a while, drank the clean salt air, and rebelled at the thought of going back inside. Somehow he could not bear that now. Maybe the hangover was catching up with him. He needed sleep, rest. He went down the veranda steps, walked toward their own house next door to Willi's, rented from a British actor who had gone home immediately to join some regiment of Guards and had let the place at a distress price.

He climbed the outside stairs of their own veranda, went through the sliding door. The living room was still a wreck from last night's party—stale drinks, overflowing ashtrays, a fog of smoke, the excreta of pleasure. He left the door open; the radio was on. Sunday morning: a church service, a swell of organ music, the bleating of a choir. One more drink, then he'd sleep. He went into the kitchen. He had just taken the bottle from the cabinet when he heard the sounds coming from the bedroom.

He made no noise as he padded to its doorway. The door was half ajar.

The two figures on the bed, naked, locked, were wholly unaware of his presence. For a half minute Lan stood there before soundlessly turning away. It was not anything he had not seen before. In the past two years with Phyllis he had seen a lot. He was not surprised that her companion on the bed was a girl—a starlet from Willi's party.

He could have walked in and joined them; neither would have objected. Instead, carrying his drink, he went back out to the porch without making any sound. There was in him a tiredness almost lethal. His body felt immensely heavy as he leaned against the rail staring out at the Pacific's lambent blue. The cold, clean water, he thought, the ultimate baptism, the final shriving. Behind him the choir kept on singing. He took a swallow of his drink, rubbed his eyes, head bent. He was not immediately aware that the chorused hymn had stopped suddenly in mid-stanza. Then the excited, almost stuttering, voice brought him around to face the radio.

"We interrupt this program for a special news bulletin. Pearl Harbor, the U.S. naval base in the Hawaiian Islands, has been attacked without warning by air and naval forces identified as Japanese. The surprise attack occurred about seven-thirty A.M., local time, even as peace negotiations were under way in Washington between a special Japanese envoy and Secretary of State Cordell Hull. Some American warships have been damaged and casualties may be substantial. A number of Japanese planes have been shot down. This is an act of war by Japan against the United States. The fighting is continuing. A statement from the White House is expected momentarily. Please stand by. . . . We repeat . . ."

Lan stood there rigidly as the announcement was completed. He stared out across the ocean into the cloudless sky, suddenly hostile now. "So," he said aloud, and he threw his glass out into the sand. He did not think the two women in the house had even heard the news.

When he moved, that weary heaviness no longer weighed him down. He knew exactly what he would do now, and there was no time to lose. He went quietly down the steps, walked swiftly around the corner of the beach house. By the time he reached his parked car, he was running.

BOOK THREE
Ravens Feeding
1944–1945

1 THEY HAD ALL EATEN their last real meal and taken
—except for the Communist—their last communion;
and now they spent the minutes remaining to them in various
ways as they waited for the hand of Death to reach into the cell
and pluck the first one to go. The thief, a smash-and-grab artist
convicted of looting the window of a butcher shop, sat slumped
in a corner mumbling something incoherent that might have
been a prayer. At the table the Communist was scribbling
furiously, producing, Martinus supposed, his own final mani-
festo. The lawyer who had been caught with the illegal radio
paced the room chain-smoking the twelve cigarettes given him.
Martinus, all letters written, all prayers said, only waited, sitting
on the cell's single cot. He was almost glad that the ordeal was
nearly over. For nearly four years he had been shuttled from
court to court, prison to prison, all across the Reich. Now he
was back where he had begun—in Vienna. The "Poor Sinners
Cell" they called this cubicle in a dingy wing of the *Landes-
gericht*, the combination courthouse and prison in which the
circuit of his life was finally closed. What lay beyond, down the
corridor, was the guillotine. After that—he had inquired and
been told—the body would be crammed into a cheap sheet-
metal box and either sent to the Medical School at the University or transported by the "Black Raven," the infamous
corpse-hauling truck now waiting in the courtyard, to the
Central Cemetery, to be buried without ceremony.

309

His body did not concern him; he had long since written that off. Only his soul mattered now, and it was at peace.

It had not always been so. He had for months assumed total guilt for the disaster he had brought to so many who if they had not believed in him might still be safely home with wives and families. And for the disaster suffered by his order, too, and the Stift at Altkreuzburg. Not long after his conviction before a people's court, the Gestapo had swooped down on the monastery in force, dispersing all the *Chorherren,* who had been forced to seek refuge with other orders. They had cleared it out and confiscated it and all its holdings, turning its enormous buildings into offices for the State bureaucracy. After almost a thousand years, Stift Altkreuzburg had ceased to exist—mainly, if not wholly, because of him.

And yet, how could he have ever known that the Goerlichs— that childlike dumpy couple with their press, typewriter, and shortwave radio—were traitors? In the beginning, he was certain, they had been sincere, but the Gestapo had played on their love for each other and broken them.

He had learned all the details in the countless trials, processes, inquisitions he had endured. The owner of an electrical shop in Altkreuzburg had got drunk with a soldier home on furlough whose specialty was radio repair. The shopkeeper mentioned the components he had sold Herr Goerlich in 1937 for a set which the old man—without previous experience, imagine!—had built himself. The soldier wondered idly if they had turned in the illegal radio; the shopkeeper did not know. Later that worried him; if they still had it and it were discovered, he, with his knowledge, might be judged accessory. The only way to be safe was to report the matter to the police. They, of course, promptly passed it on to Gestapo headquarters on the Morzinplatz in Vienna, the former Hotel Metropole. The Gestapo at once raided the Goerlich villa, but in secret. Sensing that they were onto something big, they put unbearable pressure on the Goerlichs: betray the resistance movement or die, separately and painfully. Probably each could have faced his own death with silent courage. It was to save the other that they yielded. So for nearly three months they had fed data back to the Secret Police: then the roundup of the suspects, the secularization of the Stift. Yes, the Gestapo were clever, knowing precisely how to turn love into betrayal. And now the Goerlichs were still alive and free, with new identities in the Tyrol, while a dozen others had gone to the guillotine and more soon would go.

Ironically, he was grateful for the completeness of the couple's betrayal. Their knowledge had been so extensive, so accurate, that the Gestapo had felt no need to torture him or any of the other leaders, and he had been spared the final, crucial confrontation between his body and his conscience that he had for so long dreaded. He had never been certain of his physical courage; joining the order had been one way of avoiding putting it to the test in the rough world outside. If they had put him on the rack, he himself might have become the crucial traitor.

Anyhow, the Gestapo had followed every lead meticulously. The scooping up of his own group had led them to others, and finally the whole resistance movement around Vienna had been brought crashing down.

But thanks to German thoroughness, it had taken a very long time. Each part had to be fitted perfectly into the whole. Months had passed before his own trial, at which he had been condemned to death; and then, for some inexplicable reason, his execution had been postponed for years. In that interval he'd been whisked from one prison to another, spending days and weeks in solitary, interrogated and reinterrogated, but no one had seemed quite able to work up the courage to take responsibility for the actual execution of a priest.

Until now, he thought wryly. This time there would be no postponement. The Twentieth of July had changed all that.

The thief let out a kind of sob. Martinus rose and went to the corner where he slumped. Kneeling, he put a hand on the shoulder of the man. "My son, you've made your peace with God."

"Yes." Still, teeth chattered in a lean face not yet thirty. "Yes, Father, but I'm still afraid. Oh, God, I'm still so afraid."

"It's only a passing through a door," said Martinus gently. "On the other side Christ is waiting to take you by the hand."

Pen stilled for the moment, the Communist twisted in his chair. "If he does, friend, you'd better count your fingers! Father, why don't you stop that goatshit? Have you no shame at all? If

311

it weren't for your kind, none of us would be here. And still you feed that poor fellow that lousy line! But your Catholic Dollfuss destroyed Parliament and smashed the workers, your Catholic Schuschnigg refused to take the workers back and let us fight the Nazis, and still you go on."

The lawyer stopped his pacing, whirled, face furious. "Now, see here, you—"

Martinus raised his hand. "Let him say what he likes. Here at least we have free speech without regard to consequences."

"I've said it," the Communist grunted.

Martinus smiled. "Well, I'll not quarrel with you, brother. The final answer to all our questions lies too close; debate now would be only academic. Allow us our comforts, and you take yours. We are convinced we go to meet the Almighty. If He turns out to be Lenin, the last laugh is yours." He sobered. "Yes, we have made mistakes, all of us. But only because we're human, and to be human is to be fallible. But He is infallible and all-forgiving." He turned to the thief. "Cling to that."

"Yes," the man said, but his teeth kept chattering and he dropped his head, staring at his bent knees. The Communist picked up his pen. But it never touched the paper. Outside in the hall, cadenced footsteps resounded. Martinus' heart seemed to leap into his throat and stick there. Everyone turned to stare at the door, where two uniformed warders holding keys and handcuffs appeared. For a seemingly endless moment they stood in utter silence, eyes raking over the quartet in the cell. The thief stopped his whimpering; there was not even the sound of breathing.

"Friedrich Preisser," the taller of the guards said at last.

"Oh, sweet Jesus," moaned the thief.

"You will come with us." And the guard unlocked the cell.

After that there was no more talking, only the feverish scratching of the Communist's pen. Martinus sat on the cot, lit a cigarette, ashamed at his surge of relief that he had not been the first to go, that he still had moments more of life. He was not afraid; it had been a good life, richly textured, more perhaps than he deserved. God had been good to him. And now he bore no guilt, either, for what had happened to the others in his group or to the Stift; it had been inevitable, but it had not been futile. Hundreds of people had borne witness with their lives and freedom to their belief in Austria and the nobility of man.

The record of that remained, beyond expunging, and the time was coming soon when it would count. Because now, in August 1944, the Nazi monster was doomed, and everyone could see that, even a prisoner like himself.

Even in prison it was surprising how much news one could acquire—and indeed news more accurate than that on the outside, spoon-fed by the Progaganda Ministry and its hirelings. Prisons were where they put people who knew the truth and dared to speak it, and one absorbed it somehow, from brief contacts with other prisoners, from friendly guards, from chaplains, and from firsthand observation.

He knew everything of any consequence that had happened since his arrest four years ago in 1940. Of England's determined resistance; of the invasion of Russia and the debacle at Stalingrad; of America's entry into the war, the defeat in Italy, and the invasion of France this June. And in being shuttled from one prison to the other, he had seen the rubble and indeed had heard the sirens and the fall of bombs and knew that Germany was being pulverized, though Austria, so far, thank God, had escaped. He knew, too, of the Twentieth of July—how only a month ago a group within the Army had very nearly assassinated Adolf Hitler. But the anti-Christ's luck still held; he had been only slightly injured by the bomb Colonel von Stauffenberg had planted underneath a conference table, and Hitler's vengeance had been terrible and was still going on. Now, though, notice had been served on him and on the world that resistance to evil was not dead in the breasts of the German people. Martinus and his group had been the first, the pioneers; but they were not alone, and the seed they had planted had not been unfruitful.

He had heard of other things almost too ghastly to be believed. Rumors of camps in the east to which all Jews in Europe had been sent; but even after years in prison, with firsthand knowledge of the possibilities of bestiality, he could not wholly credit these. They posed a theological problem with which he could not cope. If they were true, then God Himself must have looked away or gone insane; besides, his people, his Germanic people, surely could not be capable of *that*. Martinus had shut those rumors in a closed compartment of his mind, would not take them into account; but he kept remembering that urn of ashes Frau Sattler had put before him.

He ground out his cigarette and lit another. The Communist

had stopped writing now, had folded his pages and placed them in an envelope. They had all been given the materials to write last letters, which, Martinus knew, would mostly never reach their destinations. Possibly his would—to his parents and to the former *Propst* of the Stift. They had been entrusted to the *evangelisch* chaplain of this death row. The Protestant pastor, unlike his Catholic counterpart, had already become a legend for his compassion toward the condemned of every confession and for the personal risks he took on their behalf. Rieger would see that they got out. Martinus had passed that tip along to the Communist, but the man had snorted. He would rather take his chances with official routine than deal with a priest.

Now that the thief was gone, the cell was absolutely silent. For Martinus, there was nothing left but to pray. They had left him his rosary, and now he knelt.

The footsteps sounded in the hall again. His fingers froze on the beads. Then they were there once more, the guards. Still on his knees, Martinus turned.

The tall warder savored the endless moment of suspense. Then his eyes came to rest on Martinus. "Chorherr Dr. Martin Peter Fischer," he said.

Martinus swallowed hard, stood up on knees gone weak. "I am here," he said, and crossed himself.

The cell door opened. "You will come with us."

Martinus closed his eyes, then opened them again. "Yes," he said.

The lawyer put out his hand. "We'll meet again. Soon." He smiled faintly.

Somehow Martinus managed an answering smile. "Yes. Peace to you, brother."

The Communist stood up, face dead pale, also extending his hand. "Forget what I said a while ago, Father. Good luck."

"And the same to you," Martinus said, and then a warder said, "Come on," and his hands were wrestled behind his back and cuffs snapped on. Holding him by each arm, they led him from the cell. In the corridor waited Dr. Rieger. After the last communion and confession the Catholic chaplain considered his duties discharged; the Protestant never let anyone go to the blade unaccompanied unless his presence was declined.

Earlier, before transferring him to the death cell, they had stripped Martinus naked, then given him cheap, ill-fitting prison jacket and pants and felt slippers. The slippers made a hissing sound now on the corridor floor as he shuffled along between the guards. They went at a smart, efficient pace, half dragging him; he found it hard to keep up. The pastor was on his right; his voice was firm yet gentle as he said the Lord's Prayer. Martinus' own voice matched his automatically, word for word. Then they had reached a door.

"Amen," said Dr. Rieger, and Martinus echoed it. The pastor touched his shoulder as the guards halted. "I may not go further with you. But now you shall find the peace that passeth all understanding."

"I'm not afraid," Martinus said. "After all, this is the moment toward which my whole life has been pointed. Thank you, Pastor Rieger, God bless you, and *Wiederseh'n.*"

"God bless you. *Auf Wiederseh'n.*"

The doors were opened then and Martinus pushed through.

He found himself in a large brightly lit dingy-walled room, divided in two parts by a black curtain hanging from the ceiling. At a long table in the fore part sat three men, the one in the center in civilian clothes, the ones on the flanks in SS uniforms. Martinus was hustled before them. The civilian glanced at his file. "You are Chorherr Dr. Martin Peter Fischer?"

"I am."

"All pleas, requests for postponement and/or pardon have been denied. The death verdict of the people's court will now be carried out." He raised his arm. "Heil Hitler!"

"Long live Austria," said Martinus quietly.

The civilian jerked his head. The two warders led Martinus toward the curtain. Just this side of it they halted; his handcuffs were unlocked, the jacket thriftily stripped from him. His wrists were then quickly bound with thongs. He stared at the curtain, and it was true, he was not afraid. Indeed, he was exalted. If he believed anything, it was that this was no end, only a beginning. All that remained was to comport himself as a man.

But, oh God, there were so many memories and life here had often been so sweet. He sucked in breath, felt tears running down his cheeks. He looked at his warders. Father, forgive them, he thought. Then anger welled in him. No! No, they should be unforgiven, they— Once more defiance, and this time he tried

315

to yell it. *"God bless Austria!"* But even as he opened his mouth, a warder dropped behind him, yanked his ankles. He toppled forward, and as the other caught him, a huge piece of adhesive was clamped tightly across his mouth, stopping his defiant cry. Then, like a carcass in a butcher shop, he was picked up by both of them and carried through the curtain.

He saw it then—the frame, the poised blade, the blood-spattered walls beyond, the stack of sheet-metal coffins—had time to glimpse all that and the rolling platform, mounted on two rails, before the guillotine. He even saw the mechanism near the blade which, when tripped by the platform, would automatically bring it down. Then he was thrown face-forward on that conveyor, rough hands shoved him. He rolled forward at frightening speed. Mary, he thought, Mother of God, pray for me now . . .

2   THE LITTLE *Kino* in Ferndorf was jammed, its darkness rank with body odors and perfumes accentuating, not masking, them. There were only a few reserved seats—wooden chairs with backs—otherwise the audience sat on benches. Naturally Kreisleiter Robert Schellhammer and Christa had the best seats in the house.

The film was a rerun of *Das Wunschkonzert,* a musical confection based on the most-loved broadcast of the German radio— every Sunday between three and five the musical requests of soldiers at the front and their loved ones at home were fulfilled, messages passed, even the crying of a newborn baby broadcast for its faraway father. Music, bittersweet romance, happy endings—the hunger for such fare was insatiable nowadays, and people almost fought for tickets to two hours of nepenthe in darkness. Christa was no exception; for that interval she found release in mindless entertainment. Around her, women sobbed and sniffled unashamed; even Robert felt the impact of the sentimentality up there on the screen, pulled her closer to him. Yet, at the moment when the lights had gone down and the film had started, she had thought involuntarily of Lan. She remembered how she'd laughed, cheered, clapped once in this very theater when his name had shone up there clear and bright as the credits of an American comedy unreeled. *"You* wrote it!" she had squealed. *"You* really wrote it!" And she had sat enthralled and proud throughout it. But that had been years ago, in another world that now was a remembered dream.

So was the era portrayed by the movie. Nineteen forty was as remote in time as the Garden of Eden, almost, as innocent, as carefree. German armies then were victorious everywhere, no Stalingrad; no El Alamein, no Normandy invasion. It had seemed impossible back then that the English would come back to Europe, or that the Americans would come at all. Now, in this October of 1944, everything had changed. Now all the victorious dreams were turned into nightmares. And so one sat here in darkness watching Ilse Werner and Carl Raddatz play out their tender, naive love story, savored the sad and lively songs, and for a while forgot that the Reich was encircled by its enemies in a ring of iron. One forgot the thousand-plane raids on the Old Reich, the Hamburg firestorm, the ghastly destruction of the proud ancient cities—and tried to forget that only last month the bombers had finally reached Vienna, too, and that now they came every day with brutal clockwork regularity, and there was nothing in the skies to stop them. Nineteen forty, already the good old days, and when the show ended, there was applause and a universal sigh of regret.

Christa's hand was on Robert's arm as they filed out into the garden separating the *Kino* from the Gasthaus Semmler. The night was crisp with autumn, the smells of farm, garden, woods, and fields all mingled in the air. Most of the crowd flowed toward the public room, reluctant to go home. "A glass of wine?" Robert asked, and they followed the throng, he accepting and answering all the respectful greetings.

Behind the blackout curtains the place was dimly lit, pungent with the smoke of the dreadful home-front cigarettes. There was the clink of glasses, the chatter of voices. Except for the men in uniform, one would almost have thought there was no war. But there were a half dozen of them of various units, most gathered around their long *Stammtisch* drinking heavily, and not a one of them not somehow maimed—lacking hand or foot, arm or leg, or in one case blinded. The war had had its way with and was finished with them. Christa could not bear to look at them as she and Robert took seats at the other long table, where the more prosperous and important villagers were gathered. And yet, she thought, only half hearing the fawning welcome Robert reaped, they were luckier than Ernst, who had been torn from behind his piano in Poland and shipped east during the last throes at Stalingrad. They had received half a dozen letters from him before word came of his "heroic death for the Fatherland." She could not bear to reread a one of them. Somehow she must remember Ernst as he had been before he had ever worn a uniform, not as suffering and dying in that frozen hell.

The wine came, she became aware of what Robert was saying: "How do I interpret the situation, Herr Kubiak? Well, certainly not in any defeatist way. One must look beneath the surface, beyond the obvious; then all is clear. Our supply lines are shortening, those of our enemies are lengthening. They are springs stretched to weakness; we are a spring compressed, powerful, ready to explode and strike. And that we shall when the time's right, never fear! When they are at their weakest and our compression at its greatest, then the hammer blows will fall. Guided by der Führer's genius, aided by the secret weapons even now in production, we'll turn the tide. Already we're saturating England and the Allied supply lines in France with jet and rocket bombs, and our revolutionary new fighters are like hawks to sparrows in the air; they can knock out anything the enemy can put up. But they're only the beginning. Believe me, there are other technical miracles in the works that will change the whole picture overnight. All that is needed is for everyone to stand fast, do his duty, and . . ."

She had heard it all before, tuned it out, though the others lapped it up. Robert himself believed it, she knew, and of course so did she; after three years of total indoctrination by Robert Schellhammer, she had become an expert at believing anything. Otherwise how could you keep going? They knew, all of them, that it was a fool's paradise they had constructed around themselves, and faith was the glue that kept it from falling apart. Anyhow, what choice was there? Not to believe was treason, and treason meant death. And anyhow, who knew? What Robert said might very well be true. They were told so little, but he was on the inside.

318

And making this appearance, doing his best to keep up their morale. They were, after all, proud of him, this lofty presence who was still one of their own. So there was a purpose in his holding court here tonight and—

The door opened, a young man swung in on a crutch, the left leg of his rumpled Wehrmacht uniform cut and sewn to cover the stump that ended just above the knee. In his middle twenties, he was lean and handsome, hair blond, the eyes that he blinked against the sudden light a bright steel blue. A little awkwardly he closed the door behind himself, then made his way to the bar, teeth clamped on his underlip as he hobbled across the room. Christa thought he looked familiar, but until Robert spoke she could not remember who he was.

"Ah, so! Herr Glaser! I had forgotten! Congratulations on the return of your son Jochen and on his remarkable heroism at Minsk! And I have great news for him—and for you, for all of us—if you will call him over."

Yes, she knew him now from the Gymnasium, Jochen Glaser— a strong, quiet, bookish boy, friendly, gentle, but dangerous once his temper was aroused, the kind who'd defy the sternest teacher. Jochen's father, who owned the largest grocery in Fern-dorf, was a man in his fifties. He glowed with pride, turned, beckoned.

Then Robert, with sudden tact, said, "No, wait. I'll go to him." He shoved back his chair and strode across the room, booted feet thumping solidly; all eyes were fixed on him, as he intended.

Jochen Glaser tossed off his cognac, held his glass out to be refilled, waiting until it was before turning to face Robert.

"*Grüss Gott*, Heil Hitler, Gefreiter Glaser!" Robert's voice was bluff and brisk.

"*Grüss Gott*, Herr Kreisleiter." Glaser's face was frozen, with-out expression, as he shook Robert's hand.

"Corporal, it's good to have you back with us!" Robert went on. "As I told your father, I have some news for you—good news, which reflects great honor on your family!"

"Oh?" Jochen drank the second cognac, dragged his hand across his mouth. His eyes blinked rapidly. He had, Christa realized, been drinking somewhere else before coming here.

"Oh, yes. You knew, of course, that you'd been put in for

319

the Iron Cross, First Class, for your heroism in combat at Minsk."

"I seem to remember something to that effect," Jochen said mildly. His eyes raked up and down Schellhammer's resplendent uniform. "Never heard anything more about it."

"Well, now you have! It has come through! In my office I have the papers and the medal itself. And I think it should be presented in an appropriate ceremony in the near future here in Ferndorf! Perhaps a special *Zapfenstreich,* with units from Vienna and a band! That can be arranged." He grinned, put his hand on Glaser's shoulder. "You must be properly honored—"

The flare in Jochen Glaser's eyes was fierce and instantaneous. "Take your hand off me!" he snapped and knocked it from his shoulder. A hush fell across the room. "And," Jochen rasped, "take your Iron Cross, Herr Kreisleiter, and shove it up your arse! That's an appropriate ceremony!"

"Jochen!" his father bleated.

Robert stepped back, lips thin, face flaming. "Corporal, you are drunk. And your sacrifices have damaged you psychologically—"

"Psychologically, shit!" Leaning on his crutch, Jochen moved away a pace from the bar. He pointed at his left leg's swinging stump. "You think this is psychological? You damned rear-echelon fancy-pants, who the devil are you to tell me it's psychological! Why don't you put on a Wehrmacht uniform and pick up a gun and go out there and finish what you started— you and your kind—and see how psychological it is! You're shit! Ah, it's all shit." He turned his back on Robert, stumped away through utter silence.

"Corporal Glaser," Robert snapped, voice hard.

"It's all shit, I tell you!" Glaser whirled, eyes staring, screamed the words, his face brick red. "All of it! You and your fancy words and medals and your bands and military tattoo and your goddamn swastika, and— And you're finished, do you hear me? You are finished, *we* are finished! They can't be stopped! And what we'll get we'll deserve, because you've betrayed us, betrayed all of us with what you've done—and in our names!"

"My son, Jochen—" The older Glaser was on his feet, face dead pale. "Jochen, listen—"

"No, you listen, all of you!" The young man was still screaming every word. "You listen and hear about what I've seen out there, what all these great Party and SS men do in our names! Have they ever told you about their death factories for killing Jews? Where they gas 'em by the thousands and put 'em in ovens and burn 'em up?" His head swiveled. "Women and children along with the men! Little babies! Little girls and boys— they burn 'em!" Breaking off, he drew in a sob. "It's factories for burning people! You don't believe me, do you? Well, they're there, I've seen 'em, and I've seen *Einsatzkommandos* shooting 'em, too, by the hundreds, and I've seen—" He broke off, voice choked in his throat. "War's one thing. Th-that is another. And I'm ashamed, do you hear? I'm ashamed to be a German soldier! But I'd rather be a German soldier than a shit like you! Anyhow, they're coming and we can't stop 'em, and what they do to us when they get here— Well, you and der Führer can thank yourselves for that! Maybe they will burn our babies, too."

He stood there for an instant, silent. Then, in the hush he said contemptuously, staring full at Robert, "Shit." And he whirled on his crutch, walked toward the door.

After one frozen second, Robert instinctively started after him, face tallow-colored. "Young man—"

An awkward scuffling of feet drowned the words. They were standing up, too, the other soldiers at the *Stammtisch*. Robert halted as a young one-armed private moved out to block his path. "Herr Kreisleiter," the young man said thinly. Then three or four others were moving in around Schellhammer, encircling him in gray. The blind man at the table began softly to sing the most-loved song of the German *Landser:* "Once I had a comrade ..."

Robert halted, head turning, looking at the men surrounding him, enduring the contempt in their eyes. "Your friend," he said presently, "is very drunk. In this case, allowance will be made for him for that reason, for the limb he has sacrificed, for the heroism he has shown. If you are truly friends of his, you'll make sure there are no more outbursts. Otherwise, hero or no, he'll have to take the consequences, which, I assure you, will be severe. Now, if you will be so good as to stand aside ..."

They moved. He turned, strode back toward the table where Christa sat. Jochen's father clawed at his elbow. "Herr Kreisleiter, you must believe—"

"The matter is ended," Robert said shortly. "The Iron Cross will be sent by post to Gefreiter Glaser tomorrow. Come, Frau Condon." The *Gastwirt* was already holding her coat for her. "And you, Herr Semmler, be more careful about whom you serve. He was already intoxicated when he came in." He put on his own coat, turned. "Heil Hitler!"

The older men in the room returned the greeting in a shout. Robert and Christa went out into the night.

He was grimly silent as he drove his official Mercedes through the village, and she knew better than to say anything. Indeed, she sensed, he was shaken in a way she had never seen before. Was it the humiliation he had endured, or was it possible that even his faith had been rocked by the intensity of Glaser's jeremiad? And that business about burning babies—factories for burning babies. What nightmare madness had put that in the soldier's mind?

Robert turned up the hill toward the Christina Hof, driving slowly, with utmost care, the red blackout shields cutting the reach of the headlights to almost nothing. It burst from her without her even realizing that she spoke: "Robert, what did he mean about those places—gas and ovens?"

"The man was drunk! Drunk and crazy. He meant nothing!"

"He sounded as if he had seen them. He said he had."

"What he has seen are simple concentration camps. There are many in the east. Naturally they are prisons, not rest homes. Sometimes prisoners die, are cremated." He paused. "There must be facilities for disposing of the bodies. He has, perhaps, seen those. But as for the rest... Well, most of the Russian propaganda is created by Jews, and you know how clever they are. With his brain weakened by combat, he would be susceptible. I hope he knows how lucky he is, the young fool. If there had been any SS there tonight, I'd have had to take decisive action. Fortunately, there weren't. And if someone denounces him, maybe I can save him. But..." She did not miss the hurt in his voice. "But he was grossly unfair to me."

"Darling, of course he was." She put her hand on his thigh. She had, after all, been sleeping with him for three years; they had needed each other desperately; he had been kind to her, had saved the Christina Hof. And so she loved him and felt protective toward him. "Don't I know how it galls you to have to stay back here when you'd rather be commanding a unit in the front line?" That was true; whatever else Robert might be, he was no coward.

"You know it; they don't." His voice grated. "I could transfer to the Waffen SS with equivalent rank at any time. I've half a mind to do it; I'm getting tired of all the names—Golden Pheasant, Bombproof. Tired of that and of the look in their eyes."

Fear rose in her; she dared not lose him. "Now don't talk foolishness." She patted his thigh, stroked it. "Anybody can carry a gun. But who could administer this *Kreis* the way you do? Like it or not, you're worth ten times as much to the war effort as someone like Jochen Glaser; it would be very unpatriotic of you—cowardly—to yield to your own preferences."

She felt him relax a little. "I suppose you're right. That's what von Schirach tells me." He meant the young Gauleiter of Vienna, former leader of the Hitler Youth, self-styled poet and patron of the arts. Robert's efficiency had made him one of von Schirach's confidants. "He's in the same boat, he says."

"You all are."

"No. No, the truth is, in a way Glaser was right. The higher you are in the Party, the less likely you are to have to fight. We're accused of sending non-Party members first and giving National Socialists favored treatment, and . . . well, damn it, it's all too true. A lot of people do use their pull to stay out; but you know I've never done that. They just won't let me go."

"And very rightly." They had reached the gate now, and he got out, opened it with his key, slipped back behind the wheel, drove through, relocked it, and pulled into the courtyard. She turned toward him, hand sliding up his thigh. "Will you stay the night?" Genuinely she hoped he would; despite the ugliness of the aftermath, the romanticism of the movie had aroused her.

"*Leider,* I can't tonight. I wish I could, but Charlotte—" He looked down at her a moment, then pulled her to him, and they kissed; and then, for minutes they were locked together, hands caressing each other, mouths hungry. Suddenly he pushed her away, straightened up breathing hard, and smoothed back his hair. "Tomorrow night," he said softly. "I'll be here tomorrow night and stay over." He gave her one last kiss. "Good night, my darling."

"Good night." She touched his face, slid out of the car. Lips crushed and swollen from the pressure of his mouth, she waved briefly as he backed the Mercedes, turned it; she then let herself into the Christina Hof.

As always, as soon as she had hung up her coat her first move was to check her father. And, as always, she was apprehensive when she knocked on the door of his apartment. He answered instantly: "Come in." She entered, wondering if he would recognize her tonight. More than half the time he took her for her mother. This time she cued him. "Papa, shame on you. So late and you're still up." She went to him where he sat slumped in the easy chair and ruffled his hair and kissed him.

Helmer looked up at her, blue eyes watery in the shrunken shell of the once strong face. His mouth drooped at one side, lips slack. His hair was now silky white, and he had lost fifteen kilos, which the doctor said it was unlikely he would ever regain; his clothes hung slackly on his gaunt and bony frame. But there still remained something of his old presence in the taut corner of his mouth when he smiled, and his teeth were still white and perfect. "Why, Christa," he said, "you're home early from the ball."

"Yes, Papa."

"Aren't you enjoying Fasching? Your mother and I went out every night." A sliver of spittle drooled from the slack corner of his mouth. "We used to like to slum, you know. The Plumbers Ball, the *Fiaker* drivers ... Strauss captured the crowning of the Fiaker Millie very well, you know, in *Arabella*." In his smoking jacket and pajama pants, he straightened up in the chair. "Incidentally, you missed a glorious concert. Ernst played the Waldstein sonata for me. It was marvelous."

Christa's heart seemed to turn to ice. He had been recovering nicely, almost phenomenally, until the day he had learned by accident from that stupid Traudi that Ernst had been thrown into combat against the Russians. She had come home to find him victim of another stroke, maundering, something about wind in sunflowers. He had since plummeted downhill, and there was nothing anyone could do. He had never been informed of Ernst's death. Now he added, "Your mother was so proud."

"Yes," said Christa tonelessly, "I'm sure she was. We are all so proud. Now, Papa, you must go to bed. I will leave for two

324

minutes, and when I come back, I want to find you under the covers." She took his arm and lifted. "Up. Up."

He came easily. She stripped away the smoking jacket, was glad to see that he had his pajama shirt on beneath. "Two minutes, mind you." She went out into the hall. When she re-entered, he was in bed, snoring slightly. She touched his head. He was so docile. She hated that feminine docility of his; it had nothing to do with the father she had known.

Mitzi was in the kitchen, sleepily waiting up. She had made a few sandwiches in case Robert came for the night. Christa sent her off to bed and, though she did not really want it, drank an *Achtel* of wine and ate a sandwich, chiding herself that she would get fat. But, of course, if she put on weight, that would please Robert. He worried about her leanness. "If you would just gain some weight," he said so often, "then you could conceive."

And always she told him, "No, it's quite hopeless," knowing all the while that he desperately wanted a child by her. "Dr. Walzer says so."

"Dr. Walzer! Why do you go to that quack? Go to the Primarius at the *Spital*."

"I've told you, I won't go near him. There's a difference between an examination and being played with. He's obscene." And when she had drawn the line that firmly, he had not protested. But Charlotte had given him two daughters in four years and was pregnant once again. He loved his children, even if he did not love his wife; but, she knew, a child, a son, by her would be for him an absolute culmination. For her it would be a surrender to ... what? An inevitability, a Rubicon she could not bring herself to cross. And Dr. Walzer had been very understanding. He had fitted her with the pessary and given her the spermicidal douche as back-up. The douche she needed only rarely; Robert was a model of unimaginative regularity in his lovemaking. Almost always she was ready for him before he mounted her, the diaphragm in place. The possibility that he would discover it was minimal. He was a stallion, and a stallion knew only one way of having sex: to thrust and hammer. Any more unconventional way would have been decadent and un-German. Of course, she herself would never have known the difference if Lan had not spoiled her.

325

So, having made it through the first week safely, she was ready from then on. On those times when he caught her by surprise, she managed to use the douche in time. Thus, to his disappointment and bafflement, that final commitment that she could not bring herself to had been avoided; though it took a lot of doing, a lot of cheating, and it was a dangerous game. Everything now was a dangerous game.

She finished the sandwich, drained the last of the wine, and started for the stairs. But there was no real hope of sleep. The various excitements of the film, the incident in the *Gasthaus,* and the wrestling with Robert in the car had wound her up like a clock. And the night outside was a fine one, though nearly moonless.

By now, of course, everyone would be asleep, even the three Polish women detailed to them by the *Kreis,* poor things. They'd had them for two years now, quartering them outside the *Hof* itself with women whose husbands had gone to war. They were strong, humble, grateful, and spoke fair German now: hard workers, but also lusty. There was the problem of forbidden intercourse with the Ferntal men. By now they would probably take anything; she knew the feeling. Anyhow, they saddened her, and Robert dealt with them, as he dealt with everything that might burden her.

She went to the closet, took down her coat, donned it, and tied a scarf around her head. Closing the blackout curtains carefully behind her, she went out on the terrace. Below her the whole valley lay dark, no longer a jeweled spangle. So far the bombers had not come at night, but there was no guarantee of anything.

Every day now at noon they surged through an iron ring of anti-aircraft fire to pound the industrial suburbs of Vienna. Now everyone planned his day around the raids; even this far out they had to count on being in the cellars from noon till two, And when the all-clear sounded, it was sickening to emerge and see the great roils of smoke in the distance lit underneath by flame, to know that people were dying in that inferno. At least, though, the Amis had shown some vestige of civilization; so far the Inner City with all its fine old buildings, the cathedral and the Opera, had been left comparatively untouched.

It was amazing how the onset of the bombing had changed everybody's thinking. Many Austrians had never quite considered the Americans their enemy. The Russians, yes, everyone feared them; and there was no doubt that the British were implacable. But until recently, except in official propaganda, one heard few words of hatred for the Amis. But now there was no longer any doubt; they, too, were an enemy without mercy, hated as they had never been before. Even Christa felt hatred for their strength and the brutal way they used it on the powerless. She wanted to cry out to those bombing planes, *Stop it! Don't you understand? You have the wrong targets! Turn against the Russians, they are the enemy! Save us from them and then we can all have peace! We didn't want this, we didn't have a hand in it* ... But what could you expect? They even bombed the French, and the French were on their side.

But one thing she was sure of—Lan was not up there in those planes. Flyers must be very young; he was too old. Besides, she knew him too well. He might be fighting somewhere, yes, but he would never lend himself to the slaughter of children and old people and women, of helpless civilians.

Looking out at the valley, she forced the thought of Lan from her mind. Maybe he was already dead on some battlefield halfway around the world. Maybe he had left another widow to mourn him; perhaps she had been divorced without even knowing it. Anyhow, she must not think of Lan, and usually she was very good at that. It was only going to the *Kino* tonight that had stirred her up.

Think of Robert. Robert would be home now, undoubtedly draining into Charlotte the lust she, Christa, had aroused in him. But tomorrow he would stay the night, before going to his office in the former Stift at Altkreuzburg. It was curious; she could not bear the thought of Lan with another woman, but she did not mind sharing Robert with Charlotte. Nor feel any shame at the general knowledge that she was his mistress; what would have been viewed in the old days as a delicious and typical scandal of the Viennese sort was now considered matter-of-factly as a manless woman's duty to the State. The only scandal was that she had never conceived. In any case, no one but Papa could have objected, and he did not even know, or at least did not comprehend.

She was tired of thinking. Turning from the wall, she crossed the terrace, went down the steps. She crossed the parklike lawn, reached the far stone wall that encircled it, and turned to follow its length, striding briskly, wanting movement to drain the tension from her. Two circuits of the wall, then to bed; and if she still could not sleep, she would take a drink of rum.

Factories for burning children. Imagine! What rotten propaganda the Russians spread! She shuddered. And yet . . . the Gestapo and the SS seemed to be capable of anything. Who knew? Still, that was too fantastic, too vile. She walked more swiftly. Following the wall to its corner, she stopped, turned. Children. Here, in this heavy thicket of lilac bushes, she had played as a little girl; deep in those bushes had been a secret place that had been hers alone. In May, when the thicket abounded with blooms, the air in there had been so sweet it had actually made her dizzy. Of course there were no blossoms at this time of year; there were—

The bushes shook, leaves clashing. Christa jumped back as something rushed from the thicket, and her mouth opened in a scream. Then he was on her, the man breaking from the lilac bushes. One hand seized her hair, jerking her around with pain that filled her eyes with tears; another slid between her teeth, filling her mouth, turning the scream into a muffled gagging sound. She was pulled hard against a thin, bony body, and she smelled sour rankness, dirt, and sweat.

The voice in her ear was a savage whisper. "Christa! For God's sake, don't scream!" Then brutally she was dragged back into the shrubbery, jerked to the ground. A man's weight covered her, hand clamping across her mouth. "Don't scream!" he rasped. "You hear? I mean no harm. Christa, it's Josef Steiner!"

"Josef!" she blurted, mind freezing with incredulity. His clamping hand stifled the single word.

"Yes, it's I! Christa, please don't cry out! I don't want to hurt you, but if you cry out, I'm a dead man!" But then, quite suddenly, he released her. "I'm a fool," he whispered. "I'm no more capable of hurting you than I am of running any farther." And he rolled off her, sprawling on the leaf-littered earth beside her.

Christa sat up. "Josef Steiner, what— Where did you—? I thought you were dead."

"I have been, several times. Why I keep being resurrected I don't know." His voice was a thready whisper. "All I know is that I can't go on any more. Maybe . . . maybe you can help me. But if you can't, just call them. Go ahead and call them. I'm tired. I don't know what they could do to me now that I could feel."

The grove was silent, save for his raspy breathing. Christa's mind struggled to comprehend this. Of course, he was a fugitive, from a concentration camp or somewhere. And, God, if he were found here, if he were harbored, sheltered . . . A fierce resentment rose suddenly in her; this man had cost her Lan, had cost her everything. What right had he now to still be alive, come back to haunt her, endanger her once more by his very presence?

"I can't," she whispered.

"All right," he muttered dully, "then let me rest a moment. If you could give me a little bread, that's all. Then I'll be away."

"You— Oh . . ." She got to her knees, rubbing palms against her coat. He lay sprawled, forearm over his eyes, only a darker blotch beneath the lilac bushes. He stank like a bear. And this was the sleek Josef Steiner she once had almost loved? She shook her head. It was not fair; it was not fair at all. She should go call Robert this very minute, she should—

Murder him? Her hands dropped. It came to that. Of course she could not. She drew in a long breath. Fight for a little time, give him a chance to rest, find out how it was that he was still alive. A strange kind of thrill surged through her. The past was not wholly lost after all. Here he was from it, tangible, not long since destroyed as she had thought. Almost like a sign. "Josef. Can you get up? Can you walk?"

"To where?"

"Upstairs in the Christina Hof. Everyone's asleep. If I could get you to the attic . . ."

"Yes. Yes, I can make it that far." Panting, he scrabbled to hands and knees.

"Wait." She crawled to the thicket's edge and peered out. Thank God that since Papa could no longer hunt Uncle Max had taken all the dogs. Everything was tranquil, of course; no reason for it not to be. "Come." She half dragged him to the edge of the lilac clump, then helped him to his feet.

He leaned against her as they stumbled across the lawn. Leaving him in the corner of the terrace, she made sure the way inside was clear. It seemed to take forever to get him through the house and to the stairway; she had visions of Mitzi or Traudi appearing suddenly: *Anything wrong, gnae' Frau?* But, of course, they were long since asleep.

They made it to the second floor. There she unlocked her own apartment, brought him in, closed and locked the door, switched on the light. He blinked, like some night bird dragged suddenly into day; and she herself, at first full sight of him, let out a muffled cry. Bearded, filthy, his clothes no more than rags, this was not Josef Steiner but a parody of him.

Yet somehow he found a smile. Two of his teeth, she saw, had rotted away to jagged stubs. "Yes. You have not changed, but I have."

"Shhh. Wait." He slumped in a chair. She fumbled through the key box, found the *Dachboden* keys, slipped them in her pocket, got the flashlight she kept by her bed. When she turned, Josef had gone to sleep in the chair, and she had to shake him awake.

3   ABOVE THE CEILING of the house's highest floor, under the very eaves, there was the *Dachboden,* the sprawling attic: one huge storage room and four smaller ones in the constricted space beneath the dormers. In a pinch the little rooms could be used as bedrooms, but now, like the main one, they were packed with obsolete furniture, old books, papers, travel luggage, and the like: repositories of thrift. Once every two or three months, Christa and a team of cleaners went through the whole attic complex, dusting, straightening, and rearranging; otherwise the *Dachboden* was rarely entered.

Further, for every door and every cabinet, chest, or wardrobe drawer there was a lock; for every lock a key. That had always been the central European way: trust no one, control your property. Lan had been amazed, then derisive of this obsession with security. "Good God, back home we never locked a door. I didn't even know we had a key until we sold the house." Aunt Alma had been appalled at such stupid carelessness, such blind trust of others. Everyone knew the world was full of thieves.

The locks and keys remained under the total control of Christa, who kept, as Aunt Alma had, most of them tagged in boxes in her room. For the main house there were two hundred and fourteen altogether, classified with an intricate numbering system. Duplicates of those commonly used and with which the servants could be trusted hung in the pantry downstairs on a big board. In addition there were another eighty-five keys to outbuildings and other storage areas locked in the cabinet in her father's office, which she now used, though some of the people on the place had duplicates. Keys were symbols of authority; it was Christa now who kept them and controlled every space in the sprawling labyrinth of the house, and to her that everyone must come for access to any attic room.

This one was small, three by four meters, maybe, set under the sloping roof of the south wing, and contained a bed with three straw mattress segments in place to form a whole, a coverlet and a piece of muslin over the coverlet to catch the dust. The rest of the room was filled with junk.

Josef Steiner sank down on the bed, eyes closed, groaning softly with the pleasant pain of rest. "Ahhh," he whispered, "ahh, God," as Christa took off his shoes, stripped away foul stockings turned nearly to paste, wincing not so much at the rankness as at the blisters, puffed or broken, on his feet.

"I'm sorry I'm so filthy," Josef whispered.

"Never mind. Drink some wine. Eat."

"I'm too tired to eat. Just let me sleep."

"No, you have to eat. Here." Holding his head up with one hand, she gave him bread and cheese. He chewed slowly, reluctantly; then, appetite flaring, wolfed it, washed it down with wine. Sighing, he eased back, eyes closed. His face was like a skull, skin stretched parchment yellow over raw bone.

"Thanks, Christa. Am I safe here?"

"Absolutely, if you make no noise."

"I'll be quiet. I know how to do it. I've been living in a room like this for years."

"All right. Sleep. When you wake up, don't move around, don't show yourself, don't get off the bed. If you walk, someone might hear you. Do you understand?"

"Perfectly."

331

"I'll be back soon," she said, but he did not hear her. He was already sound asleep.

Christa stood there indecisively, shutting off the flashlight she had used to light their way. Josef snored softly. With some effort she rolled him over on his stomach to minimize that much sound; she knew how much noise men sleeping on their backs could make. Then she went out, locking the door behind her. In her own apartment she leaned against the wall for a moment, hand at her breast, feeling the thudding of her heart. Now what? she thought. What do I do now?

It was after one and she was exhausted; morning would come soon and the day would be long and taxing, but for the moment she was far beyond sleeping. She rubbed her face, then poured herself a drink of brandy. Her body still ached from the bruises he'd inflicted when he'd dragged her into the lilacs....

Now, fed and sleeping, the *Dachboden* locked, the keys in her possession, he was, for the moment, safe. Or was he? Where had he come from? Who might be pursuing him? Had he escaped from prison or a *KZ-Lager*? She shuddered. Suppose police were on his trail? They hunted fugitives with dogs, she knew. He could not, must not, stay here long. Tonight, tomorrow, well, tomorrow night, too, for Robert would be here all night long. That thought almost caused her to panic: Robert here, Josef just above him in the attic. Then she told herself that she must keep her head. If she stayed cool, she could manage all; but if she got rattled, disaster would surely follow.

It was possible that she might not even see him for a full two days. When something was needed from the dusty *Dachboden,* a servant was always sent; if she herself were noticed by one of them scuffling around in the attic, that would arouse at least curiosity if not suspicion. And with Robert here tomorrow night, there would be no chance. During that interval there would be much that he would need.

Although she should have given them to the Winter-Help, all of Lan's clothes, fresh and clean, were stored in a chest; she had kept them as if they were talismans. Now she took out underwear, shirt, pants, jacket, socks, meanwhile mentally ticking off his other needs. For the next three-quarters of an hour she was furtively busy, assembling and taking to the attic everything she could imagine that he would need: food, wine, cigarettes, water for washing and drinking, soap, towels, a chamberpot, a magazine to read. She was taut with excitement, heart pounding, feeling a burglar's guilt in her own house. He did not stir as she arranged things in the little room, and she left a note for him on the food:

Here are supplies for two days. You should be safe as long as you are quiet. Don't walk around. Robert Schellhammer will be here all night long just downstairs tomorrow night. Be sure all blackout curtains on the Dachboden windows remain drawn. I may not see you for forty-eight hours. Then we will talk.

She did not sign the note. When she left the attic, she locked every door behind her as she went, imprisoning him, and hid the keys and duplicates in her dressing table; no one could possibly enter his hiding place without first getting her permission. Then she undressed, washed away the attic dust, fell into bed. Strangely, instead of tossing restlessly as usual, she fell asleep almost at once, her mind occupied now with something besides futility.

All the next day the attic drew her like a lodestone, and half a dozen times she almost entered it, drawing back each time at the last moment. She was always on call; what if one of the servants sought her out and found her there? She must excite not the least suspicion; the moment she had not turned Josef over to the police, she had committed high treason. And after all these years she knew where the ultimate loyalties of the servants lay.

Then Robert came and her tension grew until she was certain he would read her guilt through her skull, as if it were emblazoned on her brain, and her temples were transparent. Before and after the evening meal there was business to be attended to; and it took every ounce of will to pretend to concentrate on it. Yet, she must have brought it off; he seemed to suspect nothing.

He and Uncle Max ran the Christina Hof's farming operations along with their own, taking care of the financial aspects and the multifarious government forms and regulations. And so the

333

Christina Hof was his second home; and she, if not the second wife in his harem, was at least his concubine. She neither knew nor cared what Charlotte Schellhammer understood or thought about the arrangement, and it seemed to be a matter of indifference to Robert, too. Anyhow, he spent as much time in Christa's bed as in Charlotte's, and maybe more.

For her it had been good to have an intimate relationship, to have her sexual needs fulfilled; and, yes, it was somehow delicious no longer to have to think or reason for herself. To relinquish will was to be a child again, free of responsibility for her own life. As Robert was to der Führer, so she was to him.

That night in bed, though, she felt no security in Robert's arms, took no pleasure in his lovemaking; all she could think of was Josef up there in the attic. At two in the morning she awakened; Robert lay beside her snoring. She turned on the light; he did not stir. She could bear it no longer. She put on robe and slippers, like a thief, watching him all the while, and took the keys from the drawer. Then soundlessly she was out the door, taking the flashlight with her.

It seemed to take forever to reach the cubicle in the attic. She did not knock, only quietly unlocked the door. "Josef," she whispered, "are you all right?"

He was sitting up in bed blinking. The room smelled of his discarded dirty clothes, the contents of the chamber pot. "What—Christa?"

"Shh. Are you all right?"

"I . . . think so." His whisper was barely audible.

"I can't see you again until tomorrow night."

"Yes. Thank you. Don't worry about me."

Not answering, she locked the door again, once more imprisoning him. She padded down the stairs and hurried to the bathroom at the end of the hall, noisily flushed the toilet. When she reached the bedroom, Robert still slept. Heart pounding, Christa hid the keys, undressed, crawled in beside him, instinctively snuggling closer to his warmth. Despite that, she began to shiver as if she had a chill. Not until she edged away, across the bed, did it cease. The source of that familiar warmth was now malevolent, would, if he could, kill the helpless man upstairs. She could feel only relief when Robert went away in the morning.

Midnight. Even through the closed windows she could hear the chiming of the distant bells of the Stift, mingled with the lesser strokes from Ferndorf. Josef Steiner drained the glass of beer, sighed, leaned back in the chair. He looked around her apartment with wonder in his eyes. Then quietly he said, "Thank you, Christa."

She had had the food and drink waiting for him when she had carefully led him down the stairs through the sleeping house. Before daylight came, of course, she must erase all signs of this meal. But that could wait. For the time being they were utterly safe here, and they must talk.

Josef's hand trembled as he lit a cigarette. "I know," he said. "You must have thought I was dead. I could only hope that you and Lan were not. And"—he shook his head, lips trembling— "and I am sorry, truly. If I had known it would go so sour, so wrong for all of us . . . But I thought we had a few more days. If we'd had just one more day . . ."

"How did you escape them?"

His eyes were huge, haunted, in the skeletal face. "Waiting for Lan in Horn, I saw them moving in on me. Their kind is easy to spot. By then I knew what was happening, that the game was up. I ran. Somehow I dodged them, escaped into the out-skirts, then into the hills. After that I was an animal for a while. I am no outdoorsman, and it was hard on me. At last I found a summer house, broke into it, stole food, fresh clothes, cleaned myself up. Then I dared go to the highway, take the postbus to a railroad station. I rode the train to Vienna and had no difficulty and somehow made it to my apartment near the Hernalsergürtel—the 'black' one." He smiled faintly. "They had not yet connected it with me. I destroyed all incriminating evidence it contained; and in preparation for just such an emer-gency I had false documents waiting for me. After that, I became a *U-Boot*, a submarine, hiding out.

"But there was no way I could get out to Switzerland or Italy. I had to stay there in the city. Then they began closing in on me. Fortunately, by then I had made a connection with a Christian family who were secretly anti-Nazi. They had their own house in Hietzing, and they took me in. That little room" —he gestured toward the attic—"for two years I've lived in one much like it, not daring to let myself be seen, coming out

335

only at night to join them, living off what they could share from their own rations. They were magnificent to me. But then the bombers came, and of course I could not go to an air raid shelter. All I could do was wait, hope—and four days ago my luck ran out. The house blew up around my ears."

He closed his eyes, rubbed them hard. "By a miracle, I wasn't harmed, but the game was up. While everything was still in turmoil from the raid, I ran. In the confusion, after the electricity came on, I caught a tram to Grinzing and then I faded into the Wienerwald. Then what? I asked myself, and all I could think of was you, the Christina Hof. I knew nowhere else to turn. I wasn't even sure whether you were still here; I thought maybe Lan had taken you out. You see, I'd had no news of you. But even if you were in America . . . General Helmer had banked with my brothers, and I hoped, was willing to risk . . ."

He paused. "For four days I've been walking through the forest. I stole some vegetables from a garden. At nights I almost froze. But finally I was here and with just strength enough to get over the wall. Just as I made it, a car drove up. I hid in the lilac bushes; after a while I heard your voice and knew you were still here. Oh, the sweetness of that sound, the sound of hope. I waited, planning to break in somehow, find you— but then you came to me, straight to me, almost as if . . . as if you felt me there. And . . ." He stood up, Lan's clothes hanging on him like bags. "And now I've rested and eaten my fill and I shall soon be on my way."

Christa stared at him. "To where?"

"I haven't the faintest idea. And if I had, I wouldn't tell you. You've already risked enough without being involved any further. Except, perhaps, if you could lend me a few marks." He smiled wryly. "I'm afraid my investments haven't prospered lately."

"Josef, of course." She went to her pocketbook on the vanity. "How much do you need?"

"Whatever you can spare. Then if you'll let me out, I'll be over the wall and gone and no one will ever be the wiser. And I shall eternally be in your debt. Of course, I already am, having, it seems, very thoroughly ruined your life and Lan's."

"It wasn't you. It was everything."

336

"You're too generous. It was I. It—"

She cut in, turning, money in hand. "Josef, you *must* have someplace to go. You can't just . . . wander."

"I'll find someplace. If I don't— Well, I've had a good run anyhow. There's only one thing in this life that ever really mattered to me that I never had." He came to her and took the money, his hand brushing hers. "Aside from the collapse of all my plans to change the world." He counted the money instinctively, put it in his pocket, stood there looking down at her for a moment.

She met his eyes; they had changed. They were only ordinary eyes now, devoid of any arrogance, assurance; as if he did not want her to see the fear and weariness in them, he looked away. "Thank you, Christa," he said quietly. "Don't worry. It will all soon be over. The war can't go on much longer and there is no longer any chance that the Reich will win. A few more months, and then one day Lan will come to the door of the Christina Hof and ring and take you with him."

Suddenly she turned away. "No. No, don't say that. That's the one thing I can't allow myself to think."

"But of course he will."

"No," she said thickly. "No, he won't."

"Have you had bad news of him? Has he been—"

"Killed? I don't know. How would I know? No, I've had no news of him. But he is through with me; I know that much. We were apart too long." And she heard herself, still not looking at him, tell Josef about the letters and how shortly after the war had started they had stopped coming. "I couldn't expect him to wait any longer. He was right to make some kind of new life. Find someone else. So you see, it was finished even before the Amis came in. And if it wasn't, if he did what you say, if he's still alive and did that, how could he want me anyhow? I have been . . . sleeping with Robert Schellhammer for three years." She drew in breath. "Maybe if it were someone else, but a big Nazi leader like Robert. After what happened to *us?* What a nice whore that makes me."

Josef was silent for a moment. Though her back was turned, she could feel the pressure of his eyes on her. "And so my guilt deepens. But I think you misjudge Lan. He would know why you do what you do; he is no fool. You are no Nazi. That I am here

337

now is proof of that. And if I were he, I would— Well, no matter." He was silent for a moment. Then his hand touched her shoulder. "Christa, please get your coat. Time is passing swiftly. I need as much darkness as possible in order to get as far from here as I can."

But she did not move. He had stirred too much in her, ripped loose too many things she had thought securely fastened down.

"Christa—"

"Josef," she heard herself say, "why can't you stay here?"

When seconds passed and he did not answer, Christa turned. He stood there, face drawn and pale, in the ill-fitting clothes, his whole body tense. Then slowly he shook his head. "I think I have enough on my conscience already. With Schellhammer in and out of here every day... What do you want, for me to give you the *coup de grâce?* Complete the destruction I began?"

But now the idea was fastened in her brain. It was almost as if his presence here offered her some kind of salvation. She could not entirely grasp that thought, define her feelings; it was only important all at once that Josef stay and that she somehow keep him safe. "It wouldn't be that," she heard herself answer with intensity that startled both of them. "There's no way Robert could know, if we're careful. You'd be locked in the room up there all day, of course, and could only come out at night, on certain nights, like this; but I have all the keys, can keep the servants out, the food's no problem. And Robert— Don't you see? He guarantees the rest of it. There'll be no surprise Gestapo search or anything like that." She gestured. "Since Aunt Alma and Ernst are gone, the next floor above is empty now, and that's extra insulation, you might say. And maybe you're right. Maybe it won't be for long. A few weeks, a few months..." She paused. "But, of course, if you don't trust me—"

"Trust you? Don't be a fool." Relief flooded Josef's face with such startling suddenness that only now did she realize fully how he had dreaded going. "If I could only be sure you wouldn't be hurt by it."

"I won't; we won't. And maybe even helped. If... if what you say comes true, if it's all over soon and we lose, then that we tried to help you may count for something."

"Listen, after what you've already suffered, you don't need

338

more credentials. But maybe you're right." His smile suddenly had a different quality and his eyes changed, he looked younger. "If you're willing to take the risk, God knows I am. To know I'll have a roof over my head again, someone to talk to. You. To—" He broke off, came to her. "Thank you, Christa," he said softly and kissed her forehead. Then quickly he stepped back. "And now," he said, "since I am staying, do you suppose . . . May I have a real bath before daylight comes?"

"Yes," Christa said, and she laughed with real amusement for the first time in weeks. "And Lan's razor's still here, if you want to use it."

4 THEY HAD SPENT almost all of that interminable March day deep in the cellars under the Christina Hof. The alarm had sounded earlier than usual, just after eleven in the morning. Christa had been walking with the General in the garden when she heard the sirens in Altkreuzburg blare, and Mitzi screamed at her, "They're coming! The Amis come!" Almost as if the baby heard it, too, it kicked within her. She raised her face to the cloud-tattered sky instinctively, one hand laid on her swollen belly. There was nothing to be seen up there, but the sirens went on howling, shrieking the world's end.

"Papa!" She seized his arm, pulled him around.

"Yes, Christina," he said mildly.

Heart pounding, she realized how deeply sunken he was into the past. "Kurt," she said. "We must go to the cellars. There is a problem with the wine."

"Ah, yes. Well, it can't be anything serious. Have the curtains you sent for come?"

"They'll be here soon. Now, Kurt, come with me. Hurry!"

"All right, if it's so urgent." He came with docility, but breathing hard from the exertion. So was she, awkward now with pregnancy going into its sixth month. Through the pressing house, then down the cellar stairs, but before they passed through the wooden door, she turned, stared at the house across

339

the courtyard. Josef was up there, helpless in his attic room. If a stray bomb should hit the house . . . Two had fallen in Altkreuzburg last week, not five miles away; the lower market place had been wiped out.

But there was nothing she could do. Clinging to her father, she hurried down the mold-slick steps, through the upper cellar, to the deepest one, its walls massive and ancient, relict of the castle that once had stood here. There was food, water, and, of course, wine, cask on cask of it; they had installed chairs, cots, and wiring for a radio. It was as good as any *Luftschutzkeller* in Vienna or Altkreuzburg; most of the shelters were old cellars like this one. Robert had sent in a team of experts to thrust up air pipes, improve its ventilation. Even so, for a while they had been careless about using it; they were, after all, so far from the main targets. Then one day after the all-clear had sounded, they had emerged to see a single American Flying Fortress circle back from the south. Like a wasp sprayed with insecticide, it wove back and forth across the sky, drunk and dying. Everyone had stood watching, fascinated, had seen three parachutes disgorged, watched them drift down into the Wienerwald miles away. The anti-aircraft guns were not even shooting; their gunners could see that the plane's wound was already mortal.

Around and around it lurched, zigging, zagging, dipping, trying to rise and failing, trailing black smoke now. Turning northward, it came, one wing down and careening crazily, straight toward the Ferntal. Suddenly Christa had realized that it would crash nearby. It was she who'd screamed the alarm, but it was already too late. The plane was already directly overhead, so low she could see the white stars on its wings, the pieces tearing off its fuselage, the flames around its engines. The sound it made was loud, stuttering, and terrible. It plunged into the valley, tried to rise again, and failed. Then, before their eyes, with terrible impact, it plowed into the hill across the Fernbach, directly below the Schellhammer Hof. It did not explode, only flew apart in a shower of fragments scattered by the terrific impact.

"Maybe there're survivors!" Mitzi had yelled. "Get a pitchfork!" Before Christa could stop them, the servants had seized farming tools, were running down the hill. People were pouring from the Schellhammer Hof as well. Christa hesitated, then ran after the others.

But when she reached the road that ran beside the Fernbach, she halted, and a scream broke from her throat, and then she turned away, vomiting. It had been thrown all the way across the stream, had landed in the middle of the road; it sat there obscenely, looking at her—a head, undamaged, of a young man with dark brown hair and wide-open eyes, affixed to the upper half of a torso, balanced on gleaming white ribs protruding from bloody flesh, the bust, exactly museum size, of what had been an American airman, sculptured by war.

The face was not even bruised. She would never forget the staring eyes, the astonished mouth. She knew there were no survivors, and she went no farther, only threw herself into the cold winter-killed grass and waited until she had strength enough to climb the hill again.

But it had been a near miss. It could have as easily plowed into the Christina Hof. Since that day, she insisted that everyone go to the cellar the moment the alarm sounded.

Down here now, she sat by the General, his gas mask and hers on her lap. He had fallen silent, as if he vaguely understood that this was serious. There were only two men besides himself left on the place, and both were nearly seventy, too old even for the Volkssturm, which, with the Russians driving ever closer to the Austrian border, had been mobilized to stand before Vienna. They had tapped a cask, were drinking. So was one of the Polish girls; there was no way to stop them. Nobody cared about anything any more, it was ever harder to enforce any authority. In fact, she herself hardly tried. There were only three people important to her any more: her father, Josef, and Josef's baby inside of her.

It kicked again as she leaned back on the bench. She put her hand on it, mouthing the words silently, "Be quiet, my darling." She thought of Josef up there in his room; he could hear the sirens, too. But he was locked in; he had refused to take a key, though she had tried to press one on him.

"No," he had said, lying beside her in the bed in her apartment. "No, I won't be responsible for any miscalculation, any extra risk. It's not myself I'm worried about, you understand. But if Schellhammer ever found out, if our signals got crossed and I made a blunder . . . No, it's up to you to say when I can come to you and when I must stay here." And he had stroked her

stomach. "Take care of him—or her. He's what counts now."
And he had buried his face in her neck. "I've got all I've ever
wanted. I've had you . . . and you've had my child. For myself,
I will not jeopardize either of you in the slightest way."

So he would not take the key. She had to go up and get him
and bring him down every night when the coast was clear.

One of the Polish girls began to sing something incomprehensible. Another joined in. Traudi turned her sharp face toward
them. "Hush that barbaric noise."

"Be quiet, Traudi," Christa said, "and let them sing. It's a
pretty sound; I like to hear it."

"I don't like to hear anything I can't understand. Who knows
what sort of slop they're singing, these ugly Slavs."

"Be quiet," Christa said.

"Yes, *gnae Frau*." Traudi yielded reluctantly to her authority.
The Poles went on singing. Christa wished she could smoke
a cigarette. But she had given up smoking for the baby's sake.
Robert had insisted on that. "Smoking is bad for unborn children! I will not see my son maimed by your self-indulgence!"

Momentarily Christa felt a twinge of pity for him, a thrust
of conscience. Her lie had made him so ecstatic. It was as if his
manhood were finally vindicated. But what else could she do?

She felt motion inside her abdomen once more. Automatically
her mind ran back to that night in late October. . . .

Josef had lived in the attic for nearly a week by then, and
maintaining him there was far from simple. Food was the main
problem. They were better off than people in the city, but
nevertheless Robert was strict about seeing that everything above
allowable rations went to market, to the war effort. Unlike most
farmers, since Robert controlled the place, she could hold out
nothing, and she could not, like the city people, take advantage
of the *Schleichhandel*—the black market. Besides, the servants
always knew exactly how much there was of everything, especially
Mitzi, who had been trained to count and weigh every gram.

Fortunately her father ate almost nothing nowadays; she
herself cut back and salvaged leftovers for Josef. She stole a
little, juggled supplies, and had managed so far to see that he
was fed without anyone the wiser. And when she was certain that
Robert would not stay the night, she would go up to the *Dachboden,* release him, bring him to her rooms.

342

Their second night together they talked endlessly, reveling in the chance to speak their minds. Freedom of speech! She had almost forgotten what that was like—to have a listener to whom you could say anything and who would not betray you. Having such a confidant was better than any wine, better even than sex. She had been starved for mental intimacy, and obviously so had he. It was nearly daybreak before he went back to the attic; she went to bed exhilarated, totally alive.

Two days later they had another night together. Bathed, shaved, he emerged from the *Badezimmer* in Lan's robe. For the fraction of a second she was startled, as if Lan himself had materialized. He saw the expression on her face. "I feel like a usurper," he said, half smiling. "But am I usurping Schellhammer or Lan?"

He had already changed, was filling out a little, his gaunt, haggard look diminishing. And he was full of energy, pacing the room barefooted, soundlessly, methodically taking the exercise denied to him in his cell. Watching him, she remembered that first afternoon in the absurd apartment off the Hernalsergürtel, and she could not help smiling at the image of herself as she had been. Now he was neither frightening, mysterious, nor overpoweringly fascinating; they were equals now, only a pair of mortals of different sexes. Yet they still had power over each other; she felt the magnetism that he still gave off.

And he felt hers. At last he stopped his pacing, turned, looked at her strangely. "Well," he said sardonically, "it's taken a long time and a wide way round to come to this, hasn't it?" He smiled. "After all, it was all I ever really wanted. To be alone with you in your bedroom."

Then he came to her, touched her cheek. "How many years? I've waited for this so absurdly long—and imagined it a million times. Christa, who knows whether we have ten thousand nights left, or only this one night? Do you understand me?"

She didn't even answer, only moved into his arms, sliding her hands beneath the robe, feeling the hard, ribby warmth of his flanks. He drew in breath. Just before he bent and kissed her, she thought of Lan. This was a betrayal of him—and yet somehow a coming closer to him. He and Josef were all mingled in her mind. Then his mouth found hers, and she was not thinking any longer.

When Josef finally raised his head, he laughed breathily. "You

343

may have to show me how." He grinned and pulled her toward the bed. "It's been so long, I may have forgotten."

He had forgotten nothing, she thought now, deep in the cellar beneath the pressing house. But she had; she had forgotten until then what it was to make love with mind and body simultaneously, to *want* to give and not just take, to be even more emotionally excited than physically. With Josef there was no need to hold back; she could give all of herself to him and he would do the same for her. So she had learned again what making love with someone whom you could love was like.

And so for months now they had played it out, their weird midnight drama, both of them living always on the knife-edge of discovery and danger. It was worth it. She was alive again, once more had identity, self-respect.

But that very fact made the nights with Robert agony; she dreaded and was sickened by them. She saw him now in a new light, and not a lovely one. She could make all the excuses for him—his sincerity, his belief in a dream he conceived to be magnificent, his scrupulous honesty, his kindness—and none of that made any difference. For one thing, she knew that if he ever got the chance, he would kill Josef Steiner promptly and without compunction. Not because Josef had ever wronged him, not because Josef was her lover. Even ignorant of that, he would have killed Josef simply for what he was—a different kind of man.

Factories for burning people! She had mentioned that to Josef, who was instantly alert and grim. "I've been locked in so long I know nothing. But who would put it past them? The people who hid me had heard rumors; that was why they took the risk for me they did. They'd seen the trains come through, bound east, they said, with people—Jews—packed in worse than cattle. They'd heard talk of camps out there—and in Germany—where there were mass executions. But only rumors, never any confirmation in the papers, on the radio. I wonder . . ."

Once she was determined to know, it was fairly easy to find out. She went with Robert to all sorts of Party functions and private entertainments where he could not be represented by a butcher's daughter. And, pretending bitter anti-Semitism herself, she learned things that chilled her blood. The brassy wife of an SS colonel made it plain one night in the ladies' lounge of

344

the Hotel Sacher, where—in surroundings of red damask, veined marble, and crystal—they were freshening makeup and perfume. "The Jews? Forget them, darling. They've all gone up the chimney."

"What?" Christa stared, then remembered and casually opened her compact. "How curious! And where do they go when they go up the chimney?"

"Where smoke always goes, of course! All those dirty creatures one used to see on the street are now floating around up there in the air. Thank God it's the Poles who have to breathe them in, not us!"

"You can't mean they burn them?" Christa's stomach knotted.

The colonel's wife belched; she had drunk a lot of *Sekt.* "Oh, not alive, you goose! First they're put out of their misery—quite painlessly. You see, they think they're going to the baths. But it's a shower of gas they get, not water, and they never know what hit them. It's absolutely humane, Gotthard says. And then cremation, and hey, presto! they've vanished from the earth. So"—she belched again—"one thing you can be sure of about the postwar world: there'll be no Jews to clutter it. That's *one* problem that's been solved forever!"

"But there must be millions—"

"Oh, there *are.* But it's all so *organized,* don't you see? The SS has it all in hand! It's very efficient, and they feel absolutely nothing, no pain at all."

Christa closed her compact. In the mirror she could see the bone-whiteness of her face beneath the rouge. "But surely not the little children!"

"Nits make lice, Gotthard always says!" The woman's voice was airy. "Now, are you *almost* ready? They're waiting for us."

In the private dining room they were all more than a little drunk. "You took long enough," Robert said and grinned, putting his big hand on her wrist as she sat down beside him.

"Fràu Colonel Kupferschmidt and I were talking about the handling of the Jewish problem in the east." She watched his face intently. "It sounds quite efficient."

"Well, that's one thing you can count on the SS for—efficiency." He took the whole matter for granted, asking her no questions about what she had heard. And she knew, with a chill around her heart, that it was all true, and that Robert knew all about it and approved. She moved her hand from under his, and where he had touched her she felt as if she had come in contact with something of unbearable noisomeness. They stayed the night at the hotel, unexpectedly, and he was full of drunken lechery. He hardly noticed her stillness beneath him and the diaphragm she had inserted not at all. For her part, when he was finished, she knew how a whore really felt after making love for money to someone loathsome.

When she told Josef, he nodded gravely. "In the context of their thinking, it makes perfect sense, of course."

"Josef, I can't stand it. I absolutely can't stand it. It makes me want to scream and scream just to think about it. And when I look at Robert and I think— My God, how can I go on sleeping with him?"

"You must," said Josef. "If not for my sake, for your own. But it won't be long now. The end is in sight. I hate it, too. But look. If you do it for me, it's not complicity—it's resistance." He was silent for a moment. "The bastards," he said at last. "God knows when this is over what the verdict of history will be on Austria. It will have to take into account the Roberts. And it will not ignore men like Martinus. But what about all the others—people like you who resisted, then yielded, doing what you had to do? Or like me, who perhaps should have found a gun and died fighting them, but chose to hide to save my skin? And what about the couple in Vienna who risked their lives to take me in? What about those who were just deluded and those who were completely powerless? I am afraid that guilt, like rain, will fall equally on the just and the unjust. I hope when the winners come they'll make allowances for those who knew no better or who could do no more. But I hope"—and his voice roughened—"they will hang every bastard like Robert Schell-hammer out of hand."

After a moment he went on. "Anyhow, if he becomes suspi-cious—"

"I know," said Christa heavily. "All right. I shall try. But—" She shuddered. "Up the chimney. Smoke . . ."

The radio buzzed and crackled as Traudi fiddled with it, but Vienna was not sending, lest it provide a beacon for the bombers. Christa glanced at her father. Slumped on his bench, he laced

346

and unlaced his fingers, staring at nothing. Maybe his answer was the best one, she thought: find a private madness as refuge from the general one. Then her hands moved over the roundness of her belly, a strangeness grafted on, and she felt better.

In December, six weeks after Josef's arrival, she had realized her pregnancy. For a moment there had been panic. Then she knew it could not be Robert's child; her precautions had been unfailing. But with Josef, completely committed, she had taken no precautions whatsoever.

An almost eerie delight had overcome them both. Under the threat of death, both responded fiercely to this intimation of immortality. *"Schatzi, Schatzi,"* Josef would say, holding her tightly. And jubilantly he would kiss her belly, caress it. "You must take good care of him—or her," he whispered. "At least here is one who is innocent of everything. And every scrap of innocence that's left must be fiercely guarded."

What was startling was that Robert's response was almost identical. Seeing a way out of her dilemma, she told him at once; and he, too, was ecstatic, as if she carried within her his justification, maybe his redemption.

She used her condition against him ruthlessly, and he never complained. Now when he wanted to make love to her, she was always a little sick. Charlotte never had been, during her two pregnancies, but, of course, Christa was made of stuff far more delicate than a butcher's daughter. Robert never doubted her. Of course she had to go to the Nazi Primarius in Altkreuzburg, but even he knew better than to tamper with her now that she finally bore a child for der Führer. He cautioned Robert against sex with her at this juncture, and Schellhammer was happy to make that sacrifice. Pregnant women received extra rations; he heaped food on the household, and that made it simpler to feed Josef. Sometimes she felt a pang at the deception she was foisting on him; then she remembered the maimed soldier in the *Gasthaus*, what the colonel's wife had told her, and she knew she would never pity him again.

Anyhow, though she bore the burden of his solicitude, she no longer had to bear his body on top of hers. And maybe, somehow, if she could keep Josef safe for a few more weeks...

What was today? The twelfth of March. The anniversary, she realized, startled, of the *Anschluss*—seven years from the day

347

that she had last seen Lan. Again she touched her stomach, and she swallowed hard. As much as she loved Josef, he was not Lan. She would have given anything for the child within her to have been her husband's. And she felt a chill. Suppose Lan were still alive? Suppose somehow, when all this ended, he came back and she had to confront him as the mother of another man's child? Mistress to two men, not just one, and what explanation could she offer, how could he ever understand? But, of course, he was not coming; he would never come, maybe he was not even alive, maybe he was like— She remembered that torso in the road, sickness rose within her, and then the radio sputtered into life. "It's the all-clear," said Mitzi.

When they came out into the iron daylight of the late March afternoon, they stared in awe. The whole eastern horizon was black with smoke, the bright dance of great flames on the underbelly of the billows. "Joseph and Mary!" Traudi breathed and crossed herself. "The whole city's burning up!" A few minutes later, back inside the house, the radio raged that the barbarians had deliberately bombed the Inner City. The cathedral had been damaged, the Ring near the Stock Exchange smashed into rubble, and the Opera had been destroyed totally.

When Christa heard that, she was startled at the anger that rose in her, the hate. Why? Why had they done that? It had to be deliberate, a gesture on this anniversary of their rape by the Germans, one so callous, so brutal, and unnecessary that there was no response but hatred. Indeed, even the servants felt that rage, and they had never been inside the Opera. That did not matter; it was a symbol. In that moment they were all one—patriots, defenders of a homeland attacked by ruthless destroyers. By nightfall the radio was playing every propaganda note on that wanton ruination.

Even Josef, when he heard, cursed, turned grim. Then he sighed. "The just and the unjust," he said. "The bombs don't know the difference either. But by destroying the symbol of the Vienna we like to think was the real one, they can only stiffen the resistance. Because they've shown their impartial hatred and contempt for us along with the Germans. The other bombing —factories and railroads—people can understand. But this— Still, it's war."

"It's all so senseless."

"People have been saying that for centuries, and it makes no difference. Anyhow, the destruction of the Opera proves one thing, and maybe that's what they wanted to prove. We are at their mercy. If the State can't protect the Opera, it can't save anything. It's a sure sign the end's not far away."

"Then why don't they just give up?" Her voice rose. "Why let it go on and on? Why don't they surrender to the Amis, throw everything against the Russians until the Amis get here and let it all be finished?"

"That's not the nature of the beast. The dying dog snaps at everything in sight, the dying scorpion flagellates itself with its own sting." They were lying on the bed. Now he stood up. "Christa, Robert's got to get you out of this. You've got to tell him, make him do it. You and your father—he's got to send you away from here, send you west. To the Tyrol, anywhere as far west as you can get, out of reach of the Russians. Then when it ends you'll be under the protection of the British or the Americans."

Christa stared at him. "Leave the Christina Hof?"

"Yes. If you don't, and the Russians get you..." His voice hardened. "Don't you know what could happen to you... and the child?"

"But I can't. What about you if I go?"

"I'm not the one who matters. He is." Josef touched her stomach. "You are. I've survived this long; I can survive a few weeks longer. You've got to do it, promise me. Tell Robert he's got to get you out of here."

She looked into his face. Everything within her rebelled against it. Was this what she was doomed to, always to be separated from any man she cared for? But Josef's eyes met hers, and she knew he was right. Her shoulders slumped. Her life was not her own, and once again she must do whatever she had to, whether or not it was what she wanted. "All right," she said. "I'll talk to him. I'll try."

5   THAT TIME there was nothing they could do about it; he had already been sworn into the United States Army before they knew. And because in an hour the temper of the country had wholly changed, as if a sudden thunderstorm had cleared unwholesome air, there was no way the studio could challenge him. Indeed, his contract contained a War, Insurrection and Act of God clause that worked two ways. Matthews, the last time he had seen him, in the living room of the O'Donnell house, had assured him there would be no blowback. Matt and Willi Orlik understood, and they were gravely happy for him. But Phyllis, of course, was almost in shock. "You could have told me." The cords in her neck stood out; she was pale, the only one drinking at all, but she was drinking heavily. "Now what am I supposed to do?"

Willi touched her shoulder. "There'll be more to do than you can imagine. A lot of people will need you. This is going to be a very long war. Lan, I understand why you enlisted as you did. But you must not be wasted as a foot soldier or the like. You have too much special knowledge. The studio would join with Matt and me in getting you a commission—training films for the Signal Corps—"

"No," Condon said. "That's the last thing I want to do. I thank you, Willi, and when the time comes that I need your influence, or Matt's, or even *theirs,* I'll call on you, never fear. But right now you can help me most by keeping the studio out of my affairs. I know what I'm about, what I intend to do."

"Yes," said Willi, looking at him. "Yes, I'm sure you do. Well, Lan, *leb' wohl.*" The two men shook hands with him and left.

When they were gone, Phyllis had poured herself another drink. "Well. I feel like I've been shipwrecked. All right, so they gave you time to settle your affairs. Did you have to take them so literally?"

"I'm sorry."

"That Sunday afternoon. Why didn't you *tell* me? Why did you just run off?"

"You were . . . busy," he said.

Her face paled; then she nodded. "Touché. Okay. If you can't get what you want, you take what you can get. And what I wanted you kept locked up inside you where I couldn't reach it. I tried everything I knew and I never found the combination." She tossed off her drink. "Well," she went on, wearily, "I guess, being as you're off to war, the patriotic thing to do would be to take you upstairs and screw you until your eardrums popped. But I'm not going to prolong the agony. You can go your way." Reaching for the bottle, she thought better of it. "Now I have to rethink my life completely. Maybe I will prowl the waterfront and make the sailors happy. Maybe I'll scrape lint for bandages or whatever they do nowadays. But I think we ought to break clean here and now. I'm going out to have a drink at Frenchy's. When I come back, your stuff ought to be gone. Okay?"

"Okay."

"Then so long." Picking up her bag, she started toward the door. "Oh, God damn," she said, halting. Then she came to him and threw her arms around him and kissed him briefly, fiercely. "All right," she said when she broke away. "Good luck, do you hear? I hope you find her. I would like for somebody in this world to have one damned thing turn out right." She wheeled, ran out the door. Condon went upstairs and packed his books and papers to be stored, his clothes to go to the Salvation Army.

Even before he had stepped forward with the others and taken his soldier's oath, his major objectives were roughed out in his mind. Though it might take years, he had to get back to Austria —and Christa—by the shortest route. So he had to be sure that they did not send him to the Pacific. Also, he must, as much as possible, stay out of combat. Not that he was a coward, but this was going to be a long war, and if he fought in the line the chances of his surviving to reach her were, he knew, almost nil. So he had to find some assignment that would take him overseas, keep him moving on, yet not subject him to constant danger. He had a little time, a few months anyway, he knew, to size up the situation, decide how to proceed. Meanwhile, combat training would not hurt him; indeed, it might save his life someday.

Assuming perhaps that he was too old for the infantry, they sent him to Fort Knox, Kentucky, where, for a brutal interval he endured basic infantry training anyhow, learned the artillery-man's trade and tank driving, maintenance, and tactics. It

351

turned out to be more complicated than being a simple rifleman, but it was less physically taxing. Nevertheless, it was still hard enough so that grown men cried at night in the barracks from sheer fatigue, confusion, and frustration. There were times when he, too, reached his limits, gaining a new self-knowledge. It was, he supposed, no worse than hoboing around the country in the early 1930s, but he had been a lot younger then.

The Army itself, he perceived, was indeed just another studio. It claimed to be a monolithic clockwork mechanism of supreme efficiency; actually it was a vast empire subdivided into countless lesser kingdoms, duchies, baronies, and fiefdoms, each ruled by its own tyrant.through fear or favor, each with its own court, its rivalries and intrigues. What it accomplished it did so in spite of itself, usually through fortunate blunder; and because everyone was afraid of everyone higher up, countless levers protruded from the structure, only waiting to be pulled and pushed by the imaginative. He had long since learned to survive in surroundings of that kind, and by the time his training was almost finished he knew where he wanted to be and how to get there.

It took some doing and a little pressure from Willi Orlik and Matthews, but presently he was there—Fort Ritchie, Maryland, attending special schools in language, prisoner-of-war interrogation, and the analysis of captured documents. All along he had counted on his fluent German, kept fine-honed by conversations with Willi and his coterie of exiles, to get him into Intelligence. And now there was no danger of going to the Pacific, or, for that matter, being exposed to the full blast of combat.

When he left Ritchie, he was already a man marked by his performance, drive, and capability for advancement. His record there earned him an almost immediate giant step toward Christa. As a second lieutenant, he went with the First Armored Division to North Africa, and there he met war firsthand. Like scavenging ravens, after the fighting had receded he and his team prowled battlefields searching the corpses of the enemy for documents, letters, diaries, anything to yield a tatter of intelligence. It was repulsive work.

The bodies themselves were bad enough, but one almost became accustomed to the varieties of death they represented; it was the violation of their privacy that was obscene, his immersion in the outpourings of the spirits that had once inhabited those pathetic, blasted shells. They missed their women and their children, their parents and their friends, their woods and hills and rivers or their flat and sandy plains, their farmhouses or their flats, their *Weisswurst* or their *Sachertorte*, their lilacs and their linden trees. They missed the bodies of their women and the sustaining touch of them, the sound of their laughter and their voices. He could not help grieving for them, being racked by sympathy; and presently he had to struggle against the tendency to see the world, the war, even his own army, through the eyes of the German dead. They were all in the same boat in the long run, no matter which side they fought on, whether dogface or *Landser*.

Then at last, just before he reached the inevitable breaking point, he was mercifully transferred to the interrogation of the living. The insight, the odd rapport with the German soldier he had established from those corpse gleanings, lent him a magical advantage—and he scored coups, built a reputation, moved up in the hierarchy of Intelligence. He made connections and used them to push himself forward, ever closer to the goal which he never once lost sight of, from North Africa to Sicily, from Sicily to Italy. Promoted to major now, exposed to minimal risk and hardship, he was sometimes even privy to advance planning. When he came due for rotation home, he refused it, lest he lose all the ground he'd gained. Three years slid by, and with each passing month hope rose higher in him. Until, like the Allies themselves, he found himself stalled in northern Italy. By that morning in January of 1945, what he felt was close to panic.

His section was housed in a shabby villa above a village that had somehow escaped destruction; well out of reach of the enemy artillery, it was still close enough to the lines so that he could hear the sullen rumble of the guns. His office had been a library; even with the oil burner going full blast, the cold was omnipresent, seeping constantly from the old thick walls, which for two years had never been fully warmed.

He had finished with the morning's digest of captured documents, had a few moments to himself. Going to the window, he looked out at a truck convoy rumbling past along the old

Roman road below, headed north. The Germans were backed up hard against the River Po, and standing there. In German, *Po* was slang for the human rump, and the Wehrmacht was rife with bitter jokes about the situation. *I've spent so much time on the Po I think I'm turning queer....* Condon's mouth twisted. Jokes or no, they'd keep on holding that line, the only solid one left.

He called out, "Gunther!"

Almost at once the master sergeant appeared in the doorway, a big blond second-generation Bavarian from Yorkville. "Sir?"

"Get my jeep, I—"

"Sir," Gunther interrupted him, "I was just coming to tell you there's a British officer outside. A brigadier. He says he's got to see you right away."

"Oh." Condon sank back in his chair. "Well, send him in."

"Yes, sir." Gunther turned. "Sir, Major Condon is free, now. Major Condon, this is— What was that name again, sir?"

"Gorton," said the man in the doorway, blocked from Condon's view by Gunther's bulk. "Brigadier Mark Gorton."

For a moment Condon only stared. Then, as Gunther goggled, Lan whooped like a Sioux and hurtled from behind his desk. The two men embraced. "Jesus Christ, Mark!"

"I say, Lan, I—" Gorton broke away, stepped back, a squat figure muffled in a heavy overcoat. He had put on a lot of pounds; his wind-reddened face was almost perfectly round. His blue-gray eyes were keen with pleasure.

"Leave us, Gunther," Lan ordered. "And don't disturb us unless it's urgent."

The sergeant withdrew, closing the door. When he was gone, the two men looked at each other for a moment in silence. "Hell, I thought you were dead," said Condon finally.

"Very nearly, several times: Greece, Crete, Malta ... Lan, you have changed." His eyes were colder now, appraising.

"I'm seven years older now than the last time you saw me. That's a long time, Mark. It makes a lot of difference."

"Yes, it's been a rough war." Mark said it heavily.

"Here, let me take your coat. Sit down. Some coffee?"

"Fine. And if you've got a spot of brandy ... I've been a long time on the road in the cold gray light of dawn."

"Ask and it shall be given; seek and ye shall find." Lan went to the door, passed a few words with Gunther. Almost at once the sergeant was there with two steaming canteen cups and a bottle.

When Gunther had gone and closed the door, Lan spiked the coffee, passed a cup to Mark. *"Pros't."*

"Pros't." Mark drank. He sighed, shivered, drank again, and took out cigarettes. Then, soberly: "How is she, Lan? Have you had any recent word?"

"I've had no word at all," Condon said. "Not since we lost touch in 1939." His voice thickened. "I've read a million letters, questioned a million soldiers, but I've never had news from the Ferntal or Altkreuzburg."

"Well, I have," Mark said.

Lan tried to speak, but no sound came.

"Quite by accident. I'm presently on Alexander's staff, as I'm sure you are not aware. From time to time I rove the line outfits and buck them up a bit in their interrogation procedures. I happened to look in on the South Africans last week when they'd taken a nice lot of P.O.W.'s and I sat in on the interrogation to see how well they handled it. Do you remember a *Konditorei* in the High Market in Altkreuzburg run by a family named Leder?"

"No," Lan said.

"Well, apparently there is one. And the oldest Leder boy was a platoon sergeant in an infantry company making a reconnaissance in force. Our chaps surrounded them and killed their officers, and he took it on himself with good *Schlappschwanz* pragmatism to surrender the whole outfit. When I heard where he was from, I took over the interrogation personally. And when he found out that I knew the Ferntal and the Helmer family . . . well, he was a veritable *Chambers's Repository* of local gossip. He'd been home only six months before and was quite *au courant*. Lan, she is well."

"She is well. She is well?" Condon heard himself repeat the words numbly.

"Or was six months ago. Living at the Christina Hof. The General is still alive, too, though not in good health. Ernst, her brother, was killed in Russia."

"Oh," Lan said. "Oh, hell. That sweet kid . . ." He grieved with his wife and for her. "But she—"

355

Mark looked down at his cup. "Yes, physically, she's all right. There's more, though. Do you remember a man named Schellhammer?"

Condon hardly heard him. For the moment the knowledge that she still lived, was where he had left her, was all he could absorb. He saw again the great house on the hilltop, the white script on its flank: *Christina*. Her home. She was there. "Robert Schellhammer," he said automatically.

"Yes," Gorton said. "Well, it's only gossip, but you might as well know it all, the worst. Schellhammer's a Party official, a *Kreisleiter*. Leder says that he's also Christa's lover and that she's his mistress."

He had, throughout all these years, prepared himself for almost anything. Not for that specifically, but for worse than that while hoping for better. Still, something seemed to pierce him, though he was certain that his face did not change. "I see," he said almost calmly.

Mark looked at him oddly. "I could not find out a great deal more. Schellhammer's married. To some butcher's daughter." He paused, frowning. "Richter, she was. Charlotte Schellhammer, *geboren* Richter."

"I don't know her either."

"It doesn't matter. She stays in the background. It's Christa who accompanies Schellhammer to all the Party functions." He drank some coffee. "There you have it, all he knew, all I could get. I hope it helps."

Condon did not answer directly. "Thanks, Mark." He took a long swig of spiked coffee. He had, after all, long since assumed something like this. He knew from the letters he had taken from the bodies, from the live ones, and those of his own men that he had censored. Men went off to war and the women they left behind were not made of marble. *Dear John . . . Lieber Hans . . . Caro Giovanni. . . .*

"You are welcome," Gorton said. For a while the room was silent.

Then Mark stood up. "Lan, I should like to know—and don't ask me why—the reason you tried to join our forces in 1939 and why you enlisted on Pearl Harbor day in 1941. Patriotism? Revenge? Or Christa?"

"For God's sake, Mark. You know!" The words burst from him.

"I thought I did," said Gorton. "But, as you said, it's been a long time."

Condon stood up, went to the window. The trucks were still rolling past down there in the village. The drizzle was laden with random flakes of snow.

"What do you intend to do when you find her?" Gorton asked.

"I don't know," Lan said. "I just have to find her."

He was aware of Mark getting to his feet behind him. "And what would you do if you did?"

"I don't know that, either."

"It may be that some things are better let alone. That when some things are ended, it's better to leave them so. I've been through that with two women: my wife and Marietta. There are times when it's better to let go than to keep hanging on. Why, Lan? Why do you want to find her?"

"I told you." Lan turned. "I don't know. I just know that I have to. We're still married. She's still my wife. I . . . was happy with her. There is unfinished business, and I want . . . I want . . ." He gestured vaguely.

"Listen," Mark said. "Has it ever occurred to you that you're looking for something that may no longer exist? If you find it and it isn't what you think it is, what happens then?"

Condon looked at him. "Do you think I'm a child? Don't you think I've been through all that with myself?"

"Well, then—"

"None of it matters. I have still got to get back to her again. I am under no illusions. Maybe when I do, it will all be gone, just a dream, and none of it ever counted. But the Russians will be there first, and by the time I ever find her, God knows what will happen. I just keep thinking that if I tried hard enough, if I did everything I could . . . Anyhow, it was the only thing I had to hang on to, and— There's no chance now, anyhow."

"There may be," Mark said. "But first tell me this. What about Schellhammer? Doesn't he make a difference?"

"I don't know yet," Lan said. "Until I know why. Sometimes people have to . . . do things."

"Yes," Mark said.

Then the rest of it sank in. Lan straightened. "You said there may be a chance?"

"Yes, I rather think there is. But first I had to know how you felt about it all. If my interpretation of the file was right—"

357

"The file?"

"On you at Alexander's headquarters. Supreme Command, Med Theater." Mark smiled faintly. "It's all there. To one who knows, it's plain as day. You've homed in on her like an arrow to the target. Pushed, shoved, maneuvered, bucked, risked... Your whole history's there, along with all the requests and wild schemes you've bucked up and had denied: being dropped in Yugoslavia to join the Tito partisans, transfer to the OSS to go into Austria— You almost made that one, but Fifth Army decided you were too valuable to be released."

"Mark," said Condon thickly, "who the hell are you?" He took a step toward Gorton. "I won't be played with this way. I've already backed the wrong horse. I thought there'd be an invasion through the Balkans, and—"

"And it didn't come off. Yes. Well, I won't drag this out any longer. In a couple of weeks I'm going to Hungary on a liaison mission with the Russian Army—Tolbukhin's Third Ukrainian Front. Our guess is they'll be the first to reach Vienna, which is my eventual destination. If you want to come along, I'll be glad to take you with me."

Somehow the village church had escaped undamaged. Now, above the rumble of the convoy, its bells chimed nine. Condon said, "Vienna? Take me—"

"Right." Gorton's voice was crisp. "Essentially this is something the Prime Minister has cooked up personally. He's always seen Vienna as crucial to postwar settlements; the whole idea of the aborted Balkan operation was to get there before the Russians. Well, that's out. All the same, there are some things that can be done, if you follow me. Perhaps Anglo-American liaison teams attached to the Second and Third Ukrainian Fronts can at least keep the Russ honest and salvage something. We've more or less been rammed down Stalin's throat, but permission has finally been secured. Officially, it's to coordinate air operations with the Fifteenth Group Air here in Italy, heavy bomber stuff, so I'll be taking in a lot of flying officers. But I'll have other staff as well, including a team expert in captured documents and prisoner interrogation to travel with the forward elements. The whole idea, essentially, is to make sure the West doesn't get screwed in Vienna; we want to know who's on our side there and who isn't and make sure the Reds don't wipe out our people without our knowledge. Now, as to who I am, what you don't know won't hurt you. But I have been in intelligence work for a long, long time. May I have another spot of brandy?"

He helped himself, went on. "Anyhow, I'd not forgotten you. In 1939 I got a cable about you, could have used you then, but something went wrong, I don't know what. When I found your file this time, there was no question—except that I had to be sure you were prepared for what you might find when you got there. Apparently you are, as well as any man could be. So if you want to come along, just say so and I'll have your orders cut. General Alexander will see that no one blocks you this time."

"Want to go—?" Lan stared at Mark, could find no other words.

Gorton smiled. "I take it silence means assent. Then done and done." And he put out his hand.

The Russians received Gorton's mission with grudging, wary correctness. Lan had been familiarized with the language at Ritchie, had been boning up since that day with Mark, and he could speak a little. Master Sergeant Finch, his assistant, was fluent, as was Gorton after years of roaming the Balkans and beyond. Communication was no trouble; a lot of Russians had had the opportunity to learn German in the past four years.

Gorton, remaining with Tolbukhin's headquarters, assigned Lan and Finch to the combat intelligence section attached to an armored corps. Here they sat in on the interrogation of prisoners, writing separate reports which they forwarded to Gorton, and, not without frequent difficulty, were given access to captured documents.

There were fewer captives than he had expected; on this front the Wehrmacht fought to the last ditch, its soldiers convinced that death was preferable to capture by the Russians. It was, Lan soon observed, a belief not wholly without foundation. The Soviets observed no Geneva Convention rules on the treatment of prisoners of war—but neither did the Germans where the Russians were concerned. Few of the veterans of the Russian campaigns gave up; it was mostly the very young and very old who surrendered. But harsh as it was, the treatment they received was not much harsher than that of the ordinary soldier, the

Vanka of the Red Army, by his own commanders.

This was an army unlike any Lan had before encountered, almost medieval despite its mastery of the technology of modern warfare, lacking all the amenities modern soldiers took for granted. No frills were expected; life in Russia had been mostly devoid of frills ever since the Revolution. There was plenty of ammunition, gas, basic rations, basic clothing; whatever else the soldier needed he stole or foraged. This was an army of farmers, villagers, backwoodsmen, hard-faced Asiatic tribesmen; and they ripped up great houses and museums for firewood, converted priceless tapestries to cloaks, blankets, rags for cleaning tank engines, with no sense of destroying something that was precious. And they took women, too, in the same spirit; they took the women of the enemy as he had taken theirs—by force, ravishing indiscriminately, from mere children to crones in their dotage. The armies that had devastated Europe during the Thirty Years War must have, Condon thought, behaved identically.

Their morale was high, superb; they needed no lectures on what they fought for, though the commissars saw that these were plentifully given and fully attended. They knew why they fought: their land had been invaded, their homes burned, their families brutalized or killed; they fought for revenge. They had seen the mass graves outside of every village, and if they had had any illusions left, they had been dispelled by what they were now discovering as their northern wings drove into Poland.

When Condon was first shown photographs of the camp called Maidanek outside of Lublin, he was incredulous. There had been rumors, but he had discounted them as propaganda. There was no discounting the pictures, the affidavits, or the look in the eyes of a few officers he encountered who had been at Lublin. "It's beyond belief," a colonel who spoke fluent German told him. "They burned all those people. And do you know how they disposed of the ashes? They used them to fertilize a cabbage field outside the camp." He swallowed hard, shook his head. "You never saw such cabbages as there were there, in that field."

At Tolbukhin's headquarters he found that Mark had already seen the data and more besides. Gorton was sunk into a deep depression. "I knew and yet I didn't know," Mark whispered.

"I didn't really want to believe. I wanted to think these people made it up. But, Lan, it's true."

"The goddamn *Pifkas*," Condon rasped. "The *Sau-Preuss*—"

"No," Mark said. "It wasn't only the Prussian swine. Look, we know now the decision was made in 1942, and Hitler approved it; Hitler is an Austrian. And I've checked the documentation, made my own little list—analysis—of names. It was an Austrian show as much as German; they were key men at every step." He rubbed his face. "I don't know; I don't know how to come to terms with it. I spent the best years of my life there, I felt I knew them. I would never have believed— We must revise our thinking, Lan. You and I especially. We must not let the charm ever mask the guilt, the music drown out the screams."

"But most of them didn't know," Lan said. "Could not have known. Christa could not have—"

"Schellhammer did," rasped Gorton. "You can bet on that. Don't be too sure of Christa. Don't be too sure of anyone, ever again, Lan Condon. After all, don't they call her father the Butcher of Galicia?"

"Stop it, Mark."

"I'm sorry," Gorton said. "If all this is true, then I must think about the world a whole new way. Even about myself. There are so many questions I have to ask myself that I can't answer: What would *I* have done? At what point would I have laid my life on the line to scream, 'Stop it, *this is insanity*'? If the papers had crossed my desk for signature and I had never had to see what they represented, would I have signed?"

He rose, went to the window of the villa on the outskirts of Pest. "When Hitler dies, as he surely will, it should be smiling. Because his legacy will live on. Not just in the Germans. We're all infected with it now, his concept of total war. We British, you Americans, the Russians, too. Because he found a key to human beings that no one else had ever touched—and if we're not careful, that little Austrian bastard will make Jesus Christ look like the village idiot when it comes to his influence on civilization."

Mark turned. "Sorry. I didn't mean to rant. Of course Christa is innocent. You can bet that Schellhammer has never told her. Probably they have kept it secret from everyone."

Lan drew in a deep breath. "I don't know." He picked up his

361

helmet. "I think now I'd better go back to my outfit."

"Yes. Well, if there's anything you need, let me know." And Gorton saw him to the door.

Budapest fell at last. On the northern fronts the Reds drove on across Poland, hammered at East Prussia. In the west the Allies reached the Rhine. In Italy negotiations for surrender were under way. Still the Wehrmacht fought fanatically, often gallantly; and men—and boys too young to shave—kept on dying.

Striving to save Vienna, Hitler threw tank divisions profligately into a counteroffensive on the Hungarian plain—Operation Spring Awakening. It was a lovely name for slaughter. For a time the Panzers even pushed the Russians back; then they ran out of fuel. After the savage fighting at Balaton, the huge lake halfway to Austria, the Germans fell back on their Southeast Wall, the fortifications at the Austrian border. The Reds drove on. By the time they reached the Wall, the Wehrmacht had no forces left to man it; what remained were drawn in tightly around Wiener Neustadt and Vienna. At last, on March 29, 1945, Russian tanks crossed the *Grenze* at the tiny hamlet of Klostermarienberg.

Condon, in the wake of battle, forced himself into a strange suspension of emotion. Now, after all that effort, all that risk, the circuit was nearly closed; he stood here on Austrian soil again, and she was somewhere over yonder in the misty distance; he could almost see that far. Now it could not be more than a few days. But he had no illusions about war left; he knew its caprices, its ghastly ironic jokes. To count on anything at all beyond the moment was a serious tempting of fate. He might hope, but he should not expect; that was the worst luck of all. Instinctively he tucked his thumbs into closed fists, a German gesture equivalent to crossing fingers, and looked out across the plain.

Wisps of greasy smoke fingered blackly against the gray of sky, seeping from the blasted vehicles that had interposed themselves against the advance of the Russians. Bodies—of animals and men—were scattered flecks against the earth, like fallen leaves on the churned fields. The nearest village and the one beyond it were ringed with parked Russian tanks. From the horizon came the crackle of small arms fire, interspersed with the stomping thump of tank cannons. High above the plain black dots circled: ravens, rooks, and crows, building nerve to come down and feed. With almost manic devotion to routine, the bell of the tiny *Kloster* in the closest hamlet chimed the hour.

And if in days or a pair of weeks, thought Condon, they did find each other once again, what then? Seven years, and the last of his youth was gone; he was forty-two now, sliding into middle age. And he had changed; he knew how he had changed. Over that period, physically and literally, every cell in his body had replaced itself; his flesh was not even the same flesh it had been, nor would hers be. Neither was his spirit; it was possible that when this was over no sentient human would ever perceive the world again as he had before; certainly he would not. What he would think, feel, and want if he survived would be wholly different from seven years ago.

And, of course, it would be the same with her. She had been almost a child then, both in years and knowledge; now she would be nearing thirty and might well bear no resemblance to the vision he had pursued so long. She could be fat now, or ugly, or scarred, inwardly or outwardly; she might hold dear all sorts of things she once had loathed. She might even be his enemy.

He drew in breath. So, he thought, he might be a fool. Anyhow, soon he would have to make a choice: hold the vision intact and be satisfied with that or face reality, for better or worse.

Then he shook his head. It did not matter. He had come too far now to lose his nerve. The game must be played out to the end.

He got back into the jeep, gestured toward the Austrian village. "We might as well go on down," he said, and the sergeant put the vehicle into gear.

6 IN THE LIVING ROOM of the Schellhammer Hof it was very still. Early April sunlight slanting through the windows projected the pattern of the lace curtains in a shimmering dance on the wall opposite; and somehow, in this instant, Robert was acutely sentient to the fall of light on all

the polished, homely surfaces of the furniture and objects he had known all his life, that were almost part of him. A few seconds of suspension—the present merging into past, the solidity, reality, of both heightened by the threatening future. Then his father worked the rifle bolt, and its loud significance broke the spell. Robert shuddered slightly, looked at the old man in his field-gray uniform, his lined face creased in a smile as he hefted the Mauser Gewehr 98. "It's a good gun," said Max Schellhammer. "It feels good to hold it."

"*Vati*," Robert said. "You don't have to—"

"Yes, I do," Max said. His blue eyes glinted; he chuckled softly, hands stroking the receiver of the piece. "Don't worry about this old badger, boy. I know all the tricks. I learned them before you were even dreamed of." He shook a cigarette from a pack, thrust it between his lips. "Hell, it's like being twenty-five again."

Robert struck a match, staring at the hard weathered face while his father inhaled. A surge of admiration filled him; the tough old man was actually looking forward to combat, as chipper as if he were going to hunt hares in the vineyards. All the same, he had never counted on this—that Max Schellhammer would have to leave the *Hof* to fight in the streets of Vienna. He felt a queasiness of guilt, mingled with frustration. "Damn it, I should be there with you."

His father blew smoke. "No. You've got your own duty. Maybe we can knock the bastards back; we'll sure as hell give 'em a bloody nose. But somebody's got to keep things running while we do it, or otherwise we don't have a chance. That's your department, son. This"—he patted the gun—"is mine."

He savored lungfuls of smoke a moment. "You know, I never went overboard for Hitler the way you did. When you're my age, you know damn well no one man is God, no one man has all the answers. I guess I half expected it to work out this way. But you know what? Maybe it was worth it. Even if we're losing now, at least there was a time when we got back our pride. The Party did that much, anyhow—it showed the world, by damn, what it means to be a German, and they'll never forget it ever again. Without him, we'd never have had that. To me that's worth a lot."

Grinding out the cigarette, he went on. "What happens to me

doesn't count. Shit, killing Russians is just unfinished business as far as I'm concerned. But, you listen. What happens to you *does* count. Whatever happens, you save yourself." His gesture encompassed the *Hof*. "And what you can of this. Most of all, though, save our pride, you hear?"

He paused, groping for words. "We've lived through it before. The bastards ground us down, it took twenty years for us to finally come back. Well, they'll grind us down again; and, by God, we'll come back again if it takes another twenty years. It's gonna be up to you and your generation to see we do that. Kiss their boots and lick their arse if you have to, but inside yourself remember what you are. And wait, be patient. And next time we won't make the mistakes we did this time. You see what I'm driving at?"

"*Vati,* yes," said Robert thickly.

Again silence. His father looked around the room once more with a kind of hunger, then glanced at his watch. "Time for me to go. I think I'll just ramble on down the hill."

"Papa, I'll take you in my car."

"No, you've got other things to do. Besides, my joints need the limbering." He cradled the rifle in his arm, pulled his son to him, and they kissed each other. Max patted him hard on the back. "*Leb' wohl,*" he said.

"*Leb' wohl,*" said Robert thickly.

"So—" They shook hands. Then Robert in the doorway watched the jaunty figure in its home-guard uniform saunter down the hill, rifle slung, until it was out of sight. Feeling grief and a chest-bursting pride at having sprung from such loins, he turned back inside the house.

Its emptiness made the sound of his footsteps hollow as he prowled it. In the bedroom doorway Robert halted, staring bitterly at the bed. *She.* She had gone to safety in the Tyrol with the children. *She* had taken up the transport space that Christa should have occupied. Just as she had taken up the space in his life that never should have belonged to her, she and the two sniveling daughters that were in her image, so much like her that he found it hard to love them.

But there was nothing he could do about it. He still had duties, but almost no authority. The SS had usurped that. Had set itself above the Party, above the Wehrmacht, had gathered all the reins in its hands. Once he, as a *Kreisleiter,* could have conjured up a whole convoy of vehicles; now he was down to a few gallons of gas in his car, with no idea where he would get any more, unless, crawling to the SS, he could beg some.

Still, they'd given him transport to move his family westward to haven in the Alps, fitting them into a convoy transporting the families of other dignitaries, plus a lot of sensitive records that must not fall into Russian hands. His *family*—that meant Charlotte and the children and his mother, not Christa and his son she carried in her. And there had been nothing he could do about it. He had not realized the depths of his mother's hatred of Christa until she made it clear that unless Charlotte went, she would not go, and that if Christa went she would not go. So there'd been no way around it; his allocated space went to his rightful wife, his mother, his lawful children; Christa and his child by her and the General had to stay. He grunted a curse. What was worse, she had not seemed at all distressed, had merely shrugged it off. She was acting strangely, refusing to take his orders, had, in fact, declined even to cross the valley to the safety of the Schellhammer Hof when they had put the tanks over there on the ridge.

He had argued bitterly with the officers who'd brought the three Tigers up the hill and dug them in only a few hundred yards from the Christina Hof. "Don't you fools understand? You put those tanks up here, they'll draw all sorts of fire. That whole *Hof* there will be smashed and all the people in it!"

The Panzer captain had looked at him with sour, weary eyes. "Herr Kreisleiter, I have my orders." He gestured. "Observe the road to Altkreuzburg, also the one in the valley behind us. Also, we can to some extent employ our guns as anti-aircraft." He looked at the three huge vehicles under camouflage in the orchards. "Besides, even if I wanted to, I couldn't move 'em. No *Benzin.*"

So he was powerless—as much so with Christa as with the captain. "Don't you see?" he ranted at her. "Now that those guns are up here, they'll pound this ridge with everything they have! They'll blow the Christina Hof to bits! You've got to move to the Schellhammer Hof. Please. Charlotte isn't there now." He took her hand. "Think of our child."

He read uncertainty in her eyes. Then she shook her head. "No, Robert, I won't go."

"Think of your father!"

"He wouldn't go. That's part of it. We'd have to carry him out out of here. It might give him another stroke—a final one. And even if he would, I wouldn't."

"For God's sake, why not?"

"Because this is our home. Look, there's no use moving. If planes come over, they'll hit the Schellhammer Hof as well. It's too nice a target, all white and clean over there. And the cellars here are much deeper and safer. No." She invoked the ultimate argument. "We'll not leave our property, abandon everything we have to looters."

He argued on, to no avail. Appealing to the General got him nowhere; the old man only looked at him blankly. Finally he gave up. "Promise me you'll go to the deepest cellar at the first sign of danger."

"I promise," Christa said.

"Very well. I'll check in as often as I can. But I've got so much to do, I don't know . . . And, of course, if they break through, I'll be fighting."

She was silent for a moment. Then she raised herself on tiptoe, touched his face, looked into his eyes. Her kiss was warm, lingering, and gentle. "Good luck," she whispered when she finally broke away. "Be careful."

"I'll see you again," he managed. "I'll be back. I—" Everything seemed to be falling around his ears. He must not show any signs of funk. He got a grip on himself, and his arm came up. "Heil Hitler."

"Heil Hitler," Christa answered.

Then he left her, cursing fate savagely as he strode to his car, cursing the Russians and the Amis and all the rest, his heart full of hatred for the destroyers of the dream he knew would never leave him.

The Russians could not be held. Four days after they crossed into Burgenland, Wiener Neustadt fell. Now they bombed and shelled the outskirts of Vienna itself. The Stadtbahn and most other public transportation no longer ran. Nobody was allowed to leave the city by car, truck, or horse-drawn vehicle without a permit; the Volkssturm was called up right down to the very bottom of the barrel; the SS, the Waffen SS, and the Army braced themselves for the final shock.

His preference would have been to fight with them; and when in his capacity as a Party officer there was nothing constructive left for him to do, he would assert his automatic rank as colonel, join a unit in the thick of the action—and then he'd show them, all of them, that he was no ordinary Golden Pheasant. Let the others run for cover like their namesakes in the beet fields when the dogs were working them; he was a Schellhammer, a German, a National Socialist, and he would serve his country and his Führer to his dying breath.

But, he told himself, turning away from the bedroom, there was still one thing imporant that he must do here. There were no house servants; every man on the place had been sent to the Volkssturm, he had ordered the women, including the Ukrainian slave laborers, to stay inside. He wanted no one spying on him now.

His father had spent a long time yesterday disassembling, greasing, and packing all their hunting arms. Added to them were the guns of General Helmer, which Robert had appropriated lest the General hurt himself or someone else with them. They made an enormous bundle, a heavy load, fitted out with rope shoulder straps. Robert wrestled the huge pack on his back and looked carefully around before he went out the door. He also made sure the coast was clear before he passed through the gate. Then, walking swiftly, he struck out along the ridge, heading for the woods.

The spreading beech forest, stippled with the first tentative green of spring, enfolded him. He felt a sense of shelter gained, tense muscles relaxing slightly. Over the whisper of wind in the trees, though, he could hear the faint vibration of distant artillery, more a rippling of the air than a sound as yet.

Presently he reached the cluster of wattled buildings in the clearing. Unlocking one, he found a pick and spade, which a few days ago he had used to bury certain records and valuables that could not be taken in the convoy. Now, some distance from the house, well down in the ravine where the brush grew thickly, he began to dig after taking a bearing between two enormous landmark trees on opposite slopes. Within an hour he had the guns deeply, safely buried and all signs of the digging erased. Straightening up, he sighed, smiling grimly. Partisan warfare, harassing occupiers, was a game that two could play at. Francs-tireurs and partisans had shown what they could do in Yugosla-via and Poland and in Russia; soon it might be the turn of Austrians. One could use a few guns to get more guns, and . . . If he could, if he lived, he would fight on for twenty years or thirty, if that was what it took.

Carrying the pick and spade, he entered the chill, musty dim-ness of Busch's house. For a moment he stood there assaulted by memory. God, he thought, what dreams had begun or been played out here! The old days, with a handful of illegals meet-ing, Busch on guard against the police.

And Christa— He turned toward the bed. Emotion swelled in him, every second of that autumn afternoon recalled in sweet and painful vividness—the perfume of her hair, musk of her body, taste of her mouth, the great triumph he had felt, and the peace afterwards. And now, his baby in her . . .

Robert paced the hut, conscious of time's pressure. Even now he should be in Altkreuzburg. There was still structure to the *Gau,* orders coming down to every *Kreis.* He still had work to do. As long as that structure held, he would hold; if it collapsed, then he was free. And once he was free, he would find some *Benzin* somewhere, fill his car, force Christa and her father into it, give them all sorts of passes, make her go northwest, to meet the Amis. Much as he hated them, better they than Russians. Then he'd find himself a Schmeisser and join the battle. Take to the woods if it came to that; he knew every path and hiding place in this area of the Wienerwald. Gather men around him and . . . Let others give up. If he lived a thousand years, his loyalty lived with him; and if he died tomorrow, it would stain the sacred earth of German Austria around his grave, impregnate whatever grew out of his rotting body.

He could linger here no longer. Carrying the pick and spade, he hurried back toward the Schellhammer Hof. Already the thunder in the distance was perceptibly closer, and toward the east the April morning was black with smoke. But even as he loped across the meadow, hope rose in him. It was the one thing they all had left to cling to. Sooner or later the armies of the

Allies and the Russians would collide, and when that happened there would surely be a brand new war, and the British and Americans would see the need of German help. A month from now he might find himself fighting alongside the English against the Reds. And that was all right, too. It might happen. The idea was something to sustain him. At the *Hof* he put the tools away, got in his car, drove to Altkreuzburg. The Volkssturm truck had long since picked his father up, and the old man would be somewhere in Vienna, going into combat.

Robert trembled with fear and pride.

7 THE OLD WOMAN and her two fat daughters they had found hidden in the cellar had been clay-faced with terror. "You must understand," the oldest girl implored in her thick dialect. "We were never for Hitler. Not Nazis. Please." She had gestured to the dining room of the *Gasthaus*, full of Russian officers. "Please explain to them. You must."

"Yes, I'll tell them," Condon had said wearily. There was, of course, no explaining he could do. By now they really did not know what they were. They were whatever they were required to be in order to survive. "Now listen. If you do exactly as you're told, you should be in no danger. Colonel Ognev has issued orders protecting civilians. But you must stay here in the *Gastwirtschaft;* don't go out on the streets." He left the women and returned to the dining room, where Gorton, who had just come up from the rear, was conferring with Colonel Ognev. Though Gorton's Russian was excellent, Ognev insisted that he speak English, which a Russian interpreter then translated. It was one of those eerie tactics the Russians were so fond of for putting any stranger, outsider, at a disadvantage. It also made it impossible for Gorton to confer with Ognev without a third party present; thus the colonel could never be tempted to divulge anything in secret, a Party precaution.

Anyhow, he could see from Gorton's face that Mark's request had been denied. He had never thought it would be granted. Which, of course, meant that his own had been turned down as well. Ognev had already turned him down twice; he'd hoped that Mark, as leader of the mission, would draw more water. Even as Lan watched, Mark raised his hands, dropped them, and turned away. Then, seeing Lan, he jerked his head. They went outside.

The little town north of Wiener Neustadt, actually on the very city limits of Vienna, had fallen without a fight. The enemy drew ever more tightly back on the city itself, which now was visible in the distance beneath a pall of smoke.

They walked up the street a distance, and then Mark halted. So far the town had taken no artillery fire; its little plastered, tile-roofed houses and cobbled pavements remained intact. In the distance battalions of tanks accompanied by infantry crawled toward the actual city, the southwestern districts of Vienna, sheltered by the flank of the Wienerwald. *Katyushas,* truck-mounted rocket launchers the Germans called "Stalin organs," lit the twilight as they sent hundreds of warheads arcing simultaneously toward strongpoints on high ground.

"I should have known it," Mark said bitterly. "Tolbukhin said the decision must be left to the forward commander. Of course, secretly he's passed the word to Ognev under no circumstances to let us go. The last thing they want is me sitting in on their negotiations in Vienna."

"What the hell *is* going on? What brought you down?"

"Well, I didn't have much time to explain when I got here. But, as I said, I had a signal from my opposite number with the Second Ukrainian Front, the northern wing. It seems there's a resistance group in Austria after all—O-five, they call themselves. *O* for the first letter in Oesterreich in the plain spelling, *five* because the second letter, *e,* is the fifth one in the alphabet. The other day a Wehrmacht sergeant made contact with the Second Ukrainian; he was an O-five messenger. It appears Wehrmacht officers and civilians alike are involved, and they have a plan for an uprising when the Russians give the signal. It took a lot of convincing, but the Soviets finally bought it. More, the leaders from the old days who've either been in jail, underground, or in Coventry are forming up again, getting ready to present the Russians with a provisional government—and, God be praised, a coalition one."

His mouth twisted. "Socialists and conservatives alike, fifty-

fifty, the kind of thing that if they'd done it seven years ago, Hitler would never have had a chance. And, bluntly, my assignment is and has been all along to be in on any such negotiations, to make sure the Reds don't Communize Vienna before we get our own people there. In short, to strengthen the conservative hand, make sure there's no purge. But of course the Russians won't let me go; I'm stuck here until the city is secure, they say, too valuable as an ally to risk. Well, I'll signal the Prime Minister direct; I daresay he'll jar them. But it will take some time. Meanwhile, I seem to be stuck well behind the lines. So are you, I'm afraid. I did the best I could with Ognev, but he wouldn't buy your proposition at all. He understands your concern for Christa, he says, but he'll not allow you to go off on your own to find her, and that's final. I agree, and I'm not going to tell you again."

"God damn it, Mark." Condon turned to stare at the humped, mist-shrouded hills, darkly wooded, in the near distance. "Only an hour in a jeep, I know every road. Just one hour, I'd be with Christa, find her, bring her out."

"Don't be a fool. You know as well as I do the German line's anchored in the Wienerwald; you wouldn't stand a whore's chance. Damn it, Lan, this is no cinema romance; you've been around long enough to know one man can't swoop in there and knock off half the German Army and rescue the heroine. You'll have to wait. Meanwhile, when the area *is* secured, I have Ognev's promise that Christa will have the full protection of the Red Army."

"The full protection of—" Lan turned away. Down the street a high-cheekboned, slant-eyed soldier in rumpled uniform emerged from the courtyard of a house dragging a woman in her sixties, his arm around her waist. She nodded numbly, whimpering as he shoved her across the street into another courtyard.

Condon spat onto the cobbles. "And if it's a patrol of Kazakhs or the like that take her?"

"There's nothing more I can do." Gorton's voice was flat. "The more I buck Ognev, the more I jeopardize my own chances of getting into the city early on." He put his hand on Condon's shoulder. "I know. But there's no help for it. Lan, it's been seven years. Two days more, a week— Hell, they may surrender tomorrow for all we know!" He paused. "Anyway, Schellhammer will be watching after her. Maybe he's already moved her west. After all, by all accounts, he loves her, too."

Presently Condon said, "And that's what I pin my hopes on? That Robert Schellhammer loves my wife?"

Gorton did not answer, and his hand slipped away. At that instant a voice called Lan's name, in English.

He turned. Starschii Leitenant Nechiev, standing beneath the wrought-iron vines and grapes of the *Gasthaus* sign, beckoned. With the first lieutenant was the warrant officer who was personal interpreter for the regimental political officer. Nechiev was the chief interrogator for Regimental Intelligence, and the warrant officer monitored his questioning sessions and submitted a separate report to his chief. Only the enlisted men in the Red Army trusted one another or took anything on faith.

"We have a few more," Nechiev said in German. He was a genial man who had worked in a Moscow bank before the war. "Just brought in. Not too much—some Volkssturm, a couple of Wehrmacht noncoms, and one medium-sized fish: an SS captain. I'm going to go ahead and get them out of the way and send them to the rear tonight. Care to join me? I could use some help with these damnable Austrian dialects."

"Go ahead," Mark said. "Let me have a report when you finish."

"All right," Lan told Nechiev. "I'll meet you." And he went to get his briefcase, moving briskly, ravenous now for every scrap of information from Vienna.

The prisoners were in the house adjoining the *Gasthaus*. Its furniture had been thrown into the courtyard to make room, and there a tank crew had built a fire with part of it, was cooking chicken and drinking wine. One of its members squatted in a corner, voiding his bowels; a fair percentage of the Red soldiers were not even housebroken, wholly ignorant of modern plumbing or even privies. A tall private with a hatchet was chopping an ornately painted peasant chest to splinters.

In what had been the parlor, the interrogators took their seats behind a long table, Lan joined now by Sergeant Finch, who in turn would monitor exchanges in Russian between Nechiev and the warrant officer. Nechiev turned to a waiting corporal. "Bring in the Volkssturm."

Downy-cheeked boys, some as young as twelve, old men or ambulatory cripples, they knew almost nothing. The home guard had been thrust out as a screen to give the regulars and Waffen SS time to fall back. They were only pawns, sacrificial lambs and rams, and even the Russians seemed to feel a certain pity for them. But they were prisoners of war, and they would be shipped east with the rest, to be worked as slaves, making good with their labor the destruction the professionals had wrought.

The boys, fresh out of or still in the Hitler Youth, were the most arrogant and defiant in the beginning, but also the most easily broken down. One or two were crying before Condon was through with them. The older men were not defiant at all; most cooperated eagerly, with the usual plea that they had been pressed into service, weren't Nazis, never had been, that planting time was coming, and that unless they were sent home to till the fields the women and children were bound to starve. But there was nothing anyone could do; they were taken out.

"*Scheisse*," Nechiev said with bitterness and produced a bottle of *Barack*. After they all had drinks, the Wehrmacht noncoms were brought in. Two were *Altreich,* genuine Germans, and despite their hollow-eyed fatigue they were like iron; it would have taken physical torture to wrench anything from them. The third, from a different unit, was not only Austrian but Viennese. Before they could begin to question him, he bowed, clicked his heels, introduced himself, and began to talk. He had been, before the war, a *Fiaker* driver. If the *Herrschaften* were in Wien after the surrender, which, God willing, would be soon, they could find no better guide than he. It would be his pleasure to show them everything, and he knew many exciting and voluptuous attractions. He answered every question volubly and thoroughly. The interrogators made furious notes. Only later, Condon thought wryly, would the Russians realize that he had told them nothing except that he always opposed the Nazis, could have got them cut-rate tickets to the Opera if it had not been destroyed, and that they were free to keep the pornographic pictures found in his wallet.

Still bowing, he was dragged out, and they reviewed their notes. So far they had learned nothing new, pinpointed no new positions, units, movements, and had only added tone to a picture of destruction already painted by other prisoners, one that Condon could take no vengeful satisfaction in. The Opera smashed, damage all through the Inner City, the outer districts ground to rubble, the great city gashed and scabbed by war. Never had he felt the senseless waste of all of it more keenly. He had read once about Indians in Washington and Oregon who held rituals at which they gave away or destroyed all their possessions, impoverishing themselves to prove their prestige and power. War, he thought, was one enormous Potlatch: nations blowing up their substance to prove their potency.

But it had to end. The enemy had nothing left—that was becoming clear. If it weren't for the SS, resistance would have long since collapsed. But it hovered in the background, ready to deal brutally and summarily with anyone who faltered, more dangerous to the German soldier caught in the middle than the Russian assault itself. He could summon little hatred for the poor bastards of the Volkssturm or even the Wehrmacht, and nothing but sad contempt for the smarmy *Fiaker* driver. But his hatred for the SS—the hard-core, death's-head, jackbooted, ruthless true believers—was implacable. They and Party officers like Robert Schellhammer, so far as he was concerned, might as well be shot out of hand. Some of them were, and anyhow, not many of them surrendered. The captain they would question next was a rarity, and his interrogation would be extended and not necessarily gentle. Condon felt a certain gloating, brutal eagerness. "Let's bring in the big fish," he suggested to the Russians. "He's stewed in his own juice long enough."

There was a report on the circumstances of his capture, which had been peculiar. A patrol had surrounded an isolated house with a walled garden in the country. Condon formed a picture of it in his mind: not a villa or a *Schloss,* just one of those pretty little summer cottages to which the Viennese loved to retreat for weekends or vacation, to putter among their flowers. As the Reds approached, there was gunfire from the garden; they lobbed in grenades, and it soon ceased. When they attacked, a black-clad figure had scrambled over the wall, dashing for the safety of a nearby clump of trees. The Reds closed in on the grove; presently the SS man, found in a thicket, had surrendered, ammunition exhausted. In his flight he had thrown away all papers and they could not be found.

375

In the garden there were three dead Waffen SS soldiers. In the house itself the Russians found two more bodies, a well-dressed couple of elderly civilians, each shot neatly through the head. They had obviously been victims of execution, and the noncom who led the patrol had thought it worthwhile to search for and bring in their papers of identity. Herr Professor Adelbert Wenzmer, retired from the University of Vienna, and his wife Gerda, both on pension now. No Party membership cards were found.

The captain's name was Emil Hofstädter, and he once must have been Hitler's very dream of the man he himself would have liked to have been: lean and muscular at twenty-five or thereabouts, blond and blue-eyed, handsome. But his captors had worked him over. His black uniform was muddy, torn, the right side of his face was one enormous swollen bruise, and his lips were puffed and cut. Yet he tried to bear himself with defiance and flatly refused to give more than his name, rank, and serial number. Nevertheless, Condon knew from experience, it was impossible for fanaticism to sustain a man indefinitely in such a situation; all sorts of fears, uncertainties, smashed hopes were fermenting beneath that sullen defiance. It was necessary only to bring them to the surface.

By experience Lan and Nechiev had worked out a routine. The Russians treated prisoners of war exactly as they pleased, unbound by any Geneva rules, and it was not necessary to observe the delicacies of interrogation to which Condon had been limited with his own army. The SS captain knew that— every German soldier did—and right now his imagination would be working overtime. Sizing him up, Condon did not think it would be necessary to use force, but if it came to that, all right. He'd simply wash his hands, stand aside, let Nechiev bear the guilt. The SS and Gestapo were one and the same, and their people knew from the beginning exactly what they had signed on for. Like the Russians, he and Finch kept their faces professionally merciless during the preliminary questioning. When Hofstädter refused to answer, Nechiev ordered tersely, "Strip him."

The guards promptly did so. And piece by piece, as the black uniform with its silver flashes, trappings, the black leather boots, were peeled away, so was Hofstädter's identity, his arrogance.

When he stood naked before them, while they smiled contemptuously, as if to mock his manhood, he was reduced in rank from SS officer to trapped, vulnerable humanity, for all his efforts not to show it.

They let him stand like that for a while as among themselves in German they discussed the procedures to be followed in the questioning. This was a charade; they never said in so many words what would be done with him. "I suggest we go to Step Four immediately," Nechiev said harshly. "Why waste time on the bastard?"

"Well, I can't stop you, but I'd like to try Step Two first. Of course, if he doesn't respond . . ." They argued briefly while the prisoner's gaze swung from one to the other like a spectator at a tennis match. He began to shiver, his skin goose-pimpled, and, Condon guessed, not entirely from the chill in the room; the whole object was to let the fear of the unknown work on him for a time.

At last Nechiev gave in. "Very well, try it your way. But you Americans are too soft. You may have ten minutes. If he cooperates, all right; if not—" He spread his hands.

Condon came around the table, perched on one corner of it, leg swinging. "As you've gathered, I'm an American officer. Let me make clear, I'm only an observer; I have no authority. Your final disposition is up to the lieutenant here. If you are cooperative, I might be disposed to use my good offices with him; if you don't, to the devil with you, I'll not interfere. The choice is yours." He looked at Hofstädter for a long moment. The man had a faint accent that had rung a bell in his mind; he thought of vast pine forests, rolling fields, huge castles on beetling, craggy cliffs, weekend excursions, and one two-week vacation with Christa. He waited. Hofstädter's eyes flickered, shuttled away.

"How old are you?" Condon asked.

The man bit his lip. Condon could read his mind: That question was innocuous, why not answer it, win that much time and credit anyhow? "Twenty-five," he said at last, and Condon knew that he had won.

"Your place of birth?"

"Vienna."

Condon's mouth twisted. "You're lying to me, Hofstädter. You're from somewhere in the Waldviertel." He slid off the table, threw up his hands. "Well, if that's the way you want it—"

"I was born in Vienna. But I was raised in Raabs on the Thaya."

"That's better," Condon said.

"Now. Your unit?"

Hofstädter hesitated. Condon gestured toward Nechiev. "The lieutenant maintains a list, Hofstädter. You have two minutes to answer. If you don't, the names of Hofstädter and the town of Raabs-an-die-Thaya go on the list. At the end of this day's work that list will be turned over to the NKVD, the Russian secret police. When the Waldviertel falls, as it surely will any day now, any relatives you have in Raabs will pay for your refusal to cooperate. Do you understand?"

Hofstädter's mouth twitched, fearful images racing through his mind. The truth of that was something he had no reason to doubt; in his own experience that was how such matters were handled. He drew in breath; and now it was not for himself that he yielded, but for his parents. With that out for his self-respect, and realizing anyhow that the game was up, he began to talk.

He had been a political officer with a squad of Waffen SS under him attached to a Wehrmacht battalion to watch for any sigh of faltering, to make sure it fought, and to execute summarily anyone whose nerve broke. The SS was taking responsibility for all units of Wehrkreise XIV, which, with a lot of Austrian officers, was riddled with unreliability. "If they do not fight," Hofstädter said, "they die."

"I see. But the old man and woman in the house. They were not soldiers, but they were executed. Why?"

Hofstädter was silent for a moment, and Condon thought at first he might rebel. Then the Nazi said, "They were on my list."

Condon sat up straight. "*Your* list?"

Hofstädter managed a wry smile. "You are not the only ones who have one." Then he sobered. "Each of us was given a list of the unreliables. Of those who might conceivably be useful to the enemy. I don't know who made them up, they came from Gestapo records, I suppose. All I know is that if we found it necessary to retreat, those people must be located and disposed of."

378

Condon felt a strange tingling in his wrists, a knotting of the stomach. "Where is your list?"

"I threw it away when I was running. Somewhere out there."

"What kind of people were on it?"

"Everyone who might have been of any usefulness to the occupiers. Everyone who had ever been suspect of showing opposition to der Führer, the Party. I suppose everyone who ever ran afoul of the Gestapo in any way. *They* scorched the earth when we came into Russia. Well, we can do the same. Only not just farms and factories, but people." Suddenly devoid of arrogance, as if wondering at it all, he shook his head. "Some of it makes no sense. It's almost as if they picked the names at random—village officials, teachers, farmers, even women. Our orders were that as we fell back to leave nobody you could use. Those two in that cottage were on my list. Naturally I had to carry out my orders."

"Naturally," Condon said. He mastered his revulsion. "How many names were on your list?"

"Twenty-five, I think."

"Can you remember them?"

Hofstädter fell silent. Nechiev, face grim, said, "We can help your memory."

The man licked his lips. "I remember some of them," he said and, concentrating, began to recite. Nechiev started writing and Condon followed suit; such people would be valuable to the British and Americans, too. But he was not concentrating. *Everyone who ever ran afoul of the Gestapo* ... Then he could sit there no longer looking at that battered face, listening to that recital, scribbling with a pencil while— He shoved back his chair. "Finch, I'll leave it with you," he said in English. And then he walked out.

It was late now, long since dark, the houses, except those already occupied, locked and shuttered, no lights showing. The street swarmed with drunken soldiers; some of them were singing. Not far away a woman screamed, a shrill sound of terror stifled abruptly. Trucks were still coming in, military police directing them; their engine-growl filled the night. On the horizon there were the dry-lightning flares of artillery, and star shells made magical brilliance in the sky. Every muscle in Lan's body felt as if it had turned to lead, unbearably heavy with a sickening weariness. He grappled with what he had learned. Yes, the Gestapo, the SS, the Crossed Arrows—which was the Hungarian Nazi organization—had done it in Hungary, retreated in a bloodbath. But here in Austria? German people? Just to wipe out generally anyone their enemies could use? Or take revenge at last for disloyalties real or imagined? And every SS officer had such a list.

Condon walked through the village. Once he paused near a house that flanked the street; inside a woman sobbed hysterically. Again a drunken soldier lurched against him, fell around his neck, breathing wine from a mouth that had never known toothpaste full into his face. *"Tovarich . . ."* Condon pushed him loose, walked on, hand dropping now to the holstered Colt automatic on his hip. The wind was cold; he turned up the collar of his jacket. Even if he's sent her west, he thought, even if the Russians don't get her . . . He reached the hamlet's border. Beyond, there was a vast bedground of troops, vehicles, an awesome spectacle of armies massing, regaining balance for one last crushing knockout punch. And, past that, a darker blackness against the sky northwestward: the Wienerwald. Like pagan campfires on distant hills, flames flared and died. German artillery chopping at the Russian flank; Red counterbattery.

Lan stood there for several minutes. Presently he walked back through the village. Entering the *Gasthaus* by the back door, he saw that Mark was still in the public room with Russian officers, and he went quietly up to the room they shared. There he picked up the Russian PPSh submachine gun he had been issued, along with several box clips of ammunition. He slung the gun, put the clips and a few cans of C rations into a musette bag, and went quietly back down the stairs to where his jeep was parked beneath a huge old plane tree. Its tank was full, and there was a five-gallon jerry can in addition, plenty for a round trip of less than forty miles. He fumbled for the key to the lock that chained the jeep's steering wheel. Then, from the darkness behind him, Mark's voice said, "Lan. No."

Condon started, turned. Mark's blocky figure moved toward him in the darkness, and then Mark's hand gripped his arm. "No. You wouldn't stand a chance."

"God damn it, Mark, I've got to. You don't understand."

Mark's fingers never relaxed their grip as he told Gorton about the SS man and the lists. "They'll have her on one, the General, too, and—"

"I'm sorry, it can't be helped," said Gorton. "You're not going. It would be suicide. Through our lines, and then through theirs? Lan, you wouldn't stand a chance."

"I—" Lan jerked his arm away. "Mark, I've come this far. If when I find her she's dead because I didn't make that one last try— I won't let you stop me."

"I'll stop you. I'll put you under arrest." Gorton's voice was hard. "The closer we've got, the more I've been expecting something like this, and when I saw you slinking down the stairs ..." Then his tone eased. "Lan, I know how you feel. But no. Not until tomorrow."

"Tomorrow?"

"I've been talking to Ognev. He's just got orders down from Army. Before daylight tomorrow he's to swing two battalions out through the Wienerwald, an armor-infantry task force that's to go like hell. Want to know its objective? The road junction at Altkreuzburg. When they go, you can go with them if you want to. Nobody knows what resistance they'll meet, how long it will take. They may make it in three hours; it may take three days. But they'll have Air ahead of them all the way, and if they secure the Altkreuzburg junction, we'll have Vienna just about pinched off south of the Danube." He paused. "Well?"

"Mark," Condon whispered, something unclenching within him.

Gorton was silent for a moment; then he squeezed Lan's arm again, this time in a different way. "All right. Let's go in and fix it up with Ognev."

8 WHEN THE TANKS CAME, emplacing themselves in the orchard, she had been terrified. Surely their crews would demand to be billeted in the house, and undoubtedly they would find Josef's hiding place. To her relief, the captain in command of them had no such plans; they would sleep near their

vehicles. "And you, *gnädige Frau,* you must not stay in the house either. In fact, you and everybody had better get out—go down there in the village or somewhere. They'll spot us sooner or later, and then all hell will break loose. This house hasn't got a chance."

Except for Josef, she had never seen a man with a face like his. It was so unutterably weary, devoid of hope, that it was hardly human. With those sad, soft eyes and his unshaven ginger beard, he looked like a tired, bedraggled dog. "I am sorry, Captain. My father is in no condition to be moved away. Besides, I will not leave my property. This is my home, and I don't care what happens."

He was too tired to argue. "Very well, then. Stay if you must. But for God's sake, stay where you can get to the cellar on a moment's notice. Once we start firing, the Russians will know where we are, and their Stormoviks will be down on us like hawks on mice. How much wine do you have?"

"A great deal, both in casks and bottled."

"You must give me the keys to all your storage areas. It has to be disposed of."

She stared at him. "Our *wine?* But—"

"Yes, for your protection—and the whole valley's. Look, I was in Hungary. Sober, the swine are bad enough; drunk they are beyond belief. If you insist on staying, you mustn't have a drop of alcohol on the place. Please, your keys."

So she had given them, and save for a few bottles for themselves, a week's supply for her, they had destroyed all of it, smashing the bottled wine, staving in the casks, careful to avoid damage to their historic carved heads. Until the cask wine drained to the lower cellar, it flooded the upper one to a depth of two feet.

There was more. The captain ripped out all of the house's plumbing fixtures, hid them beneath a woodpile. "I know you won't believe this," he said, "but in Hungary, a great many people with flush toilets and running water in their houses were automatically shot as bourgeois or capitalists. There's something about this plumbing that inflames a certain kind of Russian. You're much safer without it." Before they did that, he and his men had enjoyed a final bath and shave, but he still looked dead tired and dog-faced. And then, while they were on the terrace drinking wine, and it might have been a pleasant

382

prewar Sunday afternoon save for the smoke filling the eastern sky and the distant rumble of artillery, he asked, "Do you have a pistol in the house?"

"No," Christa said. "You've seen my father's condition. We used to have a lot of guns. But we were afraid he'd hurt himself, so we got rid of all of them."

A strange expression crossed the captain's face. "You've seen the Amis' Wild West films? Where the Red Indians surround the wagon train?"

"Yes, of course."

"Then you remember that the hero always gives the girl a pistol. Do you remember why?"

Christa stared at him a moment, then said numbly, "Yes."

"With my compliments," the captain said, and unsnapped his holster and handed her his sidearm, a P-38. "Do you know how to use it?"

"Yes. Kreisleiter Schellhammer showed me when he practiced."

"Then good. If you will not leave, keep it with you every hour of the day. Do you understand?"

"I understand," said Christa, and she opened her blouse and thrust the gun in the waistband of her skirt. It was hard and cold against her stomach, even through her slip.

"So," the captain said, draining his glass. "For the moment, this is the front line, what there is of it. We have more guns over there, directly across the valley. But we have little ammunition, and once it's exhausted we'll be drawing back deeper into the Wienerwald. If you have the opportunity, would you send this letter to my wife in Karlsruhe?" He bowed, kissed her hand, and left her.

"Damn it," Josef said fiercely, "do what he says! Get out! Don't you understand? You've got to get away from here, you and the child! Go to the village, go somewhere."

They were in Christa's bedroom. She had not seen Robert in four days, and doubted whether she would ever see him again. She had sent all the servants and the two Slav girls to the village; only Mitzi had been reluctant, but Christa had insisted. "In a few days, if everything's all right, you can come back."

After that she had wrestled with her conscience. Her father— she owed him safety, too. But he had solved that problem for

383

her. He had sunk into deepest funk; somehow it had been impressed on his mind that the Russians were coming, his worst fears realized. "They'll put me in a cage," he mumbled, "and drag me through the streets of Moscow. And then they'll ram me on a stake." He was lost in some fog of agonizing terror, reduced almost to gibbering—except when she sought to take him from the house. Then, understanding what she was about, he not only regained a measure of rationality, he fought so violently that she feared another stroke. "I will not leave!" he roared in his old deep voice. "It's on the wall out there, don't you see? The *Christina* Hof! Do you think I'd leave you to them?" Short of binding him, there was no way she could get him out, and she ceased trying. If this was where he chose to die, then she had no right to deny him that. "All right, Papa," she said. "All right. Here is where we'll stay."

And a load had lifted from her as well. It was as impossible for her to leave this place as for him, but for a different reason. She told herself that it was Josef; he had no place to go but here. And now, standing at the window as he urged her again, she turned. "No," she said. "No. It's quite impossible. For Papa's sake and yours."

He was silent for a moment. Then he said, a little wryly, "All right, Christa, come off it."

"What do you mean?"

He sat there on the bed in Lan's pajamas, looking at her. He had filled out, was almost the old Josef of years ago, save for the deep-etched lines in what had once been a smooth face. He puffed on a cigarette; she still had several packs left, gifts from Robert. "It's not the General," he said quietly, "and it's not me. It's just that if he comes back, this is where he'll look for you."

Christa was silent for a moment. Then she said, "Josef, he won't come back."

"You know damned well that if he's alive he will." Josef stood up. "Or else you don't know Lan the way I do."

Christa touched her belly. "And if he did, what difference would it make?"

"I don't know," said Josef. "I know how I would feel."

"How would you feel?"

He didn't answer. Instead he said, "Christa, darling, please. For my sake, go."

"I'm sorry, Josef."

"Then I'm right."

She turned back to the window. "I don't know whether you're right or wrong. I just know that I will not leave."

"Then I'll go. Maybe it will change your thinking."

She whirled. "Josef, you will not!" Her voice rose, broke. "My God, Captain Weber said the SS are all over. If they find you—" She came to him, clutched his hands. "No. You have to stay with me. Don't you understand? If not for me, for Papa. But we have to have—"

"The credit that I represent? That much-wanted Jew that you saved? I had forgotten that aspect of it. You put me in a bad position. But— All right. Then we'll tough it out together. But will you make me a promise?"

"What?"

"Once it's over, if it turns out that Lan is dead or . . . doesn't want you, and if we are both still alive, will you marry me?"

"You know I will," she said at once.

Josef smiled. "If I survive, we'll not be poor. I've plenty hidden away in Switzerland. There's only one thing." He sobered. "We'll leave Austria. I won't say forever. Maybe nobody like us can ever leave forever. But what I dream of now is getting out of here. I want to go somewhere that will evoke no memories, not require me to think about anything. America, or South America or somewhere—" He looked into her eyes, then shrugged. "We'll talk about that later. But soon. Soon we can make plans. If we can manage it with the Russians. For now . . . My poor darling. You look so tired. Come lie down beside me and let me hold you while you go to sleep."

She lay on his arm, eyes closed, heard his heavy breathing. Sleep eluded her; Captain Weber had given her the latest information received on his tank radios. She needed only to look out the window to confirm it. Today, the eighth of April, Vienna was burning up. The cathedral was in flames; the Russians were in the southwestern districts pouring artillery fire into the Inner City; a fall-back had begun to the north bank of the Danube . . . It could not be long now. Then she began to drift into sleep. In drowsiness her fears and doubts dissolved. Not long. Soon. Soon Lan would come again. She dreamed of a night in the Tyrol . . .

Below, in his own room, General Helmer heard the thunder

of the artillery in the distance. But they had all left him; he was at the mercy of the Cossacks, and he bit his thumb to keep from whimpering. But then it was all right. Christina came to him across the ballroom of the palace. . . .

9   ROBERT SCHELLHAMMER had not taken off his clothes for four days, and his Party uniform was rumpled, stinking. The offices of his *Kreis* in the Stift at Altkreuzburg had been a madhouse for forty-eight hours, and in that interval he had not even lain down to rest. Contradictory orders poured in, from the Gauleiter of Niederdonau, from Berlin, from Vienna. Frightened citizens had besieged him, wanting everything under the sun—safe-conduct passes west, gasoline, food—and there were even a pair of absolutely mad old people who wanted their dog's license renewed. Then the Gauleiter, whose offices were in Vienna, had simply disappeared. No more orders came; phone and teletype were dead. Nor could he reach von Schirach, personal friend of Hitler, moving spirit in the Hitler Youth, Gauleiter of Vienna, and thus real ruler of the Ostmark; he had dodged out, too. In his office only a few clerks remained. Of course, Robert told himself, they've gone out on the line. Where I should be.

It was finished now and there was nothing more he could do here. He dismissed his staff, what few of them had showed up, told them to seek what safety they could. Then he flopped on a couch, slept like a dead man. Early next morning he was awakened by the buzzing of the switchboard.

Blearily he groped his way through the deserted offices to it. He fumbled with the plugs for several seconds before he found the right one, and then he had trouble with the earphones. A crisp voice said, "Kreisleiter Schellhammer, *bitte.*"

"Speaking," Robert answered.

"Lieutenant Trappner, SS, speaking here. Herr Kreisleiter, I have sad news for you. I was with your father when he died."

"My father . . . died . . ." Robert rubbed his eyes. "Oh . . ."

"Yes. He died in my arms. A grenade. His last request was that

386

I notify you. Herr Kreisleiter, my sympathies. He died a hero of the Reich."

"Yes," said Robert. "Yes, of course. Where are you calling from?"

"Why, I am in—" Then the line went dead.

"Halloo?" Robert yelled. "Halloo?" But there was not even a buzz.

Groggily he shoved off the earphones. He stood up, not even aware that he was crying. *Vati* dead, old, strong Max. A grenade. How? Ripped open? He stumbled across the office, opened the windows. From this height he could look out across the whole valley of the Danube. Vienna was a roil of flame beneath a pall of smoke. Killed in action. Well, they had both expected that. A hero of the Reich. My God, there *must* be Valkyries to swoop down and carry a man like that to a Valhalla. He was too big, too great, too lusty for any ordinary Catholic heaven. Such a death, Robert thought, demanded pagan grandeur. An ordinary heaven was not fit for such a warrior; like Busch, he wanted mead and great joints of meat and full-bodied women and a place to hunt— Robert dropped onto the couch, sat there with head in hands for a long time.

Presently he rose, and in the bath down the hall removed his shirt, sluiced down face and torso. *The German soldier regardless of the temperature will wash in cold water to the waist every morning.* The eyes that looked back at him from the mirror were bloodshot, weary, strangely dead. There was gray at the temples, some in his beard.

It was nine o'clock when he returned to his office. Still no one had come in. The whole enormous Stift was like a warren from which all the rabbits had fled. Everyone had run west or gone home to shield his family from whatever came, or else was out foraging for food. Despite all his efforts, the distribution system in his *Kreis* had broken down; everything had broken down, ground to a halt. He dropped into the operator's chair at the switchboard, tried every line to Vienna; they all were out. He found himself ringing other numbers at random; vaguely he felt that he should tell someone about his father. No one answered. He tried the Christina Hof. But there were no central operators on duty in Altkreuzburg, it seemed. After a while he gave up. He went out into the corridor. Usually the benches there were full of supplicants, people with official business with the *Kreis*. No one there today.

He rubbed his face, returning to his private office. The red of the enormous Party flag hanging behind his desk was that of blood. Robert went to a closet. From it he took an MP 38/40 machine pistol and a cloth bandolier of ammunition. Now, gasoline for his car; he must find enough to fill it. He had no idea where. Christ, the whole country had run down like a clock. But he would get some, drive to the Christina Hof, get Christa and the General on the road, and then find a unit somewhere with which he could fight. They had killed his father and his country and his dream, and he would fight against them for as long as he had breath. Then he heard footsteps in the corridor.

Unslinging the weapon, he went into the outer office. Its double doors opened and two men entered. Robert relaxed; they both wore black, with the death's-head insignia on their caps. There was something solid and reassuring about a couple of SS officers, as natty as if on parade in full rig; here were men who did not panic.

One was a colonel, the other a lieutenant. There was no doubt or faltering in their Heil Hitler salutations. Robert responded in kind, pleased at the firm timbre of his own voice.

The colonel had a knobby, reddish face with black brows like crayon marks. "Herr Kreisleiter Schellhammer?"

"I'm he."

The SS man put out his hand. "Colonel Mittler; here is Lieutenant Dorfmann."

They shook hands. Mittler looked around at the empty outer office. "Business is slack," he said, grinning slightly.

"Yes. What can I do for you?" It was good to hear the voices in the empty room.

"A few minutes of your time." Mittler hooked out a chair with a booted foot, sat at a desk, opened a dispatch case. "Just some information."

"Of course." Robert took a chair at the same desk. "You've come from Vienna?"

"Yes."

"What's the situation there?"

Dorfmann let out a barking laugh. "Begging your pardon,"

Mittler said, "but, Herr Kreisleiter, the situation there is shit."
He took glasses from his pocket, put them on. "The Russians
have almost reached the Ring. So far we've held the highway
from here to Vienna open, but they'll cut it soon. I may as
well be frank. Preparations are being made to fall back to the
north bank of the Danube. We'll consolidate there and then blow
all the bridges."

Robert let out breath. "That bad?"

"Yes. You'll soon be cut off from the city, at least on this
bank of the river. It's pretty much written off. They have another wing coming through and around the Wienerwald, but
the main thrust of their drive is toward Vienna; we're going
to let them have this whole area. But"—he glanced at the
machine pistol—"if you intend to join the fight, there'll be
some units farther up the valley, if you can reach them, who'll
fight a rear-guard action."

"You make it sound hopeless."

"Only if one is afraid to die," said Mittler calmly.

Anger welled up in Robert. "This morning I had word that
my father, a member of the Volkssturm, was killed in action."

Mittler looked contrite. "I am very sorry. Now, time presses.
If we could have a little assistance." He laid a typewritten list
of names and addresses before Robert. "We're strangers to the
area. Could you help us locate these addresses?"

"You mean go with you?"

"Oh, no. Surely you have a map. If you would just pinpoint
them on the map, by numbers one, two, three, so on, that's all
we need."

"Of course." Robert went to another desk, opened a drawer,
took out a map of Altkreuzburg and the area, one of many
printed for tourists, with all the local attractions shown. He sat
down by the colonel again, taking his mechanical pencil from
his pocket. Then he froze.

"May I ask," he said, his voice seeming to him to come from
far away, "the purpose of this list?"

"No disrespect, but that is a secret SS matter."

"I am a Party official with rank equal to yours."

Mittler looked at him a moment, then made a careless gesture.
"Very well. Obviously you're one of the Old Fighters and have
been the distance, and it's your *Kreis*." He took off his glasses.

"A few days ago a plot was discovered within the Vienna command of the Wehrmacht to betray the city to the Russians. Certain officers were in touch with members of a resistance group known as O-five. Yesterday the officers responsible—a certain Major Biedermann, a captain and a first lieutenant—were taken and tried. This morning they were hanged in public by the Floridsdorfer Bridge, where they will be left as an example."

Robert stared at the list. "These people are members of this— What did you call it?"

"O-five." Mittler shrugged. "We don't know whether they are or not. What we do know is that the Morzinplatz has flagged their files and . . . they are considered hostile to our cause. Anyhow, we're taking no chances. If we should have to go underground, there's no reason to leave all these people alive, intact, for the Reds to use. So— As many of them as can be located, Lieutenant Dorfmann and I will deal with today."

"Kill them," Robert said numbly. He raised his eyes, stared at Mittler. "All these? Only the two of you?"

"Yes, we're all that could be spared to handle this immediate area. Now you see why we must hurry. If you'd just mark the map . . ."

"But these people— I know most of them. There are some who don't belong on here. Some mistake's been made."

"Too bad for them. No time to correct it now."

"But I tell you, there are names that should be taken off that list." His voice rose, and Mittler looked at him oddly.

"Herr Kreisleiter, you know better than that. The Morzinplatz put them on; only the Morzinplatz can take them off. I have no authority—"

"Well, I do!" Robert snapped. "This is my district and—"

"Herr Schellhammer"—and Mittler's voice was cold—"I beg your pardon. You have no district and no authority." His eyes met Robert's. "And it does you no credit to show concern for such traitorous types. True, they are your neighbors, I suppose, but what does that count against the larger interest? An Old Fighter like you need not be told that. But"—his indrawn breath was a kind of hiss—"if you insist too much, you do so at your own risk. A name cannot be taken off the list. One can be added. Do you understand me?"

They were both looking at him now, hard: the colonel and

the lieutenant. Robert swallowed a thickness in his throat. "Yes," he said. "You are right. Forgive me. I was overwrought. My father . . ."

"Naturally. You have our condolences and sympathy. Now . . ."

"That can be quickly done," said Robert. He bent over the map, jotting numbers on it in a firm hand, circling each. Signing, he thought, death warrants.

But his hand was steady as he shoved the map at Mittler. "There."

Mittler handed it to Dorfmann, who folded it and stood up. "Thank you, Herr Schellhammer. Now . . . until we meet again, good luck."

"The same to you," Robert said huskily. He raised his arm. "Heil Hitler."

"Heil Hitler," the two men answered. When they had closed the door behind them, Robert stood there as motionless as if carved from wood. Then he began to tremble. He did not know what to do. The list was in alphabetical order. The third name on it had been Christa's. The eighth had been her father's.

It was not fair, his mind screamed. Der Führer had no right to ask it of him. But der Führer had not asked it. If he had known, he would never have asked it. But . . . Robert closed his eyes. Not only Christa. But the baby that she carried, the baby that was his son, his vindication of the past, his link with the future. But they would not spare her because she was pregnant.

He drew in a deep breath, let it out. He picked up the Schmeisser and ran across his office into the hall, toward the stairs. There were three flights of them, broad, made of marble with marble rails. He heard the sound of the booted feet of the two officers as they reached the bottom flight. He ran after them, making the lower landing just as they were about to open the massive door.

"Colonel Mittler!" he called, halting on the landing. "One moment. You forgot—"

They both turned. Robert had held the Schmeisser behind his back. Now he brought it out and up. Their eyes widened as they saw it; Dorfmann opened his mouth to yell.

Expert with the gun, as he always had been with any sort of firearm, Robert killed the two of them with two short bursts.

10

THERE WAS ALMOST NOTHING LEFT TO EAT. She had given each servant, even the Polish girls, baskets of food when they had fled to sanctuary behind the lines. Apologetically, Captain Weber had requisitioned rations for his men, and meanwhile a party of infantrymen with all sorts of papers of authorization had come through and slaughtered the pigs, driven off the cattle, and killed most of the chickens. There was, she had realized, nothing she could do about it anyway, and so she had made a great show of patriotic willingness—anything to divert suspicion, get them gone as quickly as possible without a search of the house. It had worked. And now, incredible as it seemed, the once endless resources of the Christina Hof had dwindled down to almost nothing: only a few loaves of bread, a couple of hoarded jars of marmalade, and a sheaf of unused ration cards not worth the paper they were printed on, since no more stores were open.

With the house empty of everyone except themselves, there was no need for Josef to stay confined in the attic room. All the outside doors were safely locked, and anyhow Weber would not let his men barge in unannounced. While Robert still had keys, he had not been seen or heard from in four days, and Christa supposed that he had either gone to fight or that he was dead. There was no getting through to his offices in Altkreuzburg by phone. The thought of Robert dead moved her more than she had expected; she felt grief not for the *Kreisleiter* who had been an accomplice in horrors she would not let her mind dwell on, but for the gold-bright young dreamer who had shared her childhood afternoons.

Anyhow, if anyone came unexpectedly, there were plenty of places Josef could quickly hide; and so they took the chance. He sat at the table with them in the dining room as they ate breakfast.

It had been his first encounter with the General, and although Christa had prepared him, Josef had been shocked. When Josef had last seen him, her father had been in his prime; now he was a wraith of that self, lost in some secret world of his own. Maybe, she had thought, he was better off. In that world his wife and son still lived, and grief and loss and fear could not enter except on those occasions when he had some sort of wartime hallucinations; but those never lasted long, and she had always managed to calm him.

The soldiers had been very good with him. Captain Weber had shown him the tanks and tried to explain how they worked and had discussed their field of fire, the way they commanded the roads and surrounding terrain, interlocking with the guns behind the Schellhammer Hof across the ridge. And—a miracle —there had been several minutes when the General had become quite lucid, discussing the disposition of the guns with, said Weber, wisdom and authority. "You must not give up on him. There is something left there, and I hope later he can have proper medical attention."

But this morning he was back in that lost place of his, displaying neither recognition nor curiosity, accepting Josef's presence passively—if he was aware of it at all. As usual he ate almost nothing, but he fed himself with neatness and precision. She told Josef what Weber had said.

"Yes. Well, when we get to Switzerland, I'll see that he gets the best care money can buy."

"Switzerland." This was a fantasy they had built, one she never tired of now—a fantasy of freedom, of the end of fear and chaos. "Do you think we'll really—?"

"Of course. Once this thing is over, I'm sure it will be simple. I still have a lot of money there, and that's the thing about it— money. It's like a parachute. If you've got lots of it somewhere, no matter where you fall from, you can always come down easy, on your feet. And the Reds, I imagine, are as susceptible to money as anyone. When they come, I'll work it out with them. A year from now we'll be in Zurich, or maybe even in America. And by then I'll wager we'll have started to forget." He shoved his plate toward her, a slice of bread remaining on it. "Here."

"No, you—"

"Don't argue. It's for *him*. You think I want my son stunted for lack of proper prenatal nutrition? Eat."

She did, without regret; she was always ravenous nowadays. She used Josef's last ration of jam as well, savoring its sweetness. The child within her seemed to appreciate it, shifting so that she had to adjust the pistol which she still carried in the waistband of the contrived pregnancy skirt.

393

There was still half a slice on the General's plate. "Papa," she said, "finish your breakfast."

Like a good child, he picked up the bread. Then a bell rang. Christa tensed. "The back door. Josef—"

But he was already up, heading for concealment in the pantry. She gave him time to lock himself in before she answered the insistent ringing. Captain Weber was there, sad-terrier face grave.

"Frau Condon. We have a radio message. A lot of Russian planes are shooting their way up the line through the Wiener-wald, coming in this direction. We are to retaliate with anti-aircraft fire. That means inevitably we'll draw down their fire on us, and ..."

Christa's heart leaped, her throat constricted. "Our house?"

Weber was apologetic. "I'm sorry. But I told you—even if we weren't here, they'd target it anyhow; the ground it occupies is simply too strategic. Now, you and your father take cover in your cellar at once. *Sofort!*" Then he tensed, cocked his head. "The devil! They're already— *Wiederseh'n, Frau Condon!*" He whirled, ran toward the orchard.

Christa heard it, too, a strange thunder from not far away, the harsh rasp of diving aircraft. The bread and jam rose in her throat. Now she saw them, high above the Wienerwald, above the next ridge over, circling, then swooping down, and smoke and dust roiling from the woods. She whirled back into the house as there was the slam of cannon fire and the chatter of machine guns from the orchard.

"Josef! Papa! Air raid! *Josef, help me!*" She seized her father, dragged him into the corridor toward the kitchen; they had to get across the courtyard to the deep wine cellars beneath the pressing house. But as she reached the kitchen, the whole hilltop seemed engulfed in thunder. The scales fell off the wall; glasses jumped from the cabinets, jingling. They were engulfed by sound, vibration, and crumbling plaster. "Josef!" she screamed.

Then he was there, seizing her father. The old man stood, head raised, listening, staring, as if that familiar roar had triggered associations in his mind. For one wild instant she thought that he was normal; he seemed the man she once had known.

There was no hope of getting across the courtyard. Christa ran to another door. "This way!" She pulled her father by the hand, and Josef pushed him down the steps to the wash kitchen—the laundry with its stove, tubs, lines. Now the roar above was muffled. Christa found another key on her ring, fumbled it into another lock. The door swung open, and they went cautiously in darkness down the steps of a second, deeper cellar, storage for kitchen supplies of potatoes and the like. She had not known any potatoes were left, but the floor was strewn with a dozen. One rolled beneath her foot in the total darkness and she went sprawling on hands and knees, dragging the General down with her. "Papa! Josef, help me!" They scrambled in darkness and finally regained their feet. "Papa! Are you all right?"

"*Ja.*" His voice was toneless.

"Good. Over here." She led them to covered storage bins that would serve as benches and eased her father down on one. There was vibration, a muffled roar from overhead. Violently the baby kicked, and she clutched at her stomach. In the fall, the pistol Weber had given her had slipped from the waistband of her skirt, but for now that did not matter. Josef was beside her then, and she clung to him while the stones of walls and floor jarred in their mortar. Above, something enormous fell, shaking even this deep a burrow in the earth. . . .

He sat in darkness, his back against a cold stone: a dugout, of course. Artillery was firing somewhere close by. But he could not quite grasp the situation. He did not know where his units were. For a moment he felt a certain urgency, knowing he should be out there commanding; then it slipped away. Once more there was the calm in which nothing mattered, people had no faces, words no meanings. He heard the barrage above; mingled with its thunder was Christina's voice, a man's voice answering. He wondered whose, then ceased wondering. The brief flare of thought had been as much as he could sustain. Anyhow, there was the other thing to think about that he had found among the potatoes in darkness when he fell.

11 THEY WERE THE FIRST HUMAN BEINGS he had ever killed. There in the Stift he stared at them a moment, not so much in awe as in curiosity. It was not really different from shooting deer or wild boar. The red that stained them was the same. *Sweat,* he thought, in hunter's lingo.

He rubbed his face. He had never thought to kill two SS men. Good God, if the Gestapo ever pinned it on him! Then he remembered and he scooped up the dispatch case that contained the list. This must not fall into anybody else's hands. If they had only been reasonable ... But, of course, they'd had their duty. So had he—to go along with them—and he had violated that. But he would make it up somehow. Once Christa was in safety and he went into combat, he would kill enough Reds to pay for them and expiate what he had done. But for now ... the gasoline.

He shoved through the big iron-strapped door. Their small car was parked hard by the wall in the deserted courtyard. Instead of a key it had a standard military switch; and when he flicked it on, the fuel indicator rose to nearly *full.*

Robert let out a breath. The car would hold Christa, the General, and himself; and its range of a hundred miles would be enough to get them out of the Russians' way. Laying the machine pistol on the seat, he slid behind the wheel, started the engine.

He wheeled the vehicle through the courtyard, out the high arched gate, and rushed down the hill to the lower town. There was no traffic, but half a dozen armed Pioneers were at the main junction in the lower market. The SS pennant on the fender was pass enough without question; they waved him on. He turned west along the Danube road, then took the Ferntal cutoff. It was too bad about the SS men. What was worse, he hated the thought of the others on the list missing their punishment. Undoubtedly they had it coming to them. But Christa was a different case. She had been a pawn in Condon's hands—and Steiner's. Exploited by a Jew. The Gestapo should have taken that into consideration. If it could have been explained to der Führer ... Robert shook his head, feeling light, strangely disembodied, his ears buzzing. He had, after all, eaten nothing since . . . When? Four or five yesterday afternoon. And he'd had two jolting shocks this morning. *Vati,* then the list.

Now he had left Altkreuzburg, was entering the Ferntal. Here it was almost possible to believe that there was peace. The chestnuts along the Fernbach were just putting out their leaves: horse chestnuts, not real ones. People could not eat them; but deer loved them, and *Vati* and the General used to pay children to gather great sacks full of the nuts to be put at the winter feeding stations for the game.

Driven by urgency, he stamped down on the accelerator. He had not seen Christa in four days. He felt a sudden, overpowering need to hold her, touch her, tell her about Max, have her weep for and with him. The car responded magically. Then, without warning, the hills on both sides and the road itself seemed to explode. Dirt, pavement, smoke, a roar like the world's end, and the car jumped, whirled sideways by concussion. That was his first knowledge of the airplanes. Jamming on brakes, he sat for a frozen second, gaping. Then a Stormovik, diving low, crossed his field of vision. He gunned the engine, shot off the road to the shelter of the chestnuts by the stream. Seizing the machine pistol, he dived from the car, hurtled down the bank, pressed himself against its cold sand, sheltered by its overhang. Panting, he looked up.

The sky was full of planes, red stars on their wings. They swooped and dived across and up and down the valley. From the ridge by the Christina Hof, tracers laced up at them from the tank guns. Then more thunder rang in his ears. He turned his head. He had not known they had put guns behind his own home, too, but they were there—anti-aircraft pumping flak at the Stormoviks. Robert grated something incoherent.

He saw one plane go whirling wing over wing to crash into the Wienerwald not far from Busch's. Then he saw the three aircraft swooping across the valley and the rockets lacing from them, and he cried out as the buildings of the Schellhammer Hof were suddenly veiled by flame and dust and smoke, masonry flying. He stared numbly, then instinctively turned his head away.

Across the valley the Stormoviks came down, flight after flight, pumping cannon shells, hurling rockets. He saw the whole ridgetop explode in white and dirty brown, trees in

397

the orchards fall away, revealing the camouflaged metal of the tanks; and he saw the spurts of tracers from the tanks cease as if someone had turned a tap and watched one and then another convulse as rockets slammed into them. The planes passed over. Some peeled off south; others turned back to renew the attack.

"Jesus and Mary," breathed Robert. Now the Christina Hof took the full fury. Tile flew, the yellow walls seemed to lift themselves from their foundation, poise, then split asunder, falling. He screamed Christa's name. His voice was drowned in the explosions. Furiously he pounded on the dirt with both hands, but there was nothing he could do. One plane banked low, away from the others; he thought then it had seen his car. He rolled down the bank into the icy waters of the *Bach*. But the Stormovik passed without firing at him, drumming instead more rounds into his home before it pulled up with a snarling roar.

Robert lay there in the water, unaware of its icy chill, face buried in his arms, while moments stretched to centuries. It was, after all, the first time he had really been under fire, and he was terrified; it was a sensation obscenely, intensely personal, primitive, with nothing noble about it, nothing heroic. If there were Valkyries, they were the enemy's, death-spitting aliens in his Germanic sky. He felt a warmer liquid mingling with the waters of the stream.

Then the roaring overhead receded; such a miracle that at first he did not dare believe it. Not until a silence, total and profound, had settled over the valley did he raise his head. Then he rolled over in the stream, staring at the April sky above the Wienerwald, filled with a curious lassitude; he had lain that way in meadows for hours when he was a boy. It seemed to take tremendous effort when at last he clambered to his feet, dripping, sodden.

Up on the hillside, smoke and dust curled up from what had once been his home. Now it was a pile of rubble, one wall only of the main house standing. He coughed, swallowed back the thick phlegm that rose in his throat. *Vati* was gone, now that. All he had left was Christa.

Suddenly his heart began to pound; he came to life. Whirling, he grabbed up the Schmeisser. He scrabbled up the creek bank and halted, staring up the other hill at the Christina Hof.

Larger, more substantial, three of its walls still stood, though its tile roofs had fallen in and the subsidiary floors collapsed, so that nothing but a shell was left. Robert licked his lips. Surely she had hidden in its cellars; she must have had ample warning. His hands shook as he started the car up again. He wheeled it, sent it across the cratered, pitted road and up the coiling way to the Christina Hof.

In low gear, the little car crawled with maddening slowness. Finally he reached the gate, which was hanging awry on the one stone pillar not blown away. The air was pungent, chalky, with plaster, brick dust, explosives. Robert got out, staring at the wall nearest him, its top segment sheared off diagonally. In its upper corner the white letters *ina* were powdered gray with dust.

Holding the Schmeisser, he ran forward. The terrace was heaped with rubble; tons of it had dropped into the drawing room. The Bösendorfer piano had been flattened under a massive weight of stone; slabs of concrete lay tilted this way and that. He realized that at least some of the planes must have dropped bombs in addition to rockets. He blinked, eyes stung by the swirling dust. Then he ran around the house to the courtyard and halted. The pressing house was a mass of rubble, too, its cellar doors totally sealed off. Oh, God, if she were down in there, then she was trapped. Alone he could not move that vast pile of masonry. "Christa!" he heard himself scream. *"Christa!"*

There was no answer. Robert stood there in the courtyard panting, not knowing what to do. God, was he doomed to lose everything today? He held his breath, but there was only the flick and clack of bits of rubble dropping like water from the eaves after a storm had passed. "Christa," he called again, voice quavering. He stood there for minutes, he did not know how many. Then, trying to think, he walked back around the shattered corner of the house. He fumbled for his cigarettes, but they all were wet.

He rubbed his face. He knew now; for him, nothing really counted except her. All he had done, all he had based his life upon, had been inspired by her, by the need for her acceptance. She could *not* be dead; he had to search.

Then he raised his head and cocked it, stood there frozen for a moment. Then he was sure, and he whirled and ran back toward the courtyard, where there was the sound of voices. And

399

there they were, the three of them, just emerging from an area-way, the outside entrance to the house's cellars: Christa, face smeared with dirt and slime, hair tousled, but wonderfully, intactly swollen with his son. Beside her, looking blankly around him, was the General. And behind her was another man, tall, lean, with black hair powdered with white dust, whom he had never seen before.

They did not see him. They were staring in awe and horror at what had happened to the Christina Hof. He saw Christa's jaw drop, her face work. Even some flicker of expression crossed the General's features. Then Christa let out a sob. "Oh, Josef!" she cried and whirled and buried her face against the chest of the man, and he put his arm around her, held her tightly.

"All right," the man said quietly. "All right." He bent, touched his lips to her tousled hair.

As if a big hand had pushed him, Robert stepped back out of sight around the corner of the shattered wall.

Then Christa: "Josef, we can't stand here like this. We've got to find someplace for you to hide. If there are soldiers left out there with the tanks, if— You can't let them take you. You've got to get back down there in the cellar."

"Darling, I— Yes, I guess you're right. But—"

Darling? Who was this man? Hide? His heart was pounding in his chest. Then he was moving up and around the corner. "Christa!" he shouted.

The man still holding her jerked up his head; his arm fell away from the woman. Slowly she turned and he saw her eyes widen, her mouth fall open, and there was no joy in her expression, only surprise and horror. "Robert!" Dismay vibrated in the single word; he was still alive, and she was dismayed.

The explosions had made his ears ring, but he was only now aware of it. "What?" His own voice sounded far away. "Who is this? Who is this man?"

"A refugee." He heard the desperate lying ring in her voice.

"Who are you?" Robert asked, turning, aiming the gun at the man.

He half raised his hands, face pale. "My name is Schmidt. Josef Schmidt, Herr Kreisleiter. I—"

But he had held her in his arms and she had pressed against him and he had kissed her hair and Robert saw the lie on his face, too, and finally now he had someone that he could make pay for all he had lost today, and he knew that he had lost more than he thought, and he was not even aware that he pulled the trigger. Christa screamed. The man, picked up by the smashing burst of lead, fell flopping on the cobblestones, kicked once, lay still.

Christa was frozen for a moment. Then she screamed, "Josef!" ran to him, dropped to her knees beside him. "Josef!" She touched his chest, drew back a red-smeared hand, and then twisted to stare at Robert. He was startled at the intensity of hatred in her eyes. "Killed," she said hoarsely. "Killed. Like Ernst. Like—" Her hand gestured to the walls above her. "Are you satisfied now? Have you killed enough and ruined enough?" Her mouth twisted, she spat the words at him, voice rising, trembling. "Have you had your pound of flesh and . . . and all the blood you want to drink? Is he happy now, your Führer, your little tin god with the sewer mind, your little pervert with the absurd mustache? Are you happy, too, you great hero, you great stupid bloody-minded idiot?"

"Christa," he whispered. "Darling—"

"Darling? When the sight of you makes my flesh crawl, the touch of you with your . . . your baby-burning fingers? Darling? You make me want to vomit. Well," she said hoarsely, "anyhow the joke's on you. Do you know who that was? That was Josef Steiner. Josef Steiner the Jew. I've been hiding him here in the house, in the attic. And every night that you were gone, he slept with me. Made love to me. A Jew, understand? Put himself inside me, made love to me . . . And he was better than you ever could be, and you took his leavings, and—" She almost yelled the words, clamping one hand on her belly. "And this is his baby, not yours! Everything you ever put in me, I flushed out of me! It's his, Josef Steiner's, a little Jew-baby that I'm carrying!"

"I don't believe it," Robert whispered.

"Well, it's true!" she shrieked. "And what are you going to do about it? Kill something else? Kill me or Papa? If you want to kill something, why don't you kill yourself?"

He said nothing, only looked at her. She stood there with hands clawed, a dust-spattered, blood-smeared harridan, face contorted. He heard a formless yell, realized that he had made it, and the gun came up and he aimed it at her belly. Jew-baby, he would destroy it. . . .

401

This was a place that he had never seen before. Yet he thought he knew it. It was ruined by war, he understood that suddenly. Something was wrong; he had not meant for this to happen. He had told her he would never let it happen. There had been a killing. Why was she screaming at that man? Yes, that was Robert. He remembered now and knew him—Robert Schellhammer. And where was Max and— What had happened to her house, Christina's house? Who had done this? He tried to follow what they were screaming. Then he saw Robert raise the gun and point it at Christina. He knew what a gun raised like that meant and what he had to do. There was a moment when his thoughts came from the tunnel in which usually they hid; they were all there in his head. It was all clear, everything, for one blinding instant. Christina, Ernst, and now the house; and Robert meant to— He felt the pistol in his hand—which he had picked up when he had fallen among the potatoes in the cellar and had hidden in his waistband—go off, buck against his palm; and then he fired again. The first bullet knocked Schellhammer around, and the second hit him in the chest, and he fell like a well-struck roebuck, the machine pistol clattering on the pavement. "So," the General said, still holding the gun outstretched. He tried to cling to that clarity, that comprehension, hold it in his mind; but it was no use. Like a live eel, rationality slipped through his grasp, disappeared into some dark hidden cavern of its own in the blackness in his head. He returned the pistol to his waistband and saw that Christina—Christa?—was sitting in the rubble crying; something pulled him to her, and he touched her shoulder. But then it had all gone away, like his wife, like Ernst, like the house which had somehow vanished; and he dropped the hand and stood there blankly, calm, with nothing real and nothing mattering.

12 AT MIDAFTERNOON of the second day, the point tanks of the Russian task force battered down the last feeble roadblock—a squad of Hitler Youth armed with a machine gun, a few grenades, and a *Panzerfaust* they never got the chance to

use. After a few minutes the children either gave up or ran for shelter in the town. Then the armor topped a ridge, spread out, and Altkreuzburg lay before them, the Stift's domed towers almost like pillars holding up the sky, sun glinting off their brazen crosses, the Danube gray beyond. "Hah!" the *Bodpolkovnik*—the lieutenant colonel—beside Lan in the command car grunted in triumph. He pointed, grinning, showing front teeth capped with stainless steel. *"Donau? Donau!"* Proud of having made it, he was also proud of his fragmentary German.

"Yes," Lan said. "The Danube." As the colonel got out, he followed suit, aware that he was trembling; not just with weariness, though he had hardly slept in the past two days and they had stretched him to his limits, but with more contradictory emotions than he could cope with, contain. He stared at the sprawling monastery, the coiling river, the huddled town, the hills beyond; and it had not changed. Nothing had changed. Then he thought, Oh, God, don't let them be forted up in the Stift.

Now, sheltered by a T-34's bulk, the colonel's staff had gathered around. Lan could hardly follow the debate in rapid Russian; at last he realized that they were trying to decide what to do about the Stift. The Russian attitude, officially, was startlingly liberal; every effort was to be made to avoid unnecessary destruction of such ancient treasures. But these men had fought their way through roadblock after roadblock in the outer Wienerwald, had seen their comrades cut down by rifle and machine gun fire, their tanks blasted by hidden 88-millimeter anti-tank guns. At first, until the air strikes, the Germans had fought savagely; then, resistance collapsing, they had fallen back or, in squads and platoons, surrendered. But it had been a bitter business hammering this far; and a fanatical regiment of parachute infantry or the like—the really die-hard professional units, of which some were still left, and which the Russians dreaded meeting—such a unit holed up in there could drag out a defense for days, and cause the town to be destroyed. From here the monastery could be pounded by the tank guns, and— Then someone shouted, and they all turned and saw the four civilians trudging up the hill, white flag waving.

It was a stiff climb; they were coming slowly. Colonel Kudrya snapped an order; a sergeant jumped into the command car and it rolled down the hill. It picked up the civilians, growled back, halted. The four men, all dressed in Sunday best, shirts starched, climbed out, faces pale, eyes shifting nervously. Condon frowned; one seemed faintly familiar. Then he recognized the paunchy figure, much older, face deeply lined—Schulz, who ran the coffeehouse in the upper market, where the hazelnut and rum cakes had been so superb, the whipped cream so rich.

Something inside Condon unclenched; he leaned against the command car, knees weak. "The Ferntal!" he blurted in German, interrupting. "Is it clear?"

Kudrya's interpreter started, glowered. The colonel motioned. "Let him ask his questions."

The delegation turned to Lan, eyes lighting as they recognized the American uniform. "Are there Americans here, too, then?" the Bürgermeister asked hopefully.

"Only I. And you'd better speak the truth; I've lived here and I know this area."

Schulz frowned, then grinned. "Oh, yes. You are the American, Herr Condon, the husband of General Helmer's Christa! Ah, so, Herr Condon!" He clapped Lan on the shoulder, seized his hand, pumped it. "Oh, a great pleasure to see you again, I have thought of you so often!"

Lan shoved him away. *"Klipp und klar.* Is the Ferntal free of German troops? If so, where is the line?"

"The Ferntal's wholly free." Schulz tried to mask his disappointment. "So is the road to Vienna from here to Klosterneuburg, at the very least. You have our lives as guarantee of that. We welcome you as liberators. And, Herr General Condon, I remember that you especially liked my *Nusstorte.* When the materials are available, I shall be honored to bake a special one for you."

"Shut up," Lan said. "My wife. Is she well? The Christina Hof?" He tried to keep his voice steady, but it broke in his throat. "Is she still there?"

Schulz looked at him a moment, then took his revenge. "One doesn't know. The Russian planes came over yesterday. It is said the Christina Hof was destroyed." He paused. "I have no confirmation, no further news."

He never knew how he did it, but Lan kept his face impassive. In fact, for five more minutes he questioned them incisively. Christa— She and her father had been at the *Hof* all along, unless at the last minute Herr Schellhammer had removed them. Herr Schellhammer was her ... protector. Schulz took his pleasure in his choice of words there, too. But there was nothing left here, no longer any structure of Nazi government, the Wehrmacht was far away, and there was not much food. The people were frightened, very hungry, and ... Surely the liberators would help them.

Lan was trembling when he turned away, and he knew Kudrya could see it. He opened his mouth to plead, but Kudrya was already speaking, choosing his words slowly in German. "We must verify all this. If Altkreuzburg is clear, we'll send patrols west and east. You may go with the one that we send west into your"—he groped for the word—"Ferntal." Then he snapped orders. The commander of the tank by which they were parked said something into his radio. Immediately the T-34s in the lead moved forward, rolling down the hill toward the Stift and into the narrow streets of the town.

It took two hours to verify that the town was clear, and for Lan Condon every minute was an eternity. As they moved into Altkreuzburg, he felt a sense of unreality, a slippage of time, with which his mind could not quite cope. It was as if he had never been away. Each street, each alley, and the individual houses were etched in his mind; the Stift seemed as it had always been. And had it been seven years ago that he had got his hair cut in yonder barber shop? After all this time, the only difference was the lull and hush of war, impoverishment, defeat. As the townspeople slowly came from their holes like frightened mice, he talked to everyone, seeking word not only of Christa but of Robert Schellhammer, who had become the most important man in Condon's life. He himself was powerless to save his wife; only Schellhammer could do that now.

And then the Bürgermeister told him that Schellhammer had disappeared. Maybe gone off to fight. Maybe he had run, like all the rest of the Golden Pheasants. But two dead SS men had been found in the Stift, shot to death. Believed to be the work of the resistance. He could make no sense of it.

Then the tanks were formed up. Five of them would thrust up the Ferntal, infantry riding on them. Air cover had been called in, too, and Kudrya, with compassion and generosity that Lan had not expected, offered him a jeep. But he refused it, his decision already made. He would ride on the lead tank of the patrol. Kudrya shrugged; it was a risk not required of him, but one appreciated, since he knew the country. It would be helpful to the commander of the point.

Westward, behind the hills, the sun slipped lower, filling the hollows with purple shadows. Condon took his place behind the turret. The sergeant commanding the T-34 left the turret hatch open, riding unbuttoned. He spoke into his microphone, gave a hand signal. Loaded with clinging infantry, the tank growled and thundered into forward motion. The four behind it followed. The patrol lumbered through the narrow streets. In some places there was no room for tanks to pass. There the infantry jumped off the lead tank; then, crushing, inexorable, it battered corners off the houses to clear the way, moved on, pausing to let the infantry remount.

From the height of the tank's rear deck Condon could see into the courtyards. He saw the stacks of firewood, the spaded gardens, the lilacs putting out their first greenery, the meticulously clipped and winter-mulched roses. He saw a hundred brief and vivid epiphanies, things he had forgotten that now flooded back on memory. Then they were out of the town itself and had entered the Ferntal road, and the tanks speeded up to fifteen miles an hour. Behind them, why he did not know, or by whom worked, or whether with or without permission of the colonel, the Stift bells suddenly clanged out with full-throated brazenness, whether in joy, requiem, or simple hypocrisy he could not guess.

And now they were well into the Ferntal, and his heart pounded, his head swiveled, but he dared not hope, much less think. The chestnuts along the Fernbach were fuzzed with green. The smell of the Russians crowded around him on the tank was pungent, like an uncleaned cage of foxes in a roadside zoo. The hills towered up, green and lovely. Then he saw first the Schellhammer Hof and after that, before recovering from the shock, high up on the ridge crest the other ruins against the sky.

As the tank rolled on, he stared, disbelieving despite all the destruction he had seen so far. It had been blown to bits; it was dead; and probably she was dead. His throat closed and he hit the hard steel with his hand. To come so far, endure so much, and now, after all that, to find— Coming to his senses, he slapped the tank commander on the shoulder, and then he pointed.

The man had been briefed, but he knew the significance of that ridge, that high ground, all too well, and this was his life at stake. Lan was screaming at him, disregarded, as the turret slowly turned and the T-34 halted. Then, with Condon howling, shaking the tank commander, the long gun belched first one round and then another.

The first went over, the second fell a bit short in the orchard; and as Lan froze, the third went home. He saw the ruins lift and tremble, one of the three walls fall in. Then another round for effect, and a second wall came down. Lan saw it fall with a kind of slow, majestic stateliness. But of course she could not be there. Or if she was, she must be already dead. It could not be those last two rounds that killed her. God would not do that to him.

Then he thought, Yes God would. He could only hope He would not do it to *her*.

"You bastard," he moaned in English, but the commander ignored him. Now he swung the tank and, followed by another, it ground up the hill.

Slowly it climbed, Lan erect on its deck. Presently the whole Ferntal lay below them. Then they were in beech forest, out again, then next in spruce. After that they were in the open once again, and Lan was already thinking of what the rest of his life would be like without her. He had no idea how he would get through it. What did you do when you had no dream left? How could anyone live without something out there, something lost or never found to search for? Without that, there was no existence; the dream was everything. Then they topped out near the orchard, and from among shattered trees blackbirds flapped up cumbrously, forsaking their feast on what was sprawled near the toadlike hulks of shattered tanks. Something ran awkwardly through the grass—a roe deer, a doe, holding one foot high—probably it had been hit in the bombardment.

The tank rolled on through the ruined gate, halted. Infantry piled off, spreading out, guns up. Condon leaped down, staring at the bleakness of the ruins. Plaster dust clogged his nostrils.

"Christa!" he yelled, but there was no answer. He waited a moment, yelled her name again. Then he clambered through the ruins.

He almost fell off a pile of rubble into the courtyard. The cellars— But the pressing house beyond had collapsed; its fallen bulk sealed them. Condon coursed around the open area of the *Hof* like a hunting dog; and then he saw the bodies.

He had seen so many corpses that he was inured to them; they had not at first registered on his consciousness. Then he realized that he was looking into the upturned face of what had been Robert Schellhammer, torso half buried under fresh-fallen masonry. It was swollen, dark, but there was no mistaking it, and Lan's last hope died. It had been up to Robert. It was Robert he had counted on.

He walked to the other body, free of rubble but equally distorted with the puffiness of death. Sprawled on its back, teeth bared, its dark eyes stared upward. Condon frowned. He knew that face, knew it from somewhere. It had changed since last he'd seen it, but—

Raucous shouting and a thick hammering sound made him turn. The Russian infantry had found a door, obviously the entrance to a cellar. Lan searched his mind. With everything blown up and fallen, it was hard to orient himself. Then he thought, The wash kitchen. The Red soldiers picked up a fallen timber, battered with it. Lan hurried forward just as the lock broke and the door gave inward; and he jumped down the steps, pushed the Russians back, and entered.

When finally she had regained her wits, she had dragged her father back down here, the only shelter left. The wash kitchen was still intact, and so was the food cellar underneath. She found matches on Josef's body, and she knew where the oil lamps were in the lower cellar. By the light of one of them, she gathered up the dozen potatoes there and carried them to the wash kitchen. She thought about the car parked outside; she could go somewhere in that, but she could not think of anywhere to go. She was too dazed. She knew, too, that she should have buried Josef and Robert, but where, how? She left them where they lay. The cellar was enough for now, its locked and sealed-in darkness. She took the pistol from her father and kept it; there were bullets in it still. Maybe later they would use them. The flue of the wash kitchen's stove had been destroyed, so they could not cook. She ate a potato raw, and later, still hungry, another one. The General would not touch one. He only sat passively in a corner. Mostly she kept the lamp turned out; they sat in darkness.

She tried to pass the time by talking to her father. He did not respond, but he was another presence anyhow. "Papa," she said, "how did all this happen? I can remember how happy we all were. You must have been happy too and so was Mama. Papa, what was she like on your wedding night? Was she afraid? I wasn't. I wasn't a bit afraid. Do I shock you telling you this? I wasn't afraid at all. It's too late anyhow for modesty. Do you suppose *she* ever had a lover? What did she do while you were gone? Who knows? Am I even your child, Papa?" But no rawness evoked response from him or from her, even.

"It's funny," she said. "I guess Josef was better than he was—Lan, you know? Lan always held back a little. Josef had no inhibitions. He was uncanny, the way he knew ... Do you know, Papa, I'm talking to you as if you were Luisa. But it was never the same with Josef either. I'll bet you had other women, too, Poles, I suppose, and Italians, while you were at the front. They couldn't have been the same, though, could they, Papa? Wasn't there always something missing? I've been lucky, Papa. I've never had anybody who didn't love me make love to me. But that's not the same as loving whoever is loving you, is it? Or is there any such thing? Why didn't you marry again after she died? Papa, there are so many things I want to ask you. Why won't you tell me the answers?"

But he only sat there. Still she kept it up; it made the hours go more swiftly and relieved her of the need for action. She could not act anyhow, she was drained of energy and emotion. "Papa, how do you believe in anything? Or do you? Why don't you answer?"

Sometimes, stretched out on the cold stone floor, she slept. She knew that sooner or later she must leave this place. "Papa, do you miss her as much as I miss Lan? Are you the one who found the answer?"

After a full day had passed, her head was clearer, mind

409

sharpened by hunger. They could not stay here. "Papa, why was it him instead of Josef? Or Robert?"

A few more hours and they'd venture out. If the coast was clear, maybe they'd take the car and drive west after all. She did not know. But she knew the child was hungry from the way it kicked.

"Papa," she said much later, "maybe we had better think about leaving here. Do you understand? Maybe we had better—" Then the whole wash kitchen jarred and she heard the dull, muted thunder of falling rubble. With strange calm, she thought, Now this is the end of it; the Russians have come. Her hand groped across the table, even as the ripple of aftershock continued, and it found the gun she'd put there when she took it from her father.

It was loaded and ready to go with the pull of a trigger. That was good. The rumbling subsided overhead. Then, vaguely, she was aware of shouting, and suddenly the courtyard door shook and bulged. Whatever had slammed against it slammed again. Christa gripped the pistol more tightly and lit the lamp. That had to be the Russians. Papa thought they would put him in a cage, but she would never let that happen. She could see now how to shoot him when the time came. She lined the pistol on his head. He appeared not to notice.

The door burst open. Now, she thought. First him, then me.

"*Christa!*" a man's voice yelled above the alien Russian babble. Surely she was dreaming, surely. Then light rayed into the wash kitchen, and she turned her head, though never moving the muzzle of the gun. "Who—?" she said thickly.

She saw the silhouette against the lighted doorway. Tall form with mushroom head, that would be the helmet. Then the voice shouted in English, "Christa, are you there? Christa, is that you?"

She turned, rising. Of course it was not true, but— Then a flashlight played on her face, blinding her; she could not see the man behind it.

"Do you have to?" she said. "Do you have to play that kind of trick on me?"

"Are you Christa?" the voice said.

She stood there, squinting into the glare. "I'm Christa, Lan," she said. "If you're Lan, I'm Christa." And, hand shaking uncontrollably, she let the gun fall to the table.

410

Condon stared at the woman in the lamplight. Her hair was frowsy, tangled, dirty; her face was smudged. Her belly protruded enormously with a baby underneath it, and her breasts had changed their shape, and, blinking at him, she did not smile; but one corner of her mouth twisted up in a kind of leer. "Lan?" she said.

"Yes, it's me." But he did not run to her, simply walked slowly. Only her voice was recognizable. She stood there by the table, one hand on her belly as if trying to push it out of sight. He halted, staring at her.

"It's Josef's," she said frantically. "Believe me, it's not Robert's, it's Josef Steiner's. I hid him and—" She raised a hand and dropped it. "It's Josef's."

He said nothing, found no words. He did not understand at all. But it was Christa. Then his paralysis broke and he ran toward her. He seized her and she fell against him and he held her. The smell of her hair was sour. That did not matter. Her flesh had a special feel beneath his hands; he could feel it through the cloth. "It's all right."

"But there are Russians."

"It's all right," Condon said.

"Papa's here. But he's . . . he needs someone to help him."

"Someone will help him," Lan said. "Christa—" He pulled away from her, led her up the steps. Outside in the courtyard they looked at each other.

She was not what he had dreamed of, not what he had expected. As she stared at him, he saw, too, the puzzlement in her eyes, the assessing of the changes in him; but he swung her around, looked down into her gaunt, smudged face. Much of the dream had vanished, but there was enough left, enough to build on. There had to be. They stared at each other, mute with things it might take them years to find the words to say; then Lan put his arm around her gently, almost as if he were holding a stranger.

"Oh, God," he said, "I thought you were dead."

"No," she heard herself answer. "I'm not dead yet. I've made it somehow. Are you really Lan? Are you sure you won't hate me? Anyhow, I'm not dead yet."

"Oh, hell," said Lan. "Hate you—?" He turned, swinging her around. Only the single wall of the Christina Hof still left standing stood between them and the sky.

411

ABOUT THE AUTHOR

A native North Carolinian, Ben Haas has now returned after three years during which he and his entire family made their home in a small town in the Vienna Woods. They were the first American family ever to live in that district when they first attempted a trial year of it in the mid-1960s, and they returned in 1972 so that the author could research and write The House of Christina. *Today he and his wife and two of their three sons live in Raleigh, while the other son continues his education in Europe.*

A prolific writer for over fifteen years, Ben Haas is best known for his stirring novels about the American South, several of which have been major book club selections, most notably Look Away, Look Away *and* The Chandler Heritage. *His books have been translated into a dozen languages.*